THE BODYGUARD

THE BODYGUARD

LEENA LEHTOLAINEN

TRANSLATED BY JENNI SALMI

amazon crossing

This is a work of fiction. Names, characters, organizations, places, events, and incidents are either products of the author's imagination or are used fictitiously.

Previously published as Henkivartija by Tammi Publishers, Helsinki. Translated from Finnish by Jenni Salmi. Published by agreement with Tammi Publishers and Elina Ahlbäck Literary Agency, Helsinki, Finland.

Published by AmazonCrossing, Seattle
www.apub.com

ISBN-13: 9781477826607
ISBN-10: 1477826602

Cover design by Laura Klynstra

Library of Congress Control Number: 2014910551

Printed in the United States of America

1

Croatians call lynx *ris*, Norwegians know them as *gaupe*, and Germans use the term *der Luchs*. Finns call them *ilves*. In Finnish folklore there are three different types of lynx: the cat, the fox, and the wolf. I could recognize each of them by their spots and tracks. They were to blame for my unemployment.

I had been working for Anita Nuutinen for a year, and now I was following her as she went to check out ornamental Easter eggs in a jewelry store in one of the fancy new malls in Moscow. In order to enter the building, you had to pass through a metal detector, which of course went off as soon as I walked through it. I was told to leave my 9-millimeter Glock behind.

"I need it to do my job," I explained to the heavily armed security guards, but it was no use. If I had any intention of following Anita into the mall, I would have to part with my gun.

"We'll make sure no shady characters enter the building," one of the guards told me in English. I highly doubted it. Anyone could be bought with enough money. But Anita was ready to take the chance.

"We might as well check it out, since we're already here. Anyway, I'm the one who would be in danger, not you," she said with a tight smile. I did not smile back.

Anita bought her Easter egg without incident. It cost three times what she paid me per month. Obviously it wasn't a genuine Fabergé egg—that would have cost ten times my annual salary. However, the tchotchke wasn't enough for Anita; she wanted to take a quick look at the furrier next to the jeweler's, too.

Usually I ask my clients not to wear flashy clothes like expensive fur coats, but Anita had never heeded my advice. Though I didn't particularly enjoy seeing dead mink and silver foxes draped on her, I generally tolerated them. My tolerance ended, however, with the fur coat made out of lynx.

Lynx is *ris* in Russian, too. I estimated that a dozen lynx had been slaughtered for the ankle-length coat she was admiring. Sensing my own growing agitation, I tried to calm myself down with the breathing techniques I had learned, but none of them worked.

As Anita tried on the lynx coat, both of the sales clerks rushed over to help her fasten the clasps and buttons correctly. They were close enough to Anita to stick a knife in her or inject her with poison. I should have moved in and made sure she was safe, but I didn't.

"Lynx. Very beautiful," said Anita to the women in English, and then switched to Finnish to speak to me. "Hilja, how about it? Isn't it just magnificent? It makes me feel like a real cat."

Anita didn't have a clue regarding my feelings toward lynx. I had told her only the basics about my life. She wasn't interested in knowing more—she was too full of herself to care about anyone else.

"The fur sure looks pretty—on live lynx." The tone of my voice visibly startled her.

"What did you say?" She wrapped the coat tighter around herself, stroking the soft fur, and then turned back toward the mirror.

"Whatever. I don't care what you think." Anita switched to English again to tell the ladies she wanted the coat.

She removed it and started rummaging in her purse for a credit card. She had four of them. She had used the AmEx to pay for the Easter egg; now she had her Visa out. The clerk began wrapping the purchase gently in tissue paper. Judging by the dark spots on the fur under her hands, I could tell that this particular coat had been made out of cat lynx.

"If you buy this coat, I'll resign immediately," I said.

"What on earth are you talking about?" Anita turned to me, credit card glimmering in her hand.

"You heard me. I don't work with people whose actions I cannot condone."

"It's just a fur coat."

"A *lynx* fur coat."

Now it was Anita's turn to get upset. Anita always expected to get what she wanted. I had seen her attacking incompetent minions and ineffective customer service representatives countless times. Lowly staff members like me should keep our mouths shut. I wouldn't be resigning, she yelled. Instead, she'd fire me. I yelled back at her that I didn't care. I knew I was red in the face now, sweating. I was close to kicking the coat racks and shattering the store mirrors, but I controlled myself—barely.

The clerks watched our shouting match in stunned silence while the store's mustachioed security guard, a real goon, appeared from the back room in a cloud of sauerkraut stench. Neither he nor the women spoke any Finnish, so they couldn't understand what our fight was about, but they could tell which one of us had money.

"*Idite*," he suggested, using the polite form to ask us to leave. Polite or not, I knew it basically meant *get lost.*

"Don't you even dare think of using me as a reference!" Anita screamed. "I'll make sure you never work again, at least not in Finland!"

"You're not as important as you think," I spat back. When the security guard grabbed my arm, I did my best not to shove him into a mirror.

I snatched my gun on the way out of the mall, not sticking around long enough to explain to the security guards why I was leaving alone. I had learned a bit of Russian during our trips, and *durak*—idiot—had become my favorite word. I hissed it at one of the guards when he tried to stop me from leaving without Anita. Our driver got out of the car to open the door for me, but I stormed by him without a word. Our hotel was only a half mile away from the mall, and I had no trouble finding my way there. A map of Moscow was imprinted on my brain.

I rode the elevator to the tenth floor. As always, our rooms were next to one another, joined by a door. Anita couldn't stand the idea of sleeping in the same room as me, but I still had to be within earshot. Most of the time we left a baby monitor on for security.

I realized I had timed my resignation perfectly. It was the first of September, and I had just been paid for August. Anita would be pissed off when she figured out that she couldn't use me as free labor. Knowing her, she might still find a way to get out of compensating me for the vacation time I had coming.

I went online with the hotel Wi-Fi to see if there was room on any flights that day. Anita and I usually flew business, but there were no seats available in any class; all the flights were completely booked. I called the train station, but the evening train was completely full, as well. Luckily there were still seats for the train the next day. I reserved a seat in an otherwise empty three-person compartment. Once I had called the hotel next door to get a room for the night, I packed my things and took off without even leaving a note. Even just thinking about the lynx coat made me upset, and I didn't want to hear from my newly former employer ever again. I slammed my keys on the reception desk and ignored the porter's reprimand.

I refused the doorman's offer of a cab and walked over to my new lodgings. My room there was tiny and smelled of cigarette smoke, but anything would do for one night. My cell phone started ringing: it was Anita. Silencing it, I walked down to the hotel restaurant and ordered a plate of *blini*, some caviar, pickles, honey, sour cream, and wild mushroom salad. And vodka. Georgian red wine had been crossed out on the menu, a reflection of the ongoing war. In addition to the vodka, I opted for strong Lithuanian beer, and downed it in two long gulps before asking for another.

I had never liked Anita, but that had never really mattered. Seven years earlier I had graduated with honors from a security academy in Queens, New York. There weren't many female bodyguards in Finland, so I had always been able to have my pick of jobs. Anita Nuutinen paid me double what anyone else had. She traveled between Helsinki, Moscow, and Saint Petersburg at least once a month and needed protection. Apparently her real estate business was bordering on shady, but as long as I didn't take part in anything illegal, I didn't have to worry about losing my badge. Not being able to use a client as a reference was a different story. Mike Virtue, the head trainer at the security academy, would have been disappointed. He always stressed that a good reputation was a necessity in the bodyguard business. Sure, mistakes happen sometimes—like when that one bodyguard he told us about hadn't been able to protect a client from multiple hidden assassins—but a client's trust had to be maintained at all times. By the time I finished my second beer, Mike was giving me a lecture inside my head.

Of course, Anita would try to convince me to come back. I knew too much about her, including the details of the security systems at the Nuutinen household and her office. This information would be extremely valuable to anyone who might be tempted to threaten Anita's life.

I had eventually convinced her to tell me who she thought her enemies were; bodyguards need to get into a criminal mind-set to predict criminal moves. Anita's husband had disappeared from her life years before and moved to somewhere in northern Finland, and Anita's only daughter lived in Hong Kong. I had always made sure that Anita was never alone, and sometimes slept at her two-thousand-square-foot condo in Lehtisaari. First I revamped the home security system, because the main threat to Anita was her former lover, who had been in the house multiple times. Valentin Feodorovich Paskevich was a real estate kingpin from Moscow, and he did not think kindly of the Finnish woman who had torpedoed his well-established summer cabin business in Finland's lake region near the Russian border.

My phone rang again. Anita. Let it ring. Was she freaking out, scared of every passing car, startled by oncoming pedestrians? Had she locked herself in her room and bolted the door? Our driver, Sergey Shabalin, had been devoted, but I suppose even he had his price. Anita knew that security was only guaranteed by being the one who could spend the most money. She believed that everyone was like her, only interested in covering their own asses. With Anita, I had adopted a persona: not the brightest bulb, yet strong and alert. She never knew that I had carefully recorded all her movements, for her own protection, of course—but having all this information meant that I could make Anita's life a living hell if I wanted to.

The vodka and beer went straight to my head, despite the substantial meal I'd had. After paying the check, I went for a stroll.

By now it was dusk, and people were swarming the city streets. I went to a kiosk to buy a soda and a bottle of sparkling water. Prime Minister Putin's eyes met mine from the cover of the latest issue of *Pravda*, in which he commented on the situation in Georgia. Paskevich supported Putin, another reason why Anita was afraid of him.

"Kak diela, devushka?" asked a male voice next to me. Out of the corner of my eye, I checked to make sure he wasn't one of Paskevich's hit men.

"I'm not your girl," I replied in Finnish and walked away while the man kept shouting *devushka* at me. I hoped he didn't think I was a prostitute; nothing in my appearance would have given him that impression. I was five foot nine, 165 pounds, and my hair was cropped like a young boy's. I dressed for the job of bodyguard: jeans, a short leather jacket, and the steel-toed combat boots I had changed into before leaving the hotel. Walking through metal detectors while wearing them would have made getting into malls impossible, so they didn't get much use in Moscow. But it felt good to know that with one swift kick, I could knock a grown man unconscious.

I walked back to the hotel where Anita and I had stayed. I found her window, the location of which I had committed to memory: the light in the window could easily reveal an intruder in her room. And what do you know—Anita did have the light on and the shades up. Stupid cow, doing exactly what I had told her not to do. It would serve her right if she got into trouble.

Despite these thoughts, Mike Virtue's voice echoed in my head. It was wrong of me to leave a client alone, it said—but Mike wouldn't have understood why Anita purchasing a lynx fur coat would set me off.

Mike had told us that we all needed to decide who to protect. Some bodyguards were employed by criminals; I had seen Paskevich's small army of hired muscle when he dated Anita while I was still working at Chez Monique, a restaurant where they used to have dinner. I had managed to protect Anita from a group of grunts like that. I should be proud of myself, not ashamed.

I made sure that the employee at the reception desk of Anita's hotel wasn't the same one who had chided me earlier. I marched in and headed to the hallway where I had previously spotted a public phone. I called Anita's room, but when she answered I hung up. She was fine. Anita would return to Finland on an early flight on Wednesday; she'd manage alone until then, I reasoned. She only had one more meeting with the person who managed her Moscow properties. Anita knew how to get there and Sergey would drive her. I was free to do as I pleased until I left town.

The man at the reception desk was staring at me. Come to think of it, as I'd walked toward the phone, the security guard near the elevators, who checked everyone's key cards before letting them upstairs, had stared at me, too. I had warned Anita not to trust him too much. Then there were the cleaners. They had access to all the rooms, and we knew nothing about their backgrounds. Suddenly, the entire world was a threat to lonely Anita.

I heard an elevator come down and backed myself into a recess in the wall as soon as I saw the familiar toe of Anita's patent leather boot emerge. She wore the lynx fur coat, but had left the buttons unfastened. She rushed directly to the main exit, where I saw a familiar cab waiting for her. It was Sergey. This was curious, as she didn't have any appointments for the evening. We were supposed to be ordering room service and turning in early to catch up on sleep. What made her change her plans?

A couple other cabs were outside the hotel, so I hopped in one owned by a company I had used before. I told the driver to follow Shabalin's car, and with a grunted *da* the driver took off. We drove along the Kremlin down to the site where the Rossiya Hotel had once stood, and then crossed the river, heading south. Apparently we were going toward the properties that Anita had managed to scam from Paskevich. Had she moved up her meeting with the property manager?

During the worst of the depression in the early '90s, Anita had inherited hundreds of acres of shoreline and small islands in Eastern Finland's Savitaipale region from her mother. Construction was nearly at a standstill at the time, and given the high unemployment rate, Anita was able to negotiate a favorable development deal with surprisingly little effort. The local council calculated that the construction would create jobs and the future vacationers in their new summer cabins would be a boon to local businesses. All Anita still needed was funds to begin building.

She had run into Paskevich in nearby Lappeenranta, where he was making inquiries about available villas for his Russian customers. Paskevich was a rising Russian oligarch, with connections to both the oil and natural gas industries. This was right after the economic upheavals in Russia; in that crazy environment, anyone without scruples could succeed. Anita's husband had just disappeared, and, bereft, she was charmed by Paskevich. In her state of temporary insanity, swayed by his fortune, she joined him not only in bed but also in business. Paskevich and Anita began construction on three small summer cabin resorts and a couple magnificent island villas on Lake Saimaa. They assumed there would be plenty of rich Russians interested in the properties. Paskevich was also making money in Moscow with his real estate business, and Anita applied for an enormous loan for the privilege of becoming his partner.

He predicted that the Finnish depression would eventually end, so it made sense to invest in Russia. For a couple years, this strategy seemed to work: Anita's investments in Finland and Moscow bore plentiful fruit, enough for her to pay off the loan at a pace that stunned the loan officer.

One evening, Anita arrived at their Moscow penthouse unannounced and found Paskevich in bed with two barely legal models. It didn't take long her for to discover that this wasn't the first time these girls had visited him. Anita didn't react. Instead, she walked out of the room and then returned with a bottle of champagne and four glasses. After pouring them each a drink, she said she understood—after all, she had grown bored of Mr. Nuutinen after ten years of marriage. Paskevich swore that he was not tired of Anita; he just couldn't commit to one woman.

After that, Anita let Paskevich have his little adventures, because he always came back to her. In the meantime, she undertook an escapade of her own. It began a couple of years before I started working for her. I didn't know all the details, but as a result of her machinations, Anita managed to own outright a summer cabin resort and two single-family houses along the Moscow River. I suspected that she must have drugged Paskevich, or he had been clueless about the content of the papers he was signing. The signatures were nevertheless legally binding, so Anita had the law on her side.

After discovering Anita's work, Paskevich put out a hit on her, so she stayed within Finnish borders for the next couple of years. But she did not completely trust her Moscow property manager, and she had needed to visit more often. Her previous bodyguard had been forced to quit; he had severed his Achilles tendon and was never going to run again. Anita didn't buy his story about an after-hours accident—she suspected that he had either been bribed or attacked. The man had since moved to Florida to run a gym.

I saw Shabalin pull up to a familiar building. My cab stopped close behind his. My driver asked what our next move should be, and I told him in English that we would wait and see. Shabalin watched and made sure that Anita got into the building after entering the door code. He then made a risky U-turn, which led to a lot of honking from oncoming traffic.

The building had a bar downstairs called Bar Svoboda. I decided to get a window seat so that I could see when Shabalin came back for Anita. I paid for the cab and realized that I had only fifty rubles left. But it would be enough for at least one drink in this nondescript, harshly lit, and nearly empty bar.

Although the decor was limited to the wooden tables and tall, plastic bar chairs, everything seemed to be saturated with cigarette smoke. I had no problem finding an empty window seat. I ordered a beer and made sure the cap hadn't been tampered with before the bartender opened it for me. Obviously insulted, he glared at me but didn't say a word. I took the beer to my seat and began the waiting game. It was half past eight.

Within fifteen minutes a group of men came to the bar. Regulars, judging by the way they greeted the bartender. I didn't recognize any of them. I could keep an eye on the bar from its reflection in the window, so I witnessed a full bottle of vodka being brought out and the men doling out shots. A plate of pickles and containers of honey and sour cream also appeared from somewhere. The guys were loud and offered the waiter a shot, as well. He obliged. No one paid any attention to me. At first.

There was hardly any activity outside. It was one of those upper-middle-class residential streets, where the only businesses were the bar and a small grocery store. Though not luxurious, the condos Anita owned were still out of reach for a working-class resident of Moscow. Each unit had its own private Finnish-style sauna, which only added to its value. I looked again at the distorted tableau in the glass and noticed a man staring at me. When I saw him get up and approach me for a chat, I took a sip of my beer and let my hand rest right next to it. He offered me a smoke, but I declined by shaking my head. He started babbling in a Russian dialect that may as well have been Greek, so I didn't even need to pretend that I couldn't speak Russian. Another man appeared next to me—I was now wedged between the two of them. I didn't feel like provoking a fight because I had some waiting to do. Maybe I could get Anita to give me a decent reference after all.

Now a third man appeared, in an attempt to stop the other two from bothering me. It was rude to decline a cigarette in Russia, but I honestly could not have cared less what these strange men thought of me. Then, through the window, I saw Anita walk out the front door. She stared at the empty street, looking flabbergasted. I guess she had been expecting Shabalin to wait for her.

When she walked back in, most likely to call Shabalin, I drained my beer and walked out on the three men without a word. There was no time for a bathroom break, either. I hated having to grovel and I knew Anita would not let me off easily. Reluctantly I walked out to wait for her so we might resolve our differences. The building door was solid wood, without a peephole. There were no cars on the street, just a single dog running between the houses.

Next thing I knew, I woke up in an unfamiliar room with a strange woman yelling at me. I had a headache, everything smelled of vomit, and I had somehow lost over twelve hours of my life.

2

The woman yelling at me worked at the front desk. Apparently I was supposed to have checked out more than two and a half hours ago, so I needed to pay extra, both for the time and for the cleaners who had to deal with the mess I'd made. Just to get rid of her, I promised to leave by six and to pay for everything. I was dizzy and nauseated, but there was nothing left in my stomach to throw up. When the woman finally left, muttering to herself about drunken Finnish tourists, I slowly got out of bed. I was terribly thirsty. The bottles of soda and sparkling water from the day before should have still been in my backpack. I scanned the room and found the backpack next to the wall. Was the rest of my gear intact? I had passed out with my clothes on, except for my shoes and jacket, which was crumpled on the floor. My cell phone was in the jacket pocket, and my wallet was in the breast pocket of my shirt, still containing whatever rubles I had left after buying the beer. My gun was under the blanket on the bed. So I had not been robbed.

I drank some sparkling water, took a pill for my nausea and two painkillers. I stripped off my clothes so I could get a good look at myself in the mirror. I didn't show any signs of having been punched, though my ears were ringing. There were some scratches on my knees, so it looked like I had fallen over, even though the palms of my hands weren't scraped up. I didn't feel any pain or bruising in my groin, either, so I knew I hadn't been raped.

I showered and thought back to what I'd previously ingested. If my dinner at the hotel had come with a drug-spiked beer, I would have felt the effect sooner. At the bar I had kept an eye on my drink as if it were my only child. Or had I? When Anita came out of the building, for a split second, my focus was solely on her. Did one of the three men slip something into my glass while I wasn't looking? I cursed out loud and wrapped myself in a small towel that barely covered my torso. I closed the curtains and called Anita's cell phone. She didn't pick up.

Had I met her? Had we made up? How did I get to the hotel? I tried hard to remember. I called Anita's hotel room, but nobody picked up there, either. The operator confirmed that Ms. Nuutinen was a guest there, but she could not give out any additional information.

Who would know what Anita was up to? Her assistant, Maya Petrova? The cab driver, Sergey Shabalin? I didn't have Petrova's number and Shabalin's line was busy. The unbearable busy signal bore a hole in my head. I had to lie down again. I pulled the blanket over myself. It smelled as musty as my clothes; so much for cleaning up in the shower. Turning over, I felt something silky against my legs. It was Anita's Gucci scarf. What was it doing here?

I started to panic. She would never have given me the scarf if we had parted ways amicably. I checked my gun—had it been used? There were no traces of gunpowder on it and the clip had the same amount of bullets in it as the last time I'd checked it. Then why were my ears ringing as if from a gunshot?

I had to get out of this disgusting room. My train didn't leave for hours and I was starving. Rummaging around, I found my emergency energy bar and ate it slowly so I wouldn't get sick. After showering again I got dressed and packed Anita's scarf under my ammunition clips in my backpack. My Glock was safe in its holster under my arm. At the front desk I paid for the room and got my passport back. I took the subway to the train station and picked up my ticket. I kept trying to reach Anita and Shabalin, in vain. Although Shabalin's phone was now ringing, he wasn't picking up.

I didn't want to lug my backpack around or leave it in the storage area, so I went to the station restaurant and ordered borscht and sparkling water. Fortified, I tried to recollect the events from the previous night, but it was hard to remember what had happened after I went outside to wait for Anita. Maybe we had met. Maybe she had refused to talk to me. Maybe she had absentmindedly dropped her scarf and I had picked it up, intending to return it later. Most drugs designed to knock out their target wiped the mind so clean that it was impossible to restore memories even with hypnosis or therapy. I assumed I hadn't done anything stupid. Maybe I had just taken a cab on my own volition to pass out in my hotel room. Or so I hoped. Once I was able to log on to my online banking account, I would find out whether someone had paid for the cab with my card.

The soup revived my spirits, but only until I called Anita again. This time, an unknown man speaking Russian answered. Why did this strange man have Anita's phone, a man who could now clearly see that Anita's number had been called from my number? Shit. I hung up. Maybe those men at the bar had been Paskevich's minions, along with the bartender. I didn't want to take that theory any further. The truth was that someone had managed to elude all my security measures. And whoever it was hadn't even bothered to make it look like I had been robbed, which is what scared me the most.

Once passengers were finally allowed to board the train, I found my compartment, and got comfortable on the smaller bed across from the bunk bed. I'd survive the night with my gun by my side, even if a Kyrgyzstani train robber decided to join me. Anita never took the train between Finland and Russia because the idea of sharing a restroom with who-knows-what-kind-of-people was out of the question. When I pointed out that she didn't have exclusive access to the airplane's facilities, she simply noted that lowlifes wouldn't be allowed in the business class restrooms.

The conductor yelled outside, then there was a whistle and the train lurched forward. I lay down to wait for the ticket check. We would stop in Saint Petersburg to pick up more passengers, but until then I had the luxury of being alone in the cabin. I tried to sleep but couldn't. I kept nodding off, and I wasn't entirely sure whether the gunshot still echoing in my ears was a dream or a memory. I was woken up on both sides of the border—first by the passport inspectors, then the customs officer—but they appeared in a sleepy haze, and I couldn't tell whether they were real or figments of my imagination.

Once I got to Helsinki, I took a tram to the Käpylä neighborhood where I kept most of my stuff in a shared apartment. With its lonely bed, small desk, and ergonomic chair, the dusty room felt foreign to me. The two students I shared the apartment with weren't around. They were about ten years younger than me, and were not unhappy that I paid a third of the rent for the three-bedroom apartment I was hardly ever in. They knew I worked in security; I had made vague statements about delivering valuable objects and how it kept me out of the country for long periods of time. The roommates were blissfully unaware of the dangers that living with me entailed. I was happy with the arrangement. My official address was here at 7 Untamo Road and not the cabin I rented in Torbacka, in

Degerby, where I spent most of my free time. There was no paper trail connecting me to the person I rented the cabin from, so it was safer than the apartment.

I worried that someone was still after me. Anita's business practices had antagonized the Finns and the Russians who were both promised exclusive deals. The Russians considered a vacation home in the pristine Finnish landscape a status symbol, but the value of that purchase plummeted when tens of fellow Russians shared the experience. And the usually good-humored Slavs turned into paranoid Finns at the cabin resort, hiding behind their security fences and setting up barbed wire in the lake, making sure no suspicious character could get too close. Even if I had the money, there was no way I would have stayed in the vacation hell Anita created. Parts of Lake Saimaa's shores had started to look uncannily like southern Europe's crowded strip of kitschy beach hotels.

The kitchen cupboard in the apartment was pretty bare, but I found a packet of ramen that I ate while doing my laundry. It was a small load, just underwear and a couple of shirts. I had gotten my workout clothes from the hotel laundry the morning before so I hadn't yet had a chance to use them. As I pulled noodles from the cup with my fork, I noticed a four-wheel-drive car parked on Koskela Road. With tinted windows and Russian plates.

Fuck. Someone *was* still after me, and this time neither my gun nor my black belt in judo would help. Paskevich's men were experts. I had previously told Anita that he was a poor excuse for a Russian businessman, but he had shown he was no amateur.

I did my best to move through the apartment without drawing attention. The blinds in my bedroom were always down, but only a short curtain covered the top part of the kitchen window. Jenni's door was already closed, and I shut the door to Riikka's room, as well. I went to get my binoculars, but they were useless in seeing into the dark windows. Obviously I didn't know all the hit men working in Finland, but I checked out the license plate and tried to recall any previously suspicious plates I had come across, scanning my memory for a match. A couple of mob guys I knew were so proud of their trade that they had easily recognizable vanity plates, in part to scare people.

The laundry was done, but there was no way I'd go out to the yard to hang it to dry on the clothesline. That would make me an easy target. I did own a Kevlar vest, but I didn't have a helmet. Plus, walking around with a helmet on would definitely attract attention from the neighbors. I'd use the building's dryer instead—it was fast. If my stalker was still out there when my clothes were dry, I could walk from one basement hallway to another, then leave through a different exit. Though an experienced hit man would have a copy of the building's layout and would suspect I'd pull something like this.

I didn't want to risk the hit man following me to my Degerby cabin, but there was no way I was going to stay here, either. No one would follow me to Hevonpersiinsaari, a small island near the town of Kaavi in Eastern Finland, only a couple hundred miles away from the Russian border. The name means "Horse's Ass Island" in English, as I had explained to the great amusement of my fellow students at the Queens academy. I could rent a car in Joensuu. Or I could take a plane, which was safer than the train, but then again I could always get off a train if I needed to. I weighed my options while I waited for the laundry to dry in the basement.

After my mother died, I was raised by her brother, my uncle Jari. Only later did I appreciate how lucky I had been that the social workers had decided to hand a four-year-old kid over to a twenty-four-year-old man—but at that moment it had been the best option. My uncle lived on the border of North Karelia and Kuopio in a municipality called Kaavi, on the island of Hevonpersiinsaari.

When he passed away, I inherited the cabin there, but I had no desire to go back. Our neighbor, Matti Hakkarainen, had been interested in buying it: the tip of the peninsula was stunning, and he thought he'd divide the land into plots for his five children. The plans had remained only plans, and Hevonpersiinsaari was still mostly uninhabited. I had a lifetime right to it—if nobody was staying in the cabin, I was always welcome to use it. I called Hakkarainen from Riikka's landline. My roommates had wanted to get rid of the phone line ages ago, but so far I had been able to convince them otherwise. It was safer to use than my cell phone, even though I changed the SIM card frequently. When Matti Hakkarainen answered the phone, I could hear the howling of a chain saw in the background.

"Sure, go ahead," he said when I asked about staying at the cabin. "The key is still in the old spot. I'll remove the gate that's blocking the road to the island—its lock is in the cabin. You can lock the gate again if you want," he instructed. "By the way, there's now electricity."

"Really?"

"They're building new cabins on the land owned by the Forest Administration, so they set up power lines for them. Nobody wants to stay in a cabin without electricity these days. I even installed a water pump in the sauna. Come and get some milk, bread, and eggs when you have a chance. Maija will make some pies, and the forest is full of lingonberries and mushrooms ready for picking," Hakkarainen said.

I rented a car and bought and printed my train ticket off the Internet. The Russian four-wheeler was gone by the time I was done. Whoever was in the car may have just been playing with me, so to be safe I left the building through another exit. I hopped onto a bus on Mäkelä Street, switched to the number seven tram after a couple of stops, and got off at the Pasila train station, ready for my three-hundred-mile journey to Eastern Finland. Nobody seemed to be tailing me. My roommates wouldn't even know I had been there, unless they were counting their ramen packages. Although Riikka and Jenni were poor students, I trusted them; they wouldn't sell me out to Paskevich. Riikka studied theology and Jenni theater—both were into role-playing in their own ways. Jenni was a strict vegan and an actor, whereas Riikka had talked about joining the clergy. As I listened to their discussions, it occurred to me that they'd chosen characters who were meant to be seen, whereas mine was designed to be hidden.

The train was half empty and everybody on it seemed to ignore me, but that didn't make me any less vigilant. I paid special attention to my surroundings at the stops closest to the Russian border—Kouvola, Lappeenranta, and Imatra. I had a small SUV waiting for me at a car rental office in Joensuu, about a three-hour train ride from Helsinki. The SUV would help me navigate the Hevonpersiinsaari road, roughed up by the late-summer thunderstorms. Also I felt safer in it than in a smaller car because I sat up higher and could see into the other vehicles on the road. After doing a quick check of the SUV with my explosives detector—I didn't want to draw attention to myself—I drove to a large shopping center to get some groceries for my trip: potatoes, pasta, canned tuna, lamb sausages, savory pies, and a twelve pack of beer. Screw dieting; calories were more important right now. I dropped by the liquor store to pick up two bottles of rum. One of them was a gift for Matti Hakkarainen. His wife, Maija, would get marmalade candy instead.

There were enough Russian vehicles in Joensuu for me to stop worrying about each of them. After driving for twenty minutes and passing Ylämylly, the traffic cleared, and mine was the only car on the road. Another twenty minutes and I was on the one main street in Outokumpu, which was quiet, too. I hadn't been there since Uncle Jari had died.

Hevonpersiinsaari was located in the municipality of Kaavi, but Uncle Jari had applied for my school placement elsewhere because it was so difficult to get to Hevonpersiinsaari. Back in the '80s, the grade school was in nearby Rikkaranta, but once I got to middle and high school, it took me almost an hour to reach school on foot and by bus. That didn't leave a lot of time for socializing. Uncle Jari had a car only occasionally; when he was short on cash, it was the first thing he stopped spending money on. He had a friend, a used car dealer, who offered up his Ladas and Datsuns; I grew up believing that automobiles were supposed to be full of rust.

The bushes along Munaniemi Road looked the same as they always had, and the road was covered in fist-size rocks. Late summer's willow herbs lined the logging site. Hevonpersiinsaari had always been surrounded by dense forest, which created a sense of security. As I drove farther, though, I realized how much the scenery had changed. The clear-cutting had been cruel, leaving behind a denuded forest. The tufts of willow herb seemed to be placed in the clearings to purposely soften the stark views. The areas near Hevonpersiinsaari had not been saved—a road sign indicated zoning for multiple construction projects.

The zoning folks must have given Hevonpersiinsaari a slightly less-offensive name in official documents. I'd been teased about being from Horse's Ass in middle school, but I had made sure the taunts didn't last long. Grade-schoolers didn't care about my past, but once I'd had a few of my tantrums in seventh grade, one of the teachers put two and two together. The word got around: like her namesake the lynx, Hilja Ilveskero shouldn't be messed with, and I did my best to reinforce my reputation. I was no pack animal; I didn't miss having close friends.

Soon it would be dark. It had started to drizzle. Hakkarainen had kept his word: the gate was open. Although it would not prevent other cars from getting on the island, the gate did make me feel slightly safer. The island wasn't exactly an island, but was instead a thin strip of peninsula that connected a tiny isthmus to the mainland—like a horse's ass connecting to its torso—easily reached by foot or boat. The Hakkarainens had worked on improving the island's look; heather blossomed on both sides of the road and sunflowers had been planted in pots. Brittlegill mushrooms were growing together with lingonberries on the side of the road, reminding me of Uncle Jari's tasty desserts. I could hide here from Paskevich and his goons, but not from my childhood.

When I pulled up to the yard, I noticed the crocheted curtains in the cabin windows. Uncle Jari had done his best to keep the yard neat, but he had never been one to spruce up the house, unlike Maija Hakkarainen, who would not watch TV or stop by for coffee at a friend's house without a crocheting project in her hands.

I stepped out of the car and sat still for a while, listening. It was nearly silent and very dark. People didn't come to their cabins on a weekday evening in September. I felt for the key in its familiar spot under the shed stairs. The shed had been painted, and the new layer of brown had completely hidden Frida's scratch marks. She never existed for the Hakkarainens—only my uncle and I ever knew that we had been hosts to a female lynx for a couple of years. There was that one time when Matti had commented on the strong smell of urine in our yard, but Uncle Jari had convincingly blamed it on the dogs who were allowed to run off-leash in the area.

I was eight when Frida came into our lives, in July of 1984. I remember that evening vividly. It began with Uncle Jari getting a phone call that obviously made him upset.

"Goddamned Kauppinen," he cursed under his breath while looking for his coat. "You'll need to tuck yourself in tonight. You can manage, right? I'll be back as soon as I take care of something."

"What?"

"Nothing children should worry about. Get the macaroni casserole leftovers and heat them up in a pan. Remember to add enough butter so that it doesn't burn, and don't forget to turn off the gas," Uncle Jari instructed. He packed up a couple sandwiches and some blueberry juice from concentrate to take with him. He touched my cheek quickly, grabbed both his hunting rifle and a shotgun, and was out the door.

The account of how he found Frida was one of my favorite bedtime stories, although Uncle Jari was ashamed for having played a role in it. There was a chicken farm several miles from us, and its owner, Kauppinen, had long suspected that a lynx had been casually snacking on his free-range chickens right from his yard. He'd even seen a lynx nearby. Kauppinen had a devilish dog—a spitz/Karelian bear dog mix—that he usually kept in the yard on a leash, but today he'd let the dog roam free. It had picked up the lynx's scent and chased it to its hole, and Kauppinen had called Uncle Jari and a couple of other men who weren't too concerned about shooting an animal outside of the official hunting season, which for lynx was between December and February. The chicken thief needed to go now.

The lynx had a den in some woods an hour away in Maarianvaara. When Uncle Jari finally made it there, the other men had taken the dog back home, and my uncle saw Kauppinen, Hakkarainen, and Seppo Holopainen lying in wait for the lynx right at the hole. Uncle Jari didn't get along with Seppo. The men stuck around waiting for the lynx. It must have been starving—why else would it be on the move while it was still daylight? The animal would eventually have to peek out of the hole, and when it did, it was Uncle Jari's task to prevent it from going back in.

Around three in the morning, the lynx finally appeared. It was a female, thin and small; although Uncle Jari hesitated when he saw her, he still jumped to block her way. She panicked and ran toward the forest, then came to a sudden halt when she smelled Holopainen, who had been fortifying himself with booze. He aimed and hit a tree stump. The lynx turned back toward the hole. Uncle Jari got a good look into her terrified eyes.

"I couldn't shoot, even if just one shot would have ended it there. She was so beautiful," my uncle would recollect later.

Kauppinen screamed and cursed, and Holopainen shot again and missed. Kauppinen landed the first hit: he shot the lynx in the hip. She tried to run away, but collapsed at Hakkarainen's feet. He killed her.

After binding the lynx's feet and hanging her from a tree branch, the other men started to fight about whose wife would be the lucky recipient of a nice lynx stole. They were ready to go home and celebrate with a drink. But Uncle Jari had dropped his compass, and he stayed behind to look for it.

"I had no desire to go to Kauppinen's place to party. I felt as if I had murdered someone, and I regretted even going out there to help them. When I found my compass near the lynx, I heard the most pathetic sound. A tiny lynx cub, probably the runt of the litter, peeked out of the little cave and said meow. She obviously missed her mother. We fools had broken the law twice, first by hunting out of season and then by killing a female with a cub; they were always protected," said Uncle Jari, his voice wavering every time he retold me the story. Not that he cared about the laws that much; he was just upset that he had been party to the death of the lynx.

"I knew Kauppinen would kill the cub if he ever saw her, and she would never survive alone in the forest without any hunting skills. Poor thing. She was timid but quick and slipped back into the cave, but I finally pulled her out, although it almost cost me my nose. I put her into my backpack, made sure she had some air to breathe, and hoped that she wouldn't meow and kick too hard. I wondered what she'd eat."

"And in the morning I woke up to her hunting for my toes," I added every time, providing the ending to the familiar tale. "Ever since then Frida and I were best friends."

I stirred from my reverie when the image of Anita caressing a lynx fur coat popped into my head. What else could I have done but quit? I had to do it for Frida's sake.

I carried my pack and groceries inside, felt for a light switch, and found it next to the door. The cabin looked strange in the electric light. And that wasn't the only thing that was new: I spotted a fridge, a microwave, a coffee maker, and even a TV. I walked back to close the gate and decided to take a swim.

Lake Rikkavesi was icy cold; it cut right through me. It also heightened my senses, and I listened and smelled the darkness like I had as a child, when I was envious of Frida's ability to see in the dark. Later, when I'd tried on night-vision goggles at the security academy in Queens, I felt like a true feline.

I really should become more acclimated to the dark; after all, Moscow was a testament to the fact that I was slipping. Back in the cabin, I missed the homey feel of an oil lamp and wished that Hakkarainen had left at least one of them behind. I had to admit that electricity was good for something, though. I wouldn't have to recharge my laptop in the car, and I could set up motion sensors around the cabin. A pro would notice them right away, but it would work for petty thieves. Working swiftly by the light spilling out of the cabin's windows, I set up the sensors.

We hadn't needed motion sensors when Frida was around. She had even detected a sneaky thief, who had come by quiet rowboat to steal Uncle Jari's motorboat. Frida was tame and no more dangerous than a household cat, but she did wake up Uncle Jari. He ran to the pier brandishing his shotgun, which scared away the would-be thief, a neighbor's teenage boy. He never learned that the weapon wasn't loaded.

I microwaved a couple of the savory pies, had a beer, and then went straight to bed. I had bought a high-tech, extremely light silk sheet that folded up to the size of a napkin. It was meant to be used inside a sleeping bag, and I carried it everywhere. I wrapped it around me and crawled between the mattress and the blankets. They smelled strange. Apparently, Maija had washed them with something scented.

Frida's paws had always caused the floors to creak. Ever since she was a cub, she had wanted to sleep in my bed. Uncle Jari explained that it was because my body temperature was higher than hers. In the beginning Frida was much smaller than I was, but by the time spring rolled around, we were the same size. Even in the middle of winter I didn't need more than a single blanket; I had Frida to keep me warm. As I recalled this memory, I could feel her soft fur in my toes, the breath that smelled of rotting meat. Frida had been my sister. I fell asleep next to her that night as I had so many times before.

I woke up to a terrible racket. I grabbed my pistol from the chair I had used as a nightstand. It was a bit after seven and already light outside. I peered through the window and saw a familiar character running away from the cabin. Maija Hakkarainen. She had been startled by the alarm I had hooked up to the motion sensor.

"Maija!" I called after her as I shut off the alarm. The basket bearing her gifts had toppled over on the cabin steps, egg yolk seeping through the weave. Sweet Maija had decided to bring me some fresh treats. How could I have forgotten that the Hakkarainens set their clock according to their cows? They woke up every morning at five. I shoved the pistol into my pajama pants pocket and started after Maija on bare feet.

"Hey, Maija! It's Hilja! Come back!" Maija was in her sixties and had bad feet, so I had no problem catching up to her. I blamed the god-awful sound on the car alarm and hoped that Maija couldn't see through the lie. I invited her in for coffee. Luckily only one of the eggs she'd brought had broken, and the milk bottle was so tightly sealed it hadn't leaked at all.

"Were you away in America again?" Maija asked. My going to New York had been quite an event. I told her that recently I had been focusing on Russia instead, which prompted her to tut-tut about the situation in Georgia and how Hevonpersiinsaari was simply too close to the Russian border. She did have some nicer news, though: my favorite childhood horse Cutey's foal had had her own baby the week before. I promised to come by as soon as I could. I gave Maija the gifts I had brought. She said Matti would be delighted by the bottle of rum, although she would keep an eye on his drinking.

Once she left I turned on the TV. It was still weird to see it in the cabin. The news was just starting. A grave-looking anchor turned to the screen and intoned, "A Finnish businesswoman was killed in Moscow. She was found on Tuesday morning near the subway station in Frunzenskaya. Moscow militia is investigating."

3

Although the businesswoman's name wasn't mentioned, I was sure it was Anita. The pieces came together too conveniently. The coffee I had drunk earlier seemed to be creeping back up; I felt woozy. Killed near the Frunzenskaya subway station. The police didn't mention how she was murdered or when, but she had been killed before Tuesday morning, when I was still in Moscow. I had absolutely no recollection of even being near that station. Then again, I couldn't remember anything about what happened between Monday evening and Tuesday afternoon.

I still had Anita's scarf in my backpack. How the hell had I gotten it? I took it out and thought about burning it in the sauna stove. If I threw the ashes into the lake, nobody would ever know that I'd had it.

I turned my phone on and inserted the SIM card for the number I had once given to Anita. She hadn't tried calling me. I did find ten or so other calls. The most recent call, voice mail, and text message were all from my roommate, Riikka, and they all contained the same basic message.

"Hey, Hilja, the police were looking for you, but they didn't say why. I told them you might be out of the country on business, but I didn't know where. Chief Constable Teppo Laitio from the

National Bureau of Investigation asked that you to call him at 071-8787-007 or e-mail him at teppo-dot-laitio at poliisi-dot-fi."

The National Bureau of Investigation had representatives in Moscow and Saint Petersburg, but Laitio wasn't one of them. They wouldn't find me that easily, but I understood why I was one of their main suspects. How could I even answer their questions when I had no idea where I was at the time of the murder? Chief Constable Laitio had called me twice. He'd left a voice mail and a text message. He probably wouldn't tell me a thing about the case; instead, he'd try to squeeze information out of me. There was also a voice mail from an unknown number; the call was made before Laitio had tried to reach me. It was in English.

"You don't have any idea who is behind your boss's murder. No idea . . . if you don't want to end up as dead as those lynx on your boss's fur coat. You understand?"

The speaker was male, with a thick Russian accent, the kind that would be easy to imitate. He could have been Finnish, Estonian, or Polish. I tried to recognize any similarities between his voice and the rowdy patrons in Bar Svoboda, but I couldn't remember their voices well because I had focused so hard on avoiding them altogether. That had been a big mistake.

I wanted to know more about this murdered Finn in Moscow, to confirm that it was indeed Anita. I couldn't use the Internet at the cabin, but at least there was a news service on my phone. I started scrolling to find more information, but each channel had the same snippet I had already heard that morning on TV. Did I really have to drive thirteen miles to Outokumpu to buy the newspaper for this? The Hakkarainens probably only subscribed to the local newspapers *Savon Sanomat* and *Maaseudun tulevaisuus*, which were aimed at farmers and foresters.

It didn't make sense for Anita to be near the Frunzenskaya subway station alone. What was she doing walking by herself in the middle of the city, anyway? Anita, who you couldn't pay to take a subway in Moscow. We'd spent countless hours in traffic inside cabs reeking of cheap tobacco before we found Shabalin. I tried calling him again, but I only heard a recording that seemed to indicate that the number was no longer in service. Of course. Was his real name even Shabalin? Having a business card was handy not only for giving people your contact information but also for helping to create a false identity. Had Shabalin abandoned Anita, who then had been too scared to use another cab and instead had thought she'd be safer in a crowded subway?

Frunzenskaya was southeast of the Kremlin, close to the Moscow River. Gorky Park loomed on the far riverbank. I had occasionally jogged through the area to reach the river when I knew Anita was safe behind her locked hotel room. The place itself didn't feel sketchy and there were always plenty of people around. If I were a hit man, I would try to find a more remote location for my work.

I didn't want to call Laitio back right away; I was afraid the police would try to trace the call to the cell tower where it had come from. I deleted the English threat after I wrote it down and saved it on my USB stick, where I kept all my files on Paskevich. I opened my previous notes on his and Anita's connections.

Paskevich had been employed by the KGB before the fall of the Soviet Union, but Yeltsin's era of chaotic capitalism had allowed him to nab as many properties as he could. Nowadays you could have called him a *silovik*, a person of the ruling class and protected by the president and the prime minister, which in practice meant that he operated above the law in Russia. Considering Paskevich's status, it was a miracle Anita had stayed alive even this long. Paskevich had a villa in Bromarf, in the town of Tammisaari, which gave him an excuse to visit Finland every now and then. He'd suggested to Anita that they meet a month before our Moscow trip, but she had politely declined. She didn't believe his claims about reaching a truce—she was certain it was a trap.

I pulled out my spare phone and inserted my prepaid SIM card into it. I called Riikka, but she didn't pick up. Then, through a new Hotmail address, I started typing an e-mail to Monika on the phone. The police would have to work a bit harder if they wanted to read my e-mails. I wrote her that I had left my job because I had been angry at Anita, and now Anita was dead.

I missed Monika. Ever since Uncle Jari had died, she'd been my most cherished confidante, a sort of substitute big sister and aunt. Despite its name, her restaurant Chez Monique specialized in Finnish-Scandinavian cuisine, with an emphasis on local and environmentally friendly ingredients. For her, food equaled politics. I guess this had pissed off quite a few competitors. First, someone had pulled out the cold storage fuses, spoiling thousands of euros' worth of food. Soon after, some customers got food poisoning, which was traced back to a batch of goat cheese that had been injected with salmonella. That was when Monika decided to get a bodyguard, and I happened to be the only woman available for the job.

I hadn't been working for Monika very long when someone tried to poison her. The perp had bad luck; I took a sniff of Monika's cup of tea before I let her drink it. Not everyone can detect the smell of cyanide. Worried that the news would scare away customers, she didn't file a police report. After that, I tasted all the food and drink that had not been made in her own kitchen. Three days later one of the chefs called in sick and never returned, and that was the end of the incidents. Still, Monika kept me on her payroll. We liked each other, and I ended up also working as her part-time housekeeper and chauffeur. She was a Swedish-speaking Finn, so we mostly communicated in Swedish, which improved my language skills immensely.

Mike Virtue would have been pissed off if he'd seen me using the security skills he'd taught me to do domestic work. Working for Monika was almost like being on vacation. I would have grown tired of it eventually; when she decided to turn her life upside down and move to one of the poorest countries in the world, Mozambique, I was actually relieved because it forced me to focus on my career. Monika was an idealist; she believed that everyone should have access to good food regardless of wealth, and she planned on using the money she'd collected from rich Finnish foodies to help those who were hungry in Mozambique. This created some buzz in the media, even outside of Finland, because people couldn't accept what she was doing—why would someone leave a successful institution like Chez Monique and her role as a famous television chef to live among the poor and cook them antelope or whatever it was they ate in Africa?

On the last day before the restaurant closed, Monika hosted a dinner for her regulars, and one of them was Anita Nuutinen. During the meal Anita asked Monika how she had the guts to go to Mozambique alone, while she was afraid to go by herself to nearby Moscow and Saint Petersburg.

"You wouldn't happen to need a bodyguard, would you? I have just the woman for the job," offered Monika instead of answering Anita's question, and that's how I ended up working with Anita. And as I found out, that job was tougher than working for Monika. Anita had just one goal in life: to make as much money as possible. Then again, it was pretty easy to handle a person like that. Money forced Anita to take risks, but mostly in the financial sphere—she'd already done her best to protect her physical well-being. So no, it wouldn't have made any sense for her to be traipsing around by herself near the Frunzenskaya subway station. It was an area where she would have never walked alone.

Avoiding the police would put my guard's license at risk. I needed to work with them on this case. I wished I could remember anything at all about what happened after I'd stepped out of the bar. All I could still see in my mind's eye was the solid wood door. Had that door been hiding a guard who had seen what went down on the street? Could he tell the police he had seen me leave without Anita? Or had he witnessed something else?

I knew I needed to take a break to practice my breathing or I'd have a panic attack. Once I calmed myself down, I weighed my options. I would have to give myself more time to try to remember what had happened. Meanwhile, I'd attempt to get in touch with Paskevich. I didn't know to what extent the Moscow militia was investigating Anita's case. In fact, now that I thought about it more, it was weird that someone had called to threaten me. Wouldn't that mean that Anita's death could in no way be a hit-and-run? Was Paskevich really so full of himself that he thought I'd hide in my corner like a hurt lynx?

Now I regretted deleting the threat from my voice mail. My typed version would carry no weight as evidence. Of course, I didn't know what kind of police officer I'd be working with. People didn't get into the National Bureau of Investigation because it was easy or because they had a friend there. In high school I had considered applying to the police academy, but given my history, I knew I wouldn't be accepted.

Getting my blood moving always helped me to think clearly. I put on my running pants and a sweat-wicking T-shirt but had to make do with regular sneakers. I also had my jump rope with me; it was lightweight and compact and could come in handy if I needed to tie someone up. First I checked the shed to see whether

Hakkarainen had kept Uncle Jari's old weights. Yup, still there, along with his own training contraption, a bench press of questionable safety. Uncle Jari used to go into the shed to lift weights, even if it was minus thirty outside. Now it was still warm, about fifty-nine Fahrenheit according to the thermometer. I jumped rope until I broke a sweat and then started to wrestle with the weights. First some light free weights, ten pounds per arm. I've known how to perform a perfect bicep curl since I was ten.

Uncle Jari had competed on the regional level as a weight lifter, but his career ended because he was a lousy competitor. I hadn't inherited that from him. Even in the army I had enjoyed showing off, sometimes carrying other people's backpacks in addition to my own. At the Queens security academy, I had to prove I was the strongest woman, even if it meant I might get injured. I sometimes trained by giving a double-piggyback ride to two men weighing 170 pounds each, which had made Mike Virtue howl with laughter.

He wouldn't be laughing now if he'd heard what I had done. Most likely he would have asked me to turn in my certificate from the academy. My muscles started to ache. Even if I had been able to bench press 200 pounds, I still wouldn't feel better about Anita.

A noise startled me, but it was only a squirrel jumping from tree to tree. Frida had followed a squirrel to a tree a couple of times, and we'd done our best to convince her that such a small animal was not a substantial meal for an adult lynx. Eventually, Uncle Jari took to hunting hare without telling his hunting buddies. According to their code, it was all right to break the law, but a catch had to be shared. I remember a time when Frida had gnawed happily on the hind leg of an elk that Hakkarainen had poached. He had honestly thought we would eat the gristly meat. Maija was so upset with him for keeping the best cuts for himself that she brought us some ground meat as compensation, which was a treat. We didn't use store-bought meat often and, when we did, it was usually meant for Frida. We didn't need meat; living on a lake meant we could have as much fish as we wanted.

I took a quick dip in the lake and marveled at the water pump in the sauna. I hadn't thought much about my uncle's fascination with asceticism until I reached adulthood, when it started feeling weird; until then, we'd gotten by just fine without electricity and running water. When I was in middle school, we did get a generator because Uncle Jari needed electricity to listen to his CDs. His prized musical possessions were his ABBA albums. He and his army buddies watched the Eurovision song contest when ABBA won, and he had fallen in love with the singer Frida. Yes, the lynx had been named after the most beautiful creature Uncle Jari had ever seen and I had no say in the matter, although it was hard for me to pronounce this foreign name.

I got out of the lake and brewed a big pot of black tea, but even that didn't clear my head. I still couldn't recall what had happened in Moscow. I switched to my official phone number and called Chief Constable Laitio.

"Hello, this is Hilja Ilveskero. You left me a voice mail. I'm hiking in Lappland, Norway, and there's not much cell coverage here. Could you tell me what your call was about?"

Laitio was quiet for a minute. I had come up with the Norway story while I was lifting weights. This would buy me at least a couple more days and I could pretend that I had not heard about what had happened to Anita. I doubted Laitio would start tracing my call unless the police had orders to arrest me.

"Norway, eh? That's a surprise." His voice was angrier than in the voice mail I'd received. "It's about your employer, Anita Nuutinen. When was the last time you saw her?"

In principle I always spoke the truth; you had to lie eventually, anyway.

"My *former* employer, sir. I resigned. The last time I saw her was in Moscow on Monday afternoon. Why are you asking?"

"Where exactly did you see her?"

I gave him the details and complained about the line breaking up. Laitio wanted to know how I had gotten to Norway all the way from Moscow. I claimed I had simply hopped off the train in Kouvola, near the Russian border, where I had met my girlfriend, and together we'd taken the train up to Joensuu. There we had rented a car and driven all night to reach Norway. I asked again what the call was about, but Laitio continued his lynx and mouse game.

"You were Anita Nuutinen's bodyguard. Who was threatening her?"

"It was less about protecting her life than protecting her property, sir. She had some issues with her former business partner, Valentin Paskevich, but I'd thought by now that was ancient history."

"So you didn't think that Nuutinen was in immediate danger when you resigned?"

"Sir, what is this about? Has something happened to Anita? I haven't called her back because I don't want her screaming to ruin my holiday with my girlfriend. And I have to save my battery here in the wilderness. If you don't mind me asking, why all the questions?"

Although Laitio talked to me as if I were his peer, I chose to be more formal to keep him at a distance. He asked whether I had plans to return to Helsinki and I said I didn't know. After all, I was a free woman now.

"Well, you better come back quickly. Anita Nuutinen was found dead two nights ago in Moscow."

I made a show of being shocked and enjoyed the performance. I just had to be careful not to overdo it—I was a security professional, after all, and not some high-strung teenager. I told Laitio I would talk to my partner about our plans and would get in touch with him. I hung up while he was in midsentence.

I'd given Paskevich's name to Laitio—he'd find out about him soon, anyway. I also didn't think that Anita had been as afraid of Paskevich recently as she'd tried to make me believe. I had reasons to suspect that in addition to Paskevich, there was also a Finn after Anita.

She had been renting her properties to Finnish business travelers who needed a place to stay in Moscow. I had heard her argue over the phone in Finnish; apparently a renter had wanted to pay her off the books, and Anita had refused. She sternly told the person on the phone that he was in no position to demand that she skirt the law for his benefit, and that if this information become public, it would be the end of him. I didn't ask Anita who she had been talking to, nor did I think she would have told me, but I could find his identity in the list of renters. All of them could have been subletting the condos, especially if they were eager to hide their identities, like Anita's customer was. I doubt Anita had blackmailed him, though.

I had fed Laitio a lie about having a girlfriend, though I did have some experience with women. While I was in New York I did all sorts of things, but I had never wanted a serious relationship. A love affair was the most dangerous form of human interaction, as I had learned as a child. Uncle Jari did just fine living on his own and it was working for me, too. Even the lynx pair up only during mating season, and afterward the female chases the male away. Then she takes care of her cubs for a year, unless she ends up like Frida's mother.

I decided to go check whether the Hakkarainens had an Internet connection these days; I assumed farmers had to fill in all sorts of electronic forms for the EU. I could read the Russian news from there. I packed my dictionary and hopped in the rowboat. Matti had bought a new fiberglass boat to replace Uncle Jari's old-fashioned wooden boat. I preferred this new model. The old one brought up bad memories, and I heard it had been burned one summer in a bonfire. The fiberglass boat was designed to be propelled by a motor rather than oars, but once I got the hang of it, I was able to steer it just fine. It was only about a half mile across the lake to the Hakkarainens'. I hadn't rowed a boat since my time in Queens when we rowed down the East River all the way to the Statue of Liberty, a feat that could not be repeated with today's heightened security. There was nobody on the lake except an old seagull that hovered over me until it realized I wasn't there to fish.

The Hakkarainen house seemed quiet. There was a horse in the nearby field; a clumsy filly galloped playfully around it. Maija might have gone to pick berries and Matti could be taking his daily nap. The tractor was in the yard with the plow still attached. The summer harvest was over, and now they were working on the fields before the frost would set in. I had spent many summers helping out during the harvest time alongside Uncle Jari and the other neighbors.

I knocked on the door, but nobody answered. Pushing the handle down, I knew it would be open because, out in the country, nobody locked their doors. I stepped in and looked around. Since my last visit, they had upgraded their furniture to brown leather. I called out to Matti and Maija, then made my way to the back room where the office used to be. Back then the books for dairy farms were kept in brown cardboard folders—now there was a computer. It was a desktop model, a few years old. Luckily they hadn't set up a password, so I was able to log in right away. I'd need to educate them a bit about security. I opened a browser window.

First I checked the Finnish daily papers, but they just repeated the same information I'd already seen on TV. The worst rag in Moscow, however, was having a field day, as I learned with the help of my dictionary. It claimed Anita had been an enormously rich businesswoman who was overcharging the Russians for villas. I clicked on the accompanying link. I hadn't been prepared for the shock of seeing Anita lying on her side in the street, a grotesque halo of blood around her head. The paper had had the decency to put a black bar over her eyes, but she was still recognizable. Looking at the picture, I saw that the gunman hadn't settled for just one well-placed shot; instead, Anita had been fired at multiple times, as if at random, and her new lynx coat was a bloody mess. The lynx had been slaughtered twice: once for the fur, and then again for the body it was draped over.

I stared at the image for a long time. It was horrifying. I was sure I could kill another human—it was, after all, part of my training. But would I ever have been able to slaughter Anita like that? I still couldn't remember what had happened that night. Although it hadn't been my gun that was used to kill her, I couldn't claim to be innocent just yet, not even after receiving that threatening call. Proving to Chief Constable Laitio that I was innocent wasn't enough; I had to prove it to myself, as well.

4

I turned the computer off and walked back into the living room, where I waited for the Hakkarainens for another thirty minutes. When no one showed up, I left and greeted the horse and her filly, who hobbled over to me and sucked on my fingers as if I were her mother. While I had been living here I had ridden Cutey, but she had been a work horse and not a plaything, and she didn't like wearing a saddle.

After a short chat with the horses, I started to row back to Hevonpersiinsaari. I honestly felt a bit lost without an Internet connection. I had never set it up on my phone, partly because I was worried I'd be easier to track that way. The academy had taught me that you should leave as little trace of yourself as possible if you wanted to be invisible. Neither Laitio nor Paskevich would be able to find me if I changed my service providers and SIM cards often enough and just kept on the move.

Unfortunately, it looked like Anita had been shot right after I had resigned. I almost felt bad that I hadn't struck a deal with Valentin Paskevich, but it didn't seem like I'd be of much use to him. His hit men must have been after us in Moscow for days; one of them must have been tailing me and seen me get on the Helsinki-bound train. Maybe it had been one of the men who drugged me.

The train had been almost empty, so it would have been easy for my tracker to start following me if he had a Finnish visa.

My palms had blistered from rowing, which made me feel like an overly sensitive city slicker. I walked to the forest to pick a few cups of lingonberries, which was easy, as they were so plentiful this year. Back in the cabin, I did my best to clear my head with meditation, but my thoughts kept intruding; none of the techniques I had learned were working. I knew that people who were drunk and drugged were very unpredictable and capable of doing something they wouldn't even dare to dream about when they were sober. I had been angry at Anita, and if she had been pushing my buttons, who knows what I might have done.

I stayed in the area until Saturday. It rained almost the entire time, so my hiking boots and rain gear came in handy when I went out to pick mushrooms. Laitio kept trying to reach me, but I didn't call him back. I had dinner once with the Hakkarainens. Matti reported seeing Seppo Holopainen over in Maarianvaara; it looked like his Thai mail-order bride had run away with a man from Kuopio. That explained why Seppo had been seen buying a case of moonshine from Erkki Karhu, who had been making quality liquor for fifty years.

Seppo Holopainen was the last person I had ever been truly afraid of. Even now, when I knew I could beat him in both physical and verbal sparring, the memory of that fear stirred up my hatred anew. I guess I should have been grateful to him: he was the reason I signed up for self-defense classes, guard training, and, finally, the army. By the age of fifteen, I had learned that Uncle Jari wouldn't be there to save me from all the Seppos in this world.

It was an evening in November, so Uncle Jari was out hunting elk. Holopainen had been banned from the hunting club after he had shot the city council vice president in the foot during a hare hunt. The hunting club had been in real trouble, trying to hide what had happened from the police, the health care center staff, and the wife of the injured man. They claimed that there had been an unknown poacher in the forest whose stray bullet had hit the vice president, but his wife was certain that he had just screwed up and shot himself in the foot. She made some pretty nasty remarks about her husband and his incompetence as a shooter. Annoyed, the vice president ensured that Holopainen was no longer a welcome hunting buddy.

That evening, the music I was blasting muffled the sound of the approaching tractor. To Holopainen it was okay to hop behind the wheel of a tractor when drunk because it wasn't technically a vehicle. He'd decided to pay his dear friend Jari a visit with a bottle of homemade vodka, but all he found was me.

Johanna Susi had recorded a Madonna tape for me. All the girls in our class adored the singer. I'd done my best to comb my hair like hers, slightly puffed up. I was only wearing a beige bra and purple panty hose, on top of which I had layered a makeshift skirt that I had made out of a crocheted shawl. To finish it off, I'd donned the red shoes I had found in the attic. The heels were so tall that I was almost six foot two in them. I used a broom as my microphone. "Like a Virgin" was playing when Holopainen entered the cabin. We had stopped locking the door now that we didn't need to hide Frida anymore.

"What are you doing? Is your uncle home?"

When I told him he wasn't, he didn't take it as a cue to leave, but instead sat down at the table.

"You've grown into a real woman. Great tits and all. Come over here and take a swig," Holopainen said. He dug for the bottle in his breast pocket and handed it over to me. I didn't move. I was sweaty from dancing and now I started shivering. In order to cover up, I would have to walk past Holopainen to get some clothes from my room. When I tried, he grabbed me and pulled me into his lap. He weighed at least two hundred pounds. His fat stomach kept me wedged between his body and the table. Its edge dug painfully into my back.

"Your mom used to wear those shoes to tease all the men in town. Looks like you're taking after her." Holopainen groped my breasts so forcefully that they popped out of the bra. Then he ripped off the shawl. Although I had always been able to defend myself, I was paralyzed and unable to breathe. He tried shoving his hand into my underwear, but the tight panty hose were in his way, so he pushed me onto the floor. I could feel his large stomach. A sluglike piece of meat hardened between our bodies. I was expecting to die at any moment. I knew that if women didn't do what men wanted, they'd end up dead.

Maybe I would've died, choked under Holopainen's weight, if Uncle Jari hadn't walked in. He was already angry, he'd been blamed for losing an elk, even though it wasn't his fault. He wasn't happy to see Holopainen's tractor out front. The guy had always been a bully, and he was the one who'd shot Frida's mother.

When we talked about it later, Uncle said it was a good thing that he had grabbed my microphone broom instead of an axe. Holopainen got away with bruises. He would pretend not to remember a thing, but I could tell by the way he looked at me that he did. We really should have filed a police report, but I guess Uncle Jari had been worried that I would be taken away from him. I was so shell-shocked that I didn't want to talk to anyone about it. Uncle took me to the sauna, where I scrubbed my skin bloody. We burned all the clothes, except for my mother's shoes. Holopainen's tractor caught fire a couple of nights later, and they never found out who did it. I was the only one who had smelled the gasoline on Uncle that night.

For years I couldn't listen to Madonna, until I was in New York and forced myself to go to her concert. While dancing to "Like a Virgin," I imagined what I could do to Holopainen if I ever saw him again. I could throw him to the ground a couple of times to break his bones or point my Glock at him and make him dance until he pissed his pants and begged for mercy.

By now, I wasn't afraid of him anymore. I had already beaten him in my mind, just like I would beat Paskevich and Laitio. I told Matti to tell Seppo hello from me, when in reality I couldn't have cared less if he'd drunk himself to death. It was a shame that he was still living when my uncle wasn't.

The Hakkarainens treated me like an old friend; they were a link to a past I thought was long gone. I had not kept in touch with anyone from high school—I hated that they knew all my secrets. Once I had taken my final exams, I moved three hundred miles away from home to Vantaa, a suburb of Helsinki, for guard training and then worked in various other cities. I joined the army as soon as they opened it up to women. It was an easy transition. I'd shared a house with a man all my life, and I was used to guns as household tools. The first women in the Finnish army were closely monitored, but I didn't mind being a pioneer.

During my time in the army, I had heard about the academy in Queens, a two-year program specializing in security. I was tempted to run away to New York, where nobody knew about my background. The only problem was the money, which I didn't have: the training cost 20,000 Finnish markkas, the equivalent of roughly 3,000 euros per year, and it didn't cover room, board, or travel costs.

After I finished my army service, I took on three jobs, which was crazy because most of my income went to pay taxes. While working as a guard, I would deliver free newspapers and moonlighted as a cleaner when I had the time. At first I hid my grand plans from my uncle; he already had a hard time with me living so far away in Vantaa, even though he understood why I had made the choice—there were no jobs in Kaavi. Maybe he'd secretly hoped I would have married some mama's boy from a nearby village and become a farmer's wife, but he must have realized that such a life would never work for me.

Because of my jobs I couldn't visit Uncle Jari for a while, so one day I received a call from him: if the mountain couldn't come to Mohammed, then he had no choice but to come to the mountain. Uncle felt uncomfortable in the city. He tried to avoid looking like a country bumpkin by buying a new pair of jeans, getting a professional haircut, and using pine soap because he was convinced it smelled better than most colognes.

He was surprised at how exhausted I was. Although after some begging, a coworker had agreed to take one of my shifts, I still needed to make my early-morning newspaper deliveries. When I told Uncle about all my jobs, he got upset.

"Is it really that expensive to live in the city? Isn't one job enough to support a single person?"

This was the perfect moment to bring up my dream, although I knew he wouldn't like it. After all, New York was across the ocean. He sat in silence for a while, then began pacing around the apartment like Frida trapped in the shed.

"But you have all that money in the bank," he finally said. "Your grandmother's. Fifty thousand markkas. I've kept it safe, in case, you know, you fell for a criminal, like when your mother—" Uncle Jari stopped short. He had almost brought up the unmentionable.

I felt dizzy. I had money? I could buy a car or travel around the world! Grandmother's will stipulated that unless I had my uncle's consent, I couldn't withdraw the money until I turned twenty-four. As soon as he relented, I left for New York.

My only goal was to graduate from the security academy with honors. With its strict policies and cameraderie, being in the academy was like being in the army again, although this time the group consisted of people from a multitude of backgrounds. The whole experience was as different from Hevonpersiinsaari as it could have been, but I never forgot where I came from.

On Saturday I stopped reminiscing and faced reality. It was time to take responsibility for what I had done in Moscow. As I drove back to Joensuu, I thought about how leaving Anita alone in Moscow had been the biggest mistake of my life, and I would carry that guilt forever. In Joensuu I got on the train and called Laitio to tell him that I was going to be in Helsinki soon. One of the silly teenage girls in front of me started laughing loudly, and I could feel Laitio's embarrassment over the phone when I growled at her, "You think this is funny, do you?" I got up from my seat and went to the far end of the car to talk.

"So you're on the train," said Laitio. He must have noticed the change in acoustics. "What time are you due in Pasila?"

When I told him, he said he'd come to pick me up. I didn't feel like mentioning that the train stopped in Tikkurila as well, where the National Bureau of Investigation offices were. Let him drive around if he wasn't smart enough to figure it out.

"I'll wait for you at the top of the escalators. I won't be wearing a uniform, but I'll recognize you from the pictures I have from the registry."

That sounded ominous. Luckily I'd have hours on the train to prepare myself mentally for our meeting. I was innocent, so I had nothing to worry about. I'd need to adopt that attitude if I wanted to convince him. I started feeling sleepy as I did my best to relax, and soon my thoughts drifted back to Anita and the past few days. Who had she been meeting at Frunzenskaya?

It was difficult to explain the fight over a lynx fur coat to anyone who hadn't met Frida. She had been more than a pet to me; she had been my sister. Although partly tame, like all wild animals, Frida had still been unpredictable. She was guided by her instincts, and could suddenly view Uncle Jari and me as her enemies. She never attacked us—her angry growl would let us know to stay away and not escalate the situation.

When I was truly relaxed, I became a lynx. I felt the fur coat growing out of my skin; tufted ears appeared on my head. My short tail waved from side to side for balance. The snow felt soft under my paws, and if I hit ice, I could always use my claws for a better grip. I saw a hare and went after it. I was a hunter, not the hunted.

I held on to that feeling when I got off the train in Pasila, where the rain was so heavy that even people standing under the awning were getting soaked. I spotted Laitio in an instant: he was the grumpy-looking man at the top of the escalator. Although short for a cop, his posture—simultaneously alert and relaxed—was a dead giveaway. With his dark-blue pea coat and a brimmed hat, he'd taken his fashion cues from American movies, and his substantial mustache took him back to the '70s. I cursed myself for not wearing high heels—most men couldn't take down a woman who was taller than them.

"Hello, Hilja Kanerva Ilveskero. It is Ilveskero now, right, and not Suurluoto?" Laitio wanted me to know that he had done his homework. I was a lynx and he was the hare; he could escape my grasp but was in no position to make threats. He led me to his car, a dark-blue Volvo that he apparently owned. No way the Bureau could afford such nice cars. I took the backseat as if I were getting into a cab, and I met Laitio's surprised glare in the rearview mirror.

He paid me back by driving away from the offices toward Töölö instead.

"I have a home office there," he announced. "I've been racking up too much overtime, and you can get home by tram. I hope you have a bus pass—no need to spend government money on your fare."

Why hadn't I asked him to show me his badge? Was this really Laitio and not some clever hit man who had happened to get my phone number from the Bureau? All I could see from the backseat was the long and bushy mustache he was sporting, which looked fake. His hair was hidden by the hat.

He managed to find street parking behind the Olympic stadium, and I followed him into the lobby of a nondescript building. I took a cursory glance at the list of residents for all seven floors: at least the name Laitio was there. We squeezed into a small elevator, and once its old-fashioned cage door clanged shut, I imagined Frida in the shed, scratching at the doors furiously. I looked down at Laitio's black shoes. They had ornate eyelets and black-and-white laces. He smelled of cigars.

The apartment door had the name Laitio on it, but he walked to another unmarked door and opened it. I figured it had been a service entrance back in the day. The cigar smell was stronger inside. When Laitio took off his hat, I saw that he was bald. He reached out to take my coat, accidentally grazing my back, which startled me. If Mike Virtue had seen that, he would have made me run around the block ten times as punishment.

Laitio wore a dark-gray pinstripe suit jacket and a tie with a subtle argyle pattern. He opened the door to his office, which was filled with cigar smoke. I didn't wait for him to ask me to sit down; I went for the dark leather couch. Laitio fell into his office chair and pulled open a desk drawer. Inside was a box of cigars. After he selected his smoke, he separated the cigar's cap from its head with an angry snap. When Laitio pulled the thick cigar to his lips, the sight was not attractive.

"We're not allowed to smoke at the Bureau offices, so I have this little deal here," he explained and blew smoke toward me. He probably knew the tobacco laws better than I did and would be able to enumerate the reasons why he was allowed to puff away here. Laitio may not have remembered that I was a seasoned traveler in Russia, where smoking was rampant. A little smoke wouldn't bother me.

He started questioning me about my work history. He didn't have a computer or a voice recorder in front of him, just a couple notepads. But he didn't write anything down.

"They focus on insignificant things, like the tobacco laws, but then they ignore the real issues, like murders," Laitio complained, sucking on his cigar. He suddenly switched gears. "Are you and your girlfriend planning on having a church wedding even though the bishops are still against it?"

"Is that any of your business?" I asked.

"I just wondered if you were the faithful type. Did you have an affair with Anita Nuutinen?"

"I don't fool around with my clients. And as far as I know, Anita only liked men."

"Were you jealous?" he asked. I stopped responding to his absurd questions, and let him smoke his cigar in silence, watching his mustache move. Valentin Paskevich had a mustache, too, but it was more of a European style, small and sharp.

"So you went all the way to America for security training, eh? Do you also always carry a gun?"

I wanted to reply by pulling out my pistol, but I didn't want him to confiscate it. He then asked me about people who had been threatening Anita.

"Being her bodyguard was more about general safety, but like I told you on the phone, she was afraid of her former business partner and lover, Valentin Paskevich."

Laitio sat still for a moment.

"Her lover? Nuutinen and this whatever-his-name-is had an affair?"

"Yes, for many years. I guess you haven't done your homework on Anita that well."

"Thank you, Ms. Smart-ass. Nuutinen didn't seem to have any friends. Her daughter was somewhere in Asia at the time and won't be back in Finland until later this week. Now tell me more about this Paskevich."

It seemed wise to steer the conversation away from me, so I took Laitio's cue and told him all I knew about Anita and Paskevich's business and all the scams they were involved with after their falling out. Laitio scribbled down some notes and didn't interrupt me once.

"So, you started working for Nuutinen after she and Paskevich were no longer lovers. She must have been a real piece of work," Laitio marveled. "Well, was there enough for you to do? Fighting and shooting, like a real bodyguard? Shoot men in face and kick them in balls?" he asked, as if he were reading from a script.

"There was no need for that. My presence was sufficient protection."

"Apparently. As soon as you left, Anita Nuutinen was killed. Why did you resign so suddenly? Did your girlfriend get jealous?"

"Nuutinen had decided to buy a lynx fur coat and I didn't approve of it."

Laitio burst out laughing so hard his mustache trembled. "You think I believe that story? You're no animal-rights activist; you're an army woman! Who paid you to leave Nuutinen behind? This

Paskevich character or one of his minions? Was thirty silver rubles enough?"

The lynx story went right over his head, obviously. He didn't need to know about my past.

"Or did you do it yourself? You took her to a quiet street and killed her? And now you're here, acting all innocent until you drop out of sight to live off your blood money on the island of Lesbos with your girlfriend, or whatever people like you do."

I couldn't help but detest Laitio. His suspicions indicated that the Bureau and the Moscow militia had no clue about this case. Maybe they didn't even want to be involved.

"Surely you have access to Anita Nuutinen's phone records. You can check them to see that I called her many times, apparently even after she was already dead. Why would I have done that if I were her murderer?"

Laitio let out his unpleasant laugh again.

"You think I'm an idiot, sweetheart? Of course you would have, so that you could sit here and ask that innocent question! So you regretted leaving her, eh?"

"Yes, I did. I tried calling her, and—" I was going to tell Laitio that I had gone after Anita, but his phone rang and interrupted us. He answered, and apparently he was angry with whoever was on the other end.

"Could you leave for a moment?" he spat at me. "Just go to the hallway. I'll let you back in as soon as I'm done. And don't even think about running away—I'll send half of Helsinki's police force after you!"

I did as I was told. Although it was annoying to be bossed around, it was nice to get out of the cigar smoke and into the hallway, and the balcony offered even fresher air. To my surprise I could hear Laitio's voice coming from a small window that was letting out more sound than smoke. He spoke in English with a heavy accent.

"I don't believe you. It's all bullshit and you know it. Shut up! I'll contact the Finnish Embassy and our foreign minister."

When he went quiet, I slinked back to the hallway, and soon his angry red face appeared at the door. His bald head was beaded with sweat when he pulled me in.

"Get your hands off me or I'll make an official complaint!" I shouted.

"Who'd believe you? I've been a cop for thirty-two years without a single incident. Goddamned irresponsible women like you really piss me off—you'll do anything for money. The Moscow militia found the murderer. Some homeless alcoholic who was living at the Frunzenskaya subway station. They found him dead from alcohol poisoning today, with Nuutinen's wallet and passport on him."

I stared at Laitio in disbelief. Now I understood why he'd been yelling on the phone.

"A homeless man. But wasn't Anita shot?" I asked.

"How would you know about that?"

"You said so on the phone."

"Ooh, but I didn't! I wouldn't be so stupid as to tell a suspect how the crime was committed. No Finnish media has reported these details."

I had told Laitio during our first call that I had not heard anything. I quickly came up with a story about how I had been to an Internet café in Joensuu and happened to check the Russian news sites. Laitio asked me to give him the café address, and I said I hadn't paid attention to it; it was the one near the marketplace.

The militia's story about a homeless murderer was ludicrous. They may have believed it, and someone may have manipulated the evidence to make sure that a single wallet would be sufficiently convincing. But a homeless man probably had nothing more on him than a knife and his own fists, and Anita wouldn't have gotten near homeless people, anyway. Bullshit, indeed. Laitio was right.

"So you'd been poking around Russian websites, huh? You speak Russki, or did you get a call from the killer?" Laitio was still trying to be menacing, but he had lost steam after the phone call and started to slump. His cigar had gone out, so he lit it again.

After a moment he opened the box and offered me one. When I declined he frowned and launched another tirade. "What's the matter? You're too good for the good stuff? I thought you had a reason to celebrate! Where are you keeping the blood money, huh? In a safe somewhere in Moscow? Goddamn it, if I catch you trying to cross the border, I'll have you arrested!"

I let him rant for a while, then I asked whether the militia in Moscow had closed Anita's case in light of this news. After some expletives Laitio confirmed that they had. He reached into his desk drawer again. This time he produced a bottle of cognac, skipped the glass, and drank straight from the bottle.

"Get the hell out of here, you whore," he said. "Go think about what you've done. Be happy that we found out about the killer just now—otherwise I'd have you jailed as a suspect. You wouldn't have been so stupid as to kill her yourself, but there's no denying that you're involved somehow!" Laitio took another massive swig out of the bottle and glared at me. The cognac dripped down his chin.

I stood up and imagined grabbing his cigar and stubbing it out on his bald head. I wanted to stay out of jail, so instead I grabbed my coat and headed down the stairs. Out on the street, I could hear Laitio yelling at me from his window, "And don't think you've seen the last of me! We'll meet again!"

5

Riikka was in the kitchen, but Jenni wasn't home. I pulled a bottle of beer from my backpack and opened it with my teeth. I drank half of it before I asked Riikka whether she'd seen anyone else looking for me besides the police. She said the building had been quiet; only the usual Jehovah's Witnesses had been knocking on doors. And there had been a Russian student selling paintings he'd made. Our neighbor had bought one and asked the boy in for coffee and quiche. This story about a Russian student didn't sound quite right, so I called our neighbor to invite myself over later to check out the painting she'd bought. A widow, she was delighted to have some company, and I always enjoyed her baking.

Before I went to bed, I looked around for anything out of the ordinary. I had carefully chosen my room and situated my mattress in just the right spot: I had made sure nobody would be able to shoot into the room from the street. It might be possible from the roof across the road, but the shooter would have to risk being seen. I set my Glock next to my mattress. It was loaded. Riikka and Jenni had never seen it, and I should have kept it in the gun case behind lock and key, but this time I just wrapped it in Anita's scarf. It smelled of her perfume, vanilla and patchouli, a greeting from beyond the grave.

Frida came to me in my dreams. We ran on the frozen lake, and I pulled fish out of a hole in the ice for Frida to play with. When we reached land, we heard a gunshot in the forest, and Frida was suddenly full of seeping wounds, just like the fur Anita had worn on the night of her death. I woke up, startled, and realized that the sound of someone trying to come into our apartment had woken me up. It didn't sound like a break-in; more like someone attempting to open the door with the wrong set of keys.

Slowly I stood up and reached for my gun. I peered into our foyer. When the door opened and someone hobbled in, I instinctively raised my gun. Drunk out of her mind, Jenni stared at the gun for a moment and then began to scream.

I rushed back to my room, closed the door behind me, and hid the gun in my purse. Then I came back to the foyer, pointing my flip phone at Jenni like a gun.

"Jesus, stop yelling! You'll wake the whole building!"

Jenni had collapsed in a heap in the foyer.

"But there was a gun pointed at . . ."

"A cell phone, Jenni. I thought someone was breaking in with all that noise. I was about to call the cops. You're so wasted you couldn't tell a moose from a squirrel," I whispered so that Riikka wouldn't wake up. I could hear her stirring in her room. I hoisted Jenni up and pushed her into the bathroom in case she needed to throw up.

Mary Higgins, my landlady in New York, had occasionally come back to our Morton Street apartment half unconscious from a mix of cocktails and cocaine. She'd made me her hangover maid, asking me to feed her salty foods and meds. It was a great deal, for which I had Mike Virtue to thank, as he was Mary's cousin. The location in the West Village was perfect for me, and I suppose he wanted me to keep an eye on her. She was a performance artist who'd sometimes take me to clubs where I never necessarily knew the sex of the person I was talking to. Although I was less enthusiastic about these outings than Mary, I did enjoy seeing people adopt a role for an evening.

Studying at the academy was like a full-time job, and it was a thirty-minute commute to get there. At that time the dollar was worth more than the Finnish markka, so my disposable income was limited. In Manhattan I felt disconnected from home, but I enjoyed telling strangers stories about my past and creating a new identity. One day I was a Finnish cleaning lady, Anneli; the next I was Helene, a Danish art student. I returned to Finland with a large supply of Mary's beloved antinausea pills and business cards from people I'd met; people I'd left in the morning with a promise to call but never did.

I gave Jenni a double dose of the pills once she'd crawled out of the bathroom. They'd taken a toll on Mary's memory, and the next morning, when I returned from my morning run, I hoped they'd done the same to Jenni. She was sitting in the kitchen, slowly sipping on orange juice. She was sickly pale, except for her bloodshot eyes.

"Hi. Nice to see you here," she greeted me and took another laborious gulp from her juice. Mary's pills would keep her from throwing up, but she didn't seem to remember that I'd given her anything. "Riikka told me I woke you up some time around three when I got home. Sorry. I guess we started the semester with a bang."

"No problem. I fell asleep shortly after. Can I have some of your juice? I'll buy you some more later."

It was Sunday, so I'd have to wait a day before signing up for unemployment. I had no intention of waiting the requisite three months before starting a new job, so I started looking. I checked the help-wanted ads in the newspaper and saw one for a security gig at the Helsinki-Vantaa airport. I applied for it online. While logged in, I sent another e-mail to Monika von Hertzen as well, although I didn't know what kind of Internet access she had these days. She was one of the few people who knew about Frida.

Elli Voutilainen, our neighbor, must have been at home because of the lousy weather. She'd lived here since the building had been constructed and acted as a godmother to most of the other residents. Occasionally I helped her with cleaning her windows or taking the rugs downstairs to be aired out. When I rang her doorbell, she came to the door in an apron, releasing the wonderful aroma of lingonberry pie into the stairwell.

"Well, hello, Hilja! I haven't seen you in a while, but I did notice you running out there in the rain this morning. Be careful you don't catch a cold!"

"I don't get sick easily; I'll be fine. May I come in?"

"Come, come! I was just making a lingonberry pie—I was in Nuuksio with Sylvi and Väinö picking the berries. Just another five minutes and it'll be done. Want some coffee, too?"

We sat in her living room, where the walls were covered in the miniature porcelain plates she'd produced over the years. She'd given me a couple in the past. Mrs. Voutilainen's specialty was flowers and birds, and the paintings she had collected depicted the same. I noticed there was a new print on the wall. It gave me chills.

"The girls told me you had a Russian salesman over. Is this the painting you bought from him?" I looked at Mrs. Voutilainen, who was about five feet tall and as fragile as her porcelain. "You really shouldn't let complete strangers into your home," I said, turning back to the painting, unable to look away.

"You think I'm helpless, don't you? No need to worry; I can tell who is having a hard time and who isn't. This Yuri seemed like a kindred spirit. He's a garbage truck driver during the day and paints in the evenings, and he sends all his earnings back to his family near Murmansk. He looked so hungry I had to invite him in for coffee and some ham quiche."

"Did you choose this painting?"

"No, Yuri picked it out for me. He said its colors would make a good addition to this room, and he was right—look how it matches my sofa and the wallpaper. I preferred the swan he'd painted, but I thought he'd have an easier time selling that one than the one I bought. Let me pop into the kitchen to see if the pie is ready. I'll set the table."

I took a few steps toward the painting. The signature was large and clear: *Yuri Trankov*. It probably wasn't his real name. The paintings may not have been his, either. It was easy to buy amateur paintings in bulk from some homeless person at a Moscow subway station. This Trankov wasn't a bad artist; the painting was incredibly realistic. It was small, only about eleven by fifteen inches, and in other circumstances I would have greatly admired it. It depicted a lynx leaping from a ledge to attack a deer. But this piece of art could only be interpreted as a warning. What did that voice mail say again? That I should keep quiet if I didn't want to end up as dead as the lynx Anita had been wearing?

Over coffee I tried to pry for more details about Trankov from Mrs. Voutilainen. He had appeared with a bag on wheels containing about a dozen small paintings of animals. He'd asked for fifty euros, but she had given him sixty because she happened to have three twenty-euro bills in her purse.

"Did you two speak in English? You don't know Russian, do you?"

"No, and my English isn't great, either. Yuri spoke Finnish, and very well considering that he's only been in Helsinki since last fall. Obviously a motivated young man."

Elli Voutilainen didn't have any children of her own; she loved taking young people under her wing. I asked whether Yuri had happened to leave any contact information, but apparently he was so poor that he didn't even have a phone. Mrs. Voutilainen accused me of being prejudiced against Russians—all Yuri took were three slices of quiche, and that was only after she had insisted on it. I didn't think Yuri had any plans to rob Mrs. Voutilainen; he was just a messenger, and his message had been heard loud and clear.

Because she was a skillful artist herself, I asked her to make a sketch of Yuri for me. She shook her head.

"Poor girl, you're so suspicious of everyone, but I guess it's part of your job." She'd heard the same cover story as my roommates about my work. Despite her protests she began to draw, and soon an image emerged of a skinny man with sunken cheeks, a small goatee, and sideburns. She had captured his easily recognized Slavic features: the prominent cheek bones, forehead, and small, narrow nose.

"Too bad you don't have his address. He would have liked this portrait. Can I buy it?"

"What do you mean, *buy*? Take it. Oh, and take some of this lingonberry pie to Jenni and Riikka. Which one of them was making a ruckus last night in the hallway? I suppose it was Jenni; the religious girl probably wouldn't have." Mrs. Voutilainen bustled back to the kitchen to pack up the pie and left me alone, staring at the painting.

At home I used Riikka's printer-copier combo to make copies of the sketch. She also identified Trankov as the man who had showed up at our door.

"If you see this guy, let me know," I said. "And do not let him in, under any circumstances." I'd tell Jenni the same thing the next time I saw her.

"Why?"

"He's not a nice guy. A skirt chaser. Better stay away from him."

"Did he hurt you?"

"He tried. I'd rather not talk about it, you know, for professional confidentiality reasons."

"Sheesh, what a job you have. Both the cops and the robbers are after you."

In an attempt to steer the conversation in another direction, I made a joke about how I hoped I wouldn't need her for spiritual guidance anytime soon.

I figured I could find out more about this Trankov character at the train station. Luckily, Riikka dragged Jenni to the movies later that day, and I had the house to myself to get prepared. I'd appear at the station as my alter ego, Reiska Räsänen.

I had created him a few years earlier. When Dylan Monroe, Mary's friend from Tribeca, e-mailed me about his trip to Finland to teach a class on male impersonation, I signed up immediately—I knew being able to pass as a man would have its uses. The other students went for more colorful types of men: ice hockey players, CEOs, heavy metal fans, but I opted for a typical, all-around Finnish guy. The type who sat next to me at school and who played cards with me in the army.

Reiska's hair was slightly longer and mousier than my own blond, cropped hair, and he had a thick mustache and a bald spot on the back of his head. Usually he tried to hide it with a baseball cap. His mirrored glasses were straight out of the '70s. I needed bushier eyebrows to become Reiska. To make my skin appear more masculine, I piled on foundation; Dylan had recommended a particular brand.

Reiska's clothes were pretty much the same as mine; the combat boots and jeans were gender neutral, as were the jogging pants and sneakers he occasionally wore. The brown-and-gray-checked shirt had belonged to Uncle Jari and was a bit snug on Reiska, which was okay. Most important was his gait: it was confident, manly, and sent the message, "Get out of my way." When Reiska had shown up in Moscow, prostitutes assumed he was a Finnish tourist.

His voice was the biggest hurdle. Mine was an alto, but it clearly belonged to a woman. Reiska's speech was hard to decipher, as if he had something caught in his throat. He also had a stutter, which made him appear a little less tough than he wanted. Reiska did his best not to speak with a regional accent, but often an awkward turn of phrase gave him away. His lilt made it clear he was from Eastern Finland.

Dylan had asked me, why Reiska? Why this almost-invisible everyman? His question provided the answer. Reiska wasn't interesting, which meant that women wouldn't be running after him and men wouldn't find him threatening. There was nothing enviable about him, and his dialect occasionally made him seem like a hick. People let their guard down around him.

Reiska's scent completed my transformation. He considered himself a hip fellow—his aftershave and deodorant were both made by Ferrari. It was important to hide my own scent, so, coughing, I lit up a cigarette on my way to the bus stop. On occasion I'd even splashed Reiska's clothes with gasoline. Our fingerprints would be the same, at least for now, so Reiska usually wore leather gloves, weather permitting.

Reiska knew some of the people hanging out at the train station and stopped to chat with them. A woman impersonating a man appears to be younger than her biological age. Dressed as Reiska I was twenty-five years old, a farm boy who had moved to the city.

It was easy for him to mingle with a bunch of teenagers who were hanging around the station. A group was speaking in a mix of Russian and Finnish, including a couple of thirtysomething men in leather jackets. I inched closer, and it didn't take long before one of them talked to me.

"Hey, what do you want?" I could tell from his accent that he wasn't Finnish. "These girls here are not for sale, you know."

"I'm not after girls."

"What, boys then? We don't have them, but give me a fifty and I'll give you a good lead."

"I only want one: a Russian painter guy. He sold an old lady a nice painting, and now I'd like to get my hands on one, too. Do you know him—Yuri Trankov? Drives a garbage truck, paints nature scenes?"

"I don't know any painters," he said. "But I can ask around if you want. Give me your number and a smoke, if you have one."

I handed him a cigarette, which he took with a funny look on his face. I could only smoke lights—otherwise I'd choke. Lights were also cheapest, which suited Reiska's persona as a cheapskate. The man didn't care that we were indoors and lit up while Reiska scribbled down one of my phone numbers for him; I'd need to remember to turn on my prepaid line. He seemed a bit too helpful, so Reiska moved on to the station bar to look for other potential informants. He ordered a beer so he wouldn't look suspicious.

Being Reiska was a challenge when it was time to visit the men's room. I had learned to pee standing up and to simulate the noises men made while relieving themselves, but it hadn't been easy. Urinals were out of the question, and a man who used a stall just to go number one was downright weird, especially someone who looked liked Reiska. So Reiska would need to take it easy with the beer—who knows how long he'd be hanging around the station.

It would be a stroke of luck if someone not only knew Trankov but decided to tell Reiska about him. And I didn't even know whether Trankov had sold his paintings to anyone but my neighbor, so asking around may get her into trouble, as well. The bloody image of Anita, slumped on the street in her soiled fur coat, appeared to me again. Elli Voutilainen's nephew lived in the small mill town of Loimaa in Western Finland. I doubted anyone would go after him, even if they did try to trace Reiska.

It was an average Sunday evening at the train station: students coming back from visiting their parents; soldiers hopping on the northbound train to nearby Hämeenlinna, where they'd continue on to the Parolannummi military base; country folk leaving the city after their weekend visits. Once Reiska finished his beer, he started doing his rounds. The police wouldn't pay attention to a guy like him, but security guards would shoo him away to loiter elsewhere.

Reiska hung around the station until midnight without any luck. The Russian he'd talked to earlier had left around ten, and some younger kids joined the group; they didn't seem to be concerned about having to go to school in the morning. Reiska drank a cup of tea at a café that only allowed paying customers to use their private restroom. He checked his phone—no calls. He went to catch a bus home.

One of the last buses of the night was almost empty, which is why the two young men in leather jackets sitting in the back caught Reiska's attention. He didn't hear what language they spoke, and they looked like they could have been Finns or Eastern Europeans. Reiska relaxed, but inside I was on alert.

The two men got off at Reiska's stop. Everything was quiet except for the lone cab that ambled down the street. Reiska walked confidently and didn't glance back. Young men like him were the least afraid of getting mugged, although statistically speaking they were the ones most likely to be targeted. He wasn't drunk, and I didn't want to put on an act. I wasn't comfortable with going straight home, so I walked over to my neighborhood place, Käpygrilli. I knew it closed at nine on Sundays, but I did my best to look like a man trying to find a bar somewhere nearby that would still let him in. A man just standing around is looking to be messed with.

"Hey man, give us one." The leather jacket duo was now next to me. The speaker used Finnish without a foreign accent. They were even younger than I had originally thought, barely in their teens. I pulled out my pack of cigarettes, and they lit up in silence.

"What are you looking for, old man? Booze?" the more talkative one asked. His pockmarked face was already ashen from smoking too much.

"Me, naw, I'm not looking for anything. Just thought I'd see if this bar was still open. I'm visitin' my cousin here in the city." Reiska started to walk away in the opposite direction from home. I hadn't brought any kind of weapon with me, and I didn't want to get into a fistfight, either. Unlike Hilja, Reiska didn't know judo, and I wasn't ready to break character unless my life was at stake. Plus, such close contact might reveal my sex, and and it was hard to know what their attitude toward cross-dressing might be.

"Hillbilly!" yelled the talkative one after me. "Fucking yokel!"

Reiska the Eastern Finn would have taken offense and paid these little bums back, but Hilja the Bodyguard didn't want to take any risks. Reiska turned the corner to a familiar apartment courtyard and hid in the shadows of the communal clothesline. The men had started to come in his direction, but weren't interested in him—they walked past. Reiska waited a good fifteen minutes before he took a detour home.

There were no lights on in our kitchen window or in my roommates' bedrooms. Still, I didn't want to barge in dressed up as

Reiska; instead, I used our storage space in the basement to remove the wig and the mustache. Once I reached our bathroom, I washed off all the makeup and showered, despite the fact that the noise could potentially wake up my roomies—I just needed to get rid of Reiska's smell. It reminded me of Uncle Jari and how sad I had been when his smell had slowly disappeared from the hunting jacket I had kept. I went to bed, trying to remember that smell. Falling asleep in the comfort it provided had always been easy.

My breakfast the next morning was a large bowl of buckwheat porridge and half a carton of tomato juice. My phone hadn't made a sound. After breakfast I hopped on the tram toward Hakaniemi to pay a visit to the unemployment office. No matter how often I went there, the experience was always unpleasant. At least this time I had thought to bring along a book, a water bottle, and two bananas. Nearly two hours later, I was finally face-to-face with a clerk. She was ready to move on to retirement: her eyes, enlarged by strong prescription lenses, were dull with apathy. I told her my name, social security number, and employment history.

"And the reason for termination?"

"Disagreement with the employer."

"Did you receive proof of employment from the employer?"

"No."

She clucked her tongue.

"You better get one. Otherwise it's hard to be employed again. Guards need to have proof that they can be trusted."

"Well, I can't get one now—my former employer is dead."

I immediately regretted saying this. Why hadn't I forged a document praising my work? Chief Constable Laitio, that's why. Like an idiot I had told him my reason for quitting. Laitio wouldn't have access to the unemployment office records, but it was in my nature not to lie—why risk getting caught?—unless the lie was absolutely necessary.

"Dead?" The rep perked up visibly. "What do you mean, dead?"

I didn't know what to say, so I said nothing. I signed the forms stating that I was ready to take advantage of their services. They offered me a cleaning job that would begin right away and I said I'd consider it—once my bank balance dropped to three digits. Regardless, it was important to show up at the unemployment office. This way, whoever was after me would assume my only concern was finding a new job. Such a person would have no business going back to Moscow to solve Anita's murder by herself. Not that I would dare to go back there. I'd conduct my investigation from Finland. Even if I would never find out who really was responsible for Anita's murder, I wanted some proof that it hadn't been me. But what if the evidence didn't absolve me?

I went back to the apartment to pack up my stuff. It all fit into a large backpack. My bus began the hour-long westward crawl along the coast, heading to Torbacka and my cabin in Degerby.

Once there, I heard more Swedish than Finnish. This made me think about Monika again. My cabin didn't have an Internet connection—I would need to go to the Degerby community center, and it was only open once a week. I'd purposefully steered clear of my neighbors in Degerby. Even the brother of the owners in the cabin next door had left me alone after I'd put him off a few times.

My bike was still in front of the local bank in Degerby; it was a piece of junk that no thief would want. I bought some tomatoes and beer from the grocery store and started riding toward the coast; it would take me about fifteen minutes. The potholes in the gravel road made my backpack bump up and down, requiring all of my effort to stay balanced. It was a real challenge to ride up the last hill on a bike with no gears. I pedaled slowly, cursing all the way, but I didn't give up.

Once I reached the cabin, I walked around it and peered inside for any signs of intruders. Everything seemed to be exactly as I had left it three weeks earlier before the trip to Moscow. Before I went in I deactivated the burglar alarm, then tossed my backpack to the middle of the floor. I plugged in the fridge and put my beer in it. Then I went to the shed to find a shovel.

Anita had given me the papers in early summer. Supposedly she still had the originals in her safety deposit box, but she wanted me to have the copies. She was sure I'd know a secure place for them.

The plot of land was pebbly and wide, and someone had marked a path through it with mounds of small rocks. I had added to it by piling up rocks at a spot that had more soil and grass. After removing the rocks I began to dig, and soon the shovel hit metal. Anita's box. Actually, it was more like a miniature safe. There was just one problem: I had no idea what the combination for the lock was.

6

I had warned Anita not to use a combination that could be guessed easily. Never use birth dates, phone numbers, or, especially, numbers that correspond to the letters in the alphabet to spell the safe owner's name. A random string of numbers was the only option. It would have eight numbers, each up to two digits. I didn't even want to calculate the number of possible combinations.

There was a crowbar in the shed. I placed the small safe on a rock and started banging on it. Despite the noise I barely managed to scratch it.

"It is usually better to use your wits than your muscles," Mike Virtue had once advised me, and it looked like he was right. I carried the safe indoors and decided to regroup before going at it again. I opened one of the beers and plopped onto the couch. My thoughts took me back to Hevonpersiinsaari, when I had tried to figure out who may have known that I had left Anita by herself. This would mean that we'd been followed the entire time we were in Moscow, and I had been a lousy bodyguard for not noticing. Or both of us had been tagged with a tracking device that I had not found despite my frequent checks.

Just the thought of it made me shiver. A tracker. Although I hadn't detected any marks on me besides some small bruising, which could have been caused by a simple fall, I began to worry. Maybe I had been drugged not to hurt or scare me, but to insert a tracker. My entire body suddenly felt like it was buzzing, as if I'd sat on an ant hill. I quickly stripped off my clothes and took the largest mirror off the wall. Then, with the aid of it and a hand mirror, I inspected my body inch by inch. No new scars or bumps. I combed my hair multiple times, felt my scalp, and probed everywhere with the metal detector, even in my mouth where I checked each tooth. I put on surgical gloves and felt for the strings of my IUD—everything seemed normal.

I checked the stuff I'd had with me in Bar Svoboda. My leather jacket made the metal detector beep, but only because of the zipper and the studs. I felt the seams for anything unusual and then ripped the fabric open at the elbow when I detected a weird bump. It turned out to be just an extra button that had somehow slipped between the leather and the lining. Nevertheless, I dumped the button in the trash, although I felt like an idiot for doing it.

There was no way I believed that a homeless drunk had murdered Anita, but I didn't want to give in to paranoia, either. It could very well be that no one had bribed the militia. Maybe someone had just decided that there was no need to investigate further now that there was a logical explanation. They were all overworked, and some screaming cop from Finland or our smiling foreign minister wouldn't change anyone's mind.

My frequent trips to Russia had taught me that it was a complicated place, and what was true or false wasn't always clear. However, most of the Russians I'd met were extremely friendly, and a couple of words of Russian were all that was needed to melt their hearts. Still, there were some topics that were off-limits if there were Russians within earshot. They believed that Finns should be grateful to them—without Russia, Finland would be Sweden's forgotten back-country. At least Soviet Russia had given Finns independence.

Then there had been the confusion when I tried to explain to my American classmates in New York why Finland had sided with Germany during the Second World War. I tried to make them understand that we had had two options: Hitler or Stalin. It was pretty crazy to claim that Hitler had been the right choice, but that's how it was. If we'd chosen Stalin, we would have been under Russia's thumb for decades, like our neighbors in the Baltic countries.

I turned the TV on. It belonged to my landlord, like the rest of the furniture. I'd only brought the basics when I first came here; I didn't want anyone to be able to trace the cabin back to me. The landlord took care of the cable, too. I switched from one channel to another until I saw a familiar face.

Representative Helena Lehmusvuo had been a regular at Chez Monique and she frequently helped with Monika's food project in Mozambique. Lehmusvuo specialized in human rights and freedom of speech. When the Russian journalist Anna Politkovskaya had been murdered, our leading politicians had told Lehmusvuo to stop talking to the press after she'd proclaimed that Politkovskaya was murdered at Russian Prime Minister Vladimir Putin's behest. Now Lehmusvuo was on TV, commenting on Russia's promise to pull their troops out of Georgia and on Prime Minister Putin's statement that the Soviet Union's fall had been a geopolitical tragedy. Lehmusvuo was a staunch opponent of nuclear power, so she criticized the way Finns were dependent on energy produced by the Russians, such as nuclear power and natural gas. She spoke with the usual bombast of a politician, but I didn't switch the channel. Instead, I listened to what she had to say.

"Finland has no other alternative than to stop relying on imported energy, which means that inevitably our energy consumption must be reduced."

The reporter began to grill her about national competitiveness and the looming economic downturn, but at that moment I got a text message. It was from Mrs. Voutilainen. I hastily read her report. She thought she'd seen Yuri Trankov walking along Koskela Road, near our building, but she wasn't sure.

My mind filled slowly with dread. They wouldn't go after my roommates, would they? If they'd figured out my address, they'd know that I didn't live alone. Sicilians scared their targets with horse heads, but I'd had to settle for a painting of a lynx.

I shoved my half-empty beer in the fridge, hid the safe under a pile of chopped wood in the sauna, and climbed up a nearby cliff high enough to see the ocean. In the slow drizzle, it was calm and gray like a wolf's fur. A flock of geese honked overhead; it was migration time. I could have easily pretended to be a mushroom enthusiast, or, if I'd grabbed the binoculars from the cabin, an ornithologist. Thanks to Uncle Jari, I knew my mushrooms—he'd made an effort to teach me what he's considered the most important life skills.

Thinking of him brought me back to the time in second grade when we were almost torn apart. My teacher had started a PE club for kids after school on Thursdays, but I couldn't join because I had no way of getting home after the school bus had left. The teacher lived about a mile from school and offered to drive me home afterward. She probably took pity on me, a motherless girl with mismatched socks. One day I did stay after school and we practiced cartwheels and climbing rope, both of which I mastered. Afterward the teacher drove me home, pulling up right in front of our yard. Clearly she was waiting to be invited in. I really wanted to introduce her to my pet, Frida, but I had a feeling that Uncle Jari wouldn't approve. So I just thanked her for the ride and showed her the best spot to turn around the car. Then I ran inside and called for Frida.

Frida wasn't there—just Uncle Jari. I had never seen him look that angry before. His face was the shade of a ripe lingonberry and when he yelled at me, his mustache shook.

"What the hell is going on? Why was your teacher here?"

"I told you about the PE club. She brought me home. I thought you were still at the Karttunen construction site . . ." I was about to cry. Uncle shouldn't have been that upset.

"We ran out of materials; that's why I'm home. And good thing I was! I barely got Frida inside before you two showed up. Don't you understand that the lynx is our secret? You can't tell anyone about her! They'll take her away to a zoo, or even worse—they'll kill her."

Now I was crying. Of course I didn't want to give up Frida.

"I'll never go to PE club again, I promise," I sobbed. Uncle Jari calmed down quickly, but reminded me numerous times that evening that Frida needed to remain our secret.

The following Thursday my teacher asked if I was going to stay after school for the club, and I said I couldn't.

"Why not, sweetie? I can always take you home."

"I just can't. It's a secret."

"A secret?" A frown appeared on her face. "You can share your secret with me."

"I can't! It's a secret between me and my uncle Jari!"

The teacher gasped and covered her mouth. "Dear child, a secret between you two? You should be able to talk about secrets. When was the last time you saw the school nurse? Oh, no, what should I do now?"

Her visible distress puzzled me, but when she asked, "Does the secret begin with the letter 'p'?" I got worried that she knew about

Frida. She was practically hyperventilating now. "Oh my goodness, how would you know such a word, how should I put this . . ."

"Actually, it does begin with a 'p'!" After all, why wouldn't I know about the paws that I saw scratching at the door every day? "But that's all I can say!" I'd already said too much, and Uncle Jari would be mad. "Gotta catch my bus, bye!"

Frida had scratched me a couple of times, enough to draw blood but not bad enough to show the nurse. The nurse came to our school every Tuesday, and although this year we didn't need any vaccinations, we were all still afraid of her. She had cold hands and smelled funny. When I was older, I realized that the source of the odor was probably the stale flowery perfume she bought at our local department store.

When the nurse appeared at school on Friday, all of us students got worried. She'd come on the wrong day only once before, and that was when Hannu Hakkarainen had lice and we all had to be inspected. That was in first grade. Now the school nurse demanded that I follow her out of the classroom. I could hear the other kids whispering behind my back. She took me into her office, which doubled as a storage room for maps and teaching equipment. A stuffed pygmy owl stared at me from the top shelf.

"So, about this secret between you and your uncle," she asked awkwardly. "Does the secret hurt?"

I stared at her.

"No, it doesn't hurt, it's nice. And cute, too! I mean, sometimes it scratches, but not that badly. See, the scab is almost gone!" I lifted my shirtsleeve to display Frida's scratch on my elbow from the previous week.

"Scratches . . . Listen, Hilja, you'll need to take all your clothes off." The nurse pulled a folding screen in front of the door and set a paper sheet on an old bed that was used as an examination table.

"Why?" I didn't understand what right she had to barge in to class and demand that I take off my clothes. Nothing was wrong. My throat wasn't hurting and I wasn't coughing at all.

"Just take all of them off." She sounded even more rattled than before. I'd heard from sixth graders that fifth graders would get a weiner inspection, but that was only for the boys.

I took my clothes off slowly in the cold storage room. First I pulled off my sweater and shirt, then my pants. I wore thick red leggings under my jeans and pink panties that were fraying around one of the leg openings. I left the panties on. The nurse inspected my skin and asked how I had gotten so scratched up.

"Our cat is a bit wild," I said. A lynx was a cat, after all.

"A cat, eh? Quite large claws she has, your cat." The nurse's throat made odd movements, as if she had an Adam's apple like a man. "Come now, take off the panties as well and hop up on the bed." Then she muttered to herself, "Without a proper examination table, how on earth am I going to—yes, now just lift up your legs and spread them."

I did as I was told. Then, without a warning, something cold and metallic was shoved into me and I screamed and kicked her in the mouth. She dropped the cold metal. I pulled it out and kept on screaming. When she tried to touch me again, I hissed and bit, and my cries turned into the kind of low growl that I had heard emanating from Frida. The nurse told me to get dressed again and follow her back to the classroom, where the other kids were already having lunch. She didn't let me go inside—instead, she fetched the teacher and we all stood in the hallway.

"She wouldn't let me examine her; she behaved like a lunatic. She even bit me! Which isn't a surprise, really, with her genes. Is she dangerous to the other children?"

"I haven't noticed."

"I'll have a doctor take a look at her at the health care center, where they have beds with straps. Would you be able to drive her there?"

"The grade-schoolers are done at one on Mondays and Fridays."

"Next Monday it is then. I'll take care of it. There's something fishy going on, with the way she went berserk. I'll need to ask a social worker to come with us. Wasn't Pirjo Koistinen on the Ilveskero case?" Her upper lip was swollen where I'd kicked her, and she was pressing it down with her hand. My teacher had a strange expression on her face when she led me back to class.

The kids had already finished eating, but I managed to scrape up a huge portion of scalloped potatoes from what was left in the pot. My friends asked me what the nurse had wanted, but I didn't tell them. I didn't mention it to Uncle Jari, either; I was so ashamed of what the nurse had done. Uncle had always told me that whatever was between my legs was my business and mine alone, and nobody else should touch me there. He'd never told me why, but I believed him. Nonetheless, I was proud that I hadn't let him down by sharing our secret, even though the nurse had been so nasty to me. It served her right to get a fat lip for trying to hurt me. I hadn't focused on what she'd said about jeans. What did she mean by that? What was wrong with the pair I was wearing?

Over the weekend I managed to forget about what had happened at school. Uncle Jari and I spent both days ice fishing. Afterward, he baked perch inside a loaf of bread and made fish soup, while Frida played with her gift, a perch that was still alive. It wasn't until Monday that I remembered about having to see a doctor. Before I headed out to the school bus, I petted Frida and promised I wouldn't say a word about her, no matter what the doctor said. When I got to the bus, my resolve started to falter. I remembered reading in a Donald Duck comic about a truth serum; maybe they would give me a shot and then all I could do was tell the truth. I would make sure they didn't inject me with anything.

School started with religion. The topic was the sons of Zebedee, which was one of Uncle Jari's favorite jokes after he'd had a couple of beers. "Who was the father of Zebedee's sons?" Would the teacher know the answer?

We built a snow castle during recess. Then it was time for math, where we practiced our times tables. They had always been easy for me; at home I sometimes played multiplication games with uncle's matches. Next was arts and crafts, where I worked on a piece of embroidery. I could put it under Frida's bowl. I had chosen yellow and dark-brown thread to stitch onto a light-brown piece of fabric. Other kids thought those colors were ugly, which just meant I had more supplies to work with.

I had been distracted again and suddenly remembered the doctor. I wouldn't make a sound, no matter what sort of metallic objects they put inside me. I prepared for the pain by pricking the back of my hand with a needle. I could tolerate discomfort; I'd show that doctor.

When we were in the car, the teacher asked me all sorts of strange things, such as where did my uncle and I sleep, and whether we went to the sauna together to bathe. Did he kiss me? I told her that I usually got a good night kiss from him when I went to my own bed, and of course we went to the sauna together to save on heat.

"Do you sometimes kiss your uncle anywhere else, or just on the cheek?"

I thought about it. Yes, I had once kissed him on the hand when we played king and queen, but that had been years ago. My teacher was curious about this game and tried to get me to remember more. It had started when I had gotten a new red blanket, which looked like a king's cape to me. I cut out a cardboard crown for Uncle Jari. We played this game for a bit, but then Matti had come over on his moped and that was the end of it. But kings' hands had to be kissed, at least in fairy tales.

"Remember, you need to give the doctor proper answers. He's the expert," she told me when we arrived at the health care center, which was a low, wide white building near a tall factory chimney. A bit farther away the old quarry tower was visible; it looked like a fairy-tale castle. The nurse took me by the hand and led me down the hallway, asking for directions. The whole building smelled strange, kind of like our neighbor's house.

The doctor was an old man with long white hairs growing out of his ears. I'd pull on them if he tried any funny business. A woman named Pirjo was also in the room; she occasionally dropped by our home to make sure we had enough food in the pantry. She was always nice to me, but Uncle Jari worried about her visits. If he knew she was coming over, he'd busy himself with cleaning and buying expensive meats and oranges.

They told me to wait while the doctor and the teacher stepped out for a minute. I looked around the room and noticed the weird bed-chair contraption that had horse saddle stirrups upside down on it. It looked funny. Then Pirjo and the doctor returned without the teacher and asked me to take my clothes off.

Was he really an expert? Doctors sometimes resurrected people, like Jesus had. He was a good man, this Jesus, but according to Uncle Jari, so much harm had been done in his name. Was I here because Jesus's friend the doctor was trying to take the lynx away from us?

I decided not to protest and stripped down. My teacher had told me that God sees everywhere, so I assumed he saw under my clothes, too. Then why couldn't the doctor see right through them, as well?

When asked, I explained away my scars with the cat story I had told earlier. He noticed the mark left by a needle, and I told him I'd accidentally pricked myself in arts and crafts class. He then asked me to get on the strange chair and started messing around with the stirrups. I was too short to reach them. He seemed to want to play cowboys and Indians, as he strapped my legs to the stirrups. Uncle had once read me a book about Delia, a white woman who lived with the Indians. In the story the Indians rode under a horse's belly in order to fool the white people. This peculiar chair seemed like it was meant to trick me, too. I felt better when the doctor put a warm blanket on me.

"Just close your eyes and relax. You can pretend that you are in the sauna or on a warm beach somewhere," he said calmly. He sounded nice. I didn't dare close my eyes. I had to make sure he wasn't going to inject me with truth serum. He was holding a metallic rod with a mirror on the end of it, just like the one the nurse had tried to use on me. He rubbed it between his hands. I didn't like this game anymore, and I tried to pull my legs out of the stirrups. Pirjo just sat in the corner and stared—she wasn't asked to join in the game.

"Hilja, honey, I need to examine you. If you won't behave, I'll need to tie up your hands as well. I can give you something to calm you down—then this won't hurt."

I knew he meant the truth serum, so I promised to behave. I felt the metallic object slide into me, and although it wasn't as cold as before, it still didn't feel right. You weren't supposed to put anything down there.

"Good girl," he told me, like our neighbor praising his horse. The metal was pulled out and something rubbery and soft took its place, but only for a second. It hurt a bit, but I didn't complain. I hadn't said a word about Frida.

The doctor untied my legs and asked me to turn onto my belly. I did as I was told, although I was worried because I couldn't see his hands. He touched my butt carefully, then pulled a blanket over me.

"Do you like living with your uncle?" he asked.

"Yes!"

"And you have some secrets, too. Does the secret have to do with his privates?"

"No! Who would have that kind of secret?"

I was disappointed. The nice doctor was a lunatic.

"Your uncle doesn't hurt you?"

"No, he's nice to me!" I got off the bed, still wrapped in the blanket, and gave him an angry look. "No matter what kind of truth serum you give me I'm not going to tell you! It's our secret!" I was growing angrier and angrier for having been prodded and then asked stupid weiner questions. Only the dumbest boys at school talked like that.

"I told you that Jari Ilveskero is taking good care of her. I would have noticed if something was wrong," said Pirjo finally.

The doctor let out a sigh. "Well, there certainly is nothing wrong with Hilja. Come on, Hilja, get dressed—I'll have the nurse bring you ice cream from the cafeteria. What's your favorite flavor?"

"Chocolate!" I blurted. We didn't own a freezer, so ice cream was a rare treat.

The doctor left with Pirjo following close behind. Once I got dressed, I started playing around with the strange stirrup chair, pretending to be an Indian girl who the bad white men were trying to shoot with truth serum.

A nurse brought me the ice cream and a glass of orange soda, which I consumed while doing my homework. There was a knock on the door, and my teacher appeared, looking disheveled. Her eyes were red and her lipstick had spread all the way to her chin.

"Nobody is picking up the phone at your place. Do you know where your uncle might be?"

"He's at the Hakkarainens, fixing up the barn roof."

"Can you tell me which Hakkarainen? That's a pretty common name around here."

"They have a horse called Cutey," I said, doing my best to be helpful. "I've ridden her twice, but she doesn't like to wear a saddle. She won't buck and try to throw me off, though, because we're both good girls." When I tried real hard, I remembered that Mr. Hakkarainen's first name was Matti. My teacher said she'd take me home and Pirjo would follow in her own car.

Frida. I began to worry about her. Would Uncle have time to hide her before we all got there? The teacher and Pirjo musn't see Frida. I felt sick all the way home, and once we reached our yard I started to cry. I ran to the backyard; Frida was not there.

"Hilja, can you please wait outside while we talk to your uncle?" asked my teacher. Uncle Jari came to the door and looked angry again. Oh, no, did he think that I'd told them? Instead, he smiled at me and was about to give me a hug when Pirjo told me to wait outside.

I walked to the sauna building to see if there was still warm water in the basin that I could use to wash myself. As I got closer to the building I heard the familiar meowing and scratching. Uncle had managed to hide Frida! I didn't open the door to greet her in case she'd run outside. The clean laundry from Saturday was still at the sauna where we'd set it out to dry, so I put on fresh panties after I washed myself, just like I'd been taught.

My teacher called me back. Her eyes were even redder than before, and Pirjo looked like our neighbor's dog after it had been scolded. Uncle Jari was still angry, too, but I could tell that he wasn't angry at me. He hugged me tightly.

"I should sue you two! This girl has already had enough to deal with in her short life, so I'll let it be this time. But you need to apologize to her, and make sure the nurse does the same next time she's at school."

Teacher knelt in front of me and stroked my cheek.

"Dear, dear Hilja. I was just doing what I thought was best for you. You read these terrible things in books and newspapers. I'm so sorry about the examinations; they were all for nothing." Her crying terrified me.

"Please forgive me, Hilja," said Pirjo. "I was just doing my job. We're all on your side here."

All this apologizing made no sense to me, but I supposed it was about their stupid questions and the cold metal object they'd put inside me. I forgave them, although I would have preferred to tell the nurse to get lost the next time I saw her. Uncle Jari said that after they were done apologizing, we would never bring this up again. Adults could be very stupid sometimes, and I had not done anything wrong.

Ever since that incident I have been afraid of doctors, so the checkups I needed to have for the army or work were excruciating. Occasionally, I have nightmares about being tied to the stirrups at a gynecologist's office. Only through learning judo and other martial arts did I finally convince myself that I was safe; that nobody would ever again abuse my body so easily. When I first had an IUD inserted, it felt like there was a strange object inside of me, but at least it prevented another unwanted object from appearing—a baby.

The cabin provided sweet solitude from my memories. There were no ghosts from the past, no people to protect. I finished my beer and rummaged around for a bottle of tequila I'd bought the summer before. I dipped a glass rim in salt. It would do me good to have a few drinks right now. It had been only a week since I'd left Moscow, and I would have paid a large sum to go back in time to stop Anita from entering the furrier, to convince her that we didn't have any more time to try on coats. I would have given anything not to have the death of a human being on my list of transgressions.

7

It was almost eleven by the time I woke up. The rain had shrouded the cabin in gray, with speckles of bright-green moss shining through the veil. One glance at the half-empty tequila bottle on the counter and I knew why my head felt so heavy. I took off my pajamas and stood outside in the rain, where only a black woodpecker or an elk might be watching me.

My moment of peace ended when my phone rang. I rushed back into the cabin and saw the call was from an unfamiliar number. When I answered, I could only hear humming at first, then a couple of words in French, and finally a friendly voice speaking in Swedish. Monika.

"Hey there, Hilja, still sleeping?" she asked.

Mozambique was in the same time zone as Finland, and most likely Monika had already been working for hours. I was cold, but I didn't dare hang up to get dressed in case she wouldn't be able to call back again.

"I just got your e-mails. The Internet service is pretty spotty here and I've been so busy. We're in the middle of a huge toilet building project."

"You're building toilets now? What happened to cooking?"

"I still cook a bit, but how can I focus on food when people don't have proper restrooms? Anyway, how are you doing?"

Monika's move to Mozambique had been a relief in a way—I had let her get too close. From the bits and pieces I had told her, she'd tried to put together the story of my past and on occasion it had gotten unbearable. I just hadn't been ready to remember everything yet, no matter how many times Monika told me it would only do me good. But now she was thousands of miles away, on a completely different continent, so I would let myself speak freely.

"I feel like shit. It's like a mental and physical hangover." She'd called on the prepaid line; I doubted the police would be listening in. "I'm here at the cabin, trying to open Anita's safe. She left it to me, in case . . ."

I started crying. Fuck. I couldn't get weepy right now.

"Shouldn't you give the safe to the police? Surely they can figure out how to open it."

"The police? They're useless! They and the Moscow militia both claim that Anita was shot by some drunkard who then died of alcohol poisoning."

The line was crackling and it was hard to hear what Monika was saying. Then the call ended. I stood staring at my cell phone until I noticed I was covered in goose bumps. I managed to get my underwear, jeans, and a T-shirt on before the phone rang again. This time, Monika's voice was clearer, as if she were right next to me.

"Some homeless drunk shot Anita?"

"Of course not! It was definitely ordered by Valentin Paskevich. You remember, Anita's former lover—they used to come to the restaurant. Paskevich's men threatened me by voice mail, too. But the police think the case is closed. Or at least the militia thinks so. The constable at the National Bureau of Investigation didn't quite agree, but what can he do? What can anyone do?"

"Get in touch with Helena! She knows how the Russian militia works. *Un moment, je viens . . .*" Monika's voice grew faint.

"Helena who?"

"Representative Helena Lehmusvuo. She used to come to Chez Monique, as well. *Oui oui, je viens*—I'm sorry, I need to go. Some sort of catastrophe."

Monika was gone and the phone didn't ring again. I put on a sweater over my T-shirt and brewed black tea as strong as I could make it. The oatmeal and tomato juice with plenty of salt and black pepper rejuvenated me, although I could still taste the tequila in my mouth.

I'd find Helena Lehmusvuo through information provided by the cabinet. Right now I was in no shape to get in touch with her, but I did make a call to find out how to reach her assistant. I really could have used Internet access again. Typing a long e-mail on my phone was excruciatingly slow, and I had no patience for it. I turned my phone off and left it in a locked box while I checked the shed outside for anything I could use to create an explosive. All you needed was gasoline, baking powder, and eggs, but the result would be more like a little bang than a controlled explosion that would break the lock on the safe without harming its contents. The lock was supposed to be secure. I'd need to think of combinations that Anita may have used. She had to have some mnemonics.

I still had her house keys on me—Laitio had not asked me to hand them over. The police had probably been there to search the place before they had talked to me. But had they been able to scrutinize the place like I would? The house was not a crime scene, so they may not have secured it. I knew its security system inside and out. The maid lived off-site and wasn't there often. And anyway, some of my junk was still at the house, so I had a legitimate reason to go. I made a mental note to visit the Lehtisaari residence.

I put on my rain gear and walked out of the cabin with a basket and a mushroom knife. Despite the weather I found plenty of mushrooms to pick. I also ran into a couple of campers at the Hiekkamäki campground. I've never understood the desire to spend one's holidays so close to other people, where private family disputes become public and everyone is aware of your eating habits. Because of the campground, at first I had doubted whether renting the Degerby cabin was a good idea. I knew I couldn't escape from other people completely, but so far, at least, there was no one camping on the cliffs behind the cabin.

I made sure that the rowboat that came with the cabin was still docked on the shore, and I scooped rainwater out of it. A swan glided on the surface of the rainy lake, not paying any attention to me.

I walked back to the cabin through the forest. I didn't notice the carcass until I was a couple yards away. It was pressed into the ground and so fresh that there was no smell, although the flies were already buzzing around it. The deer's coat was wet from rain and blood, its eyes expressionless and empty. Elk season had not yet begun and I doubted that poachers would just randomly shoot at animals in an area so full of vacationers. The deer was only a couple dozen yards away from the road, so I supposed someone may have run into it and thought it survived. Or maybe it had died of old age or a disease.

There was a fourth possibility, which I confirmed as I stepped closer to the deer: it had been killed on purpose, but not by shooting. The neck wounds were undoubtedly the work of a lynx, and it had had a chance to fill its belly with meat. There were broken twigs and blueberry bushes all around; the deer's antlers had been shattered in multiple places during the viscious fight.

Legally speaking, I should have called either the police or the gamekeeping association, who would have argued that the dead deer belonged to whoever owned the land, usually the local hunting club. I disagreed. The deer belonged to the lynx, who had hunted it down. Maybe it was a mother with hungry cubs.

My scent could have rubbed off on the deer, so I stepped away from it. The animal had died in a fairly open area—the forest would be teeming with mushroom hunters this time of year, some on the hunt with their dogs. Usually people avoided picking wet mushrooms and berries, so at least the lynx had the rain on its side.

I checked my surroundings. It wasn't easy to find tracks on the forest floor, which was mostly covered by rocks and small bushes, but I finally found a couple of familiar-looking paw prints. Slightly farther away I spotted light-yellow hairs that had been ripped off during the battle.

I'd felt the presence of a lynx at the cabin, and thought I'd seen its amber eyes flash in the light of my head lamp when I'd climbed to the top of the cliff to watch the storm unfold. In the past, people had told me they'd seen lynx near the river, and tracks could be found on the sea ice, as well as a few miles east in Koppernäs, where lynx had hundreds of acres of untouched lands and piles of rocks for dens. There was enough for them to eat—deer and hares—but there were also dogs, whose restless barks would carry the news from one house to another as soon as they'd detect an elk or a lynx nearby.

Sensing the lynx's presence helped me to focus. The animals were able to sit without moving for long periods of time, so still that they'd be camouflaged and almost invisible. Although the rain kept getting heavier, I walked in the forest for hours, thinking. Once I got back to the cabin, I set the mushrooms out to dry before I gave Saara Hirvelä, Helena Lehmusvuo's assistant, a call. I only managed to reach her voice mail, so I left a request for a call back and mentioned that I had worked with Anita Nuutinen and that Lehmusvuo and I had met before.

I turned on the news. There was a report about the Russian operations in Georgia and speculations about how Georgia's potential NATO membership would affect global politics. Uncle Jari had always been interested in politics and was vehemently against Finland joining the European Union. When we officially joined, he burned the Finnish flag in our yard in protest. Then again, he'd fortified himself with quite a lot of moonshine before that. Later he explained that the flag was damaged and therefore wasn't usable anymore, so it had to be burned out of respect. That same day he went to Kaavi to buy a new flag.

Before my uncle became my legal guardian, he had been in trade school, learning construction. For four years he traveled around working on construction sites before he had to settle down with me. I can't really remember what it was like before I lived with my uncle; I have a few hazy recollections, but I could never tell which were real and which I had made up. There was an apartment building, and from its window I could see a garbage truck. I'd remember the smell of mashed potatoes, hot dogs, and fish sticks. The red shoes clonking on the wooden floor, the soft red lips on my forehead. The red on the floor, all over, that smudged my pajamas and seeped through my pants, the red flame in my dad's eyes.

Monika was the only person I'd told about all of this. Now I banished the memories by thinking about the dead deer. I didn't have a camera with a telephoto lens—which was a pity, since the lynx wouldn't come close if it could smell me. I'd rather let it eat in peace than disturb it just to make myself feel better by being close to my soul mate.

I did what Uncle Jari would do. I took a nap, and soon I was in that state between sleep and consciousness, just like on the Moscow train. I was at the building door again, waiting for Anita. She stepped out, and someone immediately hit me. When I came to, Anita's cream-colored silk scarf was on the street next to me, but she was nowhere in sight. I awoke with a start when a squirrel ran across the tin roof. Was my dream a memory, or just my foolish hope that the scarf had ended up with me for some innocent reason?

My phone rang after six p.m., and although it was from an anonymous caller, I decided to pick it up. A familiar voice was on the line.

"Hello, this is Helena Lehmusvuo. My condolences. Were you there when Anita Nuutinen was shot?"

"No, I wasn't."

"Of course it's a load of crap that some homeless man shot her. We're dealing with bigger players here. Had she given you a night off?"

"I don't think we should be talking about this over the phone."

"Yes, you're right. Can we meet? Are you in Helsinki or near Kirkkonummi any time this weekend?"

Lehmusvuo lived just outside of Helsinki in Kirkkonummi and had been voted in as representative for the Uudenmaa region, which contains the capital city and its suburbs. I suggested that we meet there, so she invited me over to her place on Friday night. This bought me some time. Of course, once she heard the story, she'd probably blame me for what had happened. But at least on my way to Kirkkonummi, I could drop by the library to check my e-mail and do some more research online. The next couple days, however, I could take it easy and focus on getting into Anita's safe.

I ate a mushroom omelette and wrote down possible codes for the safe while I waited for the sauna to heat up. I tried all the ones I'd warned Anita against: her birthday, her daughter's birthday, backward, forward, and mixed up. My social security number, bank account number, our passport numbers, all the phone numbers that had some connection to Anita, including Valentin Paskevich's official phone number. None of them worked. I went to the sauna to stretch my muscles and relax, assisted only by a beer and a bit of tequila. Then I watched the ten o'clock news, but there was nothing on Anita. I read a tattered *Anne of Green Gables* I found in the cabin until sleep pressed my eyes shut.

A flock of loud cranes woke me up at dawn. I went to the bathroom, had a glass of water, and tried falling asleep again. I was lying on a field of moss, the spring sun warming my body. My uterus could not take it any longer; I had to push, and a bloodied lynx cub appeared from inside me. It rooted around for my nipple. Before it reached its target, another cub emerged, just as energetic as the first, and found my nipple. I felt my milk flow to their hungry mouths, their damp fur cooling my belly. Then a third cub appeared, just as hungry as the siblings. I thought I would not be able to feed it but as I looked down on my belly, I saw myself covered in fur, with two more nipples. The third cub grabbed the nipple right below my heart and began to suck on it. All four of us purred. I knew I would wake up soon, but I tried to prolong the dream. I was sad to return to reality.

Monika had decided that she wouldn't bring any kids into the world until everyone had enough to eat. My motivations weren't quite that pure. I just thought I wouldn't make a good mother. I couldn't guarantee I wouldn't get tired of the child and drive him away like a mother lynx does to her cubs when she is in heat.

When I was twelve, Uncle Jari met Kirsi on one of his construction gigs. She'd been providing meals for the men and had been so interested in my uncle that she'd even come to Hevonpersiinsaari for a visit. I gave her exactly one glance and took off in my rowboat, and didn't return until her gray Lada was gone from our yard. That was the last we saw of or mentioned her, but about six months later, we got a postcard from the Canary Islands. It was from Kirsi and some guy named Jomppe; they were on their honeymoon. Uncle studied the card for a moment before throwing it in the fire. As far as I knew, he hadn't dated anyone even after I moved out.

I ate an apple and decided to take advantage of the cloudy, dry morning, and went for a run. I spent the time thinking about possible combinations for the lock. I only had company when a male elk with large antlers was startled near the cliffs—he ran off quicker than I ever could have. After the run I went back to check on the deer carcass. The lynx had had a feast; it had eaten all the best parts. Now it was lying somewhere in a hole waiting for the darkness, when it could continue eating. It might even go back a fourth time, but after that the meat would get too old and the lynx would leave it to the birds, ants, and flies.

After a substantial breakfast, I turned on all my phone lines. The prepaid one displayed two voice mails: one from Cecilia Nuutinen-Kekki all the way from Hong Kong, the other from Chief Constable Laitio. I didn't feel I needed to get back to either one of them—instead, I began to work on the safe. Anita had originally given it to me so that I'd put it in my own safety deposit box at the bank, but I had brought it here to the cabin. Anita hadn't known about the cabin, and she hadn't needed to. I tried all the new combinations I had come up with during my run, but still nothing worked. The safe's gray, dented steel reflected back a hideous image of my face, as if to mock me. I was pissed off and when I saw Laitio calling me again, I figured I might as well answer—I was already in the proper mood for it.

"So, where's Ilveskero been hiding? My boys went to your place to bring you in for questioning, but they couldn't even get a whiff of you.

"I'm at my girlfriend's. I thought Anita Nuutinen's case was closed."

"We found some interesting contacts in her phone records. Apparently she'd been in tough competition over some shore properties near Kotka with her former business partner, Valentin Paskevich. Did you just forget to mention this to me?"

It was better to stay quiet now. Maybe Laitio would tell me how far the police had gotten in finding Paskevich.

"He's a former KGB agent. You know what that means, don't you?" Laitio continued. "Or were you in on this plan? Did Paskevich pay you? He and Nuutinen had both made offers on the same property in Kotka. Well played, Hilja-fucking-bodyguard. Did Paskevich give you a new passport? Because if he did, don't worry—we'll still find you."

"I don't need to listen to your threats. Good—"

"Don't hang up just yet, Ilveskero. Who chose that name for you, anyway? Don't think I don't the reason it was changed. Wouldn't it make sense for you to cooperate with the police?"

"I don't think my childhood has anything to do with this case." I couldn't wait to get rid of Laitio and attack the safe, so I threw him a bone, as if he were a lynx starving behind the bars in a zoo. "Paskevich was not just a former KGB officer, he was also a *silovik*. I hope you at least know what that means."

"And you decided not to tell me that before? Where does this girlfriend of yours live? We should meet. Shall I go to Jokiniemi or do you want to come to my place on Urheilu Street?"

I hung up without a response, removed the prepaid SIM card, and inserted another brand-new one. Why was Laitio still on this murder case? Had he gotten orders from the home secretary?

Anita and I had gone to Kotka, on the Gulf of Finland coast, some weeks before. This old lady, Julinin, who Anita had been hounding for months, had finally passed on at the ripe old age of a hundred and three. Apparently she'd kept her wits about her until the end, leaving in trust a seventy-four-acre plot with about a mile of oceanfront property, which would benefit her family for generations. But they wanted to sell it. Anita knew she'd have no problem in finding a buyer, so she'd made an offer. Before we left for Moscow, she'd mentioned something about a pre-agreement.

So, Paskevich had killed two enormous birds with one stone: he'd paid back Anita for duping him and managed to get rid of his competition in Kotka. Laitio seemed almost pleasant to me, now that he'd revealed all this information, but I doubted he'd done it without an ulterior motive. The Moscow militia had stopped looking into the murder, but Laitio wasn't about to quit. He seemed to be searching for more evidence that would warrant reopening the case. What would happen to me then? If Laitio found reasonable cause to search my home, I would have to show them my gun safe, where I still kept Anita's scarf. Why hadn't I burned it already?

I spent the evening messing with Anita's safe, but my code-breaking skills were severely lacking—by ten p.m. I was beating the thing with a crowbar so hard that the nearby cliffs echoed. The door hadn't budged. Worst-case scenario, I had managed to damage the lock so badly that even if I knew the combination, it would no longer open. As a last, angry resort I tossed the small safe into the fireplace, but quickly retrieved it when the plastic in the lock began to melt.

I tried to sleep for a couple of hours, but woke up at around five a.m. Someone was moving outside the cabin. I peered out to see if a pair of gleaming eyes would betray a lynx in the darkness, but all I could see was pitch black. When I stepped outside to the porch I could only hear the steady rhythm of the ocean from a few hundred yards away. I put on my rain gear and inhaled a cup of coffee, then immediately brushed my teeth—I can't stand the aftertaste of coffee. I set out into the darkness. Although I wore my headlamp, I didn't want to turn it on just yet. The wind was coming from the southeast, so I could approach the deer carcass without any animals smelling me.

Something was moving in the forest near the carcass. I lowered myself down slowly behind a rock, until I was hard against it and motionless. It was almost daybreak now.

The mass near the carcass was certainly not an elk. It was moving too carefully, placing its feet between mounds of moss, doing its best not to step on any large branches, which would make too much noise. It was too large to be a lynx; I could see branches moving about six feet off the ground. Although a lynx could climb a tree, it wouldn't hop from one tree to another. I held my breath when the figure stepped out onto the road.

It was a man, about six foot five, with a shaved head. His camo pants, jacket, and boots reminded me of a soldier. The sun was climbing higher now behind the cliff, just as the man appeared in my sights. I rose slightly to see his face in the sunlight, and I immediately knew who he was and in whose private army he was serving.

I'd seen him twice at Chez Monique, when Anita didn't need protection yet, when she was still Paskevich's sweetheart. He never sat at the Paskevich table—they wouldn't allow bodyguards to join them—but instead, he's positioned himself a few tables away, always on the lookout for something. It had been clear he was Paskevich's bodyguard. I had asked a waiter to give me his name from the credit card he'd use to pay his bill, just in case I'd need the information someday. I didn't think that really was his name, but I still remembered it. The man who had just moved his revolver from his belt to the holster under his arm was David Stahl.

8

Despite my rain gear, I felt moisture seep into my skin through my clothes. Or maybe I was sweating. What the hell was this Paskevich minion doing near my cabin? Where had I made a mistake? Had they bugged me or my phone? I wished I'd brought a gun to the forest. Just one shot and David Stahl would have been history. I could use the wheelbarrow at the cabin to cart his body to the rowboat and in the dead of night drop it in the middle of the lake. He wouldn't be found until spring, if then.

But I didn't have a gun on me, or any real desire to start murdering people, either, although I'd do my best to defend myself. Stahl was now wiping his bald head and put on a small cap with a brim that hid his face. Had he been wearing it a moment ago, I would not have recognized him.

Stahl looked around, as if planning his next move. Then he started walking along the road toward my cabin. I had forgotten to turn on the burglar alarm when I left, but I did lock the door. The sauna was always unlocked, but there was nothing inside that would reveal my identity to anyone.

After waiting a few minutes I started to follow him, not on the road but in the forest. I hoped he wouldn't turn around and see me. After a bend in the road, I climbed a cliff, which gave me an aerial view of the cabin. As soon as I had signed the rental agreement, I'd figured out all of the best observation spots near the cabin; now I was trying to reach the pile of rocks that I knew would hide me but not my view of the building.

I had to tread carefully to avoid stepping on branches that could crack and stones that might roll; I hoped that any sounds I made could be attributed to wild animals. I had no idea how comfortable Stahl was in the forest, how well he knew his way around. By the time I got to my hiding place, I saw that he was standing in the yard. He walked around the cabin but didn't step on the porch. After a moment's hesitation, he started walking back on the road toward the campground.

It was broad daylight by the time I dared to get up from my rocky hideout—it took me a while to stretch my limbs so they'd work again. Stahl could have still been waiting for me around the corner, so I didn't walk straight to the cabin, but instead I went back to where I had first spotted him. I saw his boot tracks and began to follow them. They disappeared in thinner sand, but would surely appear again. It was as if Stahl was communicating with me, telling me I should follow him.

His steps led from Talludden Road to the boat docks. The same steps were visible from the opposite direction, too. When I got to the muddy parking lot, his boot prints showed up clearly, along with the spot where he had parked his car. He'd headed north from the parking lot, but as soon as the car reached the gravel road, the tracks mixed with those of other cars. Following them would be useless.

I walked back to the cabin for a hot shower and an omelette. There wasn't too much left in the pantry, so I would have to go to the Degerby Deli to buy some food. I oiled my gun and left it in my coat pocket, near the door. I wouldn't leave the cabin without it, not even for a quick stop at the Deli.

Before going out I did one more search for any possible tracking devices on my body or inside my cell phone, but I came up empty. It was a good idea to get rid of the cell phone; I decided to dump it when I met with Helena Lehmusvuo. I made a few attempts to open the safe again. It was a pleasant if boring way to pass the time, and after a sudden rainstorm was over, I put the gun in my underarm holster, hopped on my bike, and started pedaling toward Degerby village.

Kisu, a household name in the Finnish rock scene since the '70s, had owned the village store for a few years, and on my first visit to the Deli, I hadn't believed my eyes when I saw him behind the counter, selling sausages and beer. Today, people were sitting at tables outside despite the weather. The tabloids informed me that the Estonian president, Ilves, was extremely concerned about how Estonia's large neighbor was conducting business in Georgia. I picked up both the Finnish and Swedish newspapers, as well as eggs, cheese, tomatoes, and some milk for my coffee. In the bread aisle, I did a double take: had I started seeing lynx everywhere, or was there really a lynx staring back at me from the rye bread packaging? Kisu noticed me grabbing the bread.

"Pretty cool, huh? Better buy it now while you can—it's a seasonal product."

Eating a lynx felt like cannibalism to me, but I assured myself that this was just a specialty bread from a local bakery, and that there had to be a reason why this particular bread had ended up in my hands. If I waited patiently, I would find out the reason later. I added two loaves of the lynx bread, a few dark lagers, and a couple of chocolate bars to my shopping cart. After paying for my groceries, I went outside to eavesdrop on the locals while I sipped hot cocoa, but all they talked about was the local elections, which were coming up in the fall.

I had just reached the corner of the petting zoo when a car driving by came to an abrupt halt right next to me. The driver rolled down his window and raindrops dotted his bald head. A familiar face turned toward me.

"Hi there. Do you know where the Kopparnäs campground is?" asked David Stahl in Swedish. I felt the weight of the gun under my arm.

"You took a wrong turn," I replied, also in Swedish. "Turn around and drive back to Hangontie, toward Helsinki. The first intersection you see is for Kopparnäs—there's an unmanned gas station on the other side of the road."

Mike Virtue would have been proud of me. My voice wasn't shaking. I looked at Stahl as if I were one of the locals, curious about a complete stranger. His car was dark gray, a small Mercedes with Finnish plates. There were no markings from a rental agency. I memorized the license plate number.

"Thank you. I must've not paid enough attention to the map. I hear there are some good mushroom hunting grounds there." With that, Stahl turned his car around in the nearest driveway and gave me a wave as he drove away.

The shaking began only after I was back at the cabin. What kind of a game was this Stahl playing? Or was he truly so thick that he'd think I wouldn't remember him? Then again, I had never sat at the tables at Monika's restaurant; instead, I'd kept an eye on Anita and Paskevich through the kitchen surveillance monitors. So Stahl wouldn't have known that I'd seen him before. That was to my advantage.

I cracked open a beer and tore open the pack of lynx bread I'd bought. It had been sliced in two: the top of the bread had an image of a lynx face, while the bottom part was shaped to look like the back of a lynx head. I decided to eat the bottom part first, breaking off a piece and inserting it carefully into my mouth, like a communion wafer. Thy body and blood shall strengthen me in battles against my enemies. Even the beer was an appropriate shade of ruby red.

The phone rang after I'd finished my snack. It was Cecilia Nuutinen-Kekki, Anita's daughter. I picked it up, even though I knew our conversation would put me in an even worse mood. We had never actually met—I had only seen pictures of this thirty-year-old woman who looked like her mother and wore well-tailored clothes, but I knew the talk wouldn't be pleasant. Cecilia introduced herself bluntly.

"The Finnish police called me a few days ago, telling me that Mom had died in Moscow. It has taken me days to get ahold of you. Weren't you her bodyguard? What happened over there?"

"I don't know much more than you do. I wasn't working for her anymore." Cecilia tried to interrupt me, but I continued. "The police say she was found near the Frunzenskaya subway station."

"Well, I know that, but why?" She was getting agitated. "Who did it?"

"Didn't the police tell you? Some drunkard, who then went ahead and drank himself to death with the money he stole from Anita."

"That's bullshit! Mom's ex-boyfriend arranged it all, didn't he? That's why she had hired you. And what do you mean you weren't working for her anymore?"

"Exactly that. I resigned before she died."

"And she was killed right after you resigned. That doesn't sound right. I'll be in Finland next week to deal with Mom's estate. Can we meet?"

If I played my cards right, Cecilia Nuutinen-Kekki would grant me access to the treasures hidden in the safety deposit box. This was an opportunity I couldn't miss. Since it looked like my cabin wasn't that safe anymore, I might as well go back to Helsinki now, where I could put Riikka, Jenni, and the lovely Mrs. Voutilainen in danger. Great idea.

I spent the rest of the day messing around with the safe without any luck. The rain was coming down hard, so I was happy to work indoors. Before nightfall I paid a visit to the deer carcass and discovered that it was now missing a hind leg. The lynx would probably not return anymore because the meat had started to smell.

My phone rang around seven p.m. and I answered, although I didn't recognize the number.

"Hello, Hilja," said a male voice, but then went silent. I had to wait for twenty seconds for the voice to start again. "This is Keijo Kurkimäki—I mean, formerly Suurluoto. How are you?"

I paused for a moment and then blurted, "I've told you a hundred times, I don't want anything to do with you!"

"Hilja, let me explain—"

I hung up. My heart was beating fast and my mouth was dry; the powdered soup I'd made for lunch was threatening to come back up. I definitely needed to change all my phone numbers. Keijo Kurkimäki had tried to reach me over the years, but none of our calls had lasted more than a minute. After his first call, he'd left me alone for two years, but after that the calls came every six months.

I hated very few people in this world, but Keijo Kurkimäki was one of them. Most of the time, luckily, I forgot that he even existed, and I didn't remember what he sounded like. I had no idea what he looked like now, either, but most likely he'd be an ugly beast with burning eyes. That's how I remembered him, and that memory had stuck with me, despite the hypnosis therapy I'd tried in New York.

Sleep wouldn't come that night, not even after downing the rest of the tequila. I lay awake, staring into the darkness with my gun by my side. I didn't know whether Keijo Kurkimäki had been let loose. Had the president granted him a pardon from his lifetime in prison? I hoped not.

It was bad enough that Kurkimäki had found out my current name. I had no idea how he'd done that, as he should not have had access to that information. And now David Stahl knew where I was staying in Torbacka. I suddenly felt insecure; even stroking the metallic sheen of the gun didn't make me feel better. I was trapped like Frida's mother, who men had hunted and slaughtered mercilessly. Why hadn't Stahl just shot me on the road when we met? Did he want to play with me like a cat with its prey?

I finally gave up trying to sleep and got out of bed. I left all the lights turned off and stared into the drizzly darkness outside. They were all waiting for me outside the cabin: Paskevich, Stahl, Laitio, and Keijo Kurkimäki. I made sure the door was still locked and all the windows were latched. I usually slept in the small main room of the cabin, but now I climbed up to the loft, placing pots and pans behind me on the stairs. They'd wake me up if anyone disturbed them.

When I awoke it was already past noon, and the weather wasn't letting up. The misty humidity made it hard to see. I was hungry and definitely tired of eating eggs. I finished my seltzer and then quickly stuffed myself with a couple of slices of bread before I hopped on my bike to get some lunch at the Kopparnäs Inn. I didn't feel like taking the longer way through Hanko Road, and dragging my bike through the forest didn't seem like such a good idea, so I decided to take the ten-minute route along the Torbacka shore to Kopparnäs. Whoever owned the shore property had tried to block the service road from car and foot traffic, but when no one was there, everyone just walked across the property. At least that's what my neighbors had told me. On the shore I stopped for a moment to look at a flock of cranes splitting the sky with their flight from west to east. A smaller group broke away from the flock, honked for a while as an independent unit, and then rejoined the main group, as if they were in an air ballet.

The Kopparnäs Inn could have been used as a setting for some of the more eclectic Kaurismäki movies. I would have loved to see Mike Virtue and a few others from my New York days in the bright-green hall with the walls covered in multicolored paintings, right there in the middle of the woods. I ordered some herring fillets, mashed potatoes, and a lager. The fillets arrived with a side of pickles and pickled beets. I was definitely in Finland.

The meal and the beginning of the bike ride back gave me a second wind. I had found a mushroom knife in my jacket pocket, and when I happened to see a broken orange plastic bucket someone had tossed to the side of the road, I had all I needed to check out the Kopparnäs mushroom situation. I biked toward the former campgrounds for employees at Fortum, the energy company. About a third of a mile before the campgrounds, I got off the bike and walked into the forest. Good thing I had worn my hiking boots instead of sneakers; the moss was slippery and the rocky cliffs were slick after the rain.

I found a lot of yellow foot and gypsy mushrooms, which prompted me to walk over the cliffs toward the shore, where I found even more gypsy mushrooms. Their purple- and chamois-colored caps had a strange, ancient look about them. Had I not been familiar with this variety, I would have left them there; they looked too much like poisonous mushrooms.

The broken bucket was a chore to carry around, so I snapped off a few willow branches and sat down on a tree stump to make a new handle. The branches were wet and twisted easily. Uncle Jari had been handy at makeshift devices. On one trip to the forest, he'd shown me how to make a cup out of tree bark, and the brook water I had from it tasted better than any other water I'd ever had.

I heard footsteps in the forest. It sounded like a human. Soon a man dressed in camo was visible through the trees. He wore a baseball cap and had binoculars hanging from his neck; from his size and the way he moved, it was clear that it was David Stah. He was still following me.

I felt for the soothing weight of the gun in my holster. I'd never been a great shot and I didn't particularly like handling guns, but they were a part of my job and I had to keep up my skills. Mike Virtue had drilled it into my brain: a gun was the weapon of last resort for defense and protection. He'd had some unpleasant encounters with the National Rifle Association because he supported the laws mandating background checks for potential gun owners.

Stahl might be a quick draw, or not—I had no idea. I pretended to whittle the branches as if I didn't have a care in the world, thinking that a mushroom knife could work as a weapon. I kept Stahl in view out of the corner of my eye. I knew my size wouldn't help me, as Stahl was clearly larger. When he stepped on a branch so loudly that I couldn't pretend to ignore him anymore, I lifted my gaze, acting as if I didn't recognize him. He walked straight up to me and I had to restrain myself from pulling out my gun. I felt the sweat forming on my lower back and under my breasts.

"*Hej*," greeted Stahl in Swedish, and then took a closer look at me. "Isn't this funny! We just met yesterday—you're the one who told me how to get to Kopparnäs. I decided to book a room at the inn for a few days. The forests here are so beautiful for hiking."

He spoke Swedish like Russians often do, with soft "l" sounds. His accent was clearly Finland Swedish, not the Swedish they spoke in Sweden. He spoke effortlessly, and based on my knowledge of the language, flawlessly. I assumed Swedish was his first language, which was a bit surprising for a Paskevich hit man.

"What sort of mushrooms grow around here? Have you found any porcini?"

I couldn't remember how to say "gypsy mushroom" in Swedish and I didn't want to start guessing.

"Not many porcini, but the yellow foot are already out. And these," I showed him the gypsy mushrooms in my bucket.

"You're obviously pretty handy," Stahl smiled, pointing at the handle, which was now ready to be attached to the bucket. The damp slivers of willow had been easy to bend into durable knots. I remembered what I'd learned at the security academy: don't let your hands shake.

"All you need is a sharp knife," I said and showed him my mushroom knife. I didn't put it back in the bucket—he could grab it from there.

"Do you live around here, or are you just visiting?" Stahl asked. I was still trying to figure out what the Russian etiquette would be for encountering a strange person in a forest. Around here people left others alone, or at least they didn't come this close to you to pick mushrooms. Stahl, however, selected one right in front of my feet, looked at it for a bit, then tossed it away.

"It had worms. I do have a knife, but I'll need to borrow a mushroom basket from the innkeeper tomorrow. They are so tasty, these mushrooms, especially with a dollop of *smetana*. There were times when my family lived on them," Stahl said.

I had to remain calm and under no circumstances let him get behind me. He couldn't shoot me without leaving some blood or other bit of evidence, but I was sure that he could break my neck in a split second. The lake glimmered behind the trees, and it would be easy to dispose of a body there. A guy like Stahl had to have a gun with a silencer. Mine wasn't equipped with one– it had been purchased legally. If I shot him first, how would I be able prove that it was done in self-defense?

I wanted to get up, but instead I focused on cleaning the mushrooms in my bucket while eyeing him in my peripheral vision. Let Stahl reveal his cards first. His camo, boots, and the army-type backpack looked a little less like soldier's gear than they had in the early morning light. He took off his cap and wiped the sweat off his brow. Was he getting nervous, or was he too out of shape to walk in the forest? His bald head was marked by small tufts of hair, which he apparently shaved since there was so little of it, anyway. When he starting taking off his backpack, I sat up. He hunched over and turned away from me for a second. Now would be a good time to pull out my gun and get the man talking. I lifted up the bottom of my anorak so I could reach for the holster under my arm. Stahl got up, holding something metallic. A thermos.

"Want some coffee? I think there's enough for two, although I only have one mug."

"No, thank you." I took my hand out of my jacket. Stahl walked a few steps away to find a big-enough rock and sat on it. He poured the coffee into a metal mug and drank it fast, as if he were quenching his thirst.

"Are you from around here?" he asked again. "How familiar are you with the forests? The innkeeper mentioned something about a tower for bird watchers. Do you know where that might be?"

"I'm not from around here, no. I'm borrowing my friend's cabin." I told him the same story I'd given the few nosy villagers who had approached me at the Degerby Deli. "And if you're looking for the bird-watching tower, you're going in the wrong direction. It's north of the inn, on the left side of the road."

"Would you be able to take me there sometime? I'm on vacation and there aren't too many other tourists now."

"I might be leaving tomorrow, and I have some stuff to do."

"Too bad. Maybe I could buy you a drink at the inn once you're done hunting for mushrooms?"

I didn't give him an answer right away. Good thing there were plenty of mushrooms in the forest clearing for me to pay attention to—even some chanterelles. I figured I had no choice but to stay with Stahl to keep an eye on him. I just couldn't believe he'd somehow drifted into Kopparnäs and had no idea who I was. If that was the case, what was he doing sneaking around my cabin in the wee hours of the morning?

Maybe Stahl underestimated me and really thought I didn't know who he was. He was playing a game of cat and mouse, but this time, domesticated feline Stahl was up against a lynx, and even a cat wouldn't know what to do when a lynx attacked.

Mike Virtue had constantly berated me for being too impulsive and taking unnecessary risks. I silenced him inside my head, turned to David Stahl, and smiled. "I can't come to the restaurant in these dirty clothes. But isn't the bar open until ten? I could meet you at around eight. Would that work?" I chirped sweetly.

A wide smile spread across Stahl's face.

"That would be great! I look forward to it. Well, maybe I'll go look for that bird-watching tower now and leave you to your business." He emptied his coffee mug and put the thermos back in the backpack, then hesitated a moment before he walked toward me. Did he actually think he had gained my trust this quickly? Was he about to attack?

Instead, he stood in front of me with his hand extended out.

"Sorry, I should probably introduce myself. I'm David, David Stahl." He pronounced his first name *dah-vid,* like a Swede. "I'm not really from anywhere, but I'm a Finnish citizen, although I don't speak the language. I'll tell you more about it this evening."

"Hilja Ilveskero," I responded and shook his hand.

"I'm sure this evening will turn out to be very interesting."

9

Once it looked like Stahl had truly taken off, I followed the shore road south. Hidden from any bystanders, I took my phone apart, but still couldn't find a tracking device. Stahl must have somehow known where I was.

I was tired of mushroom hunting, but I had an idea: the forest offered ingenuous ways to get rid of difficult people. Morel season was unfortunately over, and nobody would be careless enough to eat unrecognizable white mushrooms. But an inexperienced mushroom lover could easily confuse harmless gypsy mushrooms with web caps—even with deadly web caps if the gourmand was sufficiently clueless. Just like the morel, the deadly web cap had three crosses next to it in the mushroom guide to indicate how likely you were to die from eating it. But unlike morels, the deadly web caps would never become edible, even if you boiled them three times for five minutes each.

After searching for a while, I found two web caps. I wrapped them in a napkin I had in my pocket and, just to make sure they wouldn't touch the other mushrooms, I grabbed a bunch of fir branches and leaves to keep them separate from the others in my bucket. Two of these web caps would be plenty to kill a grown man. Stahl would end up poisoned slowly like Alexander Litvinenko, that officer of the Russian Federal Security Service: first he wouldn't know what hit him, and by the time he did, it would be too late. His organs would be irreparably damaged. And nobody could ever prove that I'd been the one to serve Stahl this deadly mushroom stew, even if the staff at the Kopparnäs Inn told the authorities that they'd seen me hanging around him.

Most likely Paskevich had sent Stahl to find out what I'd told the police and whether I connected Paskevich to Anita Nuutinen's murder. As always, I figured it was best to lie as little as possible. I'd pretend to be a lonely but libidinous single woman so that it wouldn't seem that outlandish if I was with a stranger.

Did I say pretend? It had been years since I'd dated anyone, and all my previous relationships had ended in disaster. Stahl would know about that if he'd done his homework on me.

Once back at the cabin, I sliced the deadly web caps into small slivers with my scissors, tossed them into a pan, and fried them. Then I disinfected both the pan and the scissors. I had a clean glass jar in the cupboard that was perfect for storing my homemade poison. It even fit in my purse. After that I took a shower and decided to get as dolled up as I could.

This was pretty much like disguising myself as Reiska—I just had to come up with an alternative identity. I'd bought makeup and a tight, glittery shirt for those times when I'd need to accompany my clients to fancy parties. I decided to wear black leather pants instead of my red velvet miniskirt; it would be easier to bike in them. I'd have to carry the high-heeled shoes in my saddlebag. With them on, I'd only be a few inches shorter than Stahl. They were pretty good for kicking, too—the stiletto heels had a steel core. They were red, like the ones my mother used to have. The foundation I caked on felt like a mask and my eyelashes, lengthened by mascara, tickled my face. I didn't put any lipstick on until I was ready to head out the door. The red shade matched my shoes.

My gun fit well in a zippered compartment in my purse. I wrapped the mushroom jar in a napkin and put it in the same pocket. People always assumed that women's purses were heavy and full of stuff, so nobody would think twice if the bag bulged a bit. I could also use the bag as a weapon if I got into a fight. I put a flashlight and headlamp in the saddlebag, along with my shoes; it would be dark before nine.

I felt a bit nervous, which made sense because I was technically going on a date. I took the shore road again and rode my bike slowly to avoid sweating. I left my bike in the parking lot, although there wasn't a bike rack. Lights illuminated the yard and I could hear a woodpecker at work. I took my jacket off in the foyer and stopped by the restroom to rearrange my hair. Even the jovial Botero poster on the restroom wall didn't lighten my mood—looking in the mirror, all I saw was trepidation.

Only the waitress and Stahl were in the restaurant, and they were chatting in English. He was holding a cocktail, and based on its strong odor, I figured it contained calvados. Stahl took a couple of steps toward me, took hold of my hand, and gave me a kiss on each cheek. He'd shaved his head again and I could detect a faint whiff of cologne. He was wearing a black jacket, black jeans, and a white button-up shirt, but no tie. He stared at my leather pants with an appreciative look that he made no attempt to hide.

"Hi, Hilja. What would you like?"

"Do you have any sparkling wine?" I asked the waitress. She said she'd take care of it. It was the perfect drink for the woman I was trying to be. Stahl led me to the back of the room to a table with a flickering candle on it. He put down his drink and then pulled out my chair, waiting until I sat down before moving to the other side of the table. I saw the entire room; he didn't. That setup suited me just fine.

"They have pepper steak or chicken breast with cheese on the menu tonight. I'll go for the steak—all that walking in the forest has made me hungry. I was just thinking about a suitable red wine to go with it. This will be my treat, of course. I invited you, after all. It seems obvious to me, but such matters need to be spelled out for you Finnish women."

I never said no to free food, especially when I didn't know where my next paycheck was coming from. After the waitress brought my drink, Stahl lifted his glass and we clinked glasses. The wine was semisweet and I could feel it in my nose. Then we sat in silence for a while.

"You said, 'you Finnish women.' Didn't you say you were a Finnish citizen?" I asked, doing my best to look him in the eye. His eyes were light gray and deep set. He had high cheekbones and wrinkled eyelids. Come to think of it, was he wearing colored contact lenses to change his natural eye color?

"You have a great memory. I'm a Finnish citizen, but I'm of mixed heritage. My father was a Soviet citizen, but he was born in Kohtla-Järve in Northern Estonia. My grandfather had moved there to work in the mines after Estonia became part of the Soviet Union. Or, 'was liberated,' as they used to say in those days. My grandmother was Estonian, too, from Narva to be exact, but she found her way to the mines, as well. My mother is Finnish, from Tammisaari, pretty close to here. My parents met in Tartu, in Estonia, where they both studied in the early '70s. Mother majored in Russian, and her great-grandmother had arrived in Finland from Saint Petersburg during the revolution, so I guess I have a bit more than just a quarter of Russian in me. After a couple of years of marriage and an agonizing wait, my father was allowed to leave Soviet

Estonia and move with his family to Tammisaari, where I was born. Once Estonia gained independence, we moved back to Tartu. My teenage years were tough; it was hard to live in Estonia while all my friends were in Finland. After that there were all sorts of issues, but now things are better. Where in Finland are you from?"

The waitress came back for our order, and I decided to go with the steak, as well. Stahl chose the red wine with an obvious expertise that impressed a wine ignoramus like myself. He repeated his question when the waitress left.

"Me? I'm a full-fledged Finn. I grew up in Kaavi in Northern Savonia. On my mother's side I'm a Savonian, but my father was from Lappeenranta, where I was also born."

"Was? Is he dead?"

"He's dead to me." I took another gulp of my wine that was quickly disappearing. Who cared if I told him the truth about my past? Maybe it would make him realize he wasn't dealing with some young innocent girl.

"So you don't live here, then? Do you still live in . . . what was that, Kaavi?"

"No, I live in Helsinki." He should have known that.

"Alone?"

"I have a couple of roommates. No pets." I made an attempt at a flirty laugh. "How about you?"

"I have to travel between Tartu, Moscow, and Finland because of work, but unfortunately I don't get to come to Finland very often. Last time I was here was a couple of weeks ago. I had to go to Kotka with my boss. Now that I finally have some vacation time, I decided to head to Finland and just happened to land in Kopparnäs. I thought I'd take some time over the weekend to go to Tammisaari, to see my old haunts. I haven't really kept in touch with anyone, but I probably still know a couple of people there. My grandparents are both gone, and my mom was an only child. My sisters are a decade younger than me and I never knew how to relate to them. They live in Tartu. Do you have any siblings?"

I managed to say no before the wine arrived. The waitress poured our drinks with an amused expression on her face, as if she knew that David Stahl had a fat wallet and an impressive pile of credit cards. Rich bastard, living off blood money. I could drop my fork and ask him to get me another one from a nearby table—he'd oblige, pretending to be ever the gentleman, and I'd have a few seconds to slip the poisonous mushrooms onto his plate.

"I'm an only child. What have you been doing in Moscow? I was just there last week and I'm pretty familiar with the city," I continued as the waitress walked away.

"I'm a consultant in the construction business, which is why I need to travel so much. What do you think of Moscow?"

We made small talk about Moscow bars and museums until the food arrived. I assumed Stahl would mention that a Finnish businesswoman had been shot dead in central Moscow just this past week, but he didn't even hint at it. Instead, he regaled me with stories about bouncers and women trying to hit on him, working hard to prove to me that he didn't care for prostitutes. I remembered Paskevich and his companions. I suppose his employees would have had a chance to take advantage of such perks, too.

The peppered steak was served with green-pepper gravy, garlic potatoes, and some vegetables, but no mushrooms. Darn. Then again, only a tiny sliver of a deadly web cap would be enough to destroy his liver and kidneys. I decided to wait for a while to find out what Stahl was after. If he hadn't been hired by Paskevich, I would have almost liked him. He was funny without making stupid jokes, listened without interrupting, and made me feel like a human being; my persona as a sexy, flirty woman started to feel just right.

"What took you to Moscow so often?"

"Same as you—business. I'm a guard of sorts. But let's not talk about it now—I'm on vacation, too." I looked at how he cut his steak: he handled the knife as confidently as a surgeon. Was he the one who shot Anita and then gave her stuff to the dying alcholic?

"A guard? I never would have guessed."

"Why not?" My angry tone startled him.

"Don't get me wrong—my mother taught me that women can do anything, and I have learned that the hard way myself. You just don't seem . . . you just don't seem like someone who wants to control others."

"Was that meant as a compliment?" I forced myself to smile, but inside I was fuming. Damn him. He'd pay for underestimating me. Of course he'd do his best to shake my confidence. I thought about what was in my purse: the gun and the poisonous mushrooms. Was it time to ask for that fork?

We ate in silence for a while. I looked at the life-size picture of a white-tailed eagle hung over the bar. The eagle's wingspan was easily more than six feet. Its talons were hooked, ready to attack its prey. I could almost feel the whooshing of its wings. The bird could destroy a four-pound pike, which would be no match for him.

The other paintings in the room—scenes of forests or trees in full foliage—were less aggressive, each done in a surprisingly different style. David began laughing at the song that was playing on the radio. It was by Lordi, the Finnish heavy metal band, and had won the Eurovision song contest. To change the subject, we started chatting about music. David liked heavy metal, but also enjoyed progressive rock, like the music of the American band System of a Down. I'd never even heard of them, which prompted such an extensive lecture about their work that we were almost done with dinner by the time David's talk ended. When he described music his eyes lit up—the topic was clearly close to his heart.

"Do you want to hear their music? I have a couple albums on my MP3 player. It's in my room."

"Why should I like the same kind of music as you?" My words came out in a sultry purr. My eyes narrowed like those of a lynx.

"Well, you don't need to, but I'd like you to hear it." He mopped up the rest of the gravy with the tail-end of a garlic potato and slowly lifted the fork to his lips, enjoying the last morsel. "System of a Down's music is even better than this steak. This steak is just Pink Floyd next to it. You do know who Pink Floyd is, right?"

The waitress had been eyeing us and carried our plates away before I even realized that I'd missed my chance to spike David's food. She asked if we wanted dessert. We decided on coffee, calvados, and an apple tart. The bottle of red wine was more than half empty, so the waitress poured the rest of it into our glasses. The wine smelled masculine, with overtones of sweat and leather.

"Sorry, but I have to ask. What did you mean when you said that your father is dead to you?" David looked at me over his glass.

I lifted my glass to my lips and drank. I decided to tell him the story—then he'd know I wasn't completely harmless.

"The last time I saw my father I was four years old, about thirty years ago. We lived in Lappeenranta at that time, near the Kimpinen athletic fields. I don't remember much about the town just that it had an enormous lake and that my mother would push me in a stroller in the shade of the giant beech trees. My parents got married young, when they were about twenty. They'd met at a summer dance. She was studying in Joensuu to become a teacher and he was in the army in Rissala. After his stint was over, they moved to Lappeenranta where he found work as an electrician. I suppose

Mother thought she'd finish her studies eventually. But that time never came."

The images were now filling my brain, but later I couldn't recall exactly how I had described them to David. The memories were too powerful. There was shouting, often. Mother and I were alone, Father was who knows where, and I suppose she got tired of waiting for him because our neighbor babysat for me a lot. I don't know what the truth really was, whether she had another man or if Father had just imagined that. But I do remember what happened when she and I came home that day.

The foyer was pitch black. Something smelled sweet, and he was there, teetering toward us. More shouting, bad words. Whore whore whore. He tore me away from her, yelling. Don't hurt the child; you whore will get what you deserve. I'm on the floor, there's red everywhere. She is no longer screaming, she's lying on the floor, reaching out to me, but I crawled away, I forgot how to walk. She was no longer wearing the ring with the precious stone, she didn't have enough fingers on her hand, the finger had been severed. She stopped moving. Father rocked the red mass in his lap, crying and begging for forgiveness. I hid under my bed, pants wet although it had been years since I'd needed diapers, my arm covered in a large, sticky red stain. Then the neighbors knocked on the door, a big man in a dark-blue coat with shiny buttons appeared, then a white bed and Grandmother next to it in the morning, Grandmother alternately crying and screaming, until she was taken to another hospital.

"Mother was stabbed thirty-five times. Father was sentenced to life. The fact that I had witnessed the whole thing was considered sufficient grounds for the charge of aggravated murder."

I hadn't even noticed that at some point the dessert had been served. I thought I could still smell blood, although it was actually a mixture of strong coffee and the vanilla sauce for the tart. The waitress had returned to her post behind the bar, but I could tell she had been listening. She'd be old enough to remember the Kimpinen carnage. Only one tabloid existed back in 1980, but crime reporter Hannus Markkula, or "Murder-Markkula," as his readers called him, was already practicing journalism then and he'd documented every detail. The case even made it into *A Finnish Murder,* his book about gruesome or unsolved murders, but I had never been able to read it.

My left hand was resting on the table. David took it into his.

"What a terrible story."

"His blood is in me. I could do what he did." I didn't pull my hand away; instead, I squeezed hard enough to cause pain.

"To kill?"

"Anyone could, under the right circumstances." I squeezed his hand even harder, and now he responded with a squeeze that could have broken the bones in my hand. I didn't make a sound.

"You mean for money?"

"Sometimes. Or to protect someone. Some mothers have claimed that they could kill another human being to protect their kids."

David let go of my hand and I pulled it away. He wore no rings. Given his mother's Finnish Swedish heritage, he must have been Lutheran, so he would have worn an engagement or a wedding ring on his left hand. I thought about my mother's severed finger and shivered. While under hypnosis I had screamed so loudly that the therapist had had to wake me up, telling me that I wasn't quite ready for it, that it wasn't yet time to banish the images that tormented me. It was recommended that I undergo psychotherapy, but I didn't.

I twirled my spoon in the vanilla sauce and picked at the apple tart next to it. Its aroma pushed the smell of blood out of my nose. David looked like he'd lost his appetite. Surely I hadn't scared a Paskevich minion with such a story? He must've heard of worse acts, maybe even committed them himself.

I took a sip of the calvados; its smooth apple flavor was comforting.

"Is your father still in prison?"

"I don't even know, to be honest. Like I said, everyone is capable of killing as long as the circumstances are right. I appreciate my freedom enough to keep my distance. I probably wouldn't even know him if I saw him on the street. Have you ever been in prison?"

David was visibly surprised by this question. He attempted to respond, but then just closed his mouth. The radio was now playing the main theme from Nino Rota's *Romeo and Juliet* score, and I almost burst out laughing at the contrast between my grisly tale and the romance set in Verona long ago.

"Do you think I might know your dad?" he finally asked. That thought hadn't even crossed my mind, but once I started mulling it over it seemed like a possibility. Maybe two parties had paid David to track me down.

"I never think about my father. I told you: he's dead to me."

The color of the tart's caramelized filling was only slightly different from the shade of the deadly web caps in my bag. The cooked apples were as soft as the mushroom slices I'd scalded in their own broth. They would have gone unnoticed in the fruit.

I desperately needed to go to the restroom, but how could I leave him alone? David was blocking the waitress's view, so he could easily slip something into my food or drink to knock me out. I had no choice. I just had to hold it in until I'd finish consuming everything. The sparkling wine was gone but there was still some red wine, the remains of my calvados, and the coffee. I took a swig of the wine, then a gulp of coffee as a chaser, hoping it would lighten the effects of the alcohol a bit.

"About your question. I've never been to prison, unless you include a quick stay in a jail cell in Saint Petersburg. And that was a misunderstanding—they let me out after one miserable night. I appreciate my freedom, just like you. The Finnish army was almost too much for me; I don't like being told what to do. But I suppose there would have been worse options than the marines in Dragsfjärd. At least I had a view of the ocean there."

"I liked being in the army."

"You've been in the army?"

"Yes, I have." I drank more coffee, although my bladder was about to burst. "It was good training for becoming a bodyguard. And like I said, I enjoyed it. I'm a second lieutenant."

David smiled and drained his glass of calvados. I handed mine over to him.

"You don't like apple liquor?"

"I do, thanks, but I still need to bike home, and I'd rather not wake up in a ditch."

David drank from the glass where my lipstick had stained it. "Do you really need to bike back home? There are two beds in my room. Why don't you stay over?"

A smidgen of my lipstick was now on his lips. If I kissed him, he'd have some on his face, on his chin, on his neck . . . I was getting lost in my role as a flirt.

"As a professional in the security industry, you must think about any potential risks involved. But I do believe you can take care of yourself," he continued.

"I do have a black belt in judo, among other accomplishments. Even Putin wouldn't be a match for me."

"Even during a shoot-out?"

"Even then. I've learned how to use a gun."

David stared right into my eyes. Uncle Jari used to call such intense eye contact "frying fish"; who knows why that memory popped into my head at this moment. I gazed back at David, let him hold my hand and stroke the back of my palm gently, let him wrap my hair in his fingers. Maybe I should accept his offer. It wouldn't be the first time a tough guy would blab to me about his plans while in bed. The problem, though, was that I actually wanted to get under the sheets with this guy, and I'd be the one to spill the beans. I had to leave now. I pulled my hand away from him.

"No, I should be going. I have to work tomorrow."

"Of course, I didn't mean to pressure you. I understand why you don't want to spend the night in a stranger's room." David's smile was causing butterflies in my stomach; I could feel my cheeks glowing, and I had to turn my face away so he wouldn't see the glimmer in my eye.

"I don't feel comfortable driving you home, given everything I've had to drink tonight. The police probably aren't patrolling around here, but it'd be irresponsible of me. Should I call you a cab?"

"No need. It might take hours to arrive. I'll manage on my bike."

"But you have a long way to go. Were you going to take Hanko Road or the shortcut through the woods?" David asked. "I'd better come and make sure that you get home safe."

"It's not that far, and I don't need to travel through the forest. My cabin is in Stävö."

"Stävö? I thought it was . . ." David almost gave himself away, but shut his mouth just in time. "When I saw you biking on Torbacka Road, I thought you lived somewhere close by. I guess I was wrong." He swirled his glass and emptied it in one quick gulp. He'd consumed two-and-a-half shots of calvados and half a bottle of red wine. What use would he be in bed?

The waitress came by to ask if we needed anything else. I thanked her for the meal and David asked to charge it to his room. When he spoke in English he managed to sound even more curt and confident than when he spoke in his native tongue. Then again, I'd noticed how my persona changed depending on which language I used. When I spoke Swedish with David, I was witty and purred like a cat; it was much more feminine than when I spoke Finnish or my broken Russian.

I thanked David and stood up. The waitress must've been waiting for us to leave so that she could go to sleep. David walked me toward the door, held my jacket for me, and watched with amusement when I swapped my high heels for sneakers.

"Well, it seems like you'll make it fine on your own. Will you give me your phone number? I might give you a call some time. Let me know if you're coming back to your cabin for a weekend. Here's my card."

I found the inn's business card in the foyer and scribbled down my number on the back. It didn't matter; I'd get another number tomorrow. David opened the door to a windy yard. Once we stepped into the darkness he kissed me.

I didn't resist—I had wanted to kiss him for most of the evening. The kiss lasted for what seemed like minutes, and I could feel it in my groin and nipples. I wanted his mouth all over my body. I wished I were more like a lynx acting solely on instinct, rather than a human worrying about consequences. It took all my effort to pull myself away from him. I hopped on my bike and didn't look back into the darkness as I pedaled. The bike seat was a lousy substitute for what I wanted between my legs.

On my way back, the only creature I saw was a fox; it ran alongside my bike before jumping off the road toward the shore at the bridge. I stopped at the pier in Torbacka to go skinny-dipping in the cool September ocean water. Even that didn't quell the heat inside me.

10

Friday morning I left my bike in the ditch near a bus stop. Before dawn I'd taken Anita's safe back to its old hiding place and sprinkled corn starch all over the floors and steps of the cabin to catch an intruder's footprints. The express bus to Kirkkonummi took only fifteen minutes. I got off and walked from Hanko Road to the center, where I bought a new cell phone and a couple of prepaid contracts. I also changed my number; this time I'd only share it with those I trusted. Unfortunately, I didn't know whether my roommates fell in this category; it wouldn't take much to get them to cough up the number. Maybe I needed to change apartments or at least give up the cabin in Talludden and sublease something else.

When I was done at the cell phone shop, I went to the library; I had booked my computer time slot in advance. The library was quiet: only a couple of retirees reading newspapers and a hippie kid flipping through CDs. I logged in to read my mail, which was mostly spam except for a group e-mail sent by my buddy from the New York days, a fellow student named Jim Parsley, who was letting us know that he'd been hired as head of security at a large bank for a monthly salary that would take me two years to earn. Then there was an e-mail from Chief Constable Laitio, demanding that

I contact him immediately, either by phone, e-mail, or in person. I skimmed the message and deleted it. He was the least of my worries.

I went back to the Russian websites to find more details about Anita's case, but there was nothing new. I wondered how many people Paskevich had had to pay off to get the media off his case and to convince everyone that the story of the homeless man as perpetrator seemed plausible. If people didn't buy the theory of an alcoholic murderer, then they might try to frame me next, which is probably why someone left Anita's scarf with me. Maybe that was the reason I'd been drugged, and not because I would have been able to stop Anita's killer. Even if I hadn't left Anita, I could still be held partly accountable for her murder, and even if the case was closed they could always open it again—as soon as someone with enough power demanded it. Laitio's influence probably wouldn't be enough, maybe not even the Finnish prime minister's, but I had to assume I might still be a suspect.

I did my homework for my upcoming meeting with Helena Lehmusvuo. She'd had a seat in the cabinet representing the Green League for ages, since 1995. She was forty-two and had a twenty-year-old son from a short-lived marriage to a classmate during college. Lehmusvuo had joined the Green League while still in school, where she had majored in economics. She'd been the leader for her cabinet group and the vice chair of the Green Party, but so far, she hadn't been a minister. She had moved from Espoo to Kirkkonummi earlier this year. Lehmusvuo's remarks often irked various business executives, as well as the Finnish policy wonks who were focused on the country's relationship with Russia. The newspaper articles didn't indicate whether she was currently married, nor was this piece of information listed on her cabinet profile page. Instead, I found a wealth of columns, speeches, and essays she'd written. Her doctoral dissertation, which she'd defended a few years back while working as a representative, had been about the effects of the Soviet Union's collapse on the Finnish economy, and her most recent essay focused on how property ownership in Finland was changing due to an increase in Russian buyers. She'd interviewed Anita for one of her essays before I had started working for her.

Next I ran a search on David Stahl and got about 26,500 hits—his was a common name, it seemed. I started browsing only to discover that the man I had kissed yesterday didn't even exist according to the Internet, which I had expected. Stahl had said he was a consultant in the construction business, and that could mean anything. I hadn't asked him to show me his ID card or his passport, as that would have been a bit odd, given the circumstances. Him being invisible on the Internet didn't really prove anything, not even that he may have given me a false name.

I poked around some more and then tried using the Finnish, Swedish, and Estonian language search engines and checked for images, as well, but came up empty. Honestly, it would have been hard to find anything about me online, either. I didn't have a website, and I had never created an account on Myspace, Facebook, or any of the other sites that people were using. Despite never having gained immortality among the bytes, I felt alive and important.

I made the mistake of searching for one more name: Keijo Suurluoto. This time, a long list popped up—armchair detectives were always intrigued by true crime. The name Keijo Kurkimäki didn't produce any hits, which meant that people weren't interested in his current identity. It was a relief to read that Suurluoto-Kurkimäki had not been pardoned from his lifetime sentence, which had begun in the spring of 1981.

My mom's maiden name had been Karttunen. She and Jari had no other siblings. Their father had died before I was born, and according to Uncle Jari, their mother had died of sorrow three months after my father killed my mother. My father's parents had been alive when the murder was committed, but they didn't want to raise me. After the murder my grandfather had wondered whether the child was even Keijo's. The thought of being someone else's child had felt good but, unfortunately, when I saw a picture of Keijo Suurluoto, it was as if my own face were staring back at me.

Uncle Jari had been more of a father to me than any number of Keijo Suurluotos could have been. I had never gone to see my father in prison, nor had he ever requested that I visit him. I guess he was as suspicious about my paternity as his own father was. But his mother had remembered me in her will, so I suppose she had wanted to make it up to me somehow.

My father had siblings, so there was a chance that a horde of unknown cousins was walking around, but I had no interest in meeting them. Someone might put two and two together upon seeing my name, an unusual one for my generation, but I'd let them figure it out. I didn't need to stay in touch with anyone.

I dropped by a restaurant for a vegetarian pizza before walking the half mile from Kirkkonummi's business district to Helena Lehmusvuo's townhome. The sun made a rare appearance, and it illuminated the first yellowing birch leaves. A purple peony was blooming on her front lawn, but Lehmusvuo's tiny garden looked neglected. The wilted peony blooms hadn't been plucked away and a dried-up rosemary plant stood in a pot next to the door.

I rang the bell. The lady who came to open the door looked much smaller than she did in pictures. Lehmusvuo's brown hair was cut short, highlighted with a few dark-purple streaks to bring out the shade of cocoa in her brown eyes. She wore a purple jacket and dark-gray pants, no jewelry or makeup. Her face was ashen, as if she hadn't slept in days. She let me in.

The townhouse seemed oddly spacious, like Lehmusvuo hadn't completely moved in yet. There were no curtains on the living room windows—only blinds—and stacks of books and papers were overflowing in every corner. This look of a temporary home was all too familiar: like my apartment on Untamo Road, it was just a place to park stuff for a while. Lehmusvuo asked whether I'd like some coffee or tea, and as I was thirsty after eating a pizza, I asked for the latter. I heard her rummaging around in the kitchen, so to kill time, I went to look at the piles of books that were starting to encroach on the living room floor. The floor was also home to a pile of lumber for a future bookshelf, accompanied by an Allen wrench and a hammer to put the shelves together. Some of the books were in Russian; I recognized the names Akhmatova and Dostoyevsky from the covers.

"Sorry, this place is still a huge mess!" Lehmusvuo called from the kitchen. "I moved here in the spring, which was a very busy time at the cabinet. Then I took a couple of months off in the summer to bike around Italy and France, so I kind of skipped out on working on the place. My ex-husband kept our previous residence and most of the furniture. I didn't have the energy to start arguing, especially with him threatening to go to the media with crazy stories if I didn't do what he said."

"Sounds like a nice fellow," I said, although I wasn't sure if she even heard my comment. She came back to the living room carrying a pot of tea, organic honey, a couple of mugs, and some muffins on a tray.

"Spelt, tofu, and organic apple muffins—have one. My assistant Saara is into baking. I'm living a healthier lifestyle now with her around, otherwise I wouldn't have the time for it."

Lehmusvuo had delicate, small features, with eyes that looked too large for such a narrow face. In pictures she always had a healthy glow, but up close you could see the dark bags under her eyes. It was the face of a tormented woman. We sat down on the couch together because there were no other chairs around. Lehmusvuo stacked up a pile of books to act as her table and nudged a small coffee table toward me.

"So, you were Anita Nuutinen's bodyguard. Did she hire you because she thought her life was in danger?"

"She didn't feel safe traveling alone in Russia."

"So someone had been threatening her before the murder?"

I didn't understand what right Lehmusvuo had to interrogate me, and I tried to remember whether Anita had ever mentioned her. Anita's and Lehmusvuo's politics were completely different, and I imagined that the only thing they had in common was their interest in Russia and Russians.

"She had enemies."

"Being a representative comes with death threats and personal attacks; you get used to them. I always notify the cabinet's head of security and the police about any threat that seems credible. We usually keep quiet about them, lest some crazies decide to become copycats and follow suit. Especially that speech I gave last spring at the Finnish-Russian Chamber of Commerce meeting. Some people were annoyed when I didn't condemn the way the Russians had invaded the Finnish vacation home market, and some in my own party were pissed off that I didn't criticize the entire vacation-home phenomenon enough. Then again, I was also accused of hate speech toward Russians. The strangest thing was that all those accusations came from Finns."

Lehmusvuo broke off a piece of her muffin and ate it. I poured myself some more tea. Politicians were fair game in the public eye; if you didn't like it, then you shouldn't run for office. Nobody was forced to join the cabinet. That's what Uncle Jari had told me, and he wasn't alone in his thinking.

"Most of the people who accused me online of hating Russians wrote messages from the same server. That doesn't really prove anything, but after Anita Nuutinen was murdered, I began to receive these messages again. That's what I find strange. If a drunken homeless man had killed Anita, why would I now be getting threats from people who were interested in her real estate business in Kotka?"

"Kotka? What do you mean?" Laitio had talked about the bidding war Anita and Paskevich had engaged in, and I had gone to Kotka once with Anita. And—the tea suddenly got caught in my throat—David Stahl had told me he'd been there with his boss a few weeks ago. Most likely with our mutual friend, Valentin P.

"I wish I had an answer to that. All I know is that Julinin's estate is selling her seventy-four acre oceanfront property there. The agent claims they have multiple offers."

"As far as I know, Anita's was one of them. It won't be valid anymore, of course, and I have no idea what will happen to her real estate business. Her daughter won't be back in Finland until next week. We haven't agreed on a date to meet yet."

"I'm not entirely sure it's just about nabbing the oceanfront property. There must be something else to it. I haven't notified the police about these new threats yet because I honestly don't know whom I can trust."

"Well, I didn't tell the police about a threat I received after Anita died. The message was in English. This was after I came back to Finland and the murder had supposedly been solved."

Lehmusvuo stared at me with her huge eyes, like a deer in the headlights.

"But why are you telling me this now? So I should trust you? If so, then my next question is, were you paid to leave Anita Nuutinen alone? Why weren't you there when she died?"

I looked her over before I stood up. "So that's the reason why you invited me here, huh? You're bypassing the police to run your own little investigation. And once the tabloids get ahold of the story, you'll come out looking like a hero. I'm not getting involved in that game."

"Come on, don't give up just because things are getting a bit complicated!" Lehmusvuo's doe eyes were gone and her voice was harsh enough to convince an opponent to change a vote. "I just wanted to know where you stood. I don't think Anita Nuutinen's murder had anything to do with a robbery committed by a random drunkard, and I'm very eager to find out what you know. I'm willing to pay you for any information. And to be honest, I could use someone right now who can make inquiries that I can't."

"Have you talked to Chief Constable Laitio at all?"

"Yes. He doesn't believe the Moscow militia's conclusions, either."

"And he told you that someone bought my loyalty?"

Lehmusvuo smiled. "Unlike Laitio, I actually believe that lynx coat story."

"Laitio told you about it?"

"The police's interrogation notes become public information once the investigation is closed. Come now, sit down and have another muffin."

I stared out the window. Through the blinds I could see a small yard with badly overgrown grass. There was a lonely apple tree; some of the ripening fruit had already fallen to the ground. The paint was peeling off the picket fence. A flock of small birds was resting there; they were in the middle of their choir practice. Helena

Lehmusvuo's residence wouldn't be featured in a design magazine anytime soon. What did she want from me, anyway? I flopped onto the couch and continued drinking tea. I might as well stick around to hear what else she had to say.

"Do you believe that a homeless alcoholic, who has yet to be identifed, was behind Anita Nuutinen's murder?" Helena asked.

"I don't know what to believe. And the information you've given me makes it all even more complicated. What do you have to do with Anita's real estate dealings?"

"I'm just interested in why this particular property is so hot. I have my own theory about it, and we could work together to prove it."

"What theory?"

"All in good time. That wasn't the only reason why I wanted to meet you. I was hoping you could help me with security. I remember how good you were at looking after Monika at Chez Monique."

"So you want me to help you with security? Give me some details and I'll see what I can do." I leaned back on the couch.

"I told you that I got divorced fairly recently, and the entire process was unpleasant. I was simply tired of coddling him, and it created a huge mess. It's funny; being in the public eye can offer protection, but it can also leave you exposed. Tiku Aaltonen, my ex, has given a couple of nasty interviews that were published in trashy magazines. I don't think my voters really care, but it might encourage some of the loonies to take action. Someone is following me. I'd like you to find out who."

"Following you? How do you know?"

"Well, not just following me. Some other strange things are going on. Around here our mail and newspapers get delivered to our designated boxes, but I still have a slot in my front door from the previous owner. Someone has been taking my morning papers from my mailbox and dropping them through the old mail slot. And someone keeps moving the rosemary plant around and stealing my apples. Once I found a dead hare in my backyard, and when I took it to the vet, it turned out that the animal had been poisoned. Also, someone has been walking around my backyard. I don't know how they get in, maybe by climbing over the fence?"

I stood up again and opened the door to the backyard. The small townhouse yards were fenced in with about six-foot-high wooden planks that were so irregularly spaced it would be easy to access the adjoining yard. It reminded me of the practice area at the Queens security academy: they'd had an eight-foot-high brick wall that was difficult to hold on to. Sometimes it was topped with shards of glass, sometimes with barbed wire or an electric wire supplied with eighty volts. Then there was the time when two Dobermans were waiting on the other side of the wall. Yet I'd always survived without a scratch.

"What's behind the fence?"

"A similar row of townhouses. I went over there to ask if anyone had seen a strange character lurking around, but no one had seen a thing."

"You can always pay someone to look the other way. You haven't thought about getting a restraining order for your ex?"

"So far, no. I worry that it would make him all the more eager to go public. I'm in support of the law—I helped to make it—but sometimes I feel it's only words on a piece of paper. People are threatened or killed despite the court order, and even the police can't stop all the crazies. Sorry, I suppose I shouldn't be saying this. But that's the way I feel—hopeless." Lehmusvuo stood at the window and pulled the blinds down.

"Is Aaltonen the jealous type? I'm asking because I just thought of someone who would be better for the job than me, but he's a man."

Lehmusvuo shook her head. "I don't want any men in my home—I want to live the way I have. And I need my solitude after all the hours I spend at work."

"Well, he wouldn't exactly be an ordinary man."

"Even if he were gay, it wouldn't change a thing. He'd still be a man. And, well, Tiku is jealous and possessive, so a male bodyguard might have the same effect on him as a red cape would to a charging bull. To be honest, he's been spreading rumors that I left him because I like women better. But today news like that doesn't really ruffle any feathers."

"I'm not talking about an ordinary guy—I'm talking about Reiska. Reiska Räsänen."

"Who's he?"

I didn't have any of my props with me. Still, I did my best to create Reiska's stance and facial expression, lowered my voice, and used my Kaavi dialect. I walked toward Lehmusvuo, looking her in the eye.

"Howdy, I'm Reiska Räsänen, a handyman from Kaavi. A good day to you, ma'am. I've been lookin' for a job but seein' there ain't much available, and it sure looks like you could use a fellow that's handy with tools around here. Paint peelin' off the fence like the devil . . . and it would only take a couple of dry days for a fresh coat! If we strike a deal, I'll throw in cuttin' the lawn while we're at it. A representative of the people has to have a prim and proper yard—what on earth do folks think of you livin' in this mess!"

Lehmusvuo stared at me, astonished. I put my hands on my hips, scratched my nonexistent balls and looked her up and down.

"You're not a bad-lookin' lady at all, though a bit scrawny to my likin'. And I'm not too keen on that party you're representin'. My daddy was a farmer, and nothin' grows in Kaavi without fertilizer, and he needs to hunt to get food on the table on top of all the farmin'. The lynx ate all the chicken from the coop as fast as they could, so he had to put all the animals into cages."

Helena Lehmusvuo cracked up. She had a beautiful laugh.

"Who is this guy?"

"I'm just Reiska, good old Reiska. Your basic Finnish guy. Straitlaced, though a bit of a boozer."

"How did you come up with him?"

I changed back into Hilja.

"Haven't you ever thought about how fun it would be to impersonate a man? It comes in handy. You can become invisible and take your time in situations where a woman might draw unwanted attention. I mean, you never know at first glance if a lynx cub is a boy or girl. In the Ähtäri wild animal zoo, they named a cub Ines, but then it turned out that it was a boy, so now it's called Matikainen. I'm kind of like that, too. And I actually agree with Reiska—this place could use some sprucing up. You don't think it could use a paint job? How many rooms do you have upstairs?"

"Two bedrooms and an electric sauna that I'm not using. If I end up staying here, I'll tear it down and make it into a gym."

"Then there's plenty of room for Reiska or, if necessary, Reiska can turn back into Hilja sometimes. Do you have house guests often?"

"My son, occasionally. Aapo is studying architecture in Otaniemi."

"Do you trust him?"

"Completely! He's only too happy that I've left Tiku."

"It's a deal, then. You'll hire Reiska. You'll enter into an agreement with him and pay his fee directly to his bank account."

"Does Reiska pay taxes? I can't pay him under the table!"

Hilja could keep her unemployment benefits if Reiska was the one working. I briefly considered the various possible tax scenarios, but my gut told me to play it straight.

"Maybe it's better if you make the agreement with me rather than with Reiska. But he can do the renovations. That will explain why he'll be around here for a few days. I'll let your neighbors know that you've hired a handyman from Savonia and he'll be staying with you for some of the time. The tax officials won't be peering through the window. I'll come back tomorrow if you need me to."

"Sunday evening will do. I'm traveling to Turku for a meeting tomorrow morning—the entire cabinet is working on a strategy at the Ruissalo spa for the upcoming election. I doubt anyone will come after me there."

I let out a sigh and looked into her tired brown eyes.

"Listen, Helena. You're not overreacting about your safety. Although you might think that Tiku is your most likely threat, you can't disregard any other potential enemies. Think about it: there are all kinds of accidents that could happen at a spa. People drown, slip on soap and hit their heads, or are electrocuted by poorly serviced equipment. If you're working with me, you need to remember this: there are no safe places. I've had to learn that the hard way."

Helena Lehmusvuo attempted a smile, but her lips were quivering. That was a good sign; it meant she understood the danger. I could not let her meet Anita's fate, not even if I had to risk my own life for hers.

11

Each time I take on a new case, I spend a significant amount of time doing background research. I was happy to have already done some of it on Helena Lehmusvuo. She was part of the small group of government officials I would have recognized on the street. I had never been interested in politics; I only voted when I had time in my schedule to do so. Helena had hired me, but I didn't need to get entangled in her ethics. There were risks involved in becoming buddies with a client, as Monika had shown me. I let Helena pour me more tea before I began with my basic questions.

"Do you always come back here to spend the night, or do you have another place in Helsinki where you stay?"

"I have a room in a two-bedroom apartment. Two women share the other bedroom. One is a member of our group from Oulu and the other is a member of the Swedish People's Party from Ostrobothnia. She inherited some money and used it to pay for the apartment. We haven't talked about this arrangement in public. Her constituents are pretty conservative and they would worry about her integrity being compromised if they knew she was living with two members of the Green League." Helena laughed. She then told me that her temporary apartment was in Töölö, in a newly renovated house where the front door was always locked. The apartment door had a peephole, a latch, and a security lock—Helena's colleague from Ostrobothnia was the suspicious kind. Nevertheless, I decided to check out both roommates' possible connection to Paskevich.

"I'd like to take a look at your place in Helsinki as well, but for now, let's focus on this townhouse. When I'm dressed up as Reiska, I will install a security system, including motion detectors and surveillance cameras. What about the backyard? Are there already lights out there?"

"No. And do you really think all of these devices are necessary? Do they use a lot of energy?"

"I can definitely look into more energy-efficient options. But you should think about how much energy you spend on being worried about your safety. We haven't calculated a price for that yet."

Helena thought about it for a second. She played with her jacket sleeve in a way that would not have looked good had she been on TV.

"I'll let you install the equipment, but I'm saying no to the bright outdoor lights. We'll have to make do with surveillance cameras and streetlights. I mean, come on—I've been the one in the cabinet to oppose any Big Brother legislation and now I'd be allowing it in my own yard!"

I let Helena steam for a moment. It was easy to rail against surveillance cameras when you had nothing to worry about. "Tell me more about your ex. How long were you two together? Where does he work?"

Helena had met Tiku Kunto Henrikki Aaltonen four years earlier at an election campaign event. Aaltonen had self-published a collection of environmental poems and offered to sell it at campaign events for the Espoo Green League. It hadn't worked out, but Helena had taken a liking to the poems and bought fifty chapbooks to give out at various events. This had prompted Tiku to write poems about her.

"I was such a fool! All the men I'd dated before were either economists or politicians. My son's father, who used to study economics with me, is now one of the head honchos of the Nordea bank group. Tiku is completely different from these men. First I thought it was fine to use my salary to sponsor a talented poet who just hadn't managed to find a publisher for his work. As if I understood literature at all. I'd show some of his stuff to you, but I donated everything he gave me to the library; I didn't want his books on my shelf anymore."

I didn't understand poetry, either. Uncle Jari had had only a few books on his bookshelf, one of them the collected works of our national treasure, Aleksis Kivi. When he'd had a bit too much to drink, he would start stammering the poem about a squirrel sleeping comfortably in the tree. That was the only poem I knew by heart—well, most of it—if you didn't count the lyrics of rock songs as poetry. In any case, I didn't know a thing about Tiku Aaltonen's work.

When Helena and Tiku began dating, Helena's son Aapo was sixteen years old, and he had not gotten along with Tiku at all. Having to relocate was one reason. Helena bought the family a three-bedroom apartment in Matinkylä, and although it was only a few blocks away from their old apartment, Aapo was unhappy about the move and the addition of a new family member. He retreated to his room, rarely joining Helena and Tiku for lunch or dinner, even though Helena would rearrange her demanding schedule to make sure she was around for meals, which she viewed as sacrosanct family time. Until then Aapo had been certain he'd enter civil service instead of the army, but once he found out that Tiku had done civil service as well, he began to talk about joining the army. Helena was caught in the middle between the two men in her life, each of who were acting childish. Aapo had also begun making comments about how Tiku didn't have a job; instead, he sat at bars and squiggled in his little notebooks, although he never found anyone to publish his work.

"He'd be roaring at Tiku about how he was just using me as a sugar mama; Tiku's response was that Aapo was doing exactly the same thing, that he didn't even work in the summer like other teenagers did. Jarmo, Aapo's dad, has always given him plenty of money, and it's true that he'd had it pretty easy. I thought things would calm down once Aapo and Tiku got to know each other better. Aapo lived with us until the end of last fall, but after being on the wait-list for a student apartment, he got a room with five other boys in Otaniemi. I guess that shows how much he hates Tiku; he chose sharing a student apartment over staying in a three-bedroom home with his family."

Helena said she'd realized only later that she'd made Tiku out to be better than he was, partly because she didn't want to be one of those pushovers who let her kids choose how she should live her life. Only after Aapo moved away did she begin to view Tiku in the same light as Aapo and her friends had. Monika had brought up Tiku to me once; I distinctly remember that she'd wondered why women like Helena fell for scam artists like him. Although I saw Helena at Chez Monique many times, I didn't remember seeing her accompanied by anyone.

"Do you have a picture of Tiku?"

"I have CDs here somewhere with pictures from two summers ago when we went on an orchid-hunting trip to Saaremaa. All the discs are labeled. Do you mind looking through them? I'll turn my laptop on for you to use."

"I'll check out the CDs after you tell me why you two separated. I assume you instigated it?"

"There were many reasons why. Or I suppose the underlying reason was that I felt I was being used. Tiku did live off my money for the four years we spent together. It was a classic scam, really: we'd be sitting in a restaurant and he'd tell me it was his treat, but then, oops, he left his credit card at home. I'm ashamed to tell you how naive I was when we purchased that apartment on Aapelinkuja: we each paid for half of it but took out a joint loan to pay the difference between the price of my old place and the new one. You can probably guess how much money Tiku spent on mortgage payments."

I used my index finger and thumb to form a zero; Helena nodded. The law had been on Tiku's side; half of the place legally belonged to him, even though Helena paid all the bills. Tiku tried to publish his poems. In every pitch letter, he'd mention that he was representative Helena Lehmusvuo's common-law husband and that the doe-eyed, orchid-loving woman in the poems was Helena. He thought this would interest women's magazines and guarantee poetry sales. His poems must have been terrible.

"Tiku started to pressure me into contacting my publisher, although I have absolutely no say in what they decide to print. They've only published a couple of my political pamphlets. That's where I drew the line; I told him he had to make it on his own. He cried and begged me, saying he was exhausted from being constantly misunderstood."

As Helena was going on with her story, I slid off the couch to take a look at her piles of records and books. Her CDs were in heaps near the foyer door. Her taste in music wasn't particularly surprising: Bob Dylan, Leonard Cohen, and a lot of classic jazz. Reiska wouldn't enjoy any of it. He was a fan of good old Finnish acts such as Eläkeläiset and Popeda. The picture CDs were underneath all the music.

"Finally, I simply bought myself my freedom," Helena continued. "I told Tiku I was leaving him and that he could continue to live in the apartment if he wanted to. If he didn't, we'd sell it and he'd get half of the money. Tiku went berserk—he didn't have the money to buy me out, and now I was about to throw him out of the best and most artistically inspiring home he'd ever had."

I spotted a CD labeled "Saaremaa," with a date from May of last year. I also noticed the pieces of the CD shelf leaning against the wall. Putting the shelves together would have taken thirty minutes max, so why hadn't Helena bothered doing it? She sure knew how to talk, though, just like a real politician.

"Then I did something I consider the most shameful act of my entire life. I convinced the banker who gave me the loan to give Tiku another loan that he could use to pay me back my share of the apartment. The rest of the mortgage was turned over to Tiku—and he didn't have a cent of income! This is exactly the type of loan that made banks collapse two decades ago and here I was, a guardian of society, doing exactly the same thing. The banker was sure that the apartment was enough to guarantee the loan. They'll never get that money." Helena's cheeks were glowing red and she couldn't look me in the eye. I started putting the CD shelves together while I listened to her rant.

"That's how I washed my hands of Tiku, and all I have left of him now is a few funny pictures and memories from four years of hell. Aapo asked me why I never sued the guy—he thought there had to be some sort of law I could invoke. But it was my fault for having been so trusting, and I didn't want anyone exposing that in the media. Good thing Tiku is not the smartest man and that he really thinks the papers are interested in his bizarre claims, like the idea that I'm having an affair with another woman. Even the worst gossip columnist at the most awful rag wouldn't buy that. If he knew what a mess my finances are in and leaked that to a political journalist with an axe to grind, though, I'd be doomed."

Helena's laptop had booted up. The picture on her desktop was of a rocky islet supporting a scraggly pine where an eagle stood on a branch. I picked up the machine, propped it on my lap while sitting down onto the floor, and inserted the CD. There were a couple hundred photos; I clicked through them quickly. I wasn't interested in orchids. There was Helena posing on a bike, showing off her slim legs and remarkably toned calf muscles; next, she was standing in the rough waves at the shore with her arm around a dark, slim man. Tiku Aaltonen's nearly black curls reached down to his shoulders. The red bandana around his head, the blue shirt, and the blue-and-white clam diggers made him look like a poor man's Johnny Depp trying to play Captain Jack Sparrow, but Tiku wasn't displaying any of Depp's devilish charm. Aaltonen was barely taller than Helena, five foot five at most, and he looked even skinnier than her. Unless he was into martial arts or marathon running, he'd be no match for me in close combat.

I glanced at a few more pictures; Johnny Depp was no longer present in any way. If I were Tiku, I would have used that pirate picture in an online dating ad. There were women who were especially interested in men who had dated a celebrity.

"Could you do me a favor?" yelled Helena from the kitchen where she was putting the tea cups in the dishwasher. "Just delete all the pictures showing Tiku, no matter how good they are. I want to forget that entire part of my life."

It looked like I was becoming a real go-to guy in Helena Lehmusvuo's household. I did as I was asked. Luckily, most of the pictures featured flowers and scenery. It wasn't until the second-to-last picture that my interest was piqued: first it looked like a moor at dusk, but when I looked closer, I saw a lynx running in the background. I tried zooming in, but the animal disappeared into large pixels. I clicked on the next picture but saw only birds.

"Did you see a lynx during your Saaremaa trip?"

"One ran by at dusk when I was on an evening stroll. Tiku wouldn't believe it when I told him; he said I must've seen a dog or a large fox. You also think that that's a lynx in the picture, right?"

"I know my lynx. This looks like a fox lynx." A yearning took hold of me and for a moment I could feel Frida's presence in the room. "OK, I've deleted all the pictures of Tiku. Let's deal with the paperwork now, shall we? First we need to create a contract that we can refer to should we run into any major disagreements, not that I think we will. Then I would like a detailed list of where, when, and how you have been harassed. Have you kept any notes?"

Helena let out a little laugh, but this time it wasn't so pretty—she could only muster a snort.

"I've been on the board of a national domestic violence organization for years, but as soon as I'm a victim . . . well, it hasn't been so easy to do what I know I'm supposed to. Hang on a second, I'll check my calendar. It'll help me remember."

I pulled my own laptop from my bag. I had created a folder on Lehmusvuo the day before, and now I began to make notes in it. Someone with less experience would have thought Lehmusvuo's concerns were just in her head: the wind had knocked the rosemary plant over, a neighbor had noticed that her newspaper would have gotten soaking wet outside so she'd dropped it into her mail slot, and so on. But all these seemingly unconnected events were clues, warning Helena that she was being watched. I remembered how David Stahl had been sneaking around after me in Degerby in the middle of the night. It was pure luck that I'd spotted him.

I gave Lehmusvuo an estimate of both my services and the surveillance equipment I was going to install. I'd start to plan the renovation first thing on Sunday night.

"It's easier to figure out the proper setup if the floors aren't swimming in junk. I'll put the book and CD shelves together right away, if you don't mind. And I haven't even seen the upstairs yet. Reiska has to survey his future abode, right?"

"How did you come up with that name? Is it a nickname for Reijo?"

"That's right. His full name is Reijo Juhani Räsänen. A genuine, uncomplicated Finnish name. And nobody can count all of the Räsänens in Kaavi—it's such a common name."

I went upstairs. The narrow hallway was empty, save for a large map of the world that was hung on the wall above the staircase. The bedroom facing the street contained only a simple bed: a pillow and a mattress but no sheet or blanket. It would do just fine for Reiska, who could always go to the recycling center to get materials to build a desk. Helena's bedroom faced the backyard. There was a four-foot-wide bed in the room; she'd hastily made it. I didn't look in her closets, not yet. I remembered how the tabloids had lambasted her for wearing the same black dress six years in a row to the Independence Day Presidential Ball—and she'd gotten it from a secondhand store. Apparently, the articles commented sourly, Lehmusvuo didn't want to support Finnish designers.

If someone about six feet tall stood on top of the fence in the backyard, he'd be able to reach Helena's bedroom window. If the stalker had done his homework, he'd know where the bed was. It would be simple to shoot her or throw an explosive into the bedroom. People were so clueless; it was extremely easy to do away with someone. At any moment, without warning, you could die. All you needed was to hit an elk on the road, or have a drunk driver plow into you, or marry the wrong person, or go to school with someone who had nothing going for him except his gun license. I understood why people made such a big deal about celebrating major birthdays. It was quite an achievement to make it to fifty alive, let alone the years beyond then. My mother had been twenty-six when she'd died. I'd managed to stay alive eight years longer than she had.

Something had to be done to the bed. It would be ridiculously expensive to replace the window with bulletproof glass, but if I thought that Helena Lehmusvuo really had a reason to fear for her life, I'd have to do it. The other option was for her to move. Tall apartment buildings had their advantages, especially if the adjacent buildings had fewer stories than yours. Anita had always chosen hotels where she'd be out of shooting range, unless the assassin was as nimble as Spider-Man or owned a helicopter. A chopper makes a hell of a racket, so anyone in his right mind would have enough time to take cover before it got too close.

Lehmusvuo's sauna consisted of two rooms: the steam room and a small bathroom with a toilet, sink, shower, and washing machine in it. The clothesline, strung across the room, was full of damp linen; it slapped against my face when I walked into the sauna. It was just a booth for two people, and it looked like Helena's claim of never having used it was true; the seats were piled with bulging file folders. Chicken wire, used to dry herbs, hung over the sauna stove, and a few cardboard boxes full of dishes were on the floor.

I went back downstairs. Next I checked who had been visiting Lehmusvuo recently. She could only remember seeing Aapo and the person who'd come over to install her broadband Internet. Someone had come to her door trying to sell her potatoes, but Lehmusvuo ate most of her meals at work and belonged to a CSA, which she used to order the few groceries she stored in her pantry. She'd only met some of her neighbors; like the other celebrities I had guarded, Lehmusvuo was slightly reserved when she communicated with "regular" people. You could never tell why they were actually reaching out to you. Cell phone cameras and voice recorders were everywhere.

"But you didn't check my ID—you just let me waltz right in," I told her when we were signing our contract. She blushed and said she remembered me from Chez Monique. Nevertheless, I told her, it couldn't happen again. Anyone could claim to be a reporter and ask for a brief interview at an unexpected place, such as a bar, where there wasn't a metal detector like there was at the cabinet building.

Helena said she'd be going to the Uusimaa Green League's election seminar the following weekend, at the Kopparnäs Inn. I wondered whether David Stahl was still hanging around there. Now that was interesting; the idea of meeting him again was much too tempting. I had to think of something else to stop the throbbing between my legs.

I'd chat with the neighbors once I came back to Helena's place dressed as Reiska. It was only appropriate that a Savonian handyman would be slightly nosy and a bit lonely, too. Maybe the men next door would even go out for a beer with him. My plans were taking shape. I asked Helena a few more questions while I put her bookshelves together. She asked that I'd put everything in alphabetical order so that she'd easily find what she was looking for. She then gave me a spare key, and I promised to make an appearance as Reiska on Sunday evening. In exchange for the key, I gave her my phone number and address on Untamo Road.

"One more thing. Anita's daughter, Cecilia Nuutinen-Kekki, will be in Finland next week. I don't know the exact date yet. I told her I'd meet up with her. Is that all right?"

"Of course. Is she in charge of making the funeral arrangements?"

"Apparently." The last time I'd been to a funeral was when Uncle Jari had died. The service had been at the church in Kaavi, and the memorial was held in the church community hall. More people showed up than I had anticipated—we ran out of coffee cakes and Maija Hakkarainen had to run out to buy more. The idea of Anita's funeral gave me chills, but I didn't think passing on it was an option.

After alphabetizing Helena's CDs and eating one more apple muffin, I was on my way. As I walked toward the Kirkkonummi train station, I felt oddly light, almost giddy. Once again I'd managed to find a job, at least for a while. Plus, I'd gotten rid of David Stahl. It would be easy to hide out at Helena Lehmusvuo's place as Reiska while I set up her security system, did some home repairs—and conducted my own investigation. Frankly, I was sure that Helena Lehmusvuo had told me only half of her story; maybe just a third of it. But I'd get the whole truth out of her soon enough.

12

The Untamo Road apartment was empty when I arrived there on Friday evening, and it stayed that way the entire weekend. On Saturday morning I bought some tools Reiska would need to work on Helena's apartment, and in the afternoon I rang Mrs. Voutilainen's doorbell—from the aroma of caramelized almonds, I could tell she was baking a Tosca cake. My nose hadn't fooled me. When I came in, Mrs Voutilainen was just pulling it out of the oven and brewing coffee to go with it. I asked her whether she'd seen any other salesmen recently, picture or otherwise, but only some Jehovah's Witnesses had been to her door. She showed me the latest issue of *The Watchtower.*

"I'm not scared of their talk of Hell—they're free to believe whatever they want. Those poor people; they're trying so hard. I took their magazine and gave them some blueberry pie so that they'd have energy for making their rounds."

"You haven't seen that painter Yuri again, have you?"

"No. Are you after his paintings? You can have mine if you want."

"Thanks for the offer, but I won't be home for the next couple of weeks; I wouldn't have time to admire it. But if Trankov comes back to sell you some more, can you let him know that I'd really like one of those lynx paintings, too?"

"Going after a new job? Are you traveling somewhere?"

"Ostrobothnia—a fox farmer has been threatened and I promised to check it out. The owner can't spend all his time guarding the foxes." The lie slipped out easily and Mrs. Voutilainen bought it completely.

"The gall of some people, threatening these hardworking farmers who are just trying to make an honest living. Once these activist types grow up, they'll see how easy it is to survive in the freezing cold winter without a good fox pelt. Here, have some more cake. I doubled the recipe for the topping—Jaakko, my late husband, would always complain about how this cake needed more topping."

The thick layer of almonds and butter settled in my stomach, so later I headed to the gym to work it off. By Sunday evening my roommates hadn't shown up, so I felt safe turning into Reiska in my room. I briefly wondered why neither of them had left me a message, but then again, when did I ever tell them what I was up to? I tried not to worry about it. Mrs. Voutilainen would have told me if she'd noticed something peculiar going on at our apartment. Still, the thought occurred to me that the Paskevich gang had kidnapped Riikka and Jenni in an attempt to find out where I was. What if David Stahl wasn't visiting his childhood home in Tammisaari, but instead was torturing my roommates in a place where no one could hear them scream? I had to contact Jenni. The call went right to voice mail, and I left her a message. Riikka's situation was even more worrisome: her phone repeated the message, "The person you are trying to reach is currently unavailable." Her phone might as well have been at the bottom of the sea.

I left them a note in the kitchen saying I'd be gone for at least a week. I thought about giving them my new phone number, too, but decided it was best just to tell them that I had gotten a new phone and was no longer using the old number.

The transformation into Reiska was complete once I put on the mustache. I didn't run into anyone I knew in the stairwell, nor did anyone stare at me on the trolley. Reiska rode the bus to Kirkkonummi on a route that stopped near Helena's townhouse. On the way he listened to Eläkeläiset and hummed out loud to their cover of Led Zeppelin's "Black Dog." Their new album would come out next week, and he'd be the first to rush into Kirkkonummi Prisma to buy it. It felt good to be in the skin of gentle Reiska, who didn't have someone's death weighing on him—he was able to enjoy life, especially now that he had some work to do.

I hoped Helena Lehmusvuo would be able to forget that there was a woman hiding behind Reiska's mustache. If necessary, I'd sleep as him, even if the mustache was prickly and the makeup made my skin feel clammy. I'd even considered cutting my hair to make it look half bald, like Reiska's, but made do with a short crew cut. It would be easier to wear a wig over it, like a swimming cap.

Nobody else got off at Helena's stop. Reiska carried an ice hockey bag, big enough to fit a woman of Helena's size. I estimated that she weighed ninety pounds, so it would be easy to carry her out of her home in the bag, should it come to that.

There were no people on the street when Reiska rang Helena's doorbell, but a flash from the neighbor's window blinds told me that someone was spying on Helena to see who her visitor was. I could hear Helena's footsteps behind the door, but it took a moment for her to open it. Apparently, Helena was smart enough to use the peephole. Reiska's first task would be to install a chain lock on the door.

When Helena finally opened the door, I could see her eyes, once again round like a deer's, but this time they hid a smile.

"Well, hi there. I'm Reiska Räsänen, and I'm here for that renovation." He stepped inside before she had a chance to invite him in. Displaying his poor manners, he didn't take off his shoes before entering the foyer. The piles of books were still on the floor, and the empty shelves had managed to gather dust in the few days I'd been gone.

"Hi . . ." Helena didn't quite know what to say. "You found your way here all right?"

"I had good directions. Where should I put my bag?"

"I thought you could stay in the guest room upstairs, the room that's facing the street. It's pretty quiet out here."

"Oh, I'll sleep anywhere," Reiska said. "I suppose I can't smoke indoors, can I? Or is it all right if I blow the smoke out of the bedroom window?"

"You smoke?"

"Need to take a little break with all that workin'. I can always go outside if you'd rather not have the smell in the house."

Reiska did his best to speak more formally in the presence of a politician. He took his bags up and came back downstairs with a drill, a screwdriver, and two security chains. The front door had a good seal on it and would definitely prevent someone from breaking in, but as was so often the case, the back door was made of weaker stuff. It would also be easy to break in from the large window—just toss a rock through it and then climb in. At least the burglar alarm would alert an unsuspecting victim about an intruder.

Reiska puttered about for a couple of hours. First he worked on the chains, and then he installed burglar alarms on every door and window. Helena stuck around, curious to see what Reiska was doing. I'd always thought that all the Green League members were raging feminists, so she shouldn't have been surprised that a woman like me knew how to work with electrical wiring. It was one of the most rudimentary tasks we'd had to learn at the security academy. Plus, I had learned a lot from Uncle Jari; I'd been his little handyman as a kid and later as a teen when I'd traveled around with him, installing wiring and electric outlets at construction sites. At Hevonpersiinsaari there were no men's and women's jobs; Uncle and I shared the chores. His preserved mushrooms and lingonberries were as good as any housewife's.

Around nine my phone rang. I checked the number. It was Jenni. All evening long I'd been using Reiska's slightly hoarse voice as if I had been stuck in puberty, so when I switched to my own voice, it startled Helena.

"Hi Jenni, thanks for calling. I was wondering why the apartment was empty all weekend."

"I was on a student trip to Tallinn. I didn't pick up when you first called because I didn't recognize the number—I thought it was a telemarketer."

"Some guy was tormenting me, so I had to switch numbers. Do you know what Riikka has been up to?"

Jenni started laughing. Based on the background noises, it sounded like the ferry from Tallinn was approaching the Finnish border and people were rushing to get into the tax-free shops before they closed.

"She met a guy! Some tech college student who lives with his dad in Krunikka. Riikka even bought some toiletries to take over there, and they've only known each other for a week. We might have to start looking for a new roommate soon."

"I'll be staying in Ostrobothnia for a while." Better to tell the same lie to everyone. "But please don't give this number to anyone else but Riikka. I'm keeping it private for now."

"All right. I'll save some of these chocolates for you—they were dirt cheap."

I'd come to the conclusion that the townhouse had good soundproofing and insulation when I hadn't heard a peep from next door— it would be safe to have a conversation without anyone eavesdropping, and I could switch back to Hilja's voice when I needed to. Nonetheless, I adopted Reiska's persona again as soon as I hung up. Hopefully Riikka's new boyfriend was a regular guy, not some Paskevich hitman. Anyone could be a threat.

The first night at Kirkkonummi passed without incident. I woke up a few times, first to a moped buzzing loudly at it went by. Apparently it didn't occur to the driver that people were trying to sleep. Next I woke up to the mail slot clanging. Helena and I both slept behind closed doors and I wasn't able to monitor her breathing. The morning was rainy, so Reiska busied himself working indoors.

Reiska and I had both come to the conclusion that we'd need to put a tracking device on Helena. Should she go missing, I'd be able to find her. But we'd have to figure out a way to hide it somewhere where a bad guy wouldn't be able to find it. Forget jewelry or a watch. Helena's ears were pierced, but she switched her earrings according to her moods. A device could be placed inside a tooth, but that required a trip to the dentist. We finally decided on placing the tracker at the nape of Helena's neck, where her hair was the thickest. She said she went to the hairdresser every three months, and in between visits she gave herself a trim to save time. Perfect. I sewed the device into her hair. It was made out of plastic, so it wouldn't set off the metal detector at the cabinet building, and it wouldn't be damaged by water. It would tell me Helena's whereabouts to within thirty feet.

"Letting you guard me like this means I trust you," Helena said with a smile that didn't quite reach her eyes. I made sure that the device was working before she left for her meetings.

Reiska's week was uneventful but busy until Friday. There was nobody sneaking around in the backyard or moving the rosemary plant. He went out a few times a day for a smoke or smoked while he worked outdoors. On Tuesday the curious retiree from next door had come to chat with him to find out who Reiska was and what he was up to. He must've had the phone number to *Seitsemän päivää* magazine's gossip line on his speed dial.

"That's what I told my old lady, too; that's no boyfriend, it's a handyman! So much younger than representative Lehmusvuo. Although, you do see all sorts of things these days. I'm Pentti Hirvonen. You must be from Savonia somewhere. You sound like home to me."

"I'm from Kaavi. Reijo Räsänen. Just call me Reiska."

"I'm from Juankoski, not too far from there."

When it rained on Thursday, Mr. Hirvonen invited Reiska over for a smoke and a cup of coffee.

"The missus went to her water aerobics class at the pool. Tried to get me to go with her, but there's no way I'll start jumpin' around like a fool. I'll turn on the fan so she won't notice we've been smoking."

Apparently the Hirvonens had been both excited and worried about having a real live politician next door to them. Her party was definitely not the right one—the Hirvonens had always voted for Social Democrats—but at least they could boast that their neighbor had been to the Independence Day Presidential Ball. According to Mr. Hirvonen, there had been all sorts of "googly-eyed folk" at Lehmusvuo's doorstep when she'd first moved in, but they'd all taken off when he'd opened the door and walked outside. When Reiska asked him as nonchalantly as he could why the newspapers would have been moved from the mailbox to the slot in the door, Mr. Hirvonen didn't have an answer.

"And of course we've been a bit worried, what with Lehmusvuo criticizin' that Putin and other Russian folk. It's fine and dandy to complain about America in this country—we're just a tiny speck on their radar, and probably most of them have no clue where this country even is. Or whether this is a real country at all! But Russians . . . they're a diff'rent sort altogether. Better to stay on good terms with them. I came into this world thanks to my pop's leave from the army; at least he made it back alive, though he lost a leg. You're so young you don't remember how it was when Kekkonen was president: we were sweatin' bullets, hopin' the Russkies wouldn't get pissed off with us and start a new war. Asking America or Sweden for help wouldn't have done a damned thing. Listen, son, you tell your employer that she needs to keep her mouth shut about the Russians; we don't want to invite those tanks to our borders. She doesn't want Finland to join NATO, does she? Now that would be pure madness."

Reiska told him that he'd been hired to renovate Representative Lehmusvuo's place, not to engage in political debates. It was good to know, though, that Pentti Hirvonen and his wife Eila thought that Helena might be in danger. At least they had their eyes on her. Just to be sure, Reiska asked Hirvonen to call the police or at least alert Lehmusvuo if they saw any suspicious characters sneaking around.

The townhouse complex had five apartments, and the middle one was occupied by Noora Asikainen, a twentysomething single mother, and her young daughter. She made no attempts to hide her interest in Reiska. He was used to it. Although he had a mustache and dressed like a farmer, women were constantly approaching him. He usually only flirted a little—after all, he was a nice guy and didn't want to get anyone's hopes up.

Helena came home by bus two evenings that week. She'd told Reiska in advance which route she was taking, and he waited near the bus stop hidden from view, checking to see whether anyone tried to follow Helena home. Thursday, though, was devoted to a plenary session that took longer than expected. Helena could only catch the 11:12 train, which would arrive at Kirkkonummi just before midnight.

Helena didn't want to use a taxi. It was only about a mile to get home from the train, and she said a walk would do her good after a long day. Reiska decided to go meet her. Of course women should be allowed to walk by themselves in the middle of the night, completely hammered and wearing a miniskirt, and if something unfortunate happened, the rapist or assailant was to blame. This was Mike Virtue's basic philosophy, followed by a long "but"—we had to be aware of all the risks, anticipate them, and prevent them as best as we could.

I'd often taken the subway alone in the middle of the night, met my landlady Mary's cocaine dealer multiple times, and partied in places I'd never even known existed until I came to New York. Nothing bad had ever happened, because I knew that the world was full of Seppo Holopainens who wouldn't take "no" for an answer. I had to think like a Seppo Holopainen in order to anticipate what a lowlife like him might do.

Reiska pushed through the maze of smokers outside the bar at the bus station, where he planned on waiting until he went to meet Helena on the train platform. The pub itself was almost empty, except for the patrons who seemed like regulars. If I'd walked in as Hilja, wearing red high heels and leather pants, they would have ogled me to death. But Reiska could walk in without anyone noticing. The middle-aged women in the pub already had male companions.

Usually people thought Reiska was twenty-five, and he'd brag about being well preserved if someone got his age wrong. Because we were roughly the same age, I could tell my army stories as if they were his. He'd joined the army in the first wave of the annual draft. No one ever questioned his manhood after hearing about the time he and his buddies had peeked into the shower used by the three women privates in their platoon, and had made fun of the one with the small tits. Of course, the victim had actually been me, but there had been plenty of guys like that in the army. Reiska didn't ever mention, though, that this woman with small tits had shown the jokesters: she'd carried the worst of the lot for two miles on her back after he'd hurt his leg camping in the forest and there was no other way to get him back to base.

Because nobody was bothering Reiska in the bar, he listened to music. Before heading out he'd put on a T-shirt with a slogan honoring Finnish war veterans. It read, "Thank you 1939–45." The shirt was adorned with a lion's crest. When I'd bought it for Reiska from a market in Helsinki, Riikka's face betrayed her disgust. "Ugh, how militant of you!"

Reiska drank his tall lager slowly—ordering two beers while on the job wasn't a good idea, but ordering a beer with low alcohol content would've been social suicide. Reiska had made that mistake once; he'd heard people calling him a fag even on his way out of the pub. There was soccer on TV. Reiska didn't have a favorite team, but he hated "those damned Swedes," meaning IFK Mariehamn.

The table next to him was a host to heated debate on local politics. Reiska had decided not to vote now that Tony Halme was no longer in the cabinet. Goddamn it, that man had disappointed them all. The arguing was getting loud enough for the bartender to take notice and unglue his eyes from the match on TV. Reiska wouldn't step in, but he didn't move away, either. Running away wasn't his style. He mentally went through the motions of taking cover in case he had to duck a flying pint glass. On a different occasion, Reiska decided to stop two women from clawing each other and was able to control the more vocal one with a holding technique I had learned at the security academy.

Both Reiska and I were relieved when it was close to midnight and time to head out. The Kirkkonummi train station was only a couple blocks away. Reiska waited for Helena behind the station—she would walk by on her way home, and Reiska could easily see if anyone was following her. The route home was well lit except for the last stretch. Reiska had stressed how important it was for Helena to pretend not to notice him, except if one of the neighbors happened to be on the same train or bus with her. That seemed unlikely; the only people Reiska had seen were the Hirvonens and Noora Asikainen.

Helena walked briskly. Her heavy briefcase was pulling her left shoulder down—she must have neck problems. Reiska and Helena were the only people on the street, save for a couple of cars that rushed by. Helena would've been an easy target for an assassin traveling in one of them.

Helena turned onto her street without incident, and Reiska picked up his pace a bit so he wouldn't lose sight of her for too long. When he rounded the last corner he saw Helena, who had stopped at her mailbox and was looking around in a panic. No wonder. A man was standing under the awning at her front door.

Reiska hid in the shadows. He recognized the man immediately, even without his pirate outfit. Tiku Aaltonen.

"Dear Helena, how lovely to see you!" Tiku's voice was unpleasantly nasal.

"What are you doing here?" Helena sneered, using the same tone she'd use when one of her political opponents said something inane.

"Well, you're not answering my messages or my calls. Helena, seriously, I'm in trouble. Help me just this once, please. I'm really close to signing a publishing deal with this new indie company. They have a great marketing plan and connections to magazines. I'll finally get my big break and then I can pay you back for everything."

Because Aaltonen sounded more like a lousy beggar than a dangerous stalker, Reiska decided to take a chance. He'd brought with him the remote that controlled all the burglar alarms, so he tapped in the code to turn off the alarms, walked around the block, and went into the neighbor's yard adjacent to Helena's. The residents were already asleep. Only a cat was nodding off on top of the table outside, but it took off sprinting when Reiska appeared. He had no problem scaling the fence between the yards, but instead of jumping down, he lowered himself slowly so he wouldn't make any noise. He could hear Helena's strained voice coming from the front yard.

"Get the hell out of here—I don't want to have anything to do with you!"

"Honey . . . I've written an entire book of poems for you, I've missed you so much. I'll call it *Helena the Unobtainable.*"

When Helena burst into chilling laughter, Reiska opened the back door. There was just enough light for him to walk through the living room without stumbling. The foyer door was open. Reiska had just oiled the hinges so they didn't creak. He quickly opened the front door with such force that it hit Tiku Aaltonen in the back and threw him to the ground.

"Why is this guy harassing you in the middle of the night? Helena, come in right now!" Reiska said.

Reiska couldn't tell who looked more flabbergasted, Helena or Aaltonen. When Aaltonen tried to get up, Reiska grabbed him by the shoulders and pinned his arms behind his back. Now Tiku didn't seem like a pirate at all—he was just a poor sailor, preparing to walk the plank after flirting with the captain's wife during shore leave. The lights came on in the Hirvonen kitchen.

"Get inside, Helena! I'll deal with this fool," Reiska commanded. He dragged the man for a couple blocks without any resistance, while explaining to Aaltonen in detail what would happen should he come back to bother Helena. Reiska parroted the worst threats that Mike Virtue had taught Hilja; the kind for which you'd be thrown in jail for six months in Finland. Reiska didn't think that Tiku Aaltonen knew the law very well.

"All right then, Timo-Kunto, if you know what's good for you, you'll run as fast as you can and you might even make the last train. Or you can try hitchhiking to Espoo, but be on the lookout for suspicious cars!" Reiska let Aaltonen go.

"And who exactly are you?" Aaltonen tried to hold on to what was left of his dignity.

"The man who doesn't let creeps like you near Helena. That's all you need to know. So scram, if you want to use your mouth for eating and your privates for baby-making."

Reiska let out a snorty laugh when Aaltonen took off jogging toward the town center. Reiska himself walked back with a swagger. Mrs. Hirvonen was at the door, wondering what the ruckus was about. At least Helena had been smart enough to go inside already.

"Nothin' to worry about, ma'am. You go ahead and get back to bed. That man won't bother us anymore," Reiska explained politely and even tipped his baseball cap to her.

"Who was it?"

"Representative Lehmusvuo's former husband. He has no business bein' here no more."

Inside, Helena had poured herself a glass of red wine and asked Reiska whether he wanted any. He didn't. He just turned the alarms back on and went to the bathroom upstairs. The beer he'd had earlier weighed heavily in his bladder, and in all honesty I was ready to get rid of Reiska's mask for a while. The heavy makeup was making my face break out in a rash. I went back downstairs as Hilja.

"Were you scared?" I asked Helena, who seemed to have downed her second glass of wine by then. She'd decided to work from home the next day, writing a presentation for an international conference.

"No, more like annoyed, at least at first. Then I wondered where you disappeared to—or, I mean Reiska."

"Reiska took Tiku by surprise. That guy is a real lightweight. It's good to know that he has money problems—that tells us no one has tried to buy him off yet. I'm sure he'd sell you out without batting an eye."

Helena stared at me. "To whom?"

"To anyone you haven't been ready to talk about yet." When she twitched I continued. "I know you're still testing me. That's okay. But once I get a hold of Anita's—oh, shit!"

I rarely cursed, but this time it was warranted. Cecilia Nuutinen-Kekki had been in Finland for who knows how many days already, and she may have even tried to call me—on my old phone number. I was such an idiot. I hadn't checked my e-mails, either, because I wasn't looking forward to hearing from Laitio or David Stahl. Lying awake in the darkness I had often thought of Stahl, and it was hard to keep myself from calling him. I wondered if he'd still have such a strong hold on me if I saw him again.

"I'm off to bed. Everything is fine," I told Helena. The wrinkles on her narrow face looked exceptionally deep. That's what she'd look like in ten years.

Helena slept late the next morning. I'd kept all the curtains closed, because I wanted to eat breakfast as Hilja. That's why I didn't dare to sneak out to get the morning paper, but instead I read a week-old publication called *The Green Thread*, which I had never heard of. Reiska wasn't ready to start working outside until eleven, and by then Helena was having breakfast. He turned off the alarm and began to apply another coat of paint to the fence in the backyard. Once that was done, he decided to paint the small fence that separated Helena's front yard from the sidewalk. His MP3 player was blasting *Humppa United* by Eläkeläiset, and he sang along to "Äkäinen Eläkeläinen," although his voice was hoarse and off key. He was so caught up in his warbling that he didn't hear the footsteps right away. Once the man got closer, Reiska pulled his cap down. The combat boots on the man looked familiar, so did the black jeans. The man passed Reiska and walked on. Only then did Reiska look up.

He could only see the man's back, but there was no doubt about who this tall, bald man was. David Stahl was roaming around Helena Lehmusvuo's neighborhood. When Stahl walked a couple feet past Reiska, he stopped and turned around. Reiska didn't have time to lower his gaze, and Stahl stared at him for a moment. I was sure he'd recognize me regardless of the disguise.

Stahl shrugged his shoulders, smiled, and continued walking. Neither one of us, Reiska nor I, felt the need to follow him.

13

I cursed silently to myself as I finished painting the fence. Had Stahl recognized me? Helena would be leaving for a weekend seminar at the Kopparnäs Inn, and we hadn't yet decided whether I should go with her.

My new phone was burning a hole in Reiska's pocket. I had to find out what David Stahl was up to. Because I would need to talk to him in Hilja's voice, I couldn't make the call from the yard, in case the neighbors would hear me. Helena was inside the house, so I couldn't make the call there, either. I didn't want to tell her about Stahl because I didn't yet know which one of us he was following.

Reiska went back inside. Helena gave him a brief glance before getting back to work on her laptop at the kitchen table. Reiska went upstairs to pack a backpack: a mirror, makeup remover, a bottle of water, cotton balls, a towel, and Hilja's shoes and jacket. He walked to the wooded area near Helena's home and began to change back into Hilja. After hanging the mirror on a tree branch, I removed Reiska's wig, doused a cotton ball with makeup remover and started scrubbing. I combed my hair and changed from Reiska's work shoes and jacket to sneakers and a leather jacket. We could both wear the same jeans. I looked around again to make sure nobody was watching before I pulled Reiska's crotch padding out. I had tried imagining how men's genitals affected their gait, and how men instinctively protected them if they tripped or got into a fight. There were a few times when I had been driving a car, going as fast as I could, and I swear I could feel my balls growing to the soundtrack of heavy metal, testosterone roiling inside me. Once, on the German autobahn, a client had begged me to slow down before I got both of us killed. I almost didn't want to—the speed was giving me such a high.

Before I called Stahl, I came up with a story. I had saved his number on my new phone, and now I used a prepaid card so he wouldn't recognize my number. If Stahl didn't answer immediately, I wouldn't leave a message. I tried to steady my breathing when I heard the dial tone. He picked up after three rings.

"Who's this?" asked Stahl, first in Russian and then in Swedish.

"Hey, David," I replied in Swedish. "It's Hilja, Hilja Ilveskero."

"Hilja! How nice of you to call. I didn't see your number on my screen."

"My phone was stolen—my insurance company gave me this temporary phone. But I have a pretty good idea who took it."

"Who?"

"This drug addict who lives next door. So, how have you been? Are you still near Helsinki, in Tammisaari?"

David laughed a little, and I tried to interpret its meaning. Was it, "Oh, my dear, you don't have a clue?" or "Well, you just saw me this morning," or "I'm glad you're interested!"

"Actually, I got back to Kopparnäs yesterday because the weather is supposed to be good for the next few days. There's some sort of a seminar here this weekend, but I was able to book my old room. Can you come this weekend?"

This was when I'd have to make plans for both Helena and me. I decided to risk it—there was no way David would have just happened to be back in Kopparnäs.

"You're in luck—I'm free this weekend."

"Will you invite me over to your cabin?"

"Unfortunately, no can do—my friend is using it this weekend. She's got a thing going on with a married man and they need a place for their tryst."

"And you support such immoral activities?" I could hear David smile.

"Who am I to judge? We all have our stories."

"Perhaps you're right. So, will you come? We can see if there are any good mushrooms in the forest, or try to run into the famous Kopparnäs bear. The innkeeper said she'd seen a lynx the other night."

"A lynx?" That was all the convincing I needed. Helena's seminar started early in the morning and she was carpooling with a friend from Espoo. I could ride with them almost the whole way and then claim that my friend had picked me up from the bus stop.

"Bring an overnight bag; I have room for two," David said, and I could feel that familiar drop in my stomach. Of course I would go. My plan was to get David into a situation where he couldn't defend himself. I told him I'd be in Kopparnäs around eleven, which would give me enough time to make sure that everything was set at the cabin and to get my bike. All I needed now was an explanation for Helena as to why I was in Kopparnäs. Or did she need to know? With any luck we'd be in different buildings, though breakfast would pose a problem.

I called Helena and told her that I had some business to take care of as Hilja, but I'd be back in the evening. I also told her to turn all the burglar alarms on and to let me know if she left the house. I didn't want to be checking her tracking device all the time. Helena suggested that we go swimming in the evening; she needed to let off some steam. She'd be easy to observe at the pool even if I couldn't go there as Reiska.

I took a long walk to clear my head. It didn't make sense to hide my trip to Kopparnäs completely from Helena. I hadn't told her about my cabin, so I couldn't use that as my reason for going. But then how would I explain to her where I got the bike? Should I trust her and tell the truth?

In the end I decided to go with almost the same story I'd told David: that my friend had a cabin near Kopparnäs and I had borrowed the bike from her. I walked over to the library to read my e-mails. There was one from Cecilia Nuutinen-Kekki, who was extremely upset. She hadn't been able to reach me. I replied, telling her that my phone had been stolen, and I offered to meet in Helsinki on Monday. Helena had a full day of meetings and she'd be safe among all the security guards and metal detectors in the cabinet building.

I turned into Reiska before I took my stuff back to Helena's place. I then left as Reiska and soon came back as Hilja. Helena wondered whether such switcheroos were really necessary so I had to explain to her that the Hirvonens and, most likely, Noora Asikainen were keeping an eye on Reiska. When I was Hilja I played up my femininity, especially when I walked, and I even put on makeup before heading out to the pool. I wasn't surprised when Mrs. Hirvonen stepped out into the yard just as we were leaving. Helena introduced me as her friend Hilja, and the woman stared suspiciously at my cropped hair.

"A friend, huh?" she smirked.

As soon as we turned the corner, I laughed. "Looks like Mrs. Hirvonen has pegged me as a lesbian!" I said.

It was drizzling lightly and the leaves on the trees were more yellow than green. Although it was later in the evening, you could hear the construction sounds echoing from Citymarket's site. They were building the market next to another one on a field—talk about brilliant urban planning. Kirkkonummi's city center consisted of a number of ugly boxes standing in a row. The only anomalies were the church and the library; the rest were flat buildings that had clearly been hastily constructed—a subject that Helena had ranted about multiple times.

"Well, are you?" asked Helena. "Not that it's any of my business, but you could tell me a bit more about yourself."

"I'm not."

"Chief Constable Laitio seems to disagree."

"Let him. And it doesn't matter, anyway. I don't plan to start a family with a man or a woman. Oh, by the way, I thought it would be best if I went to Kopparnäs, too, just in case. I heard from an old friend who happens to be staying there, and I can crash there if necessary. But first I was thinking of visiting another friend of mine who has a cabin in Stävö, close by."

If you ever need to massage a story, come up with something that's simple and as close to the truth as possible and then stick to it. That's what Mike Virtue had advised. I was juggling too many balls, but I had to find out what David Stahl was up to.

"I'm sharing a room with Ulla, the friend who is giving me a ride tomorrow, but we can also ask the innkeeper to bring in a cot if you need a place to stay," Helena said.

It was good to know I had a backup plan if things went awry with David. Then again, he was the one who had asked me to share a room. Helena said that the Green League members would have dinner at seven and that anyone who felt like it would go to the sauna afterward. It would seem odd if I kept my distance from

Helena now, so I told her I was in Kopparnäs not as a guard but more as a security profiler. The seminar's schedule had been posted online, so who knew what kind of crazies could turn up.

Swimming helped to burn off some energy, but even that didn't kill my growing desire for David Stahl. Not knowing what game he was playing was actually a turn-on. Helena was tired and went to read in bed before ten, whereas I memorized my cover story and packed my bags. Reiska had to stay in Kirkkonummi; this weekend was for Hilja alone.

In the morning, it was drizzling but warm, and by the time we reached Siuntio, the clouds began to break. The farmers' plows transformed the yellowing fields into mounds of soil while flocks of geese circled overhead. At the Degerby intersection, the sun finally peeked through the cloud cover. I got out of the car and told Helena and her friend that I'd meet them soon. Once Ulla's car disappeared, I fetched my bike from the ditch where I'd hidden it.

The cabin looked untouched, and the cornstarch I had sprinkled on the floors hadn't been disturbed. I also made sure that Anita's safe was still hidden. The dents on it were such an embarrassment. I hoped Cecilia would be able to tell me the combination.

It was warm enough to bike to Kopparnäs without a long-sleeved shirt. I'd lined my eyes with black and wore huge hoop earrings, although that wasn't my usual style. Even details as simple as earrings are helpful in changing your appearance, and I needed something to compensate for my extremely short hair. I looked like a white Grace Jones.

David was waiting for me in the inn's yard. The familiar camo outfit and heavy boots looked sexy on him, and I wanted to kiss his smiling lips. I was sure I was projecting pheromones like a female chimpanzee. The yard was full of cars, and the campaign flag for the Green League was affixed to the door of the main building. David offered to take my bag upstairs. There was no way I would leave him alone with my stuff, so I followed him. I had to stop myself from tearing off both my clothes and his. David's room was definitely not luxurious; it had a twin bed with small tables on each side, and a dresser table with a mirror and a chair. The upholstery was various shades of yellow, making me feel like I was inside a quaint summer cottage. The room smelled like David—I had to get out of there before I completely lost my mind. David grabbed his backpack and I spotted a thermos in it. I'd be in for some coffee.

The car was already equipped with his mushroom basket; he'd even brought a knife. I had thrown away the poisonous mushrooms from the previous week—there'd be more in the forest if I needed them. We got out of the car and started walking on Leiri Road toward the shore. I let David do the talking. He certainly didn't need any prodding. I listened for any clues that might indicate that he had recognized me as Reiska, but he didn't mention his little trip to Kirkkonummi at all. I didn't dare ask. Instead, he told me about his visit to Tammisaari and reminisced about his early days there. It was your basic childhood, really: he'd played soccer and sailed around the Hanko peninsula.

"That's what I missed the most in Tartu. I had a small boat, but I couldn't use it because the town was so far away from the water. The other day I rented a boat in Tammisaari and went around the familiar islands. It was lovely. Do you know how to sail?"

"I'm more of a rower." I bent down to pick a woolly milk-cap. David didn't seem to be looking for any mushrooms, but they weren't exactly plentiful where we were—we'd need to walk deeper into the forest. The side of the road was jammed with cars parked at odd angles, as if it were National Get-Thee-To-A-Forest Day. "I didn't ask this last time, but what does it mean that you're a construction consultant?" I asked.

"I get people and pieces of land together. Either I'll look for plots that match the client's needs, or I'll find an architect who can create the kind of building my client wants. Every day is different."

"What kind of training do you have?" I looked at Stahl with a curious expression on my face, and he hesitated for moment—it was enough for me. He even touched his ear. Anyone who's studied the psychology of body language would know that I was talking to a liar.

"I think in Swedish it's called construction architecture."

"So do you have a business of your own, or do you work for someone?"

"I have my own business."

"What's it called? Do you have a website?" I was bombarding him with questions as if I was completely smitten and wanted to know everything about him. Women yearned for information. They wanted to know the names of the guy's parents and siblings, his entire life story, favorite foods, childhood traumas, what pajamas he wore.

"I'd rather market myself by word of mouth. My services are pretty pricey because I'm good at what I do, but I've had plenty of customers. Is this mushroom edible?" David was obviously trying to change the subject. He was pointing at the side of the road where a milk-cap, barely standing up, was half covered by gravel.

"It is as long as you boil it twice for five minutes each time. So it looks like we're sort of in the same business. We're both entrepreneurs. Do you always choose your clients based on who can pay the most? Are you always able to determine your price?"

"That's exactly it. I'll work for whomever makes the highest offer. I know what I'm worth."

The sun had reached its peak. Sweat trickled down my back, and I had to unzip my fleece and roll up my sleeves. I suggested that we take a path over the cliffs and walk to the water's edge. There weren't many mushrooms on the cliffs, but we ran into some ornithologists on top of the highest cliff, observing geese and crane migration. A couple of the men spoke Swedish, so David joined in on the conversation. I eavesdropped nearby, undressing David with my eyes. Helena didn't pay me to sleep with Paskevich's allies—I could do it for free, on my own time.

The ocean was calm, the final shreds of clouds had disappeared from the sky. A flock of geese approached from the northeast; switching formation, they honked instructions to each other. One of the ornithologists estimated there were about four hundred birds. Another flock came from the east. The birds had not yet lost their way. As long as they kept to this ancient ritual of flight, there was hope for the rest of us. David's smile was inquisitive; he took hold of my hand. A wave of happiness unexpectedly washed over me. It wasn't supposed to be this way. Yet at that moment, there was no other place I would've rather been than on this sunny cliff, under a clear blue sky speckled with geese, with David.

We took the path down to the sandy beach where we had our coffee. David talked about soccer. He firmly believed that soccer was a *lingua franca*: everywhere you went the ball was round, and everyone kicked it in the same way. He'd joined pick-up soccer games in Parisian and Brazilian parks, wasn't afraid of getting in the way of the ball, and loved playing defense. I listened without hearing, and I let him run his fingers through my short hair. I'd let him kiss me if he just had the brains to do it. He'd brought some strange cookies to have with the coffee; they must've been Russian. There was no packaging to check for clues, because he had placed the sweets into a small plastic box along with napkins. Even if the coffee was spiked and the cookies were drug-infused, David would not find out anything else about me that he didn't already know, except for Helena's and Cecilia Nuutinen-Kekki's phone numbers. We sat on the beach, side by side. I wanted to stroke David's bald head and to find out if he was as hairless anywhere else.

A family of four walked on the beach. The older son's dark hair blew wildly in the wind and the mother's basket was full of gypsy mushrooms. The younger boy sang and played air guitar while walking. The older one moved like his father, and the mother, much shorter than the men in the family, had to take two steps for their every one to keep up. The father talked about stopping at the inn. The younger son picked up a rock to throw and tried to make it skip on the water. I'd remember this family for the rest of my life; they briefly intruded on the world I shared with David, and although they didn't even notice us, they remained in my overly stimulated mind as the idyllic family I'd never had. It could very well be that the kids had only joined their parents for the outing because they felt obliged to; maybe they had been bribed with the promise of getting ice cream at the inn, the mother and father disagreeing about everything else except that the kids had to accompany them on family trips. Maybe the older kid was missing his girlfriend, and the younger son felt badly that he wasn't dating yet. I didn't know about all the masks people wore; that family of four probably lied to each other about almost everything, like David and I. Still, the attraction I felt for David was genuine and true.

I got up, walked to the edge of the water, and threw a stone. It skipped five times. We started walking along the beach toward the campgrounds. I had a few mushrooms in my basket—three woolly milk-caps, one milk-cap, and some brittlegills. Picking them had been idiotic. Where would I even cook them? David kept asking about my friend who was supposedly staying at my cabin, so I came up with Reetta, who'd gone to the army with me. Her boyfriend was Matti, that's all I knew about him; he'd told his wife that he was on a fishing trip with the guys. I was making up lies for people who didn't even exist.

"Have you ever been married?" I asked.

"No. And no kids, either, although there was one close call."

"What do you mean?"

"About seven years ago, there was this woman. Gintare. She was Lithuanian but lived in Estonia. She was pretty possessive, but I liked her. Until it became clear that she was a drug addict, and then the relationship went south. I tried leaving her more than once, but there was something so pathetic about her that I always relented and stayed. And she was gorgeous, although that's never enough of a reason to be with someone."

David thought that Gintare might have used her fingernail to puncture a condom when she was putting it on him. Or maybe it was just bad luck. In any case, Gintare told him she was pregnant. David had begged her to stop using prescription drugs because they might harm the baby; after all, it was his child, too. "How would you know?" Gintare had taunted him. "I could have had any number of men; how do you know the child is yours?"

"That was the only time I've ever come close to hitting a woman. Not because of that stuff about other men, but because of the baby. I didn't want to be with Gintare, but the thought of having a child . . . it was nice. And it would've been fine for my family, too; like I told you before, there are a lot of mixed marriages in my family. Of course I would've married her."

Three months later, David got a call from the hospital. It was Gintare, telling him she'd had an abortion. When she filled out the paperwork at the hospital, she'd listed the father as "unknown."

"I grieved for that child for two years. Gintare started using heavier drugs. The last time I saw her, she was sitting in the nightclub at the Viru Hotel, waiting for the next guy to finance her habit. She was still beautiful, but her eyes were empty."

This was a good moment to take David's hand and squeeze it; that one act communicated what I was thinking, *I'm so sorry.* I let my hand linger in his, and didn't pull away even as we walked to the inn and I worried that Helena might see us.

"Are you hungry? The innkeeper said we could have dinner as soon as the rest of the guests are finished, sometime around eight. I have some cheese and fruit in the fridge and a bottle of whiskey to tide us over."

I followed David to the low-roofed building and noticed that he had neighbors on both sides of his room. These old buildings probably had poor insulation, so I was happy that the other guests had gone out to dinner. I took off my fleece and shoes and sat on the bed. The room was way too small; David seemed to take it over completely. Was his head hitting the ceiling when he opened the bottle of whiskey? David's hands were large with slim fingers, and I wondered how they'd feel on me. He handed me a glass and sat on the chair next to the vanity. Our legs bumped into each other, but I moved mine even closer to his and took a careful sip of the whiskey. I needed to know what and how much David knew about me, and how Anita Nuutinen had died. Why wasn't he making the first move, or was he just teasing me? It was understood that a woman wouldn't follow a man into his hotel room unless she was available, right? Or was I supposed to lean over and give him a kiss on the lips? I put my glass down on the table and looked at him. What are you waiting for? Kiss me.

Finally he read my mind, grabbed my shoulders, and pulled me to him, smelling like a man should. His lips were hungry, his tongue searching its way into my mouth. I let my hands wander under David's shirt, feeling his back muscles, tight and warm. I realized

I'd closed my eyes, so I opened them. David didn't ask for permission; he got up from the chair and threw me on the bed, reaching his hand into my pants behind my back, squeezing my buttocks, his mouth never leaving mine, eyes so close I couldn't tell their color anymore. I took my shirt off without David's help and reached to remove the black turtleneck that he'd revealed after removing his camo jacket. His light-colored skin was mapped in small moles and he had no chest hair—maybe he'd shaved his chest, too. He unclasped my bra and I was done with foreplay; I just wanted him inside of me. I unbuckled his pants and threw all the clothes onto a heap on the floor, our pants getting twisted up together.

David pulled back for a moment to search his jacket pocket, found a condom, opened it, and rolled it over his penis before he entered me. It was all completely right; I wasn't pretending when I rocked in his lap, accepting his rough kisses, his hands groping my breasts. I wrapped my ankles around his neck, folding myself underneath him. My orgasm took me by surprise, and I screamed out, let Helena or whoever hear, now wasn't the time to care about it, this feeling was what I cared about. I would have confessed anything as long as David didn't stop, I wanted us to go on even after I had come, onward all the way to Hell, just don't let this end yet.

Our scents mixed, David was heavy on top of me, this lovely weight, and even though coming together was supposedly the best thing ever—according to stupid porn magazines— even that wasn't a lie in this moment. Me pressing against David and not letting him go even after he'd gotten soft was all true, true, true.

14

I could've fallen asleep in David's arms, but I was starving. I licked salt off his skin, but it wasn't enough, and we had three more hours until dinner.

"Hey, where's that cheese and fruit? I mean, that's what I came here for."

"So that was the deciding factor? I'll have to keep that in mind," said David. He got up from the bed and bent over to kiss me on the cheek before he turned to look at the heap of clothes on the floor with a smirk, then pulled on his camo pants. He disappeared for a moment and came back with a tray covered with Saran Wrap, revealing cheese, crackers, and fruit.

The cheeses were still cold, but I didn't mind. I wrapped myself in a blanket and David didn't bother to put anything else on. I gorged on Brie and apple slices as if I'd never seen food before. David asked if I wanted more whiskey or if he should go downstairs and convince the innkeeper to sell him a bottle of red wine to bring up to the room. I was fine with water, but I enjoyed watching David pour himself a couple of fingers of the amber Scotch. Beyond the window, the forest's fall foliage was waving in the wind, set against a backdrop of deep blue. Wagtails congregating in the birch trees were negotiating in bird language about when to leave for a warmer climate and for food.

The mushroom basket had been abandoned on the floor—I was now hunting for something else. David was snacking on the cheese contentedly, and I pulled him over to the bed to drop grapes into his mouth. I took a sip of his whiskey then dipped my fingers in it and let him lick the liquid off me. His bite marks were visible on my left breast; I was a marked woman.

"You're free this weekend and you don't need to be anywhere. Surely you can stay the night?" he asked.

"I can." Helena hadn't called me yet, so I better check on her. I didn't know which room she was in; worst-case scenario, it'd be the room next to David's. My private life was none of her business as long as I did my job. I turned the tracker on, but all it showed was that Helena was in the area.

"Who are you protecting these days?" David moved his finger up and down my arm, amusedly checking out my biceps. "Jesus, these muscles! I better not piss you off!"

Hopefully I didn't need to use my judo skills on him. I expected him to know some sort of martial arts, too.

"This one female representative. But she might be fine and not need me anymore. She was being harassed by her ex-husband and I showed him—" I was going to use the Finnish idiom "how the chicken pees," but I didn't know how to express the idea in Swedish, so I ended up just saying, "which way the wind's blowing now." David must've understood some Finnish, having spent his early years in Finland. They spoke Swedish in Tammisaari, but he would've learned Finnish in school before he moved to Tartu. I shouldn't have assumed that he didn't know a word. Maybe he was just pretending, trying to make himself seem harmless while eavesdropping on conversations that weren't meant for him to hear.

David stopped asking about my work. I could hear children outside, someone yelling from the woods, "Karita, come over here! I found some flowers!" I sat at the vanity and looked at myself in the mirror. How could my eyes be drowsy yet twinkle at the same time? David's toiletries were strewn on the table: cologne and anti-perspirant, both the same brand, an electric toothbrush, and a tube of Russian toothpaste.

"So you're the kind of man who carries around a condom just in case," I joked in Finnish when I saw the pack of condoms next to the toothpaste.

"I don't understand you," David replied in Swedish, but I thought I could see a smile play on his lips.

"I'm sorry, was I speaking in Finnish? I just said that you're in the habit of traveling with condoms on you."

"Is that a bad thing? And what if I had bought them only with you in mind, hmm? Do you want anything else to eat?"

"No, thank you. When you take the cheese away, can you also put the mushrooms in the fridge?"

When David left I quickly hopped over to rummage through his closet. Two pairs of jeans, dress pants, a jacket, a black leather jacket, T-shirts, socks, and underwear. No gun or handkerchiefs with embroidered initials. When I heard his footsteps, I slipped back into bed and pulled the blanket over me. Maybe I should send him to get red wine. I was especially interested in checking out his wallet. I had made sure to take all of Reiska's identification out of mine, and I'd also left my calendar at home.

David took his pants off and got next to me under the blanket, here we go again, and I didn't resist. His hands were eagerly searching me; my lips were slowly swelling from his bites. I could hear voices in the hallway, luckily they didn't sound like Helena, but I tried not to moan too loudly. I got on top, moving back and forth across David's body, now my breasts didn't feel too small at all, just sensitive and enjoying the touch, the lips on the nipples, the squeeze of fingers. A phone rang somewhere, probably David's, but I didn't let him move, nor did he want to. The bed creaked—it wasn't made for this activity.

David got up and tossed me under him. I was letting him do whatever he wanted, it was Hilja vs. David, zero to six, and I enjoyed every bit of it. I was done with men who apologetically stroked my skin, not knowing what they wanted, pretending that the person they slept with somehow mattered when all they cared about was their own pleasure. David's enjoyment grew from watching mine, and I wasn't holding back; I was unashamed, totally free, moving with David until he came in one huge rush. He laughed—this man wasn't showing any signs of postcoital depression; he wasn't running away, rushing into the shower to wash himself like a sinner trying to remove all traces of evil. I sniffed him like an animal, memorizing his smell. During my academy years, I had learned to recognize my classmates by their individual scents and, in a dark room, I could tell a person standing close by just from their faint odor.

David's phone rang again, and this time he reached out to check who was calling.

"Sorry, I need to take this." He jumped off the bed, trying to put his pants on with just one hand, then left the room. I could hear him out in the hallway, where he began the conversation in Russian.

Now I'd have a chance to go through his wallet. But where was it? It wasn't in his pants pocket; I would've felt it when I was touch ing him. It wasn't in the nightstand, either, but I did find a Finnish passport there, adorned with EU stars.

I opened it. According to the passport the man was David Daniel Stahl, born in Tammisaari on October 18, 1974. There were multiple stamps showing his trips to Russia, and it was valid for another two years—yet the pages were almost full.

The passport looked genuine, but with the right connections it wasn't hard to get a forged one. Finnish passports were a hot commodity because customs officials usually gave them just a quick glance. If I were David, I would have left the passport for me to find, as evidence to back up his story.

I looked under the bed and found a suitcase. I was just about to open it when I heard footsteps in the hallway. I quickly jumped back under the covers and prayed that the slightly dusty floor didn't show any signs that the suitcase had been moved.

"Idiots! Calling about work on a weekend. That was about Permian, one of those oil moguls; he wants a summer villa in Finland—and it needs to have five bedrooms, two bathrooms, an ocean view, and easy access to the highway to Saint Petersburg! These properties don't grow on trees, you know?"

"My former employer was also in real estate, and used to work with Russians a lot. Maybe you've met her—Anita Nuutinen?"

My surprise tactic worked. For a split second, David looked disoriented.

"Anita Nuutinen . . . I feel like I've heard that name before. Oh, that's right!" David was good at pretending that he was slowly remembering the details. "Was she the Finnish businesswoman who was shot in Moscow a couple weeks ago? Were you—was she your boss?"

"She wasn't my responsibility anymore. I quit a day before she was killed."

"Wow. That's quite a coincidence. Why did you quit? Did you feel like you weren't needed anymore because Nuutinen was safe?" David sat next to me, stroking my cheek slowly. This wasn't an interrogation; it was just pillow talk between lovers, with one telling the other about the biggest professional screwup she'd ever committed. That was a sign of trust.

I repeated my lynx coat story in as much detail as I could remember. David sat listening, expressionless, but his fingers kept moving around my body, traveling slowly up toward my neck. These hands could quickly go from gently caressing to strangling.

"Are you against furs because of some principle? Are you one of those—what do Finns call them? Fox girls?" David said the last words in Finnish.

"A lynx girl, more like it." I tried to force a smile. I could hear David's stomach growl—it was almost seven. I'd have to get him drunk; there was no other way now. I got up and went to the bathroom. The mirror reflected the deep glow in my eyes.

The shower, like the bathroom, was in the hallway. I asked David for a bathrobe, as I hadn't brought one. The thick black terry cloth smelled of David, making me feel like I was falling into him. I took a shower, wrapped myself in a thin towel that barely covered me from breasts to hips, and then quickly slid back to the room, where I poured myself a shot of whiskey and splashed a bit more in David's glass. I handed his glass to him and let a sort of half smile play across my lips.

"How much would I have to pay you to wear a lynx coat?" David took the glass, but didn't lift it to his lips.

"You couldn't pay me enough. I'd never do it."

"What if someone's life was at stake?"

"Aren't you the philosopher! What is this, part of an ethics exam?"

"No. I was just trying to understand."

I began to dress for dinner. I put on the only push-up bra I owned and matching bikini underpants, then leather pants and high heeled shoes, and, finally, a tight black shirt Jenni had given me because it was too small for her. The shirt was slightly too short for me but the sliver of skin now visible between the shirt and pants was perfect for the look I was after. The question was whether it was futile to still play the hottie because David had already slept with me.

"Are you upset with me?" David asked as I got dressed in silence. He grabbed my right thigh with both of his hands, squeezing it to his chest. "I didn't mean to blame you for anything. After all, I've made some pretty stupid calls in my life, too."

"But did anyone die because of them?"

"Not by my own hand. Like in the case of your former employer. What was her name again? Nuutinen." David stood up, turned me to face him, and gave me a gentle, comforting kiss.

"Remember, Hilja, even if you had been with Nuutinen when she was shot, you may not have been able to do anything."

"I could've handled a drunk with a gun," I muttered into his shoulder. "And Anita would've never been wandering around that late at a subway station if I'd been with her."

"Maybe you could've handled the drunk, maybe not. Maybe you would've died right next to her, and we would've never met. Let's go have dinner—we can come back here for dessert." He raised his eyebrows suggestively.

I smiled and hoped his words had been said in earnest, employed to absolve me of the guilt I suffered over Anita's death. I tried to seem grateful, as if I really had believed him; on the short walk to the main building, I pressed my body against his like a little girl. People passed by us on their way to the sauna, but I couldn't see Helena in the crowd. The innkeeper would know Helena's room number, but how would I find out without David overhearing my question?

David's phone rang at the right time. I told him not to rush and I'd meet him at the restaurant in a bit. Helena was standing at the bar, chatting about a gas pipeline project with a woman sporting a blond bob.

"Helena," I blurted out because I had no idea how long I'd have. "Sorry to interrupt you, but can I talk to you for a minute?" I led her to a small room next to the bar.

That friend of mine . . ." I continued. "I'm not so sure about how trustworthy he is. It might be best if he didn't see us talking. Is everything all right?"

"Why wouldn't it be? I've spent half a day in this gorgeous scenery, and now I'm ready for a relaxing sauna and then sleep."

"What's your room number?"

"Room one in the Copper 1 building."

I let out a sigh of relief: David and I were in Copper 3. Luckily Helena didn't ask any questions. I let her leave first, then sat down at the same table where David and I had previously had dinner. Each table was set in a different color; ours had a purple tablecloth, napkins, and glasses. The waitress came over and asked if I'd like something to drink, but I said I'd wait for my friend. I hadn't filled in any sort of registration card for the inn, but I suppose they didn't need it.

"I am what I am / I do what I want / I'm capable of hate and love / and I never embrace someone / just because that's the way it should be." Jari Sillanpää's dramatic waltz was on the radio, and although I wasn't a fan of the *schlager* genre, right now this song was getting to me. It revealed my feelings to everyone within earshot, and when David stepped into the room, I was happy to be with him again, right here, right now.

"That was one of my sisters," said David. "Sofia. Told me to say hi to you."

"Why would she say that?"

"I told her that I'd met a very charming woman, and I was going to spend the rest of my life with her. And that she's Finnish, so the family traditions won't disappear. What do you say, some sparkling wine for the occasion? What's on the menu tonight? Hopefully plenty of protein."

We both chose the smoked salmon, a bit of bubbly as an aperitif, and a bottle of white wine to accompany the fish. Now I just had to make sure that David drank most of it. He was pretty talkative again, blathering on and on about his childhood, sailing, getting lost in the fog. I noticed that I, too, divulged more about my past than usual. I even told him about Hevonpersiinsaari, and that it translates as Horse's Ass Island, just like I'd told my academy friends, and it made him laugh.

"Your Uncle Jari sounds like a nice guy. You're lucky to be raised by someone like him. Who was your best friend when you were growing up? Don't girls always have one special friend, whereas boys roam around in groups?"

"Frida. Frida was my best friend."

"Frida? That's a Swedish name. I didn't know Finnish Swedes lived in that area."

"They don't. Frida wasn't human; she was a lynx. An orphaned lynx cub that Uncle Jari found and brought home."

"You had a lynx as a pet?"

"She wasn't a pet. She was a friend. My sister."

David's phone buzzed with a text message. As he read it, his brow wrinkled and his cheeks tightened. He read it again and started typing a reply. I wondered whether he could change the alphabet on his keyboard to write in Cyrillic, or whether he transliterated Russian words using the Roman alphabet. He let the phone drop loudly onto the table, and after a moment's hesitation, he picked it up again and turned it off.

"I'm sorry, but there's a change of plans. I need to leave by nine in the morning. Unfortunately, this business can't wait."

"So you work on Sundays, too?"

"If the client insists. But let's not focus on that—we should enjoy the time we have together. Tell me more about Frida."

The only photo I'd ever carried in my wallet was of Frida. I hadn't shown it to many people. Once to my landlady on Morton Street when she was properly high on cocaine, and once to Mike Virtue during a weak moment, just when I'd heard that Uncle Jari had passed away. Even Monika had never seen Frida's picture, although she knew about her. David would now be the third keeper of my secret. The picture barely fit behind the plastic window in my wallet, hidden under my driver's license.

"There. Frida is about two years old in this one. Uncle Jari drove all the way to Kuopio to get this photo developed in case someone in Kaavi or Outokumpu would see it and start asking questions."

"What a beautiful creature! We should go to Saaremaa together sometime. The lynx population there has grown to about six hundred because of the number of deer in the area."

I thought about Helena's photo from Saaremaa. Combining David and lynx sounded great. Of course I would go.

"I like islands. Saaremaa, Åland Islands, Corsica, Iceland, Ireland . . . they're all great," David continued.

"Out of that list, I've only been to Åland Islands a couple of times for work. Monika von Hertzen, my employer before Anita Nuutinen, had friends over there. My teacher at the Queens security academy, Mike Virtue, was Irish on his mother's side, and you could tell. I mean, in a good way." Suddenly I saw his red hair and green eyes in front of me, the freckles on his face washed out by the years. Although Mike spoke in controlled American English, after a few pints, he would revert to his native Irish accent, and I had a hard time understanding him.

"I promise to take you to Corsica as soon as we both have time in our schedules. Thank you; it was delicious," David switched to English to reply to the waitress who had come for the plates. "Would you like to have dessert?"

The dessert I desired wasn't displayed in a bakery case or in the freezer. I had to make do with ice cream. David had turned his phone off and I had no clue about his security code. I wanted to know who had called and texted him. I felt like my whole information-gathering project was falling apart. All I had found out so far was that David Stahl had a strong libido.

People fresh out of the sauna came to the restaurant for a nightcap. It sounded like they were having a debate about energy policy. A man with shiny red hair reaching almost down to his butt claimed loudly that plans for the seventh nuclear plant had already been drawn up and that the Green union was an unwilling stooge to a pro-nuclear government. Others insisted this wasn't true. I had no opinion on nuclear power, but Uncle Jari had been firmly against it.

David leaned over to kiss me in a way that indicated we should leave. We walked outside to the platform where summer dances were held; it was built into the cliff and we stood there, looking up at the stars. Back in the room, our clothes came off right away, and we almost fell out of bed. I didn't know where I began and where he ended.

"Where are you going tomorrow?" I panted, trying hard to remain focused on my investigation.

"I can't tell you right now. Clients don't trust blabbermouths. You know that, Hilja," was all David said. He spoke only when he wasn't making love to me, and then there was no need for words, only moans and cries. David kissed my mouth shut and didn't let go of my lips until he came. I had never in my life cried for joy, unless you included while watching a sappy movie, but now I could've shed tears. It was almost embarrassing.

"Can I tell you a fairy tale?" David asked later.

"A fairy tale?"

"That's right. There was a prince and a princess, like there always is. They aren't very young anymore, and queens and kings aren't forcing them to get married or to kiss frogs. The princess is pretty, of course, but the prince leaves a lot to be desired: he's large, and he's bald. But because they were the prince and the princess, they were meant for each other. The prince knows that the princess can kill dragons on her own, but he still wants to protect her. Because that's how princes are." David paused and pressed his head against my chest. The hallway echoed in laughter and doors slammed; someone was wishing someone else a good night. When David lifted his head to continue his story, his cheeks were wet.

"The prince had his own battles to fight, like princes always do. You know how they have to solve three puzzles and live through three trials before they get the princess. This prince knew that the princess wouldn't be waiting for him atop the glass mountain; she could come and rescue him, like some princesses rescue their brothers who have been turned into ravens, or their friends who are under the spell of Snow Queens. But right now, this prince has to fight his own battle alone, at least for a while. But should he need the princess's help, will she come?"

"She will," I replied, although I didn't even know what I was agreeing to.

"Then they'll leave everything behind. They'll take off their crowns and they'll go to a desert island or to a mountain village in Corsica where they don't need to be the prince and the princess any longer; they can forget the pressures of the throne. And they'll live happily ever after. That's how fairy tales end."

I fell into a dreamlike state in David's warmth and scent. At one point I did get up to go to the bathroom and brush my teeth. It was quiet, only the wind rattled the trees outside. I wondered whether I should give David my real phone number. After all, I'd already shown him a picture of Frida; how bad would it be to give him my number?

People began stirring in the building around seven, and I woke up before David. His face, softened by sleep, was like a boy's; I could easily imagine what he'd looked like in grade school, sailing and playing soccer in Tammisaari. I still had some time to investigate, to go through David's stuff. He'd told me he needed to be gone by nine, but I hadn't seen him set an alarm. When I sat up as quietly as I could, though, David opened his eyes and smiled at me.

"Hilja. I was afraid it had all been a dream."

I hadn't had my fill of him yet; we had to make love once more. Would I ever get enough of him? Although our lovemaking was hasty and melancholy, it was still genuine. We went for breakfast together, and the restaurant was already empty. The innkeeper told us that the Green group had gone out to the dance platform for their lecture because it was so warm outside. The sun was as hot as it'd been in the height of summer, although it was nearly time for the fall equinox. I wasn't surprised that the seasons were crazy; my world had just been shaken to its core, too.

David paid the bill and told me to keep his room if I wanted to stay a while, but I went to grab my things before I walked him to his car. I was about to kiss him good-bye when I saw Helena and a couple of others walk to the parking lot to pick up a stack of papers from Ulla's car. They didn't greet me, but I missed my good-bye kiss because of them. David just hugged me quickly, got into his car, and was gone.

While Ulla and another woman began carting the folders toward the dance platform, Helena stayed behind.

"Was this your mysterious friend, the one you weren't sure could be trusted?"

"That's the one."

"Did he go to the security academy in New York, as well?"

"No. I just happen to know him."

"Strange that he didn't seem to recognize me. I talked to him last year because of this article I was writing. We met in Saint Petersburg; a detective I know from the security policy hooked us up. Of course you know that David Stahl works for Europol. He specializes in relations between the EU and Russia."

15

I made Helena tell me her story three times. She'd met David Stahl in Saint Petersburg. His expertise was in energy. Earlier he'd been investigating black-market oil and how electricity produced by nuclear energy was being sold without a paper trail. Since then he'd switched to Nord Stream's new gas pipeline project in the Gulf of Finland. His mission was top secret, and Helena had to go through multiple channels to get into the same room with him. Although she was a Finnish politician, Stahl hadn't immediately trusted her. Helena began to regret telling me all this; she'd assumed I had known what Stahl did.

Luckily someone needed to speak with her, and I had some time to come up with an explanation. What had I just thought about my world shaking? Now the tsunami had swept away everything I had imagined, leaving behind only smooth sand. David Stahl didn't work for Paskevich; he was on my side.

I ran to the beach, took off all my clothes, and swam in the cold water. I had to feel that my body was following my orders again. In the past twenty-four hours, it had been loved so much it now responded with gratitude. I got dressed again and walked briskly back to the inn. I did some cartwheels to the amusement of the Green League members who were hurrying to lunch. I used the shower in Ulla and Helena's room, but the only dry shirt I had was the shiny black one from the night before, which still smelled like David. David, who hadn't sold his soul to Paskevich. My energy renewed, I snatched a couple of rolls from the lunch buffet before biking to my cabin to get Anita's safe. I managed to cram it into my backpack. I left without looking around the place. The seminar would be finished by two, and it was time to get back to Kirkkonummi. Lyrics from an Ismo Alanko song echoed in my mind—*I'm rudely full of life*—and I felt as if nothing could stop me.

I dropped my bike in its familiar hiding place in the ditch and waited for Ulla and Helena to pick me up on the side of the road. There were two other people in the backseat this time, so I squeezed in as the third. The vehicle was small and energy-efficient—a true Green League car—but my legs were cramped by the time we reached Kirkkonummi. Even that didn't bring me down. I took a few minutes to stretch my legs and then began to organize Helena's bookshelf again. I'd actually always loved to organize things in alphabetical order, although I didn't own more than about twenty books—a person's collection could reveal too much. At least music could be hidden inside an MP3 player.

Helena and I both went to bed early. I thought about sending David a text message, but then decided against it. He still didn't have my new phone number, but I was pretty convinced that a Europol man could find it if he wanted to. And I had to cool myself down a bit; my body remembered his touch too well, wanted it more, endlessly. In my dreams I mated with a lynx—he bit me on my neck, his feline penis barbed.

The morning bus meandered through busy Hanko Road and smaller local streets. Helena read a memo about changes in waste-water legislation; a representative of the people had to work for her salary. Anita had always sneered when talking about politicians, believing it was good that they got paid so poorly. It made it easier to influence them, maybe in the form of financing their campaigns. Anita had supported representatives from Kymi, the district in which Kotka was located, regardless of their political leanings. In other words, she supported the candidates for all three major parties.

Leaving Helena on the bus, I got off in Hanasaari and walked along the shore to Lehtisaari. I had run on these familiar paths around Keilalahti before. Whatever clothing I still had at Anita's house was tattered and ready to be thrown out. She'd provided the linen, and besides my clothes, the only personal item I had brought with me after I'd been hired was a magazine clipping of a lynx that I had pinned above my bed. Anita should have realized that lynx were important to me, but then I realized she may have never gone into my room to see the picture. The murder investigation had been closed before it really ever started in Finland, so the police had never even searched her home.

Anita had lived in a row-house condo. The residents had hired a groundskeeper, who was now raking the first fallen leaves in the yard. When he recognized me, he took a step closer and gave me a quizzical look. I quickly pressed the doorbell to get away from him; he was surely after some meaty gossip.

Cecilia Nuutinen-Kekki must have been waiting for me, given how swiftly she opened the door after I rang. She didn't look much like her mother; she was almost too skinny and small-boned in general. The black color of her hair was most likely from a bottle; it only highlighted how pale she was. Cecilia was thirty, a couple years younger than me, but her face was already etched with deep wrinkles. She held a Masters of Science in economics and business, and worked at an international brokerage company whose name I had forgotten.

"Please come in."

The condo was familiar, yet so unfamiliar. I recognized most of the furniture, including the enormous leather sofa and armchairs Anita had bought from Milan and the art she had called "investment paintings"; they were supposed to be sold for profit later, but in the meantime they made a nice pair of images. The glass table in the living room supported a laptop and an open briefcase. A wireless printer spit out paper in the middle of the floor. Anita would've hated how the printer destroyed the room's symmetry.

Although Cecilia may not have looked like her mother, her movements were similar. She walked with purposeful strides peppered with oddly jerky movements. I had once seen Anita dance, and she had absolutely no sense of rhythm. She listened to music only when she was forced to. Once I had followed her and a Russian client to the opera. While the Russian had laughed and sang along to *The Marriage of Figaro*, Anita had looked positively tormented. She only clapped at the end so as not to insult her companion. That evening's suffering paid off, though; Anita sold the client an island property in Taipalsaari, breaking the municipality's record for the highest sale price.

Cecilia wasn't sure where to start. She finally asked me to tell her again why I had quit. She still didn't buy my story. When her phone rang and she picked it up without excusing herself, I went to my old room. The cleaning lady had removed the sheets from the bed and had arranged my stuff at its foot. There was no sign of the lynx clipping. The trash can was empty, too. I tossed my old underwear there. My pajamas were a relic from the previous winter and were too hot to wear now. One of the T-shirts had a hole in the armpit, but that could be fixed.

"Where did you go?" Cecilia appeared at the door. "I had to take that call. There's a financial crisis going on in the United States, and it affects everyone, even us. At least Mom didn't have to be here to watch the value of her investments tumble."

"Are you going to inherit her assets?"

"I don't know yet. Do you? Mom had a will—you know how particular she was about money. God, I really don't have the time to organize this funeral, but it's going to be held at the Temppeliaukio church on Friday afternoon. It was the only time they had available. Her obituary will be in the papers tomorrow, and we'll have the memorial service here at home. We have plenty of room for it, that's for sure. There is a caterer to take care of the food, but I have no idea how many people are coming. You will be there, right?" It was more like an order than a request.

"If I'm welcome." I thought of Laitio. In books and movies, police always showed up at funerals when someone was murdered. But this was real life. The security academy had taught me well that reality was more horrifying than anything a storyteller could imagine; it crept up on you with unpleasant surprises again and again.

"These are mine, by the way," I said, and pointed to the clothes I hadn't packed yet.

"That's what Felicia and I thought; they weren't Mother's size." Felicia was Anita's cleaning lady, a mail-order bride from the Philippines who had grown tired of sitting in the sticks in Kesälahti with nothing to do, divorced her husband, and moved to Helsinki to find a job. At least here there were other Filipinos she could speak her own language with. In Anita's worldview Felicia was from a class below me, and Anita had done her best to prevent us from being friends. I guess she was afraid that we'd gang up on her. I needed to chat with Felicia—she'd been working for Anita for three years, even when Anita and Valentin Paskevich had still been romantically involved.

"Do you know who took care of your mother's finances? As far as I know, she had a safety deposit box, but I never found out in which bank," I asked. Anita had split her money into so many banks that the options were too numerous. The safe weighed heavy in my backpack, but I didn't want to tell Cecilia about it just yet.

"She used the law firm Mikaelsson and Ainasoja. Johan Mikaelsson was in charge of her personal affairs. I've already talked with him; they have her will. Apparently it comes with a hefty list of properties." Cecilia let her face relax for a moment, but her expression didn't quite qualify as a smile. "We scheduled the reading for Saturday, the day after the funeral. I need to get back to Hong Kong as soon as I can."

I figured that Mikaelsson would know about the safety deposit box, but it would be a bit too forward of me to mention it before the will was read. Now would've been a great time to show Cecilia what I had in my backpack, but I decided not to. We walked back to the living room where the printer was still spewing out paper. There was a pile an inch thick in front of it. The sheets were filled with numbers that meant nothing to me.

"Mother didn't want me to touch her finances, although I'm an investment advisor," Cecilia said. "It's just frustrating, waiting here, knowing that her properties could be seriously devalued if the stock market collapses."

"Are you worried that your inheritance will be gone in a flash?"

Cecilia was startled by my tone of voice. "My, aren't you prickly. I don't even know if there will be any inheritance for me. Who knows, this house may already be owned by the bank, all the way down to the doorknobs. Mother always took risks, and this is the result. By the way, some Finnish politician has been claiming that she didn't believe the Moscow militia. You know, that a homeless man had killed my mother. I haven't kept up with Finnish politics enough to remember her name. I think she was in the Coalition Party."

"Helena Lehmusvuo. Green League. My current employer."

Cecilia's eyebrows flew up so quickly I thought they'd be forever lost in her bangs.

"Well, you certainly didn't waste any time! You already have a new boss?" Cecilia took a breath. "Whatever. Let me ask you something. Who do you think killed my mother?"

"Well, they found that drunkard," I said, avoiding the question.

"Even the Finnish police aren't buying that! I had a chat with the Chief Constable . . . what was his name? Laiho something."

"Laitio?"

"That's right, Laitio. He insisted that the militia had been bribed, but the Finnish police had their hands tied, because those higher up in the government food chain don't want to rock the boat, given our lukewarm relationship with Russia. And here I was, thinking that we had finally stopped bending over backward to the East, being a EU member state and all. I'm ashamed to be a Finn! I know, I know—Valentin has friends among the politicians and the oligarchs who fund those politicians, but it's just unbelievable that such lawlessness is allowed in Russia, which is supposedly, according to Putin, doing its best to become a modern state. I'd sort of understand if the victim had been a Russian citizen, but I thought they'd still care about foreigners being killed in their country. Although I know it's a dog-eat-dog world, why on earth do we have police and a justice system when they're good for nothing?" Cecilia pulled a small silver box out of her pocket and opened it. She slipped a piece of chewing gum into her mouth. "I quit smoking a year ago, but ever since Mother died, I've been craving cigarettes again. Thank God for nicotine gum."

Cecilia's phone rang again. It sounded like it was a friend or a relative of Anita's asking about the funeral. I waited for her to finish, but the longer the conversation went on, the clearer it became that she wasn't going to hurry to get off her call on my account. I was, after all, the person who had indirectly caused her mother's death. I couldn't rummage through Anita's things with Cecilia standing there, and she had asked me to return my set of house keys.

I'd sum up our conversation in one word: disappointing. Cecilia had been gone from Finland for so long that she barely knew what her mother had been up to. They had spoken over Skype and exchanged e-mails, but Anita hadn't revealed very much about her business to her daughter. According to Cecilia, only a fool would talk about these things on such an unsecure method of communication.

"But I have to tell you, Mother humiliated Valentin so badly that he couldn't have let it go without seeking revenge. Though his real estate holdings are just a small part of his empire, he'd certainly feel threatened if he lost millions of rubles. I happen to know one of Valentin's bankers. If he ever made a mistake with Valentin's accounts, he'd be better off killing himself before Valentin's men got ahold of him."

Cecilia presented this as if it was a fact of life. The security academy at Queens had been an international school, so we were taught how to handle security threats in various countries. The Russian mafia, the Camorra in Naples, Colombian drug lords. I had been naive to think they'd never enter Finland.

"It's a shame you're already employed," Cecilia continued. "I wanted to hire you to work on my mother's murder case."

"But I protect people—I'm not a private eye. And besides, I thought you blamed me for her death."

"Oh, I do." Now Cecilia's expression did begin to resemble a smile. "That's why I thought you'd give me a discount. Maybe I should negotiate with this Lehmusvuo woman. I'm sure I can pay more than she does. And I pay my taxes in Hong Kong—or rather, I don't pay them."

The look in Cecilia's eyes reminded me of Anita's when she'd stroked the lynx coat in the fur store, and I just wanted to get out of there. But first I had to find out what Anita's safety deposit box contained and how David Stahl was connected to all of this.

"We could negotiate with Helena," I responded, deliberating. "She hired me to map out a security profile for her, and that's now done. And I managed to eliminate her most prominent threat." I smiled when I thought of Tiku Aaltonen.

I promised to be at the funeral on Friday. Helena would be at a party meeting. I went to the apartment on Untamo Road to transform into Reiska, and on my way there I rang Mrs. Voutilainen's doorbell. She didn't answer. My roommates were both out, too. I'd gotten a couple of envelopes: a ballot for the upcoming election and an ad for a car. Really exciting stuff.

Everything went smoothly until Tuesday. I was almost done with being Reiska; Helena hadn't received any threatening calls or letters, and although I hadn't mentioned Cecilia's proposal to her, I began to feel like I was wasting my time there. However, on Tuesday Finland imploded when a gunman killed nine students and a staff member at a vocational college in Kauhajoki. Helena was in emergency meetings for several days, and I hung around in her office in an annex to the cabinet building, where she'd arranged for me to have a temporary key card. Uncle Jari had always been against spending money on fancy offices and living spaces, but when I saw the piles of paper in Helena's small office, I realized why she needed more space.

"Do you happen to own a gun?" Helena asked me as we were driving home on Thursday evening, accompanied by her roommate and a colleague. "We've spent all day talking about what we should do with the gun laws." Helena turned her head to me from the front seat. Her colleague was driving well over the speed limit, probably thinking that the traffic laws didn't apply to politicians.

"Yes, I do. And I have a permit."

"Where do you keep it?"

"In a locked case, unloaded, just like the law says."

This was only a partial lie. I had left my gun at Helena's place in a locked box. The bullets were in another box, also locked. I had a gun cabinet at my cabin and a similar one in the Untamo Road apartment; it was like a safe that could be bolted to the wall, but a determined burglar could break into it. It was just unfortunate that I often forgot the gun in my backpack or in my holster, but in those instances I did keep a close eye on it. Helena's colleague began to interrogate me about my thoughts on the gun law, but I had nothing to say. Some people needed guns for their jobs, and that's just the way it was. A gun was an additional security measure; of course I didn't want to use it, but if I had to, I would.

I put on my underarm holster and stuffed two full clips into my handbag before I left for Anita's funeral on Friday. The yellow leaves on the trees contrasted sharply with the clear blue sky. Even the ocean shimmered in calm blue; it was almost waveless. I walked Helena to the cabinet building and then went to the nearby church. At the steps I hesitated. What was I doing at the funeral? Was I simply driven by some weird compulsion to punish myself by attending?

"Every one of you will make mistakes during your careers, even grave misjudgments. Many of you may even have to break the law, but please, try to at least follow the laws of whichever country you are in. When a mistake has been made, it cannot be undone. You can regret it, process it, but you can't start second-guessing yourself. You have to be ready to analyze why you made the mistake and then move on. And try not to make the same mistake again. You can't be afraid of screwing up; it will only paralyze you." Mike Virtue's words echoed in my head, refusing to disappear.

I couldn't avoid walking into the church, though I didn't especially want to hear the relentless rumbling of the organ. I'd always hated organ music. It was just a jumble of sounds that never seemed to coalesce. If there was a clear melody, it would inevitably have been taken from some angry hymn whose message was that a human being is a sinner, a miserable pawn of Satan, a lowly worm ready to turn back to dust.

The local priest had called me in New York to ask which hymns should be sung at Uncle Jari's funeral, but the only hymns I had remembered were "Suvivirsi," celebrating the start of summer, and some Christmas hymns. I guess I could've found someone in New York who had a Finnish hymnal, but I didn't bother looking, so I told the priest to choose whichever songs seemed appropriate. I had no recollection of what he'd chosen; I didn't even remember what the priest had said at the funeral. Uncle Jari had never been a religious man—he was a church member in deference to his parents. After the funeral and the memorial service, I sat alone at our house in Hevonpersiinsaari, downed almost an entire bottle of bourbon I'd bought at the duty-free shop on the way to Finland, and listened to ABBA. "I Can Still Recall Our Last Summer" was my funeral hymn for Uncle Jari.

Buying flowers for Anita had seemed hypocritical. I sat in the very back of the half-empty church. Cecilia Nuutinen-Kekki was in the front row along with her husband Joel Kekki. She was wearing a wide-brimmed hat, which made her look like a white mushroom past its prime. The organ gave way to the violins, which made my ears ache. I scanned the backs in front of me, looking for someone who looked familiar—I wished I had sat upstairs so I could've observed the crowd better. Then again, I wasn't here to protect Anita; there was nothing left to protect. She was in the coffin and would be taken to Hietaniemi to be cremated.

The priest spoke: God moves in a mysterious ways, humans do not know where their roads end. When Cecilia got up to place her flowers on the casket, she looked even more like a mushroom. She might have fallen under the weight of her wreath if Joel hadn't pulled her up by the arm to balance her. Anita's ex-husband, Cecilia's father, was among the first to lay flowers on the coffin. Their divorce had been civilized, or so Anita had claimed. Monika, on the other hand, knew that Paavo Nuutinen had found someone younger and trimmer, and Anita had made out well in the divorce.

People filed past Anita's coffin to pay their respects: business partners, friends, even a former minister I didn't realize Anita knew. He had been at the height of his political power while I had been studying in the United States, and he was among the politicians Uncle Jari had despised. I had forgotten his name, but never his face. Uncle Jari had used it as a dartboard one summer. He'd been aggravated about a decision over EU farming subsidies that the minister had forced through the cabinet. For some reason, Anita had sold this former minister a twenty-four-acre plot in the Imatra forest near the Russian border for a ridiculously low price. There was a lot of media attention about the development plans for the land, as the intention was to build yet another shopping mall located far from a town, in this instance situated right next to the highway leading to Russia, to attract Russian tourists. If I remembered correctly, the former minister had defended the plan, saying it would help the economy of poor, impoverished Eastern Finland.

The queue of flower bearers was long. Some spoke Russian, but I didn't see anyone who looked like one of Paskevich's men. Anita's maid Felicia was the most emotional; she sobbed loudly. It was quite impressive, considering how poorly Anita had treated her.

The organ started again with a familiar hymn. *O Lord, stay with me / it is already evening.* It was the same song I had heard at the first funeral of my life; the one I had desperately tried to forget. I had worn thick white tights and fancy black patent-leather shoes with gold buckles, but Grandmother had told me I better not flaunt them. The shoes were meant for mourning. My black skirt was soft, reminiscent of the dress my mother was wearing the last time I was with her, hers patterned with red flowers, or maybe the flowers bloomed afterward when Father left her to lie on the floor. The church was full of flowers, their scent intoxicating, and Grandmother wore a black veil, which I thought was exciting. I wanted one, too, but they didn't make them for children. Grandmother had put my hair up in pigtails; it was the first time I wore pigtails, and I had wanted pretty ribbons instead of the black ones I had. Uncle Jari had tried to convince Grandmother that a child didn't need to wear all black, but she knew best—she was Uncle Jari's mother, after all.

My mother had been placed into a coffin that was some sort of space capsule. It would take her to heaven. The funny man with a long black dress and a white bib had talked to me about heaven. *Your cross shall light my path, O Lord / As my road takes me to the valley of death.* The church had had a wide aisle; I could have run up and down it without bothering anyone. There were pink flowers on top of Mother's space capsule; I supposed I could take one for Grandmother so she wouldn't be so sad. "This is a celebration, celebrating how your mother is now in heaven," Uncle Jari had said, but Father couldn't make it to the party, because Father had been really bad and wasn't allowed to see me ever again. *In life and in death, you shall stay with me.* Now Grandmother and Uncle Jari got up and Uncle took me by the hand; the aisle was long and I didn't want Mother to leave, I wanted to go to heaven with her . . .

I sat at Anita Nuutinen's funeral and cried like a baby.

16

I skipped the memorial service. Instead, I headed to a restaurant on Runeberg Street and ordered a Chimay, a dark beer. And then another. I sure as hell needed to get rid of these memories. The gym would have been a better option than a beer, as would have a ten-mile run, or maybe a judo match against Vladimir Putin. Helena could fire me for not being on top of my job, and I'd be back at the unemployment office. I already pictured myself haunting shopping malls with some semi-Nazi guard—half of the time preventing him from beating up kids who were drinking beer, the rest of the time dragging drunks who'd pissed themselves away from the respectable folk and then waiting for the cops to show. What bright prospects I had!

I tried to decide between a third beer and another type of treat. I'd memorized David Stahl's number easily, and I had also saved it on my phone. The weather outside was ridiculously gorgeous, so after a trip to the restroom, I began walking back toward Hietaniemi beach.

I hadn't understood the concept of death when I was four, and because Father had been carted off at the same time as my mother's body, I had thought that he'd taken the same space capsule to heaven, although nobody had told me this. Grandmother had to be heavily medicated in order to attend the funeral, and right afterward she had to be hospitalized again, leaving Uncle Jari and me by ourselves. First we lived in an apartment building in Tuusniemi, but that lasted for only a couple of months, and I barely have any recollection of that time. Then we moved to our small cabin in the woods, and Hevonpersiinsaari became our home. Uncle Jari changed our name; given my unusual surname, he didn't want people to connect me in any way to the infamous murderer, and Uncle figured it would be better if we had the same last name. My father later attempted to gain joint custody of me, but luckily it was denied. Keijo Kurkimäki had no say in my life. At the Queens security academy, I had told people that both of my parents had died in a car crash when I was young; most strangers who happened to ask about my past heard the same story. It was the one Anita had also heard. Being a murderer's daughter didn't look that great on your résumé.

I walked through the cemetery to the beach. The red-and-yellow maple leaves flashed vividly and the ocean reflected the light so brightly that I had to dig out my sunglasses. I sat on a bench where ducks came over to beg for food. I crumbled up some of my energy bar for them, and its seeds attracted a squirrel, who didn't care about the ducks—he expertly avoided their beaks while diving for seeds. Only when I was sure no one could hear the tears in my voice did I dial David's phone number.

His voice mail launched after the eighth ring. "This is David Stahl's answering machine. Unfortunately I'm busy at the moment, but please leave a message," he said in Swedish, and then repeated the message in English and Russian. His familiar voice gave me goose bumps.

He wouldn't be able to see my number on his phone. Should I risk it and leave him a message? The beer in me said yes; luckily I hadn't had more than two.

"Hi, David, it's Hilja. Just wondering where you might be. I'll try to reach you later. It would be fun to see you again." I left the message in Finnish on purpose. I still couldn't believe that he didn't grasp at least the basics of our language. If he didn't understand me, at least he would recognize my voice and my name.

I felt miserable, and the only cure was to find some company. Helena wouldn't be free before six, and after that I had plans to follow her to a taping for a TV show in Pasila, where she was taking part in a panel discussion on climate change. Did they have metal detectors at the studio?

I hated that I couldn't stand to be alone. I wanted to be invulnerable. I'd always found company in bars, but right now I did not want to be with strangers. How about my roommates—I could always chat with them, right? Or old lady Voutilainen, next door. I decided to keep calling people. It was four in the afternoon in Mozambique, same as in Finland. I rang Monika, although I didn't think she'd answer. After ten rings I hung up, but she called me back in a few minutes.

"Hilja, how are you?"

"Anita's funeral was today." Damn, I almost started crying again. Why was Monika thousands of miles away? Why did everyone important in my life evaporate into thin air: Mother, Uncle Jari, Frida, Monika, David? I would've even sat down for a chat with Mike Virtue.

"How was it?"

"Your standard funeral. But Monika, the thing is . . . I remembered the other funeral. Mother's funeral. Uncle Jari had always told me there was no use in trying to remember. But my father killed my mother, and I saw it. Although I've tried not to remember, it's all coming back to me now."

"That's huge. Hilja, I'm so sorry. Why didn't you tell me before?"

"I didn't want to. It's all in the past—I just wish the memories would disappear, too."

"Oh, Hilja. I wish you could come over here. It would do you good to get away from everything for a while."

"I can't. I'm under contract with Helena. Except I just took a break in the middle of my workday to have a beer. I had to drown my thoughts. Maybe she'll fire me."

Over the phone, I could hear bells clanging in the background—what a strange time to go to church, in the afternoon. Or were those cowbells? I couldn't even imagine the conditions in which Monika lived, although apparently Hevonpersiinsaari had been luxurious compared to her current home. Someone was chattering away in clipped French in the background and Monika laughed.

"Jordi says I'm slacking off, talking on the phone three times a day. I've told him that Finns even take their phones to the sauna, and that priests remind the congregation to turn off their phones before a sermon. Jordi won't believe that even little kids have cell phones in Finland."

"Who's Jordi?" The jealousy in my voice was obvious even to me.

"A young man in his twenties. I'm teaching him how to cook. He's got a pretty good plate."

"What?"

"Oh, I meant *palate*! Sheesh, soon I'll forget both Finnish and Swedish—I only speak French here. So I assume you hit a brick wall with Anita's murder investigation?"

"Yes. Except that—" I thought about telling Monika about David, but then I decided to shut up. Having Europol on my back wasn't something to brag about. I let Monika talk about what she had been up to, about yams and manioc and other ingredients that were only names to me. Listening to her talk calmed me down much more than alcohol ever did. I remembered the times when Chez Monique had just closed for the evening, the last plates had been brought back to the kitchen, and the dirty tablecloths had been stuffed into the cleaner's bag. Then the restaurant changed, at least for a while, from a public place into a home. Monika would drink a glass of wine and I would have a beer, especially if it'd been a rough day. That had been a happy time, but I couldn't go back there.

My phone beeped. Helena wasn't supposed to call just yet—the meeting shouldn't have been over for another couple of hours.

"I need to go now, my employer is calling."

"Tell Helena I said hi!"

When I picked up, Helena's voice was tense.

"Available yet, Hilja?"

"Yup."

"Good. I've told the cabinet building receptionist that you'll be coming in today. Saara slipped on the stairs over there and broke her leg. I really need to get this paperwork done. I've borrowed Outi's assistant, but it's a Friday night and she has to go pick up her kids from day care. Can you get to my office as soon as you can? Take a cab from wherever you are."

I was indeed available, but there was this one *but*—the Glock in my underarm holster. I didn't want Helena to know that I regularly carried a gun. I figured she wouldn't like it.

I called a cab, asked him to drive to the train station and wait for me there. I bought a couple of newspapers from the kiosk once I got there. It was rush hour and people were scurrying through the station. All the lockers were downstairs, situated in such a way that anyone could see who was using them. I had to go to the restroom to take my gun off. I paid the offensive three-euro fee for using the restroom, went into a stall, and tried to make as much noise as I could while removing my gun and holster. I placed both of them in the newspaper.

I was sure that the stalls had security cameras, even though the law prohibited any sort of recording in restrooms. Supposedly they were after drug addicts and dealers, but I had met enough people who worked for security and surveillance companies to know that real pervs also got these jobs, and they loved watching women do their business in the toilet—and they called that working. I made myself as inconspicuous as possible, although a security guard had to be a real fool not to notice what this woman was pulling out of her armpit.

It took a while to find an available locker. I had paid for my newspapers with a twenty in order to get some change. I'd learned in New York that you always had to have change handy, or you'd be in trouble. The security cameras were aimed at the lockers, too, I bet. I could already see the scandalous tabloid headline about the politician's bodyguard—a lesbian, according to the police—who was caught storing a gun in a locker at the Helsinki train station. I slipped the clips from my purse, placed them next to the gun, and felt a twinge as I locked the door and left my protection behind. I had brought the 9-millimeter Glock from the United States completely legally, and the accompanying red tape had made me crazy. The model was the same one the Finnish police and border patrol used. As a bodyguard I could probably obtain another pistol, no matter how much the gun laws would be tightened, but I didn't want to give up my trusty colleague, who I'd only needed so far as a deterrent. The Glock was to me what phones or favorite hammers were to others. I thought about how I should get back to the range to practice shooting and keep up my skills.

The cab driver I approached was having a smoke, and looked annoyed when I interrupted him. My destination was the annex at the cabinet, but he wasn't impressed by the address.

"You can't walk a short distance like that? Or do you have some vouchers that us tax payers paid for? Jesus, you sure can spare money for vouchers and for every goddamned immigrant, but when a small business owner like myself tries to get a tax break then all I hear is *no can do, look at how much the government is in debt.* And the price of gas keeps fluctuating—at the end of the day there is nothing left of my paycheck, but my prices are controlled like in some fucking Socialist country while Russkies and Somalis drive unlicensed cabs and make three times the amount I do without paying taxes."

I'd seen all sorts of cab drivers in NYC, but this guy was a first-class racist. Unfortunately the driver had to take a longer route in order to get in front of the cabinet building, but luckily I had the ability to tune out an idiot like him. Zen and the art of dealing with morons, that's what my book would have been called.

I didn't leave a tip but I asked for a receipt, on which I made a note that the trip was from Hietaniemi to the cabinet building; I didn't need to mention that I had stopped at the train station. If Helena wondered why the cab had been so expensive, I'd tell her I had left my gloves at the cemetery and had to go back for them or something.

Helena waited for me in the annex lobby behind the metal detectors.

"You took your sweet time."

"Rush hour. What do you want me to do, anyway?"

"Type some letters. You'll need to make sure that the addresses are right."

"Letters? What happened to e-mail?"

"Some news is still best delivered by snail mail. Follow me."

The only reason why Helena's office was in decent shape was because of her assistant extraordinaire, Saara Hirvelä, who kept the piles in check. Wasn't it interesting that a representative of a political party focused on the environment was drowning in paper, or was the cabinet to blame for not going paperless? Wasn't the thrifty speaker of the house able to persuade the representatives to generate less paper?

Helena worked on her opening statement for the evening's panel discussion and replied to e-mails. She'd be safe at the TV studio people couldn't just slip in there unnoticed—so I decided to pick up my gun while Helena was on the air.

I finished the letters and Helena asked me to take them downstairs to the porter. It took me a while to find him. My temporary access pass was scrutinized at every turn, so I really had nothing to worry about. Helena would be safe as long as she stayed either in the granite colossus of the cabinet building or in this annex.

"Running errands for Representative Lehmusvuo?" the porter asked. "Good, she received a letter. Sign here, please."

I stared at the letter. Express mail, straight from Moscow. I couldn't open it on the way back to Helena's office because I wasn't alone in the elevator.

When I got back, I handed the envelope to her. "Helena, this came for you; it's express mail. Do you know the sender?"

"Let me see here . . . Anastasia Butyrskaya? Yes, I recognize Nastya's handwriting. She's an old friend of mine. I asked her to send me a collection of essays that's secretly making the rounds—it criticizes the Russian government's energy policies. I hope this is the collection I was looking for and that it made it safely across the border."

I had heard about the censorship during Soviet times, but I hadn't thought it would still be alive and kicking. Maybe the rednecks I had met at a bar in Queens one night had been right: while the political system changed, Russia didn't. It was still an evil empire that Americans needed to battle with a strong arsenal of weapons.

It was the collection. Shortly before seven we hopped onto the tram heading out to the Pasila TV station. As we passed the ice hockey arena, Helena received a text message.

"It's from Saara. Five weeks of sick leave. Crap! And we're so busy with the election and all. It's impossible to find a new assistant right now, especially someone who knows how to do the work. Everyone else is already involved with the elections. Damn!"

The car turned toward West Pasila. It came to an abrupt stop when a drunk almost walked in front of it. Helena would have hit her chin on the seat in front of her if I hadn't quickly stuck out my arm. I hadn't noticed before how slow her reaction time was, although she sure could talk. We got out of the car before it turned toward East Pasila and walked through the police station to Radio Street.

"Wait, why am I worrying when the answer is walking right next to me? You can be my temporary cabinet assistant! There hasn't been a peep from Tiku since Reiska told him to take a hike, and all my other stalkers have left me alone, too. What do you say? Let's kill two birds with one stone." Helena looked at me.

"And you don't have to pay me because I'll be on the cabinet's payroll. Thank you, taxpayers. I don't suppose you can deduct a bodyguard's pay on your taxes? Isn't it considered part of your general household expenses?"

"Thank God it's not a household expense yet," Helena laughed. "But seriously, Hilja, would you do it?"

"What's the pay like?" I asked, and when Helena mentioned a sum that was significantly lower than what I usually charged, I hesitated. Then again, it was better than unemployment and having to endure those humiliating visits to the unemployment office. "But I don't know a thing about politics! Vanhanen is the prime minister, Niinistö the speaker of the House, and Väyrynen is in the cabinet—that's all I know."

"You can be in touch with Saara on the phone and through e-mail, and she'll be happy to help you. You can go meet her at the hospital tomorrow if you want."

Helena was good at convincing people. No wonder she had received so many votes in the last cabinet election. Of course, her suggestion made sense. We had already gotten used to each other; maybe we even liked each other. I also appreciated the steady stream of money going into my bank account.

While Helena was debating environmental and energy policies on the Friday night broadcast, I went to get my gun. Between the show and the time in the makeup chair, she'd be busy for about two-and-a-half hours, so I was in no hurry to get back to Pasila. I stuck around the train station. I took an open window seat at the small bar and did some people-watching. I saw all types: folks from the countryside who came to spend the weekend in the big city, others running around aimlessly, lovers. Should I try calling David again?

That's when I saw him: a dark young man carrying an artist's case. I immediately recognized him from Mrs. Voutilainen's sketch. Yuri Trankov. I dropped my energy drink and ran after him. He ambled down the steps from the train station to the market square and didn't seem to be in any hurry. He turned toward the National Theater but stopped at the station corner to light a cigarette, and that's when I decided to take a chance. I approached him.

"Evening," I said, trying to muster the expression of a woman who is interested in the opposite sex. "Can I bum a cigarette off you?"

Trankov glared at me. "I no speak Finnish."

"Do you speak English? Would you give me a cigarette, please? I'll pay, one euro."

Trankov sighed and pulled out his cigarette case. I was in luck: it was a western brand, not some cheap Russian stuff. He lit the cigarette for me and waved his hand when I offered him the euro coin.

"What do you have in that case?" I continued in English. "Are you an artist?"

"Sort of."

"What do you paint? Hey, do you need a model?" I flashed a smile that was positively whorish and managed to not puke on my shoes with disgust.

"I don't paint people," Trankov cut me off.

"What do you paint then? Some boring squares that you see at a modern art museum?" Art galleries had been everywhere in New York, but I hadn't spotted many works of art I would have put up on my wall, except for the one of the mailman with the split beard I'd seen at MoMA. It had reminded me of Uncle Jari.

"Animals. People like to commission pictures of their pets." Trankov was now looking around, hoping someone would walk by to rescue him from this overeager woman.

"Animals! How exciting! Is your work displayed anywhere? I'd be interested in a painting of a lynx." I let my voice drop during the last sentence.

"A lynx?" Trankov wasn't fazed. "I don't think you're allowed to keep them as pets in Finland."

"It would be more like a memento. To remember a friend who had a lynx fur coat. My neighbor on Untamo Road in Käpylä bought a lynx painting from a Russian painter. Was that you?"

"Could be." Trankov threw his cigarette down and stepped on it. "You should let friends dressed in lynx fur lie. I don't paint anyone dead. Not women or animals. And it's much nicer to be alive than dead, isn't that right, Ms. Ilveskero? *Da svidaniya.*"

Trankov turned around and crossed the street, climbed the National Theater stairs, and disappeared inside. When I got there, the lobby was empty and the usher rushed over to tell me that they weren't selling any more tickets that day.

This was absurd. It was the day of Anita's funeral, the best possible day to deliver some new threats, to play cloak and dagger. But this wasn't a game. I ate men like Tiku Aaltonen for breakfast, but Valentin and I would never send heart-shaped cards to each other—only bullets to the heart.

17

The following month disappeared into thin air. I worked at the cabinet performing completely uninteresting tasks.

I met Anita's maid, Felicia Karhunen, at a café in Kamppi, but she didn't know anything more about Anita's business. I tried hinting at how I wouldn't mind coming over to Anita's place to reminisce, but Felicia didn't have the keys any longer—the condo had been put up for sale. Because I knew the security system I could have broken in, and in bitter memory of Anita I almost considered it, but at the same time I heard her accusatory voice in my head, so I didn't dare. If I were caught, I would look even more suspicious to Laitio.

Cecilia Nuutinen-Kekki stopped keeping in touch. I suppose there had been nothing in Anita's will for me. I hadn't been expecting a generous thank-you as her loyal underling, but I had hoped her will would have offered some clues about her murderer. Maybe it just really had been Paskevich's desire for revenge. But even he hadn't been able to buy the coveted oceanfront property in Kotka—the papers said it had been purchased by a businessman named Usko Syrjänen. I memorized his face from the accompanying pictures. He was going to use the land to build a gated country club for an elite group of carefully selected members.

"Finland doesn't offer private clubs of this caliber, where you don't have to worry about reporters and cell phone cameras. I know from international experience," said Syrjänen, whose womanizing was in the same category as Paskevich's, in an interview. "If there aren't enough customers from Finland, we will certainly have interest across the border to the East."

"Sounds like an overpriced brothel," sighed Helena when I told her the news. "Clever businessmen always find a way to circumvent the law."

The cabinet was a strange world for me, and I had to work hard to understand even half of what was happening. The weekend after Anita's funeral, I finished installing the rest of the security system at Helena's place, and as there were still no new threats, I became her full-time assistant. Apparently Tiku Aaltonen had been the only one who'd been stalking Helena, but Reiska's rough treatment had convinced Tiku to leave her alone. I traveled with Helena from one election event to another and took care of her correspondence and calendar. As a temporary job it was all right, but I knew it wouldn't hold my interest for long. Five weeks was nothing, though. I'd be willing to spend that much time working as a nanny or a shop detective.

There had been a big brouhaha about the way some men behaved in the cabinet during the previous spring, so I had assumed they'd learned their lesson. It didn't look like it, though: a new employee piqued some men's interest; especially the men whose eyes were at breast level when I wore four-inch heels. Helena wondered how anyone could even walk in them, and I have to say I even surprised myself. I was more used to sneakers or hiking boots. Wearing high heels and looming at six foot two, this Lehmusvuo assistant couldn't be avoided. When I was shorter and wore no makeup, I looked like a completely different person. I bought a couple of miniskirts the size of a mudflap. Those men could just blame me, which they would, if they couldn't help themselves. My leather pants also made for an interesting atmosphere in the elevator.

Because I had no idea of the pecking order at the cabinet or its cliques, I would sit with anyone in the cafeteria. I found it odd when one blond man was upset when I sat down next to him; perhaps he imagined I was trying to hit on him? A couple of days later I found out that he was the minister of defense. I did my best to memorize names and connect the faces, but I just couldn't be bothered to do so for such a temporary job. Admittedly, it was pretty amusing when groups of visitors stared at me as if I were someone important, too.

I couldn't forget David, so I was pleasantly surprised when I received an old-fashioned letter from him, postmarked Kotka. It was waiting for me when I returned to my apartment after another confusing day at work.

"*Kära Hilja*," it began. *Dear Hilja.*

I was touched that he had addressed me like that, although I knew that Swedes would call anyone a dear. David said he'd tried unsuccessfully to reach me by phone and e-mail, and then had resorted to using the phone number service to locate mine. I hadn't been keeping in touch with him—was I angry with him? He was sorry he'd had to leave so quickly and unexpectedly, but he'd had no choice; it was for an important work-related matter that couldn't wait. After that he'd found himself in Madrid, and had actually brought me something from there. Could we meet? He was coming to Helsinki on the week of October 25 and would be staying at the Hotel Torni.

It was the week before the municipal elections, when Helena had multiple speaking engagements in and around Helsinki, and I was supposed to accompany her. On Wednesday evening she was going to a cabin where members of the Green League would be holing up to work on last-minute strategy, so I could take a few hours off then. David hadn't left me his e-mail address, so I called him.

"Hi, this is Hilja. Sorry I didn't call you sooner. My phone fell into a puddle and died, and the SIM card was permanently damaged, too." David would see right through this obvious lie, but I didn't care.

"It's so nice to hear your voice! How are you?"

Just his voice made my insides quake. I was ready to go wherever he asked. We agreed to meet. After the call I just lay on my mattress and tried to calm down. A man who could provoke such a reaction in me was dangerous. Nonetheless, I was already counting the hours until I would see him again. Through the wall I could hear Riikka's music; she was playing Vuokko Hovatta's song "Favorite Animals." *And a buzzard descends fast through the clouds in Saksalanharju / and you, then you have lynx in your eyes.*

Despite my best efforts, I got caught up in the elections. Helena was an angel, listening to people complain about how her party was the brainchild of Stalin, or that it was run by a bunch of environmental anarchists, or that it was beholden to the bourgeoisie. When such comments were peppered with too many curse words, I'd take a step forward like a bodyguard.

The day before my date with David, I was going through Helena's mail as usual. Curiously, one of the envelopes was from Kotka, and because Kotka now reminded me of David and Anita, I read the letter. Usually I placed the sane letters in a pile for Helena to read; the ones from the loonies went straight into the recycling bin. Helena would be a fool to read all that garbage and upset herself. Some of the letters she received could very well have been reported to the police.

Inside the envelope from Kotka was a map. It didn't contain a cover letter or a return address. And it wasn't a regular topographical or road map; it looked like a map showing property lines. The more I looked at it, the more familiar it seemed. The map depicted a cape stretching out into the ocean, away from other properties. It was the cape Anita had dreamed of buying; the one that Usko Syrjänen had purchased. Why would anyone send this to Helena? Was it to tip her off about a suspicious business transaction involving this piece of land?

I knew Helena still hadn't told me everything, and I could play the same game. I photocopied the map and left the original in the pile of general correspondence. We'd be going straight to Kirkkonummi for the night after an election event in Siuntio, so I wouldn't have time to look at the map closely tonight; plus, I already had other things to think about, like my upcoming rendezvous. I searched the envelope for fingerprints or hair, looking for any clues as to who the sender might be. But there were none: the address on the envelope was the work of a printer and the stamp was nondescript.

On Wednesday morning I was up by six. Stars were sluggishly making their way out of the dark sky, but the herd of commuters headed toward Helsinki was already in evidence on the freeway. I was so horny I had to go for a run to burn off some of the extra energy. I would've had an even harder time that morning had I not been ridiculously busy later. Helena was going to give a speech in Swedish in Tammisaari on election day, and I'd promised to go through it because she wasn't sure of her grammar. My Swedish wasn't perfect, either, but two pairs of eyes were better than one.

The door between our offices was open while Helena was meeting with a Russian journalist, Marina Mihailova, a frail woman in her sixties, who was an editor for a blog that was constantly changing servers and web addresses because of its criticism of the Kremlin. Helena and the woman spoke in Russian, but I understood a few words here and there. They talked about a gas pipeline that was going to be laid under the Gulf of Finland and how freedom of speech was faring in Russia. I could have sworn that at one point they mentioned Kotka. Had Mihailova sent Helena the map?

When Mihailova said "nyuteenen," a Russian-accented version of "Nuutinen," I started paying closer attention.

"*Potshemu?*" Helena asked. *Why?*

"She knew what they were going to do to the place. Now it wasn't just a question of . . ." I couldn't understand Mihailova's next sentence, but then she said the name Valentin Fedorovich. There were thousands of them in Russia, but I knew that Paskevich had used Feodorovich as his alias.

Helena asked whether Mihailova was sure about this, and Mihailova said she had no doubt in her mind. Then Helena's cell phone went off and I had to answer it; she'd left it in my office and had asked me to interrupt her meeting with Mihailova only if it was extremely important. The call came from a journalist, checking in on what Helena's predictions for the election were. I said Helena was unavailable while listening to Mihailova say her good-byes.

"Good-bye, Marina Andreyevna." Helena kissed the woman on both cheeks. Marina Andreyevna Mihailova was barely five feet tall, and the usually fragile-looking Helena stood like an Olympic shot-putter next to her, while I felt like a giant.

"Good-bye, Helena, and God bless you!"

"God bless you, too," said Helena, although she was agnostic as far as I knew. "Hilja will walk you downstairs. It won't be long until the train leaves."

Mihailova was going back to Moscow. I missed the Moscow churches with their shiny onion domes. Mihailova wore a thick woolen skirt and sturdy shoes, and you couldn't have told her apart from the hundreds of *babushkas* selling knickknacks at the train station. And here she was, a dangerous dissident. When we said goodbye, her tiny hand squeezed mine firmly. I watched her walk slowly across the square in front of the building, as if each step was causing her pain. Nobody seemed to be following her, but I watched her until she disappeared between Kiasma, the modern art museum, and the Sanomatalo business center.

"I hope I'll see Marina Andreyevna again," Helena said when I returned to her office.

"Why wouldn't you?"

"She has a cancerous tumor and the Russian security police's special forces are after her. I don't know which is worse. Marina knows that she doesn't have much time, which is why she's not afraid to speak her mind.

"About what?"

"A lot of things, including Russia's energy policies. They have an effect on Finland, too. Just think about it—all those gas pipelines and nuclear waste. We're dependent on all this energy the Russians produce. Why do you think most of my colleagues keep their mouths shut about events across the border? We don't need to worry about being occupied, but if Russia decides to turn off the gas and nuclear valves, it will kill our economy."

We went for a vegetarian lunch in the annex staff cafeteria with a couple of Helena's friends; they were Social Democrats who were against nuclear power. My contract would be up in a week, and the staff was already waxing poetic about Saara Hirvelä's spelt bread and mushroom quiches. Helena probably didn't need a bodyguard. I admit the thought made me a bit sad.

The cabin that would be used by the election crew had previously been trashed by some homeless people. Like a good maid,

I rolled up my sleeves and started cleaning. When people began entering the cabin, I took off and Helena didn't ask me where I was going. Hotel Torni was only a few blocks away from Kamppi square, but I felt like I was stepping into a different world. I called David to let him know I had arrived.

I always liked to meet my lovers at hotels. They were transitory places; nobody's everyday life got in the way there. When married men invited me to their homes I always declined, even if they owned a penthouse with a view of Central Park, or an island villa near Hiittiset. I didn't want to see their children's toys, or wear their wives' slippers, or think about who had washed the sheets and towels I was using. In a hotel all of those things were mine, if only temporarily.

David came down the elevator and when I saw him, I had to muffle a cry: he had hair! The black, curly mess was obviously a wig, but why was he wearing it to meet me? He smiled at my confusion while he led me into the elevator.

"Is that the gift you brought me from Spain? You scalped Señor José in the bullfighting ring?"

"Why should women be the only ones allowed to wear wigs? A man can play with hair, too, right?" David said coolly. I remembered again how he'd passed me on Helena's street when I'd been dressed up as Reiska. Of course he had recognized me. But if David worked for Europol he had to be wearing the wig for a reason. Come to think of it, his eyes looked strange, too. Before, his eyes had been bluish gray; now they were dark-blue with small brown speckles. I wondered what name he'd used when he checked in.

When we got off on the fourth floor, David had still not made a move to touch me. I was standing next to a completely different person than the one who'd written to me from Kotka and had called to arrange a meeting. My excitement turned into disappointment, but I was still nervous. Maybe my coming here was a big mistake. David led me to the end of the hallway, to room 411. The room was dark; all the blinds were drawn and only one small lamp was on. As soon as he closed the door he pulled off the wig and once again looked like the man I had made love to a month earlier.

"This is so hot. It's like wearing a coonskin cap! Have you ever worn a wig?" David didn't wait for my reply—he shut me up with his mouth. I heard him lock the door behind him. I responded to his kiss, stroking his damp bald head. There were no mixed messages about why I was in the room. David was already tearing his clothes off and helped me remove mine, shoved away the pillows, and tossed me on the bed, biting my breasts and pushing himself into me, and all I could think about at that moment was my pleasure, David's smile, David's mouth on mine. I let him take me, I followed, responded to him, it was enough.

Later we lay side by side, so close that all I could see of his face were details: a couple of pockmarks, eyebrows that were almost joined together, black eyelashes that matched his now darker eyes and the wig. Had he dyed them?

"Why the wig and the contacts?" I asked, but David didn't reply. Instead, he pulled the contacts out.

"It doesn't matter," he said and threw the contacts carelessly onto the bedside table. Disposables. His eyes were familiar again, but they avoided my gaze.

"Oh, right, my gift." David got up and I saw how my nails had dug into his back. I picked up a pillow and propped up my head while David was going through his closet. He returned with a flat package that looked like a book.

"I saw this in a bookstore and I thought of you. Or," he looked slightly guilty, "I didn't just happen to see it. I specifically went to a certain section to see if there were any books on this topic. Come on, open it already!"

The wrapping paper was thick. I tore it off and uncovered a thin, brownish paperback. The cover depicted a lynx with mournful eyes.

"El lince ibérico. Una batalla por la supervivencia," I read out loud. "A book about Iberian lynx . . . hang on . . . 'the fight for survival.' Thank you!"

"You know Spanish?"

"A little." I had learned the basics at the Queens academy from our teacher Fernando, but I'd already forgotten almost all of it. I flipped through the book, which was printed in Spanish and had barely any white space. There were footnotes everywhere, so this was a serious scientific document. The book also contained maps for lynx habitats, and I shook my head at the information in front of my eyes: the Iberian lynx had only been seen in two small mountain regions in southern Spain, whereas a hundred years earlier, the animal had roamed all over Iberia, except on the plains. There were also pictures of lynx at a wildlife refuge—resting and playing, as well as hunting rabbits, their main source of food. Cubs with tufted ears peeked out from a tree trunk. Frida's favorite place to hide had been a pine trunk Uncle Jari had hollowed out for her. She would hide there and play-attack us if we'd pass by. Frida had been angry when she wasn't able to crawl into the trunk after she grew to her full size.

"Thank you! I do understand enough Spanish to know that this was written by people who are working to protect the lynx. There aren't more than a couple hundred of them left anymore. It's not easy to see one in the wild. Why were you in Madrid?"

"I spent a couple of days there, but I stayed mainly in Málaga. The economic crisis depressed the prices for oceanfront property there, so now's the time to buy if my employers have the money for it. I was in negotiations with this one Russian in Madrid—he's planning on investing in Spain."

"A Russian? What was his name?"

"Why do you want to know? Well, if you're so interested, his name is Vasiliev."

Not Paskevich, then. That would've been too much of a coincidence. I got off the bed and walked across the thick carpeting to the bathroom. I saw a claw-foot tub and four towels. Would Helena still need me in the evening? I could just spend the night; the bed was big enough to hold two couples.

I washed my hands with lingonberry shower gel but let David's scent linger elsewhere on my body. The following week I would no longer be under contract, and I could follow anyone anywhere. I could even go to Spain to save all the Iberian lynx, or I could join Europol. When I came back into the room, David was sitting naked on the couch, with two bathrobes next to him.

"These robes are on the house. What's your schedule like?"

"My boss is busy until eight."

"Oh yes, Helena Lehmusvuo. I found your name on the Finnish cabinet website. Who on earth are you, Hilja Kanerva Ilveskero?"

I wasn't able to interpret the look in his eyes. Was he sad, or amused, or just curious?

"I've told you. I'm the daughter of a murderer, at your service if you pay me enough. This gig is just temporary. And come to think of it, I don't really know who you are. But does it matter? We're here now." I sat on his lap facing him, brushing my lips along his shoulders. I still hadn't had enough of him.

David's phone rang. I hoped he wouldn't pick it up, but he stood up, holding me tight so that I wouldn't fall. The phone screen displayed a number, no name, and in the split second I saw it. I didn't recognize the country code.

"Stahl. In Helsinki." This time the call was in English and it had to do with cars. Sounded like David was buying a Jaguar. Or it was some Europol code he was using. I imagined David as James Bond, although I knew what a boring job being an agent actually was, even if they were sometimes in danger. He even had a blond in his bedroom, just like Bond. All David needed was a dry martini, shaken, not stirred. While the call went on, I got up and peeked into the minibar, but they didn't have any gin, let alone vermouth. I opened a bottle of mineral water and drank straight out of the bottle while I peeked between the curtains. I could see the traffic on Kaleva Street below.

"Thirsty?" David had finally hung up. "It was a broker from Amsterdam."

"A car?"

David nodded.

"Jaguar?"

"Yes."

"Red?" Then I realized David probably wasn't familiar with Finnish popular culture, much less the Jerry Cotton stories and the song about him that begins with *Who's the man driving a red Jaguar*?

"Black, actually." David wrapped his arms around me from behind; I felt him harden against my back. I only cared about this touch right now. He could be anyone and lie as much he wanted to. The outside world did not exist. I kept on repeating the mistakes Mike Virtue had warned me against.

Of course, I didn't call Helena to ask for a night off or to rearrange my schedule. I left David before eight. I would rather be the one leaving than the one being left behind, surrounded by the scents of a lover, seeing lipstick on drinking glasses, hoping there was someone else to share the large bed with. I caved in and gave David my phone number before I left. He'd have to return to Spain early in the morning, but he'd be back soon. It would serve the unemployment office reps right if I just took off to Málaga with him. If David could afford a Jaguar, he certainly could support a lover for a day or two.

Toward the end of the week, the elections ramped up and I was getting sick of the whole thing. On top of that, I had to attend a book fair with Helena because she'd agreed to be on a panel there. In New York I'd learned how to deal with screeching subway trains and streets roiling with people, but the book fair was packed to the gills and the cacophony was overwhelming. I had to muscle my way through the crowd to create a path for Helena to reach the panel table, where people listened to her as if she were their guru. She knew how to talk to a large group. Afterward Helena was stuck at the fair for hours, signing autographs and smiling for photos. I wanted to warn her about letting people get too close—nobody checked purses or bags at the entrance, and anyone posing with her could have had a knife. I wasn't authorized to search anyone.

The night before the elections, Helena slept at her apartment in Helsinki. Her roommates were there, too, so I left her with a can of pepper spray and took the tram home to Käpylä. I was happy to shed my high heels and switch back into my camo pants that I hadn't been able to wear for weeks. My roommates weren't in. Loneliness felt sweet for a change. I sent David a dirty text message and then began to investigate the map I had copied at Helena's office several days before.

I looked for the coordinates on Google Earth and, yup, I was right. This was the same area Anita had been fighting over with Paskevich. Goddamned Helena! She knew more about Anita's business than she let on. Why didn't she trust me?

There was a code at the bottom of the map, consisting of eight numbers. 1 3 91 11 77 6 3 46. It wasn't a filing number for the map, nor was it a phone number. I'd spend quite a lot of time with combinations recently while trying to figure out how to open Anita's safe. There was no way this could be the combination—was there?

I tried to not get too excited. The safe was in the same closet where I kept my gun and ammo. I opened the gun locker and pulled out the safe and, for a few minutes, I tried to stop my hands from shaking. I began to enter the combination.

When I rolled the last number into place, I couldn't believe my eyes: the lock snapped sharply. Anita's safe was open.

18

I was amazed. I hadn't expected this insane attempt to actually work. My heart beat hard as I shoved my hand into the safe to pull out its contents. There wasn't much; just a couple of envelopes sealed shut. One of them read, "Anita Nuutinen. My last will and testament." I opened it. No surprises; Cecilia inherited everything. Anita had also made large donations to the Finnish Red Cross, the Women's Bank, and Monika's charity in Mozambique. The will was dated from March of last year, when I was still working for Anita.

The other envelope felt like it contained a stack of papers. It was sealed, with no writing on it. But Anita had given me the safe to ensure I'd take action even if she wasn't around anymore. Because Cecilia or her representatives hadn't demanded that I hand over the safe, I assumed I was the only person who knew about it.

I slit open the envelope. It contained about ten sheets of paper, the topmost depicting the all-too-familiar map of Hiidenniemi in Kotka. There were also articles in Russian, printouts from the Internet, and a couple of letters. One was signed by Anita; the other by someone named Boris Vasilievich Vasiliev.

I spent the rest of the evening and well into the night translating the materials. I used Babelfish's translating website to help, but this made the letters even more confusing, and I realized I would need to take the letters to someone who was fluent in Russian. The police had an interpreter, and I could probably find one at the cabinet, too, unless I wanted to hand these papers over to Helena.

I did find out that this Vasiliev had approached Anita and asked her to act as a middleman for the Hiidenniemi deal—she could buy the place in her name, when in reality Vasiliev would be the owner. Anita had declined the offer. Her letter to Vasiliev was blunt, without any of the usual Russian niceties. The clippings and printouts were from tabloids that focused on celebrities. In one of them, a man who could have been Boris Vasiliev was shown walking into a nightclub and leaving later with two strikingly beautiful women. There was a printout from the blog edited by Marina Andreyevna Mihailova, Helena's friend, which claimed that Vasiliev had connections with Chechen rebels and terrorists. The second printout contained an image of Vasiliev posing with a rifle on his shoulder and a dead bear at his feet; next to him was a man anyone would recognize, the former Russian president and current prime minister, Vladimir Putin. The third page contained a grainy picture showing Vasiliev in partial profile, and I recognized the man staring right into the camera. It was Usko Syrjänen.

Vasiliev was a common name, but it still bothered me that David had mentioned that his business partner in Spain had the same surname. Of course, it could be a coincidence. But why on earth had Anita kept all these papers locked up? Had this Vasiliev fellow been threatening her, too? Why had Anita told me about Paskevich and his hit men, and said nothing about this guy? Were Paskevich and Vasiliev in cahoots with each other? As far as I knew, the Kremlin had always protected Paskevich, and Anita had never mentioned any rebel connections. And this Usko Syrjänen could very well pay off the politicians to help his building project run smoother, but I doubted that any Finnish businessman would be financing Russian terrorists. That would be commercial suicide; as soon as word of this got out, all those malls and amusement parks Syrjänen had built would become ghost towns when Finns stopped spending their money there.

Was this a message from Anita, telling me to stop worrying about Paskevich and turn my attention to Boris Vasiliev, whoever that was? Or was I supposed to deliver these Hiidenniemi papers to Vasiliev? The idea of running into Paskevich's goons had seemed dangerous enough, but if I was really going up against a terrorist boss here, I was in deep shit. I wasn't well-versed enough in politics to know who were the real terrorists and who were just accused of being such. It seemed to depend on who was in charge. Although Marina Andreyevna was Helena's friend, her blog post could have been inaccurate.

I had my phone on silent, and now I saw the light was blinking. It was David.

"Hi, Hilja. You're still awake, although it's almost two over there! In Spain people stay up late, especially on a Saturday evening." David sounded like he'd had more than a few.

"Yes, it's Saturday night and I'm alone in my apartment, working. Does the name Boris Vasiliev mean anything to you?"

The barely audible intake of breath on the other end of the line told me that my question had been a surprise. But I had to take this chance. I needed to know whether Vasiliev was big enough to have attracted Europol's attention, or whether he was only a tough guy inside Russian borders.

"Where did you run into him?" David wasn't even trying to hide that he knew about Vasiliev.

"In some papers Anita Nuutinen left behind. Vasiliev had asked her to be his middleman."

"In general, or just for some specific deal?"

"Honestly, I don't understand these papers. But you do know who he is, then."

"I know Boris Vasiliev, but who he actually is is a completely different issue. He appeared out of thin air a few years ago."

"So you've met him through your business?"

David was quiet for a moment. I could hear voices in the background, but I couldn't tell what language they were speaking.

"Oh, Hilja, Vasiliev is a boring subject."

"All right. How's the weather over there?"

"A bit cooler today, only about sixty degrees, and it's stormy. I couldn't eat dinner outside. Do you like seafood? They have the most delicious lobster here."

Our conversation turned to chitchat about food and scenery, and it was obvious that was David's intention. I wanted him badly. He'd be back in Finland earlier than expected, on Tuesday. Only three nights from now. I purred into the phone like a lynx and when we finally hung up, his voice still played in my ears. How could I have fallen in love with a man who constantly lied to me? Was I following in my mother's footsteps by choosing an unpredictable man, a decision that could cost me my life?

Uncle Jari had refused to discuss Keijo Suurluoto with me, but it was evident how much he hated him, a sentiment he had passed on to me. Only our neighbor Seppo Holopainen, who had gone to school with my mother and uncle, had even hinted at how my mother may have been somewhat flirty and given Father reasons to be jealous. I don't remember where my mother and I were coming from on the evening when he killed her. All I had been told was that Mother had decided to leave Suurluoto and take me with her, and that's why he'd killed her. Because of me.

I checked Helena's tracking device to make sure that she hadn't gone anywhere. She was still sleeping in her apartment. I got up to find Jenni's hot chocolate and made myself a cup. I'd get her more when I had a chance. At that point, Jenni got home, slightly tipsy, and told me a long-winded tale about some boring guy named Tero who'd tried to hit on her.

It was four a.m. before I fell asleep, and I didn't wake up until noon. I checked the tracker again—Helena was now at the Green League cabin for last-minute election planning. The city was overwhelmed by a rainstorm, so I skipped my morning run and opted for a quick series of exercises on my floor: a hundred and fifty push-ups, a hundred lunges, and another hundred sit-ups. I'd promised Helena I'd go to the Greens' election party. I had seen it on TV before, and it always seemed crazy, which is why I wanted to experience it firsthand this time. I felt obliged by my temporary gig to vote, so I did. I took my time deciding between Donald Duck and Modesty Blaise, but finally decided to go with the candidate who had treated me like a peer all the time I had been working at the cabinet. Mrs. Voutilainen was casting her ballot at the same time, so we walked together back to her place through the storm. She'd made coffee and strawberry cake to celebrate the election.

In the evening I sat at the computer, Googling Boris Vasiliev. There wasn't much information considering how well known he was, at least according to David. This guy obviously wanted to stay under the radar. Helena called, asking if it was all right for her to go to Kirkkonummi for a change of clothes. We'd meet at Tavastia, the nightclub where the Green League was waiting for the election results.

I had no idea how to dress for such an occasion, so I just wore my usual jeans, combat boots, and a long-sleeved T-shirt with an image of a lynx head on the front. I had found it in some boutique in Greenwich Village and paid a fortune for it. I wanted it to last forever, so I rarely wore it.

I associated Tavastia with shatteringly loud rock music, drunken people stumbling over their own feet, a floor sticky with beer, and cigarette smoke. The club had since banned smoking, and instead of watching a band perform tonight, people were staring at a TV screen, enamored by real-time voting results. To me it was as exciting as watching paint dry. Helena wasn't around yet. I wasn't officially working, so I ordered a gin and grapefruit juice with some ice, and chatted with a couple of assistants for a while. I didn't belong in this crowd, but being able to observe people in novel situations makes for a better bodyguard. It's amazing how people don't think about their safety when they are staring at a screen. Although the bouncers at Tavastia made sure that everyone left their jackets in the coat room, any woman could have smuggled in a handgun in her purse, along with a couple of rounds of ammo. If someone wanted to get rid of the majority of the Green League in one pop, this would be their chance—and it would be easy. People really believed in the good of others, and then were shocked when they read about school shootings and parents killing their entire family. They should have realized that anyone was capable of anything.

In Finland even the president walked around town without a care in the world—I had spotted her once in the bathroom of the Tennispalatsi movie theater sporting a tracksuit and a baseball cap. It was just the two of us at the sinks, and I could have done anything to her. But I pretended that I didn't recognize her. I could just imagine how Mike Virtue would have freaked out if I'd told him about that. He didn't even take off his Kevlar vest when he went swimming—rumor had it he wore it to bed, too. Because Mike wasn't the type to sleep with students, we were never able to prove the latter, but there were pictures of him on Long Island and at Brighton Beach, swimming in his vest.

I'd worn my vest a couple of times in Russia. Anita had refused to wear one because she thought it was uncomfortable and made her look fat. I hadn't worn a riot helmet since my training days at the academy, though—we'd fought imaginary enemies, stormed buildings, and prevented rioters from entering.

News of the projected winners was appearing on the screen, and the crowd murmured, saying that it would look better once the votes from Helsinki were counted. I asked a girl in a woolen sweater to keep an eye on my drink while I went to the restroom, where I tried calling Helena, but she didn't answer. She might have been on the train and the connection wasn't that great in the tunnels. If I knew which train she was on I could go meet her, although the idea of standing in the driving rain didn't seem all that fun. The general mood at the party was upbeat, despite the poor showing for the Greens.

When I still hadn't heard from Helena by nine and she hadn't picked up her phone, I started to worry. I went back to the restroom, locked myself in the stall, and fished out my tracker. It immediately found Helena: she was between Karjaa and Tammisaari. The green dot on the screen was moving slowly eastward on Hangontie. I tried calling her again, but the automated message told me that the number I had dialed could not be reached right now.

I looked up Tiku Aaltonen's number and called him.

"What? I'm not interested." He sounded stuffy, like he had the flu. There were no car sounds in the background.

I lowered my voice to a tenor. "Hello, this is Reiska Räsänen. Did you already forget our little conversation?"

"Who?"

"We met recently in Kirkkonummi, at Helena's house. Didn't you learn your lesson?"

"What are you talking about?"

"Where are you, Tiku? When can I see you?" I heard someone walk into the restroom. Damn, I couldn't change my voice back now.

"I'm at home, in Matinkylä. Watching *Finnish Idol.* Did something happen to Helena? Dude, did you do something to her? Or are you just fishing? Today is election day, so Helena is probably over there at their party. She didn't want you there, is that it?"

I hung up. I could check whether Tiku was telling the truth by heading over to his place, but Helena's tracker wasn't anywhere near Matinkylä—it had reached Tammisaari. I couldn't be one hundred percent certain that the device was still on Helena, but I had no choice but to assume it was. Yet another fucking mistake I'd made, letting Helena go to Kirkkonummi alone. Why would she leave with anyone? To watch the election coverage with someone in Tammisaari, really?

"Anybody here from Tammisaari?" I asked the assistant I'd been chatting with when I got back to the bar.

"I think they had their own party. Why do you ask? Look, look! There we go, the numbers are going up! Haven't we been saying this would happen?"

I wasn't interested in voting trends, but I also didn't want to make a scene about Helena's disappearance on national television and under the watchful eyes of the journalists who were in the room, waiting with baited breath for any reaction from the politicians. When the party leader took a break from interviews, I pushed my way through the crowd to tell him that Helena had gotten a stomach bug of some kind and was stuck at home.

"I told her not to eat that two-day old smoked fish, but no, she didn't want to let food go to waste. Please don't tell anyone; she's so embarrassed about this," I whispered. "I'll make sure that she's okay, poor thing."

The party leader had already turned back to the numbers on the screen, so I was able to leave Tavastia without a hassle. Helena had turned north from Hangontie. I hailed a cab at the nearest hotel. I had to get to my apartment to retrieve my gun, bulletproof vest, backpack, and a change of clothes. And I'd need a car. I asked the cab driver if he knew of a rental car place that was open twenty-four hours. The driver said he could take me anywhere, as long as I paid for the ride, but I wanted to go alone. The cab driver was a man of about sixty and didn't look like the action-hero type who would have been useful to me. He said he'd find out about the rentals while he waited for me. He was sure there'd be a place still open at the airport.

Jenni and Riikka were watching the election night coverage; Timo Soini's satisfied mug was on the screen. It was just as well that my roommates were preoccupied; I could get my gun and pack up three rounds of ammo without making them suspicious. My gun had fifteen slots for bullets; I loaded it up and then slipped it into my holster under my arm. I left the vest off for now. I also packed Reiska's gear with me just in case I needed a disguise. I asked to use Riikka's printer and made a copy of the Hiidenniemi map, although I had no idea whether it had any connection to Helena's disappearance. I dropped my passport into a waterproof bag, where I also kept two driver's licenses, mine and Reiska's. I also grabbed my laptop and the dongle I could use to connect to the web anywhere, as well as a backup battery for my cell phone. A couple of energy bars, a water bottle, moist towelettes, and thermal underwear, and I was all sct. I wore my outdoor gear because the rain just didn't want to quit.

"You should go to the airport; they have a lot of options," the cab driver told me. "Where are you going in this weather, hon? Is it far?"

"I'm not sure; it might be a long drive."

"Going after your boyfriend?" the driver asked, all sympathetic, but I didn't have the energy to come up with an elaborate story. I just said it was for work.

Getting a rental car was easy. I told them I didn't know yet when I would return it, but my credit was good so they didn't have to worry about me. When I drove the Opel out of the airport, it was raining so hard that the windshield wipers had a tough time keeping up. I took Ring 3 westward and hoped that I'd have a tailwind. The ring road was the fastest way to reach Hanko Road, and luckily most of it was well lit. I was speeding, going seventy miles an hour when the limit was forty, flying through yellow lights. If any cops were out there in this weather, I'd have a hell of a time convincing them not to confiscate my license on the spot. The Opel slid on the rain-slicked road for a moment as I passed a huge Russian car carrier, but I quickly had it under control again. The tracking device was riding shotgun with me, and I followed its green dot out of the corner of my eye. Since I'd left the airport, the dot had been moving slowly, almost at a walking pace. I tried calling Helena once more, but she didn't answer. My guess was that Helena didn't even have her phone any longer, and might not even know where it was.

In Espoo I swerved into a Finnoo Road gas station to buy a cup of coffee and to check in on Helena. I punched in the code. When the information flashed on the screen, I cursed in every language I knew: it showed she was in Tivergiken, Bromarf. *Durak*. Idiot. I should've figured this out.

Helena was in Valentin Paskevich's oceanfront villa in Bromarf. I'd let Helena go alone to Kirkkonummi, and Paskevich had kidnapped her. Yet another client of mine was about to meet her maker with Paskevich.

I paid for my coffee and downed it in two gulps, then ran to the car. Bromarf was about sixty miles away, and luckily I had already memorized the route to Paskevich's villa. I flew onto the ring road; before the two lanes merged into one, I managed to pass a slow-moving Toyota Corolla that was swerving from side to side, as if someone completely wasted was behind the wheel. I was now driving seventy-five and hoped no elk were wandering on the road.

Should I call the police? If Paskevich had approached Helena, she would have called me, as I'd told her to let me know of any changes in her schedule. Kidnapping a representative was a serious crime that couldn't be hidden from the media once the police got involved. Besides, Helena hadn't been gone long enough to qualify for a missing persons report. No, it was better to work alone, although I didn't know what was waiting for me in Bromarf.

If Paskevich killed Helena, too, I wouldn't let that bastard live.

19

I sped down rainy Hanko Road as if my life depended on it. Towns flew by: Kirkkonummi, Siuntio, Inkoo, Karjaa. I kept trying to reach Helena on her phone without any luck. I knew I shouldn't assume that Helena's tracker was still on her. They may have even spotted the device and were using it to lure me.

There was an accident on the long straight stretch after Karjaa's off-ramp. A small red Audi traveling toward Hanko had slid off the road; the police and first responders were already on the scene. There were hardly any cars on the road, but traffic was still stalled on the one lane. The driver had just been removed from the crushed metal and was being placed on a stretcher. I saw a glimpse of a woman, bleeding.

When I finally got to Tammisaari, I looked at the map and then turned north a couple of miles past the city center. The speed limit changed from forty to fifty. The road was clear; everyone was at home, waiting to see the final election results on television. A pair of glowing eyes flashed in the darkness, and a white cat braving the pouring rain stared at me as if it could've used a ride.

The route became winding, leading to an ever-narrowing unpaved road. The rain had washed away enough of the soil that I began to worry about a mudslide; I didn't want my car to end up in a ditch. I drove through the huge puddles covering the roadway without knowing how deep they actually were. I got stuck in the mud in a bend on the road, and it took a while to get enough traction to get going again. The road leading up to Paskevich's villa was so narrow that if a bicyclist had been in front of me, I would have been unable to pass him. I spotted a widened section of the road built for U-turns. I parked facing the opposite direction so that I'd be able to get out of there fast if necessary. According to my calculations, Paskevich's hideout was only three hundred yards away. I left my backpack in the car, pulled on all my gear, and brought only the bare essentials that would fit in my pockets and in a small pouch that hung from my neck.

I didn't know what sort of security system Paskevich had at his villa. The place was difficult to reach, thanks to the meandering roads; approaching the oceanfront property by water would've been much easier. I hadn't looked at the aerial image of the property, so I didn't know whether there was a fence around the estate, which included a thirty-seven-hundred-square-foot villa, a waterfront sauna, a guest cottage, and a garage. If the property's security fence ended at the waterfront, then I would need to steal a boat to get in. Paskevich may have set up a motion detector around the perimeter of his property—I might have a welcoming party of bloodhounds and armed guards waiting for me. I had to elude them if I wanted to find Helena. I worried that my tracking monitor would get soaked in the rain and conk out, so I stopped to check it. Apparently Helena was at the villa.

A gust of wind beat rain into my face; I felt the water seeping through my shell. I stepped into a deep puddle and could feel the water filling my shoes. When I was a kid, I walked around in the dark all the time, but this sort of pitch black was unfamiliar to me—except for that one time in New York when the power went off when I was on the subway. It had taken a moment for people to pull out their lighters and cell phones. The flickering flames had caused panic among some of the travelers; if a fire had spread in an enclosed space like that, it would have been a disaster. This time, I was alone in the black.

Soon lights began flashing in the darkness. I was getting closer to the yard and the windows beyond, and I didn't see a fence anywhere. I stopped again, this time to figure out where the lights equipped with motion detectors might be and where to walk to avoid setting one off. Although I waited to hear the approach of growling dogs, I didn't notice any doghouses or leashes.

Nobody seemed to take notice of me when I circled the house. The curtainless windows occasionally flashed with human shapes. They were too blurry for me to decipher. I walked over to the dark guest house, and jumped back when a light was thrown on me. It looked like motion detectors were working there, and the light spread all the way to the shore and the sauna, where smoke was coming out of the chimney. The garage doors were closed. I called Helena once more; it was no use. I would've given up a lot to hear her voice and know she was alive.

I sneaked to the back of the house again and came up with a plan to get inside. I should have dressed up as Reiska—the disguise might fool Paskevich and his men for a while, whereas they would most likely recognize me as Hilja. They'd first followed Anita and then Helena, in each case choosing the perfect moment when the bodyguard was overwhelmed and not doing her job. So what right did I have to protect myself here? I should just walk in and claim I had a flat tire, or that I was completely lost, confused by the rain and the darkness.

I was so nervous that I needed to pee. I walked deeper into the forest and unzipped my pants. Immediately, rain washed over my butt; trying to prevent the drops from getting on me was futile. I took a gulp of my energy drink, tossed the can into the woods, and begged the forest spirits for forgiveness. I was now ready to enter the lion's den. I walked nonchalantly through the yard. There were a couple of steps leading up to the front door, but the west side of the house had another door, probably for servants. I was headed toward that entrance when suddenly a bright beam of light hit my face. The side door flew open and a flashlight aimed straight in my eyes blinded me.

"There you are, finally!" an angry male voice said in accentless Finnish. "We've been waiting for a good thirty minutes. And don't start making excuses; you should've been here. Get inside already!" The beam of light was going down my body; I was still half blind.

"Are you deaf, or don't you speak Finnish? We specifically asked for a Finnish girl; that was the whole point of this deal! Get a move on. You're already late enough."

I complied just to get out of the rain, and because the other viable option—running into the dark forest and risking getting shot or having to start shooting at others—didn't sound great, either. The man motioning me to get inside was the type who spent half of his life at the gym. His red hair was shaped into a crew cut was and he had a tattoo on his neck that poorly matched his pale, freckled skin. When I stepped inside, he was still eyeing me.

"Wow, those are some clothes," he said. "Well, I guess you can't be out in the rain in something skimpy. There's just nothing sexy about what you're wearing. Let's see if you'll even fit into the clothes we have for you—you're pretty tall. Weren't you supposed to be a size four? Take off that hat."

I swiped the hood off my hair.

"Short hair . . . we should have a wig somewhere. And makeup does wonders. Where did you leave your car?"

"I was dropped off."

"What? But we had agreed on complete confidentiality, right, Sarita? Who brought you?"

"My—my friend Pete. I told him I was going to a friend's cabin to help clean it for the winter. He doesn't know why I'm really here."

"Pete, huh? Well, it's better that way. Follow me; I'll show you your room and your outfit. Valentin's gotta have his little birthday treat."

I recalled the red car on the side of the road and a young woman on a stretcher. Sarita had been on her way here, but her car flew off the road and landed on its roof in the ditch. I had better act as Sarita, no matter what I had to—I didn't want to finish that thought.

The redhead led me upstairs to the end of a hallway and then turned on the lights in the room—it looked like a scene out of a cheap porno film. The walls, curtains, and bedspread were made of red silk and velvet. A large gold-framed mirror was attached to the ceiling above the four-poster bed; another mirror stood on the floor, and the third was next to the dresser. There were black vinyl and various leather straps on the bed, and next to it were high-heeled red shoes that were at least a size too small for me. The dresser had a pile of handbags on it, with makeup and perfume spilling out of them.

"Wear these—I'll come back to check on you soon. Valentin is getting impatient."

The good news was that if Paskevich had ordered himself a hooker for his birthday, he didn't have any immediate plans to kill Helena. Or was I, or the unknown Sarita, the appetizer before Paskevich would devour the main course? Was he turned on by violence?

I took off my wet coat and pants and hung them up. I caught a glimpse in the mirror of a woman wearing a woolen shirt and thermal underwear. There were all sorts of kinky people in the world—there had to be a couple of men who'd find my current clothes a huge turn-on. My gun holster bulged under my shirt and I had no idea where to hide it. Sex shops didn't usually sell clothes that were designed to provide ample cover for a gun.

What did they expect me to wear, anyway? At least the vinyl chaps almost completely covered my crotch—but my butt was entirely visible. There were no panties included, so I assumed the idea was to walk around with everything up for grabs. The cap was black leather, and the tangle of strings was some sort of a weird shirt that exposed the breasts but made the wearer look tied up. A gun holster was under the strings. In it was a fine reproduction of a 9-millimeter Beretta that could have fooled an inexperienced bank teller, maybe even a cop who was easily flustered. The handle was similar to the one on my gun. Did Paskevich like having a gun held to his head? I had seen enough of New York and its sex dungeons that I didn't even raise an eyebrow at people's desires. If Paskevich wanted to play with the toy gun, I may not have the chance to switch it for the real one. Who knows; Valentin's preference might be to point the gun at others.

I put all the clothes on except for the holster, the shoes, and the cap. Then I went over to the dresser. The redhead had mentioned something about a wig, and I found a blond braid in a box. It was straight out of an Elovena oatmeal ad. I used bobby pins to fasten it onto my hair and hid the seams with a black leather strap that I had found in another box. The redhead peeked in through the door.

"How much longer?"

"I need to still put my makeup on. Did you have any preference on color or style? And I can't wear those shoes—they're way too small."

"You told me you were a size 7!"

"No I didn't, I told you I was a size 8! Was I talking to you on the phone, or some other deaf guy?"

"Shut the hell up! Let me see what I can find. A couple of weeks ago there was this transvestite entertaining Valentin's friend Heinz. I'll see if he left any of his shoes here. Just put on plenty of makeup: black eyes and red lips. You know, like a real naughty girl. Chop, chop!"

I was close to tossing the redheaded lumbering fool down the stairs, but I could handle name calling for now—I had more important things to focus on. He ambled back into the hallway, where I heard him open another door. I went through the handbags for powder, applied foundation on my face and lined my eyes with black. I chose dark-gray glittery eye shadow and caked on enough to scare a drag queen. I pretend to be Reiska playing a woman, a sex toy. I wanted to look extra crude, so I spread lipstick all over my nipples. All this makeup would hopefully prevent Paskevich from recognizing me right away. Getting dressed up like this wasn't too different from transforming into Reiska, or wearing a dress and high heels to Anita's fancy parties.

"This is all I could find. Hope Valentin likes them!" The tattooed man threw high-heeled black boots at me. They looked too big for my feet. It was better that way.

"What was your name again? I already forgot," I asked the man, who had apparently arranged this meeting between Sarita and Paskevich. "And when am I getting paid?"

"I'm Sami. That's all you need to know, and you're just Sarita. You'll get the money tomorrow morning—you promised to spend the entire night here, remember? I don't know if that damned Trankov has some other plan going on, as he dragged some broad here, too, but that woman doesn't look like Valentin's type at all. In her fifties and wrinkly. I'm afraid you'll be too tall for him, but he really wanted a Finnish woman. What does that even mean? Someone with a long back and short legs?"

"Fuck you, Sami," I said in a nonthreatening tone. It was more like one-upmanship, showing that I knew rough language, too. "Go over the plan once more with me, will you? What was it you wanted me to do?"

"I don't want anything—it's all for Valentin. Rumor has it that he gives himself a new prostitute each year as a birthday gift. He's turning fifty-five today. Dude's been downing Viagra for days, so get ready. Oh right, the ropes! Valentin loves it when cowgirls lasso him. Just don't tie him up too tight. Hang on, I'll go get them."

Sami took off. I wanted to kiss my heaven-sent boots. I swiftly tied my gun around my right ankle with a couple of leather straps. This was still risky; although the gun was pointing toward the floor, who knows what could happen during the rough ride Sami had promised I was in for. Unfortunately, I couldn't hide any additional ammo in my clothes.

Sami came back with the ropes and gave me a once-over.

"Hey, you don't look half bad. I'd fuck you, but I'm faithful to my wife. You know how to make a lasso?"

Charlie Davis was a Nebraskan and some sort of a teen rodeo star back in his youth. At the academy he'd shown us how to tie a lasso and throw it, and I'd even put these skills to use when I had to pull our neighbor's cow out of a bog one summer. This was after Uncle Jari had died, when I was packing up his belongings at the cabin. The neighbors had been pulling the cow from the swamp, but none of them had been able to throw a rope far enough to reach her.

I didn't quite get why a cowgirl would wear a leather cap, but you know—to each his own. Before I headed downstairs, I checked in with Sami. "You mentioned some other broad here. She's not trying to get in on my deal, is she? Where is she? I'll tell her to get lost."

"No, it was some business thing. Trankov had tried to get in touch with her for ages and today he got lucky. He took her out to the sauna, so she won't be bothering you right now. That's all I know. I'm just a janitor here and it's Valentin's show. Come on, let's get going!"

"Does this door have a lock?" I asked. I really didn't want anyone to go through my stuff.

Sami laughed. "A lock? It's up to Valentin. Guests are treated well here—don't worry about it. If he's happy with you, he might even pay you extra."

I followed Sami downstairs. The lights in the hallway had been dimmed and there were real candles in the chandelier. I couldn't tell how old the villa was; at first glance it looked like it was from another era, but most likely it was built only a couple of years ago. The room I walked into was as large as the three-bedroom apartment I lived in on Untamo Road, and it, too, had appropriate mood lighting: the dimmed bulbs gave off a soft red glow, a fire was crackling in the fireplace, and candles shimmered in the chandelier. It was warm, and after that torrential downpour, it actually felt cozy. The armchairs and sofas were covered in soft distressed brown leather, and a whiff of cigar smoke wafted through the air.

Two maids were waiting with trays of drinks. I quickly recognized Russian champagne in a chiller, cognac, brandy, and Vana Tallin liqueur. Only then did I pay attention to the maids, who looked like they were twins with dark eyes, pale skin, and black hair cut into shiny, sleek bobs. Both were wearing a traditional frilly maid's cap. Their remaining clothes were less traditional—black vinyl with such plunging necklines that I could see glimpses of their nipples. Their skirts were short, barely reaching their thighs, and were covered by a small handkerchief of white apron. Both wore stockings and garter belts. Maybe the maids were everyday amusement for Paskevich. They stared at me expressionlessly. Their extremely long fake eyelashes must have given them a headache; their lips were painted dark red. Under their tight garments, the womens' bodies were perfect; slender yet busty. Who knew if they'd had some help from an expensive clinic? Paskevich would have been able to afford what he wanted, no matter how many millions Anita had taken. Sami had been right. I was a hot mess compared to these Miss Universes. I just had to use it to my advantage.

The large armchair in front of the fireplace began to slowly rotate. Paskevich wanted to make a real entrance, it seemed. Fifty-five, Sami had said, and in this dark room, it would've been easy to believe that my dear friend Valentin was much younger. His hair wasn't gray at all—it was gorgeously chestnut, slightly wavy. Paskevich had had a mustache, but now he was clean shaven. The skin on his face was tight and smooth, his blue eyes shone, and he wore large, rimless glasses. He was wearing a black-and-red silk robe and black dress pants. The chandelier reflected off his shiny shoes.

"Finally!" he said in English and puffed on the cigar that was resting between two of his fingers. It was almost too much, honestly, the icing on the comical cake. "What a beautiful smile. What is your name?"

"Suzy," I said the first name that came to me. Suzy, Sarita, Annie Mae, whatever. Paskevich didn't really want to know my name.

"Suzy, then. Would you like something to drink? What do cowgirls usually drink? Bourbon? I do have some Four Roses."

"Sure, I'll have some bourbon."

One of the women slid toward me in her five-inch heels across the lush red carpet like a figure skater. When her skirt moved, I saw that she wore no underwear. Her tray was covered with different types of drinking glasses. I wasn't sure which one to use, so I chose a tumbler that could hold about half a cup of liquid. The woman opened the bourbon bottle so quickly that I couldn't tell whether it had already been unsealed, and she filled my glass almost to the brim.

"I'll have one of those as well, Lena." Paskevich was still sounding extremely friendly. This was turning out to be a fun party, although the only participants so far were the host and the guest of honor.

"You can go now, girls." He used the Russian plural *devushki.* "I'll call you should I need anything, but please do not disturb me from now on. Come here, little Suzy!"

As I walked toward Paskevich, memories of Seppo Holopainen and the school nurse came back to me. A large divan covered in a thick red silk shawl was behind the armchair. Beyond that was a rack that at first glance looked like it was part of a jungle gym, except that it was made of black steel. The lasso rope was heavy in my hands. Was Sami keeping an eye on the room with a security camera? Or did Paskevich think that he was untouchable here in his hideout in the middle of a forest? Could he truly be that dumb? Or maybe he already knew that I had a gun, if they'd been watching me get prepared upstairs. It was hard to believe that a big shot like Paskevich wouldn't have surveillance equipment all over the property.

I swung my hips as best I could and stopped right out of Paskevich's reach—he could make the first move. If he groped me,

I had to let him do it. I braced myself. You'll take action when the time is right, I told myself.

I quickly calculated that in addition to the two of us, there were two maids, Sami, and Trankov at the villa, but Trankov may have been down at the sauna keeping an eye on Helena. Who else was on his staff? Did the maids do all the cooking, or was there a chef? How about security guards? Sami and Trankov didn't seem to be buddies. Maybe I could turn Sami into my ally.

"Welcome!" Paskevich raised his glass. "*Prosit*, Suzy!"

"Prosit, *gospodin*. And happy birthday. I hear you turned thirty. Or was it thirty-one?"

This made Paskevich laugh. We both took a sip from our glasses. I had made sure Lena hadn't been able to slip in anything extra into mine, and because Paskevich's drink was from the same bottle, I had no reason to believe that the bourbon was poisoned. If anything he may have spiked it with drugs to aid his sex drive. I didn't want to appear suspicious, so I had to drink, but I also had to stay as sober as possible.

Paskevich pulled me closer and pushed his head against my belly. He had lowered his glass onto a side table, where he had an assortment of smoking paraphernalia, including cigar cutters. Because my hands were full, I had a hard time responding to his caresses. I moved the loop of ropes on my arm so that I could pet his head softly—before yanking his hair violently, being careful not to cause too much pain.

"Who's in charge of this birthday party here, you or me?" I stared Paskevich in the eyes. His pupils were now enlarged. I took off his glasses. "You wanted a woman with a lasso. What are you, a Russian bull? A bull that wants to be caught?"

My words made me sick, but Paskevich was buying the act. I could hear Mike Virtue's voice, telling us over and over how important it was to get the job done, always. Even if you had to steal, to lie, to break a promise, it didn't matter. Only the end result mattered. We worked in a field where the end justified the means.

"A bull . . ." Paskevich laughed. He dripped some bourbon on my right breast and lifted himself off the chair enough to lick it off. It was disgusting, nothing like David's touch—but I shouldn't be thinking of David right now. When Paskevich was done with his slurping, I took a couple steps back. If only I knew where all the cameras and alarms were. And where was the main power switch? If there was no backup generator, I could easily kill all the lights. The switch was usually in some room with other equipment; here it would most likely be downstairs. I had to get rid of Valentin for a moment.

"A little bird told me that your dearest birthday wish was a little rodeo. Yeehaw!" I yelled, just like Charlie had taught me, and hoped that Sami wasn't overcome by laughter as he looked at his security camera feed. I began to twirl my lasso; catching Paskevich as he sat in his chair was easy. I eyed the trays with bottles on the side tables where the maids had left them. I had liquid at my disposal if I needed it—good. Any wiring visible in the room? I wasn't sure I could crash all the electronics and lights in the villa, but I was hoping to at least blow a fuse in this room. I pulled Paskevich closer to me with the rope and he didn't fight back. My boots made me slightly taller than him.

"Should I lasso you again, or is it time to go for a ride?" I rubbed his crotch with my hand, but he pushed it away.

"We agreed you'd be mine for the entire night. So let's not be hasty, Suzy. We can both ride when it's time. But where's the whip? Didn't Sami give you one?"

When I shook my head, he dug out his cell phone from his pocket. He pressed a single button and Sami soon entered the room. So Paskevich didn't have a beeper for reaching his minions; just a cell phone that could easily be turned off.

"Sami, the riding crop! You forgot it!"

"No, sir. It's right here." Sami marched to the divan and lifted the blanket to uncover the crop. He wasn't sure who to hand it to. Paskevich yanked the crop away and took a swing at Sami, barely missing. The swoosh was heavy in the air.

"Get lost! Run around the house three times in the rain. When I tell you to do something, you better listen!" Now Paskevich didn't sound so playful. Sami slinked out.

"Spread your legs," he told me, and I did as I was told. He let the crop run up and down my inner thighs. I closed my eyes and prepared myself for pain, but nothing happened. How much did Sarita make for being someone's plaything like this?

The fire crackled with renewed energy, brought about by a gust of wind that ran down the chimney. At that moment I spied the fuse box, with multiple cords coming out of it, next to a bookcase on the wall. I wondered whether . . . ? I just had to be patient.

Paskevich didn't seem to really care whether Sami had gone outside to do his penance. His breathing became heavy when he lowered the crop and handed it over to me.

"Hit your shins with it, so that I can hear it. That's it, just like that . . . and now, the lasso . . ."

I caught him with the lasso again and again for about five minutes. I constantly worried that I'd accidentally lasso the chandelier candles, so I blew them out just in case. Now there were just two sources of light. I pushed Paskevich to the divan in the corner and tied the lasso around him so that he couldn't move his arms. I kissed him on his lips first, and then let my breasts brush against his lips. I used the rope to pull him up again; he danced like a puppet. I pushed him into the armchair and tied him up enough to hold him for a bit. In one movement, I grabbed the cigar cutter and the tumbler off the table, severed the electric cords, and threw some bourbon on them.

A spark, crackle, then darkness. Even the outdoor lights had gone off. I ran to check the doors to find that Lady Luck was with me—they were locked from the inside. Paskevich was bellowing something in Russian and thrashing in his chair, but he calmed down quickly when he saw what I had inside my boot. I aimed it straight at his head.

"Sometimes bad things happen at a rodeo, dear Valya. A horse may buck and kick you off, and you get badly injured. It's time for a little chat, but we can forget about horses for now. Where is Helena Lehmusvuo, and why the hell did you kill Anita Nuutinen?"

20

There was a knock on the door, then Sami's voice asking in English whether everything was all right.

"Tell him everything's fine," I hissed into Paskevich's ear. "Tell him you turned the lights off on purpose." While I talked I removed his cell phone from his pants pocket and turned it off. For a moment I thought about tossing it into the fire. Instead, I pressed the barrel of my gun tight against Paskevich's temple. I didn't like what I was about to do, but I also didn't want any more dead bodies.

"Didn't I tell you not to disturb us, you idiot!" Paskevich yelled in English. "I'll call you if I need anything." Fear was in his eyes, sweat was slowly forming on his forehead. Really? Valentin had never stared down the barrel of a gun before? Had he always let other people do the dirty work?

Sami responded with a quick "okay" and I could hear his footsteps walking away. So there were no security cameras or Sami would have known what was going on. Paskevich was an idiot.

Speaking of which, I felt pretty idiotic myself in this getup. I pulled on the leather straps to hide my breasts. My kingdom for a pair of pants! Should I take Paskevich's? But even just the thought of his pants on my bare skin was revolting. I wrapped the rope tighter around Paskevich, then bound his wrists with the leather strap I had used to wrap the gun around my ankle.

"I didn't kill Anita," Paskevich muttered. A dark stain had appeared between his legs. It was slowly seeping into the chair's leather seat.

"Of course not, you'd have someone do it for you. Who was it, Trankov?"

"No! I'm telling you, I was not responsible for Anita's murder! I know I'm the prime suspect; even the Finnish police think so. But I didn't do it. I wasn't that upset with her."

"If it wasn't you, who was it?"

Paskevich didn't reply. Yellowish liquid was now dripping onto the floor. I could have had a plastic gun in my hands and I bet Paskevich would still have been scared shitless. And I'd always thought of him as a tough guy.

"Who exactly do you work for?" he asked. "You're not a cop, are you? Finnish cops don't take quite such drastic measures as this."

"I'm not a cop. Where is Helena Lehmusvuo?"

"Why do you ask?"

I shoved my gun in Paskevich's face now, hard enough to cause pain.

"Don't! I asked Yuri to bring her to me for a chat when he had a chance."

"My intel tells me that Lehmusvuo is here, in your villa."

"Could be. I know Yuri was after her today, but I had other things on my mind. My birthday party." Paskevich let out a sob like a little kid who'd gotten a lump of coal for Christmas. "Who are you, really?"

I pulled a chair to face Paskevich and wrapped myself in the silk shawl I'd seen on the divan.

"I'm not the person you invited over. What was Trankov supposed to do to Helena Lehmusvuo? Why did you want her here?"

"I wanted to see how much the Finnish government knew about the Hiidenniemi property deal." Paskevich had a hard time pronouncing "Hiidenniemi," but I could tell what he was talking about.

"Why should the Finnish government care about the deal? Besides, Lehmusvuo isn't even a minister."

"True, but her party is in the government and Lehmusvuo is an expert on Russian matters."

"What does Russia have to do with Hiidenniemi? I thought it was purchased by a Finn named Usko Syrjänen."

"Come on, don't be ridiculous. You know who the buyer is. You work for him, don't you?" Paskevich was clearly recovering from my surprise attack. He was gaining some color in his cheeks and his sweaty brow was drying out. And he'd said *him*. So the actual buyer of the property was a man.

First things first: I had to make sure Helena was all right, and I had to prevent Paskevich from calling for help, so I'd have to knock him out. I wouldn't kill anyone unless I was forced to. I could probably make him come with me to the sauna, but even that seemed risky. Sami or Trankov could interfere.

"What's Trankov's phone number?"

"Trankov's . . . I don't remember it. It's just one of many on my phone. You can dial Sami by pressing two. Give me that phone and I'll call him!"

I took the phone and told Paskevich to give me the code to unlock it. When he didn't respond right away, I hit him. The pistol landed on his head with a nasty crunch and a bloody bruise began to form.

"Next time it'll be a bullet. I'll start with your toes. What's the code?"

Paskevich recited the number, which he'd definitely taxed his imagination for: 9876. Trankov wasn't much of a bodyguard if he hadn't warned Paskevich about using such obvious passwords.

"All right. I'll put the phone next to your ear, but remember that the gun is right there with it. Ask Trankov if Helena Lehmusvuo is with him. Speak in English so I'll understand." I turned the speakerphone on.

"But we always speak in Russian when it's just the two of us."

"Not this time. And if I catch you warning Trankov, let me remind you that this gun goes off easily. You'll get at least as many bullets as Anita Nuutinen did."

"But I didn't—"

This time, I merely lifted my hand to shut him up and didn't need to do anything more. I pressed number one on the phone. Trankov might grow suspicious if his boss spoke to him in the wrong language, but that was a risk I had to take.

"Hi, Yuri, it's Valentin. Sami's claiming that you brought some woman to the villa. Did you have a birthday gift for me?"

"Sami told me not to disturb you—apparently you have better things to do than have a word with Representative Lehmusvuo."

"Lehmusvuo is here?"

"Yeah, at the sauna. She's sleeping—or, well, she's drugged."

"What?!"

"You told me to bring her here as soon as that bodyguard woman was out of the picture. I followed Lehmusvuo all day, from the Green League cabin to the bus, then tailed the bus all the way to the station where she took a cab home by herself. When she sent the cab away I waited in my car until she walked out of the house again. I gave her a taste of my best medicine. She'll be ready to talk in a couple of hours when she wakes up."

I hoped Trankov had been careful with his dosage. Helena could be awake in a couple of hours, but she'd also feel like shit. I nodded to Paskevich to tell him he liked the plan.

"I'll give you a call!" Paskevich growled. "But for now, don't disturb me." As soon as he'd said that I turned the phone off.

"So you just wanted a friendly chat with Lehmusvuo, eh? Why the kidnapping and the drugs, then?"

"Looks like Yuri got a little too excited. Representative Lehmusvuo doesn't trust me. I've suggested meeting with her numerous times, but she's refused. She said she's not interested in sitting down for a talk with a murderer. Even she thinks I had Anita killed, but it's not true. Jesus, I admired Anita. It would take a special woman to con me, you know." Paskevich blushed—he realized he'd fallen into my trap. "Believe me, whoever you are. Suzy can't be your real name."

"Aren't you the clever one. So if you didn't kill Anita, who did?"

"Your employer."

For a terrifying moment I thought he meant Helena, but then it began to dawn on me.

"Who do you think I work for?"

"Come now. Boris Vasilievich Vasiliev, of course. He had Anita killed when she found out that this Usko Syrjänen was just a middleman for him. I only recently found out about it—not that I know much," Paskevich added hastily. "You can tell Vasiliev that I'm keeping my mouth shut. I'm not stupid. I'm not going to tell Lehmusvuo anything, either. I won't even meet with her. You two can have her, and I swear I'll never tell how she ended up in your hands. I'll pay for Yuri's silence as well."

Damn. Paskevich was practically offering Helena to me on a platter. I could get her out of here and not have to worry about Paskevich causing any trouble for either of us. It would have paid off to be allied with Vasiliev; Paskevich was obviously terrified of him. But if I left with Helena right now, I would never find out who this Vasiliev character really was, and why he had paid someone to act as his middleman in the Hiidenniemi purchase.

"For a long time, Anita thought that I was in cahoots with Vasiliev. It was such a shame that Anita had to be so petty and get upset over the girls. They meant nothing to me. A man has his needs, but Anita and I could've been a great team. We could've made a fortune together in real estate. I was so sad when I heard about her death. I even lit candles in front of Holy Mary's icon and prayed for her soul."

"You're telling me you know nothing about Vasiliev's business, but it sounds to me like you know a lot. Looks like you'll just be in our way. If you miss Nuutinen that much, you'll be happy to hear you'll be joining her soon." I lifted my gun in front of Paskevich's eyes. Even in the dim light he could see my finger on the trigger. The slippery silk shawl fell off my shoulders and I kicked it away.

"Please! I beg you!"

"Now you're going to tell me everything you know about Vasiliev and Hiidenniemi, and how you found out that Vasiliev was behind Anita Nuutinen's murder. Your journey to hell will be more comfortable with less guilt weighing you down, don't you think?"

"I wanted to know who was setting me up as the murderer! I knew someone held a grudge against Anita Nuutinen, and I would be an easy target for that person. Many people knew about our relationship, including that Finnish police officer. Anita's bodyguard had tipped him off."

"Which Finnish police officer? Did the Finnish police interrogate you about the murder?"

Paskevich told me how Laitio had been furious when the Moscow militia dropped Anita's case, and he'd contacted Paskevich personally to threaten him, saying one day he'd have enough evidence to convict Paskevich on murder charges. I wonder what Laitio's bosses, the head of police and the home secretary, would say about that. He would be tossed out on his ear.

"Syrjänen had no problems in buying Hiidenniemi," Paskevich said. "After all, he'd doled out money for election campaigns quite generously."

"Did you or Trankov make threatening phone calls to Nuutinen's bodyguard?"

"Of course not! And how would you even know about them?"

"I'm well connected to the police. Laitio happens to be a good friend of mine. But I'm not even going to let my favorite cop know that you're innocent. Let them hound you. If I were you, I'd check Trankov's background, too."

"Why?"

"The police had seen him hanging around with Nuutinen's bodyguard. They both might work for Vasiliev."

I almost believed Paskevich when he claimed none of his men had been calling me, but Trankov had still been on my tail. Did he have two masters? Was he spying on his host for an even more powerful boss?

"I can't trust Yuri, either? You're lying!" When I didn't respond, he switched gears. "My hands are going numb," he complained. Now only embers were glowing in the fireplace; a candle dripped wax onto the floor. Paskevich glanced at his bourbon glass longingly.

"Let me at least have a drink. It's my birthday, after all."

"Here!" I threw the bourbon in his face. I was angry. But I'd better concentrate on Helena and let Valentin stew.

Paskevich blinked miserably, trying to lick the burning alcohol off his face while it ran down his cheek and chin.

"Both Anita and I were wrong," he sobbed. "Anita was convinced that I worked for Vasiliev, and I assumed the same of her."

"How do you know?"

"I met her—I met her the night before she died. We were seen together. Probably by one of Vasiliev's guys—maybe it was Yuri! That's why they killed her. I should have known Vasiliev would come after me, too."

I was boiling under the leather cap so I tossed it away. The rest of my body was freezing. I wanted to get out of this disgusting getup. Paskevich could have just been buying time; maybe he knew who I was all along. He could have made up the story about Vasiliev and Hiidenniemi; it was too neat a tale. And even though Helena had claimed that the Moscow militia had covered up Anita's murder and they'd blamed an innocent man for it, Paskevich still would have been better off never contacting her, even if he agreed with her. Kidnapping wasn't making him look much better. The disappearance of a high-profile politician was huge, and the police couldn't be paid off. How could Paskevich think that Helena wouldn't go to the police after they'd had his long-desired chat? While drugs and alcohol could wipe away hours of a person's memory, Paskevich still would have been taking a huge risk in drugging her. It was a different story if Trankov was acting alone.

If I told Paskevich now that I worked alone, he'd have the upper hand—his cavalry would be here sooner or later. I did my best to summon my father's spirit from inside me, but I just didn't have that killer instinct. I couldn't shoot a man while he was tied up.

"Why did Vasiliev hire Usko Syrjänen to buy Hiidenniemi in the first place? What did Vasiliev want with the property? Couldn't he have bought it by himself? Come on, Valentin, spit it out."

"I don't know all the details, but it's got something to do with energy—that gas pipeline they're building. Vasiliev made his money with oil, and the pipeline would hurt his business. He doesn't like the project, but he doesn't quite dare to speak out against it in public, because the Russian leadership is all for it. You Finns are way too dependent on Russian energy." Paskevich had started sweating again. He was probably afraid of knowing too much, of getting shot. He'd meet the same fate if he pretended to know too little.

"Vasiliev is rich enough to buy off anyone. Finnish politicians have ludicrously low salaries and any extra income has to be carefully documented. I wanted to hear from Lehmusvuo why she was so critical of the gas pipeline. Who knows, maybe she works for Vasiliev, too. Wouldn't that be the best cover: a representative for an idealistic party? I grew up in Russia under the Communist regime. You never knew who was spying on you. Vasiliev even has a man inside Europol. He used to work for me but quit; I guess he got tired of me."

My heart skipped a beat. Vasiliev's man inside Europol; someone who'd also worked for Paskevich.

"I assume you mean David Stahl? I need to let Vasiliev know that this guy is so transparent that even slime like you can see through him!"

"No, Anita told me about him when we met for the last time. We could've been so good together . . ." Tears welled up in his eyes, and I stifled the urge to kick him in the crotch. Inside I was nothing but cold ice and black hatred, putting all my energy into finding out everything Paskevich was willing to spill.

"How about Usko Syrjänen, then? How's he connected to Vasiliev?"

"They had some joint business ventures. Vasiliev's company holds stock in Syrjänen's most recent shopping paradise. Do you know how much energy is required to run all these spas and malls? The majority of Syrjänen's revenue comes from those businesses. I bet Vasiliev is selling oil to Syrjänen for less than the market rate.

"How the hell did you find that out?" I yelled. Paskevich started to whimper. It really did pay off to pretend I was Vasiliev's ally. Maybe I could locate that killer instinct after all.

"Anita told me," Paskevich sobbed. "She discovered that Syrjänen and Vasiliev were working together. I wanted to find out whether the Finnish government knew about it. Lehmusvuo and Anita were acquaintances. Neither Russians nor Finns want to jeopardize the gas pipeline. I was doing my country a favor."

"And afterward they'd ignore your questionable business ventures, right?" It was quite amusing that even though the Russian militia had suspected Paskevich of murdering Anita Nuutinen, nobody wanted to touch him because he had friends in high places. The system had cut off its own hand.

"I love Russia. We finally have a leader who can turn the country into a democracy. We've finally gotten rid of the czar and the Communists; we're no longer a country run by an oligarchy."

"And you don't consider yourself part of an oligarchy, Valya? Well, you are a small-timer next to Vasiliev and his ilk. If I let you live, you better be careful. If you send people after me, even if they kill me, someone on my team will eventually find you. You're following your dick and letting any woman who's willing to play with you come into the house, with no security cameras installed anywhere. Even your motion detectors are primitive! You better have at least a fucking burglar alarm here!" I kicked the tumbler on the floor, enjoying my role as a psychotic hellion a little too much. This woman could blow Paskevich's balls off at any moment.

"If you work with me, I'll let Boris Vasilievich know what a good guy you are. I can tell him that you're just a harmless minnow who will never again swim with the big fish. Call Trankov and tell him to bring Lehmusvuo over here."

I stepped toward his chair. The puddle of urine under him was vile. Paskevich had sat with his legs wide apart so the liquid wouldn't get on his shiny shoes. I moved the drink tray and grabbed the tablecloth from underneath, then soaked it in the puddle and threw it into the darkest corner of the room. Then I took his pants off, and wiped him down with another tablecloth. Touching his privates didn't do a thing for me. I felt nothing, not even disgust. He was just a piece of meat.

"We've had a good time tonight, haven't we, Valya? Now I'd like to see the birthday present Trankov brought you. I would like to have a chat with Lehmusvuo, as well—after all, it's why I came. We had a tracker on her, which is how I found my way here. And I have implanted one in you, too. Don't bother looking for it; you won't find it. We are in different leagues, you and I. Next time you should choose your hairdresser with better care. Now, call Trankov, and speak in English."

Paskevich did. This was, of course, a hell of a risk, as I had no idea how Helena would react when she saw me in this bondage gear. Where were Sami and the maids? I asked Paskevich when he was done with his phone call. He was picking through his hair as if looking for fleas.

"Lena and Lyuba are already in bed. Their room is behind the kitchen."

"You don't support the oligarchy, but you treat your kitchen staff like sex slaves?"

"I pay them well. You know, no one's forcing them to be here. Sami sleeps upstairs with his wife, at the end of the hall where the guest rooms are. He keeps his cell on because he knows I might need him at any time."

I took Paskevich's phone and threw it into the glowing embers, still hot enough to ruin the phone immediately. If only I could get rid of Trankov and Paskevich for a second, I could take off with Helena. I just couldn't let Trankov see me. If Helena was still unconscious, I'd need to carry her to the car. But first I had to get some decent clothes and go get my backpack—my car keys were there.

"Repetition is the greatest teacher, dear Valya. Neither one of us was here: not me, not Helena Lehmusvuo. As a matter of fact, you know nothing about Lehmusvuo. We've been after her for so long but she's hardly ever alone, and we wanted to fly under the radar. Now I can simply take her to Boris Vasilievich. Maybe your little favor will convince him to treat you with kindness."

There was a knock on the door, and I backed toward it with my gun still pointing at Paskevich. I opened the door and checked the lock with my hand at the same time. Shit, it couldn't be locked from the outside. How about the kitchen? At least I could get out of the house through there, but I'd have to lock up Paskevich and Trankov elsewhere.

I couldn't worry about it now. When Trankov stepped into the room, dragging a dazed Helena by her armpits, I knocked him out with a strategically placed palm strike. Mike Virtue would've given me an A-plus. Helena slumped toward the wall and slowly melted onto the floor. It was better that way. Although she was a smart woman and knew I'd been following her with the tracker, there's no telling what she'd reveal in a panicked state.

I used Paskevich's pants to gag him. Bite on this, you son of a bitch. It wouldn't be long until either the maids or Sami would wake up to his muffled cries or until he loosened the ropes around his wrists, but I should have just enough time to get Helena to my car. I tossed her over my shoulder—she was lighter than I'd imagined—and barricaded the door as best as I could with an armchair and a small table from the hallway. I ran up the stairs to the chamber of horrors, laid Helena on the bed, and gratefully removed the chaps and boots. I didn't have time to figure out how to take the string shirt off, so I left it on under the rest of my clothes. I put my spare clips into my pants pocket and strapped on my holster over my shirt. Then I lifted Helena over my shoulder and wrapped my coat around her. When we stepped outside, the lights clicked on, forming a halo around the house. If this didn't make Sami suspicious, then I didn't know what would. I began running. When I got to the dark road I could feel Helena retching. I gently placed her on her feet and held her as she threw up.

"Hilja, is that really you? Where am I?"

"You're safe."

"How did I get here?"

"It doesn't matter right now. Come on, we have to get to the car." I helped her through the rain and mud; the rental car would get filthy, but it was just a car. Helena was welcome to throw up in it if she wanted to.

The car started without a hitch and rolled steadily on the rain-ravaged road. There were no other people out—the world was empty and deserted, as if just created, as if dead.

Helena nodded off next to me, waking up to the occasional bump or turn. I forced myself to focus on driving. I couldn't let myself think about the soul-crushing truth that was pounding in my head.

David Stahl was a double agent. David Stahl worked for the oil oligarch Boris Vasilievich Vasiliev. David Stahl was nothing but a bastard.

21

It was still dark when we got back to Kirkkonummi. The newspaper had already been delivered, its front page full of stories about how the True Finns party had won the election. Helena had been dozing off the entire way home, and only had enough energy to walk into the foyer before collapsing into a foul-smelling heap. I pulled her back to her feet and dragged her upstairs to the shower. I took her clothes off; Helena followed my instructions like a small child. I threw her clothes into the washer.

"Want me to wash your hair?"

"No, leave it. Where have we been?"

"In Bromarf, at Valentin Paskevich's villa. His little helper Yuri Trankov kidnapped you. Go ahead and sleep if you feel like it. I'll let the cabinet know that you'll be taking the day off. Didn't you have a post-election group meeting scheduled this morning, or is it in the afternoon?"

"I don't remember. Where's my cell phone? My schedule is in it."

Most likely Trankov had tossed her cell phone into a ditch or the ocean. My body was screaming for sleep, but I had more work to do. I dried Helena with a towel and dressed her in the warmest pajamas I could find. I even tried brushing her teeth, knowing how terrible her mouth would taste after throwing up as violently as she had. I'd wait until the morning before I'd make her talk: What exactly did she know about Boris Vasiliev and Usko Syrjänen? Why did Vasiliev need Hiidenniemi? Chief Constable Laitio had been threatening Paskevich, but Paskevich had been too scared to mention Vasiliev to Laitio. I wouldn't be.

I turned my computer on and typed up my notes on everything I knew. Reiska's narrow bed was extremely inviting. Even without sheets, it looked like the most blissful place in the world. I went to turn all the burglar alarms back on and then hit the hay.

I woke up after noon to a phone ringing. It was one of the cabinet secretaries, asking how Helena was feeling. I said she was still ill. The secretary said she was sorry to hear that, but chuckled at how many others had been tired as well after the victory celebrations. I read the paper more closely to see if anyone had reported the car accident. How was Sarita doing? The terrible rains had been the cause of multiple crashes, and the accident in Karjaa was covered in a single paragraph—the woman driving the car was critically injured, but stable. I needed to send her some flowers as a thank-you for making my job so much easier.

I brewed a pot of strong coffee and fried some eggs. Helena must have been starving after what she'd been through. I peeked into her room. She was still asleep. Her damp hair had dried and was sticking up like fuzz on a troll's head; her face was pale and narrow. She still looked so fragile. Paskevich would never bother her again, but I couldn't guarantee Vasiliev wouldn't. I thought about Marina Andreyevna Mihailova, who was even smaller and frailer than Helena; I wanted to protect them both. It had been a mistake to take Helena home—we should've gone to a safe house, somewhere where nobody could find her. Paskevich assumed that I worked for Vasiliev and I'd whisked her away. If Helena nonchalantly returned to the public eye, Paskevich would know he had been fooled. Maybe I could find a doctor who could insist she take a leave of absence. They must have doctors on staff at the cabinet, but I wasn't sure if they could be trusted to keep their mouths shut. I avoided doctors like the plague.

I ate my breakfast alone. At one p.m. I went to check on Helena. She was slowly stirring and the bags under her eyes were dark, as if someone had beaten her up. I lowered the blinds in her room. Outside the rain had temporarily stopped; the cloud cover was slowly breaking apart.

"How are you feeling?"

"My head hurts. What happened to me? What did they do to me? I wasn't . . . raped, was I?" Helena's face was pure terror. I felt sorry for her, remembering what it was like to wake up in similar straits in Moscow. Paskevich's story had convinced me about one thing—I may not have shot any of the bullets that had killed Anita, but that didn't make me any less guilty of her murder.

"No, you were dressed when I found you. You took a shower and I didn't see any bruises on you, either. Are you remembering something? Something they did to you?"

"No." Helena rose carefully. "The room is spinning."

"Are you nauseated? Should I help you to the bathroom?"

"No. I'm just dizzy. And thirsty."

"There's some water on your night table and I have breakfast ready. Get up, but take it slow."

Helena followed my instructions. I handed her a pair of slippers and a robe, and walked in front of her down the stairs, ready to grab her should she waver.

"What do you remember?" I asked when she was on her second cup of coffee, the color returning to her cheeks.

"Just flashes here and there. I came home for a change of clothes. No offense, but I needed some time alone. It's a rare treat these days. I was going to take the bus, but when I left the house it was pouring, so I thought about getting a cab. I opened my umbrella, which prevented me from seeing what was in front of me. I heard a vehicle stop right in front of me and, next thing I knew, a man had pulled me into the car and was poking me with a needle. I remember lying on some boards in the dark, the smell of smoke all around me, and then I was dragged through the rain into a brightly lit building, and there you were. Aside from that, I have no clue what happened."

"Trankov must've had you drugged the entire time. You were a birthday present for his boss. The present his other minion got him wasn't exactly what he'd wanted. Instead of the cowgirl he'd paid for, Paskevich got me." I told Helena what had happened without getting into any of the unsavory details, and then returned to the subject at hand. "So Paskevich was after you, but not for the reason we suspected. He wanted to know how much you knew about Vasiliev's business."

Helena's eyes grew wide. Combined with the dark bags under her eyes and her pale skin, she looked like a frightened panda.

"Does Paskevich know that I'm helping Marina Andreyevna to find out what Vasiliev is really up to? Did he tell Vasiliev about that?"

"Weren't you listening to me? Paskevich thinks that I work for Vasiliev, and that I took you to see Vasiliev. Who is this guy and what does he want with Hiidenniemi?" I asked.

"According to Marina Andreyevna, Vasiliev is an evil, power-hungry creep. He's upset that with Putin and Medvedev in charge, there's a limit to how much power he can grab. He doesn't want to criticize Putin's government too directly—he's worried he'll end up like Hodorovsky."

"Who?"

"This oligarch Putin put behind bars. Hodorovsky spoke out publicly against Putin and did his best to buy off Duma members. Marina doesn't know whether Vasiliev is trying to do the same, or whether he's just trying to create chaos. He's against the pipeline venture in the Gulf of Finland, so I assume that gaining access to Hiidenniemi has something to do with that gas pipeline. I doubt he's interested in the value of the land—he'll let Syrjänen handle that—but the large bodies of water around the property are a different matter entirely." Helena set down her coffee cup. "There's been a lot of talk about how the pipeline will affect the surrounding marine life, and researchers have already found evidence of increased levels of methane in the area. Marina Andreyevna suspects that Vasiliev is trying to slow down or even halt the project by polluting the waters near Hiidenniemi and blaming it on the pipeline."

"Has this Vasiliev character been threatening you?"

"No. It's been just Paskevich—or, well, actually, I don't know. I never thought Vasiliev was behind Anita's murder—I always thought it was Paskevich simply seeking revenge. When I heard about it, I was upset and went public with my suspicions, knowing that Paskevich had connections to the militia and could have paid them to make up the story about a lone drunken murderer. Anita was a Finnish citizen; they should have taken action when a foreigner was murdered. I told you how I'd also received threats in English, right? But I thought they had to do with my friendship with Marina Andreyevna. Vasiliev isn't her only target. Like I said, the security police special forces are after her."

I thought about the threats I'd received. They were orchestrated to make me believe that Paskevich was behind them. If the Russian special forces were following Marina Andreyevna Mihailova, they would probably be able to dig up information on Paskevich, as well. We just didn't know how they'd use all that information.

"So you got in touch with the Central Bureau of Investigation and Chief Constable Laitio about Anita's murder, and you told Laitio that you thought Paskevich did it?"

"That's right. And at first I thought that Paskevich had paid you off, too, but Monika vouched for you. She said you're strong-willed and sometimes a little unpredictable, but you couldn't be bought. Otherwise I wouldn't have hired you."

I would have been in a real pickle without Monika. She was a true friend. But enough with the sentiment—it was time for action.

I told Helena that she should lay low for a few days and not go into work. She claimed that it wasn't possible—people just didn't take a leave of absence from the government. The media scrutinized everything, down to what politicians were having for lunch and who they were having it with. And although hospital records were private, the public would soon be speculating about what was wrong with Helena. I asked her whether a doctor from the cabinet could stop by for a visit.

"You're still in shock after the kidnapping. Doctors can't breach confidentiality and tell anyone about that. I'll file a report about the kidnapping because you're still sick. Where can I find the doctor's number?"

"I'd rather get Krista here. She's my primary care physician. But can I at least call her myself? We've known each other for ages, and I don't want to lie to her any more than I have to."

The doctor came early in the evening. While she examined Helena, I went to buy groceries for the Talludden cabin. I also bought a phone with a wireless connection. It was ridiculously expensive, but Helena would need it while she was in seclusion. I used Reiska Räsänen's ID to register it. Then I left Laitio a voice mail. As soon as Helena's leave from work was approved, we headed out to Talludden. I'd told the rental car people that I'd keep the car a bit longer. It made my life easier, and I doubted that any of Paskevich's guys had memorized the license plate. I didn't think that the rental place would share the information with anyone else other than the police, either.

As we left the city, I turned to Helena. "I wasn't completely honest with you before. The cabin is not in Stävö but in Degerby. But it's a really peaceful place—you only run into elk and the occasional hiker. Should you tell your son that you can't be reached for a while? I would assume he's tried calling you already."

"Aapo is on a college trip to Rome and won't be back until next week. He won't miss me."

Paskevich's information about David was still burning in my mind. I felt even worse after I got a text message from him when we reached the cabin, forty minutes after we left Helsinki.

Dear Hilja, I'll be in Finland tomorrow. When can we meet? I yearn for you, David.

I wish I could've believed it. I felt sick, but I responded in kind. *Dear David, I'll be busy for the next couple days, but Thursday might work out. How about that Kopparnäs Inn? Country girl that I am, I prefer it to Torni. With love, Hilja.*

Had I truly loved David, I wouldn't have used that four-letter word yet, but now I despised him, so I felt fine lying. The cabin was cool, so I turned the heat up to seventy-five and lit the fireplace. Helena did her best to convince me that I was wasting too much energy, but she went quiet when I told her that the cabin heated up quickly. I let her stay in the main room and made myself a bed in the loft where I could keep an eye on anyone approaching from either the north or south. I'd check in the morning to see if there had been any new lynx tracks. After making sure that Helena's tracker was still working—what a blessed device—I installed motion detectors near the cabin and on its doors. Dinner was millet-eggplant stew and spelt crackers from Inkoo. I hadn't brought any alcohol with me this time—we had to stay alert. We had our late-night tea and retreated to our beds to read. Helena had dragged piles of work with her.

My cell phone was on silent, but around midnight I saw the light blinking. It was Laitio.

"Ilveskero," I answered.

"Laitio here. What's the story? I got your voice mails. Do you have something to tell me?"

"Yes, I do. I know who killed Anita Nuutinen." I heard Laitio curse, but I didn't let him interrupt me. "Can we meet tomorrow? I'd prefer the National Bureau's offices in Jokiniemi."

"No can do. I mean, I can't meet in Jokiniemi. I sprained my ankle."

"An old man like you shouldn't be pissed-drunk in the streets. Leave it to the younger guys."

"It's a sports injury! But goddamn it, there was no way I was going to take any sick days. If you want to talk to me, you'll have to come to Urheilu Street. At two. Buzz for Pepponen. And Ilveskero, this time I have your phone number. I'll find you if you don't show up." I knew these were just empty threats, but so did Laitio.

The next day I went for a long run in the morning drizzle. Sunday's storm had pulled the remaining leaves off the trees, and the raindrops sparkled in spider webs, like crystal lace. "Even princesses don't have jewelry as fine as that," Uncle Jari had told me. "And they're precious; they only last for a short while. You have to stop and look whenever you notice them."

There were no lynx tracks and just a couple of swans were out on the bay. I asked Helena to stay indoors. When the blinds were drawn, you couldn't see even a speck of light from outside. Rain began coming down harder again, so Helena could read her reports in peace while I went to Helsinki.

I left the rental car in Hanasaari and hopped on a bus. I rang the buzzer at one minute to two and wondered why the name was Pepponen and not Laitio. When Laitio's familiar growl echoed through the speaker, I told him my last name and he let me in. I walked the stairs up to Laitio's door, which was already open. He was waiting for me in the foyer.

"Come in." This wasn't the kind of meeting that began with handshakes and mild comments about the weather. Laitio was puffing on a cigar again. His outfit matched—it was cigar brown, too tight around the shoulders. He had a brown leather shoe on his right foot, a worn-out tartan slipper on his left.

"And you shut up," he said when he saw me smirking at his slipper. "These are trendy now—even rock stars wear them. They're all the rage. And that's why I fucking hate it that I can't fit anything else on this damned foot. Even my daughter said my slippers are cool. Ha!"

I sat on the familiar couch; Laitio took a seat at his desk. I was barely able to breathe in his office-cum-humidor. Laitio turned the recorder on and rattled the usual interrogation information to start off.

"So, you're here to confess, eh? Finally got a guilty conscience?" he said while offering me a cigar. I declined.

"I suppose you could charge me with unlawful battery for what I did the other evening. But that's a minor detail. You've been on the wrong track, Laitio, but then again, so have I. Valentin Paskevich didn't have Anita Nuutinen murdered."

Laitio's mustache vibrated for a second, and his eyebrows became a marquee over his deep-set eyes, almost reaching over his thin-rimmed glasses.

"What sort of a story did you and your employer cook up this time?"

"Listen. This is an entertaining one, where the bad guys get their comeuppance."

I told Laitio about Sunday evening. He tried to interrupt to ask a question, but I told him to shut up. When I described the lasso scene, he began howling with laughter and then was so embarrassed by his reaction that he kept his eyes focused on the tape recorder for quite a while. The only thing I didn't tell him was the information about David. That man was my prey—I'd let others handle Vasiliev, Syrjänen, and the lot. When I was done with my story, Laitio sat still for what seemed like an eternity. Then he offered me a cigar, again. This time I took one. I snapped the head off with the cigar cutter. I really should buy one of those for my tool kit. It had turned out to be pretty useful at Paskevich's villa.

"So you're not one of Paskevich's girls?" Laitio finally asked when I was on my second draw from the cigar. I had to admit it tasted nearly as good as Uncle Jari's pipe tobacco.

"I've never been one."

Laitio stared at me in disbelief.

"But I thought Paskevich had bribed you to leave Nuutinen alone. I was so sure of that. So damned sure! It was the logical explanation. But that this Vasiliev . . . and even Usko Syrjänen, for fuck's sake! I almost admire the man. He's not some Swedish fag flaunting his inherited money—he's a decent Finnish guy who built his empire with hard work! And now he got weak and buddied up with that Russki."

"Syrjänen might not know what Vasiliev's motives are. Are you familiar with this Boris Vasiliev character?"

"Vasiliev? I've heard the name. My colleague in Europol is on his tail. There are rumors about Vasiliev being tied to terrorists in the Middle East, connected to some kind of joint oil venture. I bet Syrjänen's cheap gasoline comes from there, too."

"Is this colleague of yours David Stahl? He used to work for Paskevich, too." My voice was now trembling, and I was sure I was blushing. At least, my heart was suddenly beating a hundred and forty times a minute. Didn't Laitio hear how it was trying to break out of my chest?

"How do you know about Stahl?"

"It's part of my job description—to know about stuff. But Stahl is not important. Do you think the Moscow militia would reopen Anita Nuutinen's murder case if you gave them this new information? This Vasiliev guy isn't on the best of terms with the prime minister. Catching Vasiliev might even make the militia look good, get some promotions going."

"Or it could be a one-way ticket to a bloodbath. I'll have to make some queries with my trusted men in Moscow. I'm trying to think of a good excuse to visit Paskevich in Bromarf. I wouldn't mind having a go at scaring the shit out of him. But I guess you already made him wet his pants real good."

Laitio's smile was distorted, his expression slightly lopsided. His cheeks and eyes were surrounded by wrinkles that made him look like a friendly but mischievous Santa Claus. A daddy figure in tartan slippers, oh dear God.

"You better be available—or at least respond to voice mails. There haven't been any official police reports about Lehmusvuo's disappearance or about anything that occurred in Bromarf that night. So far I'm the only one who knows. Here is what will happen to the tape." Laitio yanked the tape out of the recorder, mangled it, and then lit it on fire. Now the smell of burning plastic mixed with the disgusting cigar aroma. Finally he opened a window.

"What I mean is, this will be just between the two of us. And what does your girlfriend think about you staying with Lehmusvuo? Then again, Helena Lehmusvuo isn't a complete troll, either."

"I don't sleep with my clients. I never have."

"Neither have I, but that doesn't mean I didn't want to!" Laitio let out a guffaw that was supposed to indicate that us guys knew the truth about women, nudge nudge. Before long he'd be asking me to join his sports team. I took off as soon as I could. Now wouldn't that be something; Laitio and I becoming buddies.

I spent the night lying awake, listening to Helena toss and turn in her sleep. Thanks to my dongle, I had been able to check my e-mail. My friends back in the States were having heated conversations about the presidential election. Most of them supported Barack Obama, but some of the more conservative types thought that it was an abomination for a black man to serve as president. Just as I was about to turn my laptop off, I received a message Mike Virtue had sent out to the group:

> *It is our duty as bodyguards to keep Obama alive, should he be elected. Whoever you support, it is always your duty to protect our democratically elected president. Remember what I taught you: your job is to protect your clients; killing is only acceptable if it is absolutely necessary in order to do your job.*

I thought about David Stahl and I knew his time was coming. Sometimes it was necessary to kill the person you'd mistakenly loved. In his twisted way of thinking, my father had done what he'd had to do; the rest of us knew he'd been wrong. What Uncle Jari had had to do was awful, but it was the only option.

When I was eight, I was too young to understand that having a wild animal as a pet just didn't make sense. I didn't even think of Frida as a pet; she was more like a family member. Of course, she never learned how to properly hunt because she was living with us. She had no mother to teach her. She occasionally caught some mice and moles like a farm cat would, and sometimes she ran after a squirrel. But hares were always too cunning for her. Only later did I understand why Uncle Jari continued to break the laws by going out to shoot hares, ducks, even seagulls, all outside hunting season—we couldn't afford to feed Frida store-bought meat.

When Frida was a cub, she always stayed in Hevonpersiinsaari, and the first year and a half went well. Even if she took off, she wasn't gone for long. Neighbors sometimes reported seeing lynx around, and during the winter we kept ourselves busy by erasing Frida's tracks in our yard and on the lake ice. I figured the Hakkarainens had to know we were keeping a wild lynx, but as Frida never did any harm to their animals, they let it be. Hevonpersiinsaari had its own rules.

We began to run into trouble in the spring when Frida was almost two and in heat for the first time. She needed a mate. Usually she liked being alone, but on these March and April nights, her calls echoed far. There was one moonlit night when the light bounced off the lake ice so brightly that I didn't need a flashlight. Frida was in the yard, wailing, and her cries were probably heard all the way to Rikkaranta.

And then someone responded. A male lynx was somewhere near Kaavi. Uncle Jari had been pretending to sleep, but even he had to get up and watch from the window as Frida went running over the ice, heading north.

She was gone for days, but then finally returned. She was alone, but soon unfamiliar lynx tracks appeared on the ice. One warm winter night, when icicles were spontaneously cracking off the gutter, I was on my way to the outhouse when I spotted them. Frida and her mate. Frida was leaning onto her front paws, hips shot up high, and her mate pushed himself inside her, biting her on the neck. Frida growled and swiped at the male when he pulled away. I was only ten then, and I didn't know much about sex. Still, I knew I had been privileged to witness this.

Frida's heat passed. I was sad when her friend was gone, but Uncle Jari told me it was just how lynx lived. Uncle Jari also knew that I shouldn't be expecting any lynx babies; usually the first time wasn't successful. Frida turned into a domestic cat again, running on the road after Uncle Jari's car. When Minttu Hakkarainen's pet bunny went missing from their yard, we panicked. It looked like our lynx had finally figured out how to hunt, and it might cost her her life.

We never discovered who ran her over. Some lousy coward who didn't even stop to see what had happened—she had been left on the side of the road, barely alive, less than a mile from our house. I found her on my way home from school. I ran all the way to the cabin.

"Uncle Jari! Come! Help! Frida is bleeding!"

Uncle hopped in the car with his elk rifle. He told me to stay in the cabin, but I told him Frida was my sister. I was coming with him. She was still alive when we got there, and I could tell she recognized us. The car had injured her hind legs and back so badly that a vet couldn't have done anything to save her.

"Hilja, she's suffering. I have to end it. Just one shot, and she won't be hurting anymore."

I looked away when Uncle shot her, but I saw his face, wet from tears. We buried her in the Hevonpersiinsaari forest next to a large rock. Uncle Jari sang the first verse of "Suvivirsi." Later the Hakkarainen family and visitors to Hevonpersiinsaari wondered why a rose bush was growing among the heather. Uncle Jari and I knew. My sister was buried under the roses.

22

When you're going to meet a woman, bring a whip. When you're going to meet a traitor, don't forget your pistol. Of course, David would know I was armed, and would be similarly equipped. It was just a question of who would draw their weapon first.

I debated between driving or biking to the inn, then decided to load my bike into the car and drive almost all of the way there. I left the car at the last turnoff next to a pedestrian rain shelter. I rode my bike the rest of the way. It was drizzling again, so I was a little worried that David would think it was suspicious if my clothes looked pristine. I wore my rain gear, but my pants were hiding a pair of black panty hose and a red leather miniskirt that I hadn't worn since my days in New York. I'd thrown my jacket over a boxy blazer, which I'd bought because it hid my gun so well. I wanted to look sexy, to turn David on and leave him defenseless, without a gun and naked.

Only when I was parking my bike did I realize how scared I was. Luckily I'd had extensive training in biofeedback. I took some shallow breaths to lower my pulse while I dispassionately analyzed my emotions. I had to admit that the woman in me was nervous about meeting David, although I couldn't let myself fall into bed with him again. I had to keep my clothes on.

David had sent me a message about staying in our old room and that I should just go there and knock on the door. He'd also mentioned that no one else was in the building, hinting that this time nobody could hear us. How much did David assume I already knew? He didn't think I was stupid enough to believe his real estate story, did he? I planned on leaving the door to the building open.

One of the options I had was to go for a surprise attack—I could walk into the room with my Glock out. I decided to leave the gun in the holster. I had hesitated to shoot Paskevich, and this time there would be no room for hesitation. It may very well have been David who had slaughtered Anita, force-fed the drunkard enough booze to kill him, and then planted the gun in his hand. My chest was heaving like a starlet's in a 1930s Finnish movie, and I could tell my pulse was beating visibly in my neck and my wrists as I knocked on David's door. He didn't ask who it was, which was stupid. I could have been anyone, although right now nobody else was as dangerous to him as I was.

"Hilja!" David beamed. He pulled me to his chest and locked the door behind us. He wore jeans and a thin shirt. There was no sign of a gun underneath, nor could I feel one in his back pants pocket. I squeezed my left arm tightly to my side and hugged him with my right. I instantly knew that this sham would never work. David's hands were already roaming over my body, my rain gear transferring droplets onto his clothes.

"Just a second. I'll take my coat off," I said and pulled away while pushing him onto the bed. First I removed my pants, then my jacket, doing my best to keep a horny expression on my face, although I must've looked more like a jittery guinea pig. I pretended to unbutton my blazer, but instead I pulled out my gun and aimed it straight at David's head. His smile went quickly from tenderness to confusion; I could even see a hint of rage in his eyes.

"What the hell is going on?"

"Game's over, David Stahl. Or is that even your real name? That's how you're known in Europol. I know you've talked with Chief Constable Teppo Laitio. What's your code name among Vasiliev's mobsters? Hands up and put them behind your head! And stay still. I won't hesitate to shoot a rat like you."

David put his hands up but I was sure he was calculating how to get out of the situation. I didn't think he would start screaming for help—neither one of us wanted to get anyone else involved in this. I avoided yelling; my voice became a cat's rabid hissing. I didn't know how many guests were at the inn on an October weekday; with some luck we were the only ones. David probably already knew this, and I had to take my cues from the way he acted.

"Who do you work for? Paskevich?" he asked.

"Shut up! I'm the one asking the questions here. If you want to live a little longer, you'll answer them like a good boy."

David shook his head in disbelief. I searched for his gun. I really could've used a pair of handcuffs to tie David to the bed: the slats of the headboard would have been perfect for it.

"I don't need to tell you anything. Go ahead, shoot me."

"You fucking murderer! Double agent! Traitor!" I didn't know how to curse in Swedish, so I had to switch to Finnish. This only seemed to amuse David, which in turn made me grip the gun tighter. "How much did Vasiliev pay you? What were you hired to do? Your former boss Paskevich knows that Vasiliev is going after Hiidenniemi, and that Usko Syrjänen is just a front. I've shared this piece of information with Laitio. Helena Lehmusvuo and Marina Andreyevna Mihailova also know.

"And Lehmusvuo is on whose team?"

"That's what Paskevich wanted to know, too, when he had Helena kidnapped." I couldn't help but boast about how clever I had been—David needed to pay for underestimating me. "Paskevich kidnapped Lehmusvuo on election night, but I had a tracker on her, which then lead me to Paskevich's villa in Bromarf," I continued. "He thought I was one of Vasiliev's girls, but we both know that I'm not, don't we? You must at least know who's on your side, right?"

David nodded. I told him to remove his belt. I used it to tie his hands around his back and then flipped him on his side. At the security academy, we'd often practiced handling opponents with a gun in one hand, ropes or handcuffs in the other. David made it easy by not struggling at all. I wasn't confusing his behavior with submission, though. I knew that only one of us would leave the room alive. I should just stop being so inquisitive and get it over with. I could then call in an anonymous tip to Laitio and tell him that David Stahl had actually been a double agent, and that when Vasiliev had found out what a traitor he was dealing with, he'd had Stahl killed.

Footsteps approached the door; then there was a knock.

"Should I heat up the hot tub for you?" asked the innkeeper in English. I gestured to David to answer her.

"A little later perhaps. I'm still in the middle of something. I'll let you know when I'm ready, but I may not have time for a soak tonight."

"But it'll do you good. Think about it!" The innkeeper began to walk away. Now it was raining hard and I wondered what would be the point of sitting in a hot tub in the rain. I guess it felt pleasant to be submerged in such warmth when a storm was raging all around you. If things had gone differently, I would be joining David there. That's probably what he had planned. And then, oops, an electric appliance still plugged into an outlet would have somehow fallen in, and that would've been the end of me. How clever. She left behind a boyfriend and a number of former employers.

"I have to tell you, I do admire how you survived Paskevich," said David. "Apparently he's not nearly as big a player as I first thought. And he didn't orchestrate Anita's murder."

"But you knew that all along. And don't try to claim otherwise."

"I didn't. I only found out about Vasiliev in the past couple of weeks. I finally got to see the Anita Nuutinen murder tapes."

"Tapes?"

"Vasiliev doesn't trust anybody. Everything was videotaped. He enjoys it. It's all been recorded: how Nuutinen walked out of the building, how you tried to talk to her, how she was abducted, and how you pocketed her scarf. You were obviously drugged."

"What the hell are you talking about?"

"Believe me, it's the truth. You were drugged in Bar Svoboda, weren't you?"

"I was careful the entire time! I didn't let anyone near me."

"And you drank beer, right? It's easy to recap a bottle once its contents have been spiked. Nuutinen owns the property, but Boris Vasiliev owns the bartender."

I was angry and ashamed at the same time, but not quite ready to believe David. His explanation sounded a bit too convenient.

David sighed. "You're right, I am a double agent. Vasiliev paid me off and I've managed to hide it from Europol. They don't know what I'm really up to. I need the money Vasiliev has promised me to create a new identity, should my plan work. Although it looks like my chances of survival are pretty slim."

He suddenly looked tired, mournful even. A ploy for my sympathy. It wasn't going to work.

"So you do know who killed Anita Nuutinen and why?" I asked, my voice turning icy. The wind outside was shaking the trees, sending gusts of rain into the window. The curtains were open, but outside it was endless darkness.

"I don't know which one of Vasiliev's hit men did it. Most likely Platov and Ponomarenko did it together. It was a spur-of-the-moment decision made on the night you quit. Nuutinen met with Paskevich and told him she knew that Vasiliev and Usko Syrjänen were working together and were behind the Hiidenniemi deal. Their relationship had to remain a secret. Only a few people know about Vasiliev in Finland, and unfortunately, Anita Nuutinen was one of them. After Nuutinen declined Vasiliev's offer to work with him, her every move in Russia was scrutinized. Vasiliev's minions had to seize the opportunity when they saw Anita getting into a cab alone, leaving you in front of Bar Svoboda, looking bewildered." David went quiet for a minute.

"At first I was just as lost as you and Laitio about the case, and I thought Paskevich was the murderer. Initially I was sure that you worked for him; otherwise it would've been too much of a coincidence that you went from working for Monika von Hertzen to protecting Anita Nuutinen, and then after her death to Helena Lehmusvuo. But then I found out that Paskevich had nothing to do with Anita's murder—it had been Vasiliev. And if you had been working for him, I would've already known about it. That's why I had to find out where you were staying, and luckily I found your cabin. It's not in Stävö like you told me, but in Degerby, next to a cliff, and it's a log cabin that looks a bit like an alpine hut." David smirked. "You're not the only clever one here."

I swallowed slowly. I couldn't let David play with my head. It was good to know, though, that he thought I was capable of killing him. "How did you find my cabin?"

"It was a fluke. I saw you get on the bus toward Inkoo on Runeberg Street. I just happened to be behind the bus in my car, and out of curiosity I decided to follow you—I was on my way to Tammisaari anyway. You got off in Degerby, went to the Deli to fill your backpack with food, and then you biked to the cabin. I watched you for a couple of hours. This was in the early summer, well before Anita Nuutinen was murdered. Later it was easy to find you again."

Although I had been sure that David had sought my company for reasons other than finding me irresistible, a part of me was disappointed. How could I have been so careless as to drive to the cabin without checking to see if I was being followed?

"Even after the murder, I wasn't sure whose side Nuutinen had been on. There was a time when I suspected that she and Paskevich were working together after all and that both of them were going after Vasiliev. Thanks to that misguided theory, I was able to find you. Hilja, you do realize that your life won't be worth a dime once Vasiliev finds out you know the truth?"

"And who would tell him the truth? You'll be shut up for good real soon."

"There are radio transmitters, Hilja, and cameras. This room could be equipped with anything. You can't know how much footage might be being sent to Moscow right now. My cell phone could be turned on, or its video camera. Or you could be carrying a recording device, revealing to Europol what a traitor I have been, or sending footage to Laitio."

I forced my body to not shiver. It was easy to set up wireless surveillance equipment, and I had to assume that David had been recording everything, at least to ensure his safety. So I had no choice. I had to destroy him and then the evidence. My stomach churned at the thought of pressing my Glock against David's temple and then pulling the trigger. I knew how to shoot; one shot would be enough. I just couldn't raise my hand or look him in the eye.

"Let's quit playing games, shall we?" David suggested. "You really think that I'm a double agent who was sent to feed false information about Europol to Vasiliev? One should always believe the worst, right? I can't blame you—I was guilty of that, too, when I saw you in Lehmusvuo's yard, dressed up as a man, and I started thinking you weren't quite as innocent as you pretended to be. I didn't know how to read you. You had even told Laitio that you preferred women to men. Is that true?"

"I mentioned a girlfriend to him, and he interpreted it in sexual terms for whatever reason. So what? When I was in bed with you of course I was just pretending; it meant nothing to me. I've had better lovers than you. And how could you tell I was Reiska?"

"I couldn't. I guessed. Did Lehmusvuo know?"

"Of course. I've only lied to Helena when it was absolutely necessary. Is Vasiliev a threat to her?"

"I don't think that Vasiliev is going to kill a Finnish politician. Right now he needs to lay low so that no one will figure out his next move. That's why Laitio and his friends at the National Bureau want to wait before they go after Syrjänen to find out what he knows about Vasiliev. He apparently knows nothing."

David turned slightly to raise his face toward me. I avoided his gaze.

"How long have you worked for Vasiliev?" I asked.

"Almost two years. It took me a while to get close to the inner circle. The information I've been feeding him has helped him financially, but it's been worth it; it hasn't cost us any lives, except for Anita Nuutinen. I didn't know enough about her involvement."

"You think I'll feel sorry for you and let you go?"

David looked me right in the eye. "Are you recording this conversation? For whom? Be careful what you say. Like I told you, you are dead if Vasiliev finds out I've been telling you about him. I'm already in danger, and I'm probably a dead man. But I want you to know the truth, even if it puts you in danger. That's how much you mean to me, Hilja. I'm sorry, but I did fall in love with you. Or, well, I'm not sorry, I just wish we'd met under different circumstances."

"Don't lie to me, David Stahl."

"There's no way I can prove anything I'm going to tell you, but I hope you'll believe me. It's true that I'm a double agent, and it's also true that I've been selling Vasiliev a variety of energy policy information from Europol and European intelligence agencies. Some of this intelligence about stock markets may have contributed to this global recession we're in. But because Vasiliev trusts me, I was given an important mission. I'll be in command of his boat. Or rather, I'll be in charge of Usko Syrjänen's luxury yacht, called *I Believe*. I'm a certified captain, although I don't have the training to be at sea. But my certification was enough because nobody else in Vasiliev's circle had it, and he doesn't trust outsiders. Or if he did, he'd have to kill them afterward, and Vasiliev doesn't want to leave a trail of dead bodies. They're way too easy to trace back."

"But you just told me that he had Anita Nuutinen killed. You're tripping on your own words, Stahl."

"There was a perfect scapegoat for that murder," said David. He tried to change positions, but quickly stopped when I pressed the gun so deep into his skin that it left a mark on his forehead.

"Listen, Hilja. Vasiliev is against that pipeline project. He's afraid that it would cut into the billions he's making with oil. That's why he's interested in the seawater around Hiidenniemi. It gives him an opportunity to blackmail the governments who'll be using the pipeline. The bottom of the Gulf of Finland is in a terrible state, and nobody knows yet whether the pipeline will meet the environmental standards. It will go through if the people behind the project have a say in it, but if necessary, Vasiliev will move on to Plan B. It's already in the works and the delivery is going to happen next week, on the day of the US presidential election. The entire world will be focusing on the election, not on Hiidenniemi. It's my job to make sure that the chemicals are delivered elsewhere, where Vasiliev can't get at them. If I fail—which is very likely—they may sink to the bottom of the sea."

"Delivery? Chemicals? What are you talking about?"

"Strontium 90, a radioactive isotope. Its half-life is thirty years. It'll be devastating if any of it leaks into the Baltic. It's perfect for blackmailing. But I'm aware of Vasiliev's plan and I'm going to stop it. So maybe I'm not just a double agent, but a triple agent—nobody at Europol knows what I intend to do; if they did, they'd try to stop me. It's too dangerous. But it's the only way. I'll blow up the *I Believe* with a hand grenade. Whatever you think about the gas pipeline, it cannot be used to blackmail governments. That's why I have to stop Vasiliev."

In my head I pieced together the puzzle as best I could to form an image that would make some sense. Let me get this straight—David was telling me that he didn't take orders from Vasiliev; that it was just a ruse. But of course he'd tell me that if he wanted to get away. We had been lying to each other this entire time, so why would he suddenly tell me the truth? Then again, I had been telling him the truth today. I had lied only once, about not enjoying our lovemaking.

"You're telling me I should let you go so that you alone, on your own and unbeknownst to your employers, can save the world?"

"I can't save the entire world, but maybe I can save a small piece of the Baltic Sea, where I used to sail as a kid. There is no way Vasilicv will take action publicly—he'll blackmail the Russian government behind the scenes. There are many things ordinary citizens don't need to know. I'm not sure how much the Finnish government knows about the security risks involved with this pipeline. That's what Paskevich had tried to find out. We can guard nuclear power plants and oil wells, but how do you guard an entire ocean? If governments begin to restrict people from boating on the open sea, there will be hell to pay. Sailors and boaters love their freedom."

I looked at David's bound hands. He could've struggled out of the belt anytime if he wanted to. In fact, he could have done any number of things—he was as well trained as I was. And he didn't need to tell me a thing.

I realized he'd had no idea that I knew about his duplicity. I had taken him by surprise, and now he was making up stories to save his skin. He may have even wanted to see me again for the sex. Maybe he was a pervert, and he got a kick out of roleplaying like this.

Suddenly I heard Mike Virtue's voice loud and clear. "Hilja Ilveskero, you are the exact opposite of my other students. They trust too much, whereas you suspect everyone. You don't let people near you; you don't believe in their goodness. Yet you've chosen this path because you want to take care of people, not because you want to destroy them."

Oh, Mike. I wanted to ask him what I should do, but he was across the ocean. I was on my own.

"So what's going to happen next Tuesday?" I asked, buying myself time to think.

"Usko Syrjänen's yacht will take off southward from Hiidenniemi, with Vasiliev and a couple bodyguards onboard. I'll be at the helm, and we'll be heading toward Saint Petersburg. Somewhere in no man's land before we reach the Russian border, we'll rendezvous with another boat and receive the cargo. Vasiliev will get his Strontium 90, and as far as I know—and hope—it will be packed in a bomb-proof container. When the seller is far enough away, I'll jump off the yacht with the Strontium 90 and blow up Syrjänen's little boat. If I'm lucky I'll have a lifeboat with me. If not, either I'll drown, be blown to bits, or end up with a bullet in my head. If the isotope isn't packed carefully enough, I can't risk taking it with me to the bottom of the sea; I'll need to come up with another plan. Worst case, I'll have to bring it back to Hiidenniemi according to Vasiliev's original plan, and figure out how to get rid of it there."

"So you came up with this entire plan? And I'm supposed to believe that I'm the only one who knows about it?"

"I'm going to tell my bosses about it. If the operation fails, someone needs to know what Vasiliev is up to. But I won't tell them until there is no way they can stop me. This could become a major international incident, so I have to tread carefully."

The Glock was heavy in my hand, forcing my arm down so that the gun was no longer pointing at David's head. I still avoided his eyes. David's plan was insane and reckless—if it was even true.

"Do you have to act alone? Can't you have some backup, like another boat following you to whisk you away to safety after the explosion?"

David gave me a tired smile. "Vasiliev will have radar monitoring all the boat traffic in the area. And I don't want to risk anyone else's life. I've never wanted to become a professional killer, you know, and I've been good at avoiding that career path—until now. And I don't like what I have to do. There just is no other way."

"So Europol has been following Vasiliev for a long time because of the crimes he has committed."

"He wants power, both political and economic."

This information squared with what Helena and Laitio had told me. Now I had to decide whether to buy that last part of David's story. Unfortunately I had no way of confirming it. I couldn't ring up Boris Vasiliev and ask if he was really going to buy Strontium 90, nor could I ask Usko Syrjänen if he had promised to lend his yacht to a friend on November 4. There was only one way.

I leaned over and kissed David on the mouth. His lips responded to mine. Up until her last moments, my mother had trusted my father and couldn't believe that he would actually carry out his death threat. But David wasn't my father. The world was full of good men like Uncle Jari and Mike Virtue, men like David. I let my gun slide to the floor. If I allowed myself to trust this man too much, I would pay for it dearly, but I was tired of lying, of being afraid and of always expecting the worst.

I removed the belt from David's wrists, kissed his fingers, and began to take off his shirt. David followed my lead and started to undress me: my blazer followed his shirt onto the floor, then the holster, tank top, and bra. All our clothes had to go—their place was now on the floor and not on us; our bodies could not be kept apart. Spoken language was useless when our bodies spoke enough, understanding each other and knowing where to bite, suck, and stroke. If the world ended next week, or right now, we'd still have our memories.

23

"I called the innkeeper and she promised to have the hot tub ready in thirty minutes," David said when he walked out of the bathroom. "Do you want to eat before that? I've got some sparkling wine and smoked salmon here. If this is going to be our last meal together, it'd better be good."

"Our last meal? When do you have to go?"

"In the morning. I'll pick up Vasiliev in Moscow to finalize Tuesday's operation."

"Who's the seller?"

"It's better if you don't know."

"Take me with you as backup. I can drive a motorboat. I can come get you after you've blown up the *I Believe*.

"No way, Hilja. End of discussion. Sparkling wine? We don't have much time left, so let's enjoy what we have."

Sometimes life imitates romantic movies, but not even Hollywood could do justice to the bliss I felt as David and I sat in a warm wooden tub watching the bare tree branches stir in the wind. My whole life was happening right now, in this moment that would soon be gone forever. It's as if I'd been traveling toward this place my entire life, expecting it to be around the corner one day. We weren't lying to each other or making excuses. We were trying to get as close to the truth, and each other, as possible.

There were so many things to share: David's memories from Tammisaari, his idyllic childhood, his days at the police academy in Sweden and joining Europol, the sorrow of never having children. I had pushed any thoughts of children away and, so far, had never wanted to become a mother. I told David about the lynx mating on the ice and Frida's death. We both wondered whether the male lynx had returned the next spring, calling out to Frida in vain.

We weren't able to sleep that night; we only napped in each other's arms, listening to the sound of rain outside and the water running down the gutters and splashing onto the rocks below. Wild animals aren't meant to be pets, and you can't own another human being. I couldn't tell David not to go.

At breakfast we joked around, because what was the point of spending our last moments grumpy? But our conversation inevitably returned to David's plan.

"So, if I actually make it, I'll need to disappear right away and create a new identity. I can't predict what will happen after Vasiliev dies. Someone will take over his empire. Or maybe it will collapse. If I live, I will let you know in time. If I don't . . . do you believe in the afterlife?" David asked.

"I don't know. I don't think so." But I'd often thought that Uncle Jari and Frida weren't really dead, and even my mother still existed somewhere inside me, although she was just a blurry image I could barely recall. I still remembered them and loved them all. Like I would love David.

"I was raised a trusty Lutheran. My mother always told me she'd keep an eye on me from heaven. I'll say the same to you now." David held my hand and bit my forefinger like Frida when she wanted to play.

The damn merciless clock wouldn't stop ticking. We spent our final moments together lying in bed, kissing for the last time. *I'm not going to cry*, I kept repeating to myself, but I could see David's eyes well up. David would face Vasiliev the giant alone; instead of a slingshot, he would be armed with a hand grenade, and all I could do was be here for him, near him. I'd marched into the inn with only my anger and my gun, so I had nothing to give him to remember me by—just these memories we'd made.

We left the inn together. It was still raining, so David put my bike in his car and dropped me off where my car was parked. He was already late; there were hundreds of miles for him to cover before he'd reach Moscow, and he didn't know how long it would take to cross the border. I drove behind his car to the Hanko Road intersection, where I turned left and he turned right. Once I got to Torbacka Road, I stopped the car on the side of the road and screamed like Frida calling for her mate.

When I'd left I had let Helena know I wasn't sure when I'd be back in Talludden, and the previous evening I had completely forgotten to send her a message to let her know I was all right. She told me she'd been beside herself, worrying about where I would've gone for the night. I didn't know what to tell her, so I just said something about how it had to do with Vasiliev.

The weekend turned out to be sunny, so we went to Kopparnäs for the day. On Sunday we took a rowboat for a leisurely paddle around Torbacka Bay. It seemed unfair that the sun was shining so brightly and the ocean shimmered in striking blue when David was on his way to his death. We all were, but he knew the exact date, maybe even the exact time. If I told Laitio about the plan, he could use his contacts in Europol to stop David in time. Why couldn't Europol just ambush the *I Believe*? They had to have an arsenal of devices that would scramble the radar signals of ships and helicopters.

I also had to come up with a plan for Helena. She couldn't be on sick leave forever. Her assistant, Saara Hirvelä, was returning to work after the weekend, but Helena still wanted me around as her bodyguard. Once she'd recovered from the kidnapping, she'd thought about vengeance. She was going to file a police report, which would directly lead to Paskevich's and Trankov's arrests. The men would be charged with false imprisonment if they were still in Finland.

I told her to think about it first. The tabloids would have a field day with this one: the representative's temporary assistant prancing around in a porno outfit and a gun, saving her employer. Besides, Paskevich would probably be off the hook anyway if he blamed it on Trankov. If anyone would be screwed by this plan it was me. At a minimum, I was guilty of false imprisonment and making unlawful threats toward Paskevich. I asked Helena not to do anything just yet. I didn't want anything to jeopardize David's plan, and we didn't need Paskevich telling the cops about Vasiliev before that. I obviously didn't share this information with Helena.

David called on Sunday evening when Helena and I were finishing up our tea and getting ready for bed.

"It's me. Do you have a moment?"

"Just a second, I'll go outside. I'll call you right back." I pulled on my coat and slipped on my shoes. The air was still, so my voice would echo no matter which direction I was facing. I climbed to the highest point of the cliff. Because sounds usually travel upward, it would be the safest place to have a phone conversation. There were no clouds in the sky, nor were there any city lights to disturb the stars.

"Everything here is going according to plan. Vasiliev seems to trust me and Syrjänen isn't even going to be here until later in the week. Well, I suppose he'll rush over as soon as he hears his boat was destroyed, but that's not my main concern right now."

"So you're in Kotka now?"

"Yeah, on the shores of Hiidenniemi. After this I won't risk calling you. Although Vasiliev's gang doesn't understand Swedish, they don't like me talking on the phone. They're all having a sauna right now, but tomorrow we're rehearsing our plans. Vasiliev wants to go over every detail."

The darkness prevented me from getting a clear view of the ocean. David was looking at the same waters, under the same stars. I had nothing to say to him—everything I wanted to say could've been summed up in three words, but I couldn't say them. David kept on babbling, going back to the story about how he'd suspected me and how happy he was when we finally learned the truth about each other.

"Someone's here; I have to go. Take care of yourself, dear lynx."

I finally blurted out the three words I'd kept to myself, but David was already gone. I recited them again to the stars, in as many languages as I knew, as if they were an incantation that would bring David safely to shore.

On Monday I got in touch with Laitio and asked him what the police planned to do about Helena's kidnapping. He told me that Paskevich and Trankov had already left for Moscow; they'd taken the train on Wednesday. Investigators from the National Bureau had gone to the Bromarf villa and found only Sami Heinonen, the janitor, and his wife there. They had no idea when Paskevich would be back. Sami mentioned as an aside that his boss might sell the villa.

"I've also informed the Intelligence Services, as well as the prime minister and the home secretary, about this and they all agree that the Lehmusvuo kidnapping should be kept hush-hush for now. She really should get back to work. Members in the council of state wanted to know why Paskevich was interested in Lehmusvuo. The prime minister will call for an emergency session once the presidential election in the United States is over. And, by the way, you didn't hear any of this from me, but Lehmusvuo would tell you anyway. You two are getting along pretty well these days, aren't you?"

"How's your ankle?" I replied. "Still wearing your trendy slipper?"

"Ah, give it a rest!" snorted Laitio and I heard a match being lit. "This damned cigar keeps on going out. It was a gift, but such poor quality. Fuck!" I could hear Laitio messing around with his phone and then we got disconnected. I didn't call him back, although I was tempted to. Laitio and Helena could get a lot of people into trouble if they wanted to; maybe they'd put Vasiliev behind bars. David would live and Vasiliev would have to stand trial. There was still time to stop Vasiliev from buying the isotope.

Despite these thoughts, I didn't do anything to sabotage David's plan. It was his choice and I had to respect it. Helena decided to go back to work on Tuesday. There was plenty for her to do after the municipal elections, and she also needed to get back to her legislative duties. Helena lied to her colleagues as easily as I had about getting sick, and after marveling about her skills for a moment, I remembered that she was, in fact, a politician. Maybe I'd do well in politics, too, at least if speaking untruths was any indication of success. The home secretary called when Saara and I were going through Helena's mail. I wanted to tell the minister, "Don't have a meeting today—give David until tomorrow," but luckily everyone was much more interested in the US presidential election than in knowing who actually owned some property in Kotka.

Helena wanted to attend a party to watch the US elections because she'd missed out on the previous get-together. I followed right behind her. This worked for me; Usko Syrjänen's yacht would depart at dusk, and David's fate would be clear hours before the world knew who would be the new US president. My jitters could be attributed to the election. Everyone around me was passionate about politics, and to them it was only natural that a bodyguard trained in America would be nervous about the outcome of the campaign.

I didn't know whether David had brought his phone with him, or whether I could even reach him if I tried calling him. The meeting was tens of miles off the coast, and the water was freezing in November. Luckily it wasn't very windy, but on the open sea, the waves could become huge, enough to cause trouble even for a good swimmer. I hoped David had at least brought a rescue suit. Then again, how would he explain it to Vasiliev and his men? Would Captain David demand that everyone had to wear one in case their business partner decided to bring them a nasty surprise?

Reports from news correspondents around the world streamed onscreen. People sang songs of hope, anticipating that the world would become a better place overnight with a touch of a magic wand if Obama were elected president. I was watching history being made, and once the results started coming in during the wee hours of the morning, I cried along with everyone else, but for completely different reasons.

I thought I would somehow sense when David made his move. I wanted to be an eagle, flying above Syrjänen's boat and seeing what David was up to. I summoned this image during the election coverage, and soon I was soaring above a fifty-foot-long vessel. There was no one else on the open water. I spotted lights in the distance from an even larger boat. Then a light, signaling: the crew had noticed the approaching boat. What would happen then—they'd anchor right next to each other? Who had the isotope? How would David get it in his hands? The image became blurry to me then, and no matter how hard I concentrated, I couldn't feel what had happened; whether David's operation had been a success or if he was dead. At the crack of dawn, when I crawled back to Helena's apartment to sleep for a couple of hours, my mind was blank—I had given in. I could have done something, despite David's stern warnings not to, but I hadn't. Had that been the right course of action?

The following day I scoured websites for news. There was absolutely no mention of an accident on the Gulf of Finland, so perhaps David hadn't been successful in blowing up the boat after all. All the news was about Obama's win and, later, how Russian president Medvedev hadn't even congratulated him.

At five p.m., though, I spotted a mention of a boating accident on the website of one of the dailies. "Businessman's Luxury Yacht Sunk in Gulf of Finland" read the headline. Usko Syrjänen's picture was plastered next to it. I clicked through. The article mentioned that Syrjänen had been notified by the Coast Guard that pieces of his yacht the *I Believe* had been found in the Gulf of Finland. According to the reporters Syrjänen had spoken with, he was "shocked." The businessman had let a friend and business partner, Boris Vasiliev, borrow the boat whenever he visited Syrjänen's newly purchased Hiidenniemi villa in Kotka. The last time Syrjänen used the boat was the previous week, when he'd made a quick jaunt to Tallinn to attend the ballet.

Most of the reporters seemed unfamiliar with Boris Vasiliev, and the political journalists were still focused on events in the United States. I expected that Laitio would spin the truth so that the media would think that Syrjänen had been the intended victim of the explosion. After all, he had stepped on a lot of toes while donating money to various election campaigns. Usually Finland didn't consider a boat explosion a means of revenge, but after the school shootings in Jokela and Kauhajoki, anything seemed possible.

On Friday I found myself in a place where I'd never thought I'd be: sitting in a meeting room in the Government Palace around the same table as the prime minister, the home secretary, the director of the National Security Police, Helena, and Laitio. Laitio was still wearing his tartan slipper and, judging by the smell, he'd smoked enough cigars to last him for a while.

The meeting was mostly about how to make the Vasiliev case go away without endangering Finland's relationship with Russia. Helena was back to her old feisty self, saying that the Russian leaders should absolutely know about Vasiliev's plans—there could be other people who might also try to sabotage the gas pipeline Helena was so passionately against. The group around the table had found out through Europol and Interpol that Boris Vasiliev had been in touch with a man from Belarus, Ivan Gezolian, who was known for his connections with Middle Eastern terrorist organizations. An anonymous Europol agent had infiltrated Vasiliev's team and confirmed that Vasiliev had a deal to purchase the isotope, most likely from Ivan Gezolian. Europol wasn't quite sure what had happened to the deal in the end. The agent had let them know about the isotope transaction on the day it was supposed to occur, but after that he had become unreachable. A hydroplane registered to Gezolian's company had been spotted at a harbor in Saint Petersburg the day before the explosion, but no other connections between Vasiliev and Gezolian had been found.

"The waters were searched after the *I Believe* exploded, and the remains of at least four male individuals were found. They are being identified right now, but it won't be easy. These investigations take time and money. On top of that, nobody has been reported missing, except that agent from Europol," Laitio said.

"Does he have a name?" asked the home secretary. "This hero shouldn't remain anonymous."

Of course I knew what was coming next.

"David Daniel Stahl," said Laitio. "Born in Tammisaari; a Finnish citizen although he spent most of his youth in Tartu and went to the police academy in Sweden. Among his colleagues he was known as *finnjävel*, the Finnish Devil, for not being a team player and for devising unorthodox plans that involved huge risks. He was chosen for the infiltration operation because of his language skills: he speaks Russian, Swedish, and Estonian, and understands enough Finnish to get by."

David had never let on to me how good his Finnish was; maybe he didn't think it was all that important. The meeting ended with a resolution to keep any information related to Vasiliev a secret, under the highest security classification among the government and the police. It meant that Helena and I had to keep our mouths shut for now. Paskevich and Trankov were placed on a banned-entry list; if they tried to come into the country, they would be arrested at the border. Everyone seemed to hope that would never happen, as it would only attract media attention, which might then put the government and senior police administration in an awkward position.

"How about the isotope that went missing—if it even existed? Is Europol after that?" asked Helena when everyone else was already eager to finish the briefing.

"We're keeping tabs on everything, of course," said Laitio. He fumbled with his cigar, then shoved it in his mouth without lighting it. "There's a chance there was no deal, and that Gezolian was just scamming Vasiliev. Took the money and then blasted the boat to kingdom come. That's the natural order of things, you know: the bigger fish eat the smaller ones. Wish we knew who the biggest fish is." Laitio looked around and grinned. "Wait a second—will the biggest fish be me if I light up this cigar in here? Hey, Nupponen, what's the current fine for breaking the tobacco law? I can't remember. Or does the head of National Security Police have a better idea? Aren't we so goddamned lucky to be protected against such evils?"

That was the end of the meeting. Laitio was allowed to sneak out to smoke his cigar. The ministers went back to their business, and Helena stayed behind to chat with Director Nupponen about setting up protection for her in the future. The government would pay for her bodyguard in the short term, but that wouldn't be public knowledge. Helena had offered me the job, but I'd declined. I needed to move on. I had too much on my mind—and it wasn't all because of Vasiliev.

My period was a few days late, which was very unusual for me. Was I pregnant? An IUD wasn't one-hundred-percent foolproof and when we'd made love the last time, David and I hadn't even used a condom. The thought of getting pregnant hadn't even crossed my mind then.

As I stepped out to Senate Square, I saw Laitio smoking his cigar on the steps of the church. He looked like he didn't have a care in the world. I walked over to him.

"Smoke?" he asked.

"Are these the bad ones you mentioned?"

"No. I gave those to the drunkards at Tikkuraitti pub. This is a genuine Cohiba, and you look like you could use one, Ilveskero. That's a prettier name than Suurluoto, by the way."

"You're right. I can't complain about the name. Do you happen to know where Keijo Suurluoto, AKA Keijo Kurkimäki, is living these days?"

"Where he's been for the past thirty years. In the hospital for mentally ill prisoners."

"You're saying he hasn't been pardoned?"

"He hasn't even petitioned for a pardon. You haven't looked him up?"

I shook my head. That was all the information I needed for now. I wouldn't be reaching out to him any time soon. He would be safe from me, too; he would be an easy target for my pent-up rage. Laitio prepped a cigar for me and lit it. Too bad Reiska was too poor to afford cigars. They smelled better than regular cigarettes.

"Oh, and about that Yuri Trankov," added Laitio. "He's Valentin Paskevich's bastard son. A dirty word: bastard. Not really used in modern language for that purpose anymore."

"What do you mean?"

"Trankov was trying hard to get his father's approval. I guess that's why he came after you. He probably thought he could use you to find out what had happened to Nuutinen. That information would've definitely endeared him to Paskevich. The boy is smarter than his father, though. Be careful of Trankov; you might run into him again."

A busload of eager Japanese tourists fanned out over the square, taking pictures of the church, the university building, and the statue of Alexander the Second. Did they even know who they were taking pictures of? I wondered, not for the first time, why the Russian czar was featured so prominently in the Finnish capital.

"Lo, the statue of Alexander the Second still stands, stands the dead czar in the mist, missed and loved by the people. Lo, the bright eye of the lion of justice shimmers through the fog," recited Laitio out of the blue, heavy on the poetic rhythm and pathos. "Recognize the poem?"

"No."

"It's called 'Helsinki in the Mist,' by Eino Leino. It's a mist you have to get used to. Alexander the Second gave us Finns plenty of freedom, but even he couldn't do anything about Finland's geographic location. We just have to keep on fulfilling the tasks of this lion of justice. You and that Stahl, were you good friends?"

The change of subject was so sudden that the cigar almost slipped out of my mouth. I grabbed it quickly between my fingers.

"I don't think I ever told you we'd met."

"Come on! I'm a cop, you know. I don't need a lie detector to tell me when I'm being fooled. Every time we mentioned Stahl, your pupils became oddly enlarged. And why did you have to reveal that you knew him? Only because you wanted to say his name out loud. That's how women in love behave."

"I suppose so." I blinked my eyes and tried to create enough smoke to hide my face.

"Love. What a curious thing. It certainly doesn't make life any easier, but it's damned nice when you find it," said Laitio. A black car pulled in front of him. A redheaded woman in a police uniform stepped out and opened the back door for Laitio.

"Need a ride?" he offered. "I can't drive myself just yet, so I'm using these interns as my chauffeurs."

"No, thanks. I'll walk," I said, not knowing at all where I was heading.

Once I completed my contract with Helena, I took some time off to spend a few days in Hevonpersiinsaari. It seemed like the only place where I could relax. Torbacka was contaminated by too many memories: I still felt David roaming in the forests, waiting for me at the Kopparnäs Inn. I'd told the Hakkarainens that I was going to be around. Matti had offered to pick me up from the bus stop at either Outokumpu or Kaavi, but I declined. I'd rather use a rental car.

I took the train to Kuopio, and once we passed Mikkeli, I felt my period start. I didn't know whether I was relieved or disappointed; both, I suppose. I had grown up without parents and didn't want to bring a fatherless child into this world, but there was a part of me that wanted to carry David's child. Our child. It was as if I had lost the final traces of him with the blood flowing out of me.

My rental Peugot took me onward from Kuopio. Although there was no snow yet, the temperature was below freezing and the puddles on the road were covered in thin, brittle ice, just as the edges of lakes and ponds were. Darkness had already fallen by three p.m., so it was comforting to see that the Hakkarainens had placed a lantern on the side of the road. They'd even heated up the cabin and left a light on, and I found a tray of small Karelian pies on the table, carefully wedged between two napkins. The fridge was on, stocked with a mixture of boiled eggs and butter for the pies, some home-brewed beer, and two smoked whitefish.

I ate one of the pies and unpacked most of my clothes. Then I went outside. On my way here, I had purchased a small candle lantern and a bunch of white roses. Although the path leading to the rock next to the rose bush was now overgrown, I was still able to find it. The bush was bare, and the roses I'd brought would freeze in seconds. The ground was hard and covered in frost. I set the flowers in water—the tin can I'd brought to use as a vase wouldn't break, even if the water froze overnight. I lit the candle and thought about singing a song. Lyrics from various songs came to mind: *life is forever for five minutes, it was happiness only for half an hour, when your eyes have lynx in them*. I knelt next to the candle and listened to the ice on the lake began to tinkle as frost crept over the water to Hevonpersiinsaari. When the next cloud drifted above me, it began to snow slowly.

24

The metal detector at the airport went off. Because it was a female passenger that had triggered it, I stepped forward and asked her to spread her arms.

"Must've been these shoes of mine," she said cheerfully. "They always make these things beep."

Then why didn't you put them on the conveyor belt, you moron, I wanted to ask her, but I continued searching her with a blank expression and then asked that she take her shoes off and walk through the gate again. This time it remained mute.

Working security at the Helsinki-Vantaa airport was boring, which is why it suited me so well. I didn't need any more action. Nowadays I had enough drama when a teenage boy tried to smuggle nine ounces of shampoo in his backpack and the entire family started arguing about it, or when we had to confiscate one lady's antique pearl scissors she had inherited because she wasn't allowed to take them on the plane. I memorized all the rules and I stuck to them. It was a nice change.

Riikka had moved in with her boyfriend, so her room was empty. Jenni was planning on going to the UK after Easter to participate in a student exchange program in Cambridge. Our little commune was going to be breaking up forever. Jenni's sister and her friends were interested in moving to Untamo Road, so I had to look for another apartment.

"You could move in here," suggested Mrs. Voutilainen when I told her the news. "I have a spare room, and you wouldn't need to pay rent if you help with the chores I can't do anymore. These legs aren't what they used to be, and carrying grocery bags up the stairs is quite difficult."

I hadn't given her an answer yet. It was a viable option, though. I had given away my lease at Torbacka—I had no desire to stay at that cabin ever again. Once I'd returned to Untamo Road, I had spent quite a lot of time with Mrs. Voutilainen. I used to enjoy being alone, but now my thoughts were so overwhelming that the only way to deal with them was to be surrounded by other people. Mrs. Voutilainen fed me her quiches and stews and nagged me about not going for a run when I obviously had a cold.

"You'll get myocarditis! That disease doesn't care how old you are! And don't you already have enough heart problems—problems of the soul?"

I was embarrassed. First Laitio saw fit to comment on my love life, and now Mrs. Voutilainen? And I'd always thought I was impenetrable and someone who could easily hide her secrets. I had never even mentioned David to my neighbor.

"Yeah, I've had some heartaches," I admitted to her. We were sitting together over a pot of tea and an apple pie. I had just brought her rugs in from outside and hung her clothes up to dry. It was like visiting a grandma I had never had.

"Was he a bad man?" Mrs. Voutilainen asked, curious.

"No, a very good man. But he died."

"Was it a car accident? My goodness, why haven't you said anything?"

"He drowned. Our relationship was short-lived—this was when I was still working for Representative Lehmusvuo and I didn't have time to see you much."

Mrs. Voutilainen patted me on my cheek as if I were a little child.

"I won't tell you that there will be other men. There will be, if that's the world's plan for you, but first you need to let yourself grieve. Does this man have something to do with that lynx painting?"

"Partly, but he wasn't the one who sold you the painting."

"Would you like to have it? It'll be your Christmas present. And if you move into my place it'll end up back in my living room. You can take it right now. I bought it because I felt sorry for that boy, but you obviously have an emotional connection to it."

So that's how Yuri Trankov's painting ended up on my wall. It wasn't bad at all; Trankov was a much better artist than a hit man. Maybe these days he was selling his paintings near the Frunzenskaya subway station, or some other station in Moscow, and nice people like Mrs. Voutilainen bought them, and slowly Trankov was becoming a decent man.

Untamo Road had great bus connections to the airport, so commute-wise, moving in with Mrs. Voutilainen was a good idea. I also suspected that she wasn't telling me everything about her health situation. She seemed to take cabs often to go see one doctor or another. Mrs. Voutilainen was the opposite of the stereotypical senior citizen who was constantly complaining about ailments. The students at the Queens academy whined a lot more, and they were supposed to be an elite group. Mrs. Voutilainen didn't ask any more questions about David, and I appreciated that. I felt close to her; she never forced me to confess anything.

I received a Christmas greeting from Gary, a former neighbor on Morton Street. He threatened to come visit me in Finland and sent the latest snapshot of his massive cat, Angus. Monika kept in touch, too. We Skyped, e-mailed, and sent text messages whenever we could. She obviously had a thing going on with Jordi, but despite that, she kept on inviting me to Mozambique. There'd be a lot of work available, as new mouths to feed were born every day.

So that was the second option, and in the darkness of the Finnish winter, the thought of Africa was tempting. Of course I wouldn't be able to whip up anything fancy in the kitchen, but I knew how to peel, chop, slice, cut wood, and carry heavy loads. It wouldn't have been the first time I'd traveled across the ocean to find my place in the world. Back then I was after a job. This time, if I left Finland to run away from my past, it would be futile—a new location couldn't heal these memories, only time would.

I worked during Christmas. Mrs. Voutilainen had gone to her niece's family in Sipoo and Jenni went to her parents' cabin. I ate sushi and vegetarian pizza and didn't give a single thought to Christmas decorations. At work I showed some Christmas spirit when I let a woman traveling to Kuopio take her Christmas pastries on the plane, although the prune filling was essentially a liquid. Luckily my fellow guards were equally laid-back.

I thought of David every single day. There were moments when I was furious at life for giving me so little time with him, but even then I was thankful for what I'd been given. Occasionally I called Helena, and on New Year's Eve, I received an e-mail forwarded from Laitio. He advised all who received the e-mail to smoke a good cigar in celebration of the new year. As an officer of the law, though, he had to remind us that he was in no way urging us to partake of illegal activities. The message ended with a note meant only for me:

By the way, Ilveskero, you'll be interested to know that we weren't able to identify any of the bodies we found in the Gulf of Finland, except for Boris Vasiliev's. His head was almost intact and we were able to verify his DNA. No information on the other victims. I hope one of them was the bastard who killed Anita Nuutinen. Nobody has David Stahl's DNA in their files, but one of the bodies matches his age and body structure. Unfortunately, we didn't have anything to compare to his dental records, so we can't confirm the ID. I'll let you know if I hear anything more. With best regards, the lion of justice, T. Laitio.

I've always hated January. Christmas is over and there's no sign of natural light. January was more tolerable in New York than in Finland, where everything seemed to close down for the month. You had to lose weight, stop drinking, exercise, and take advantage of all the sales. The falling snow brightened up the world, but it would melt in a few days. Rich bastards who didn't care about climate change took off to Southeast Asia or to ski in the Alps. Even Mrs. Voutilainen went to the Canary Islands for two weeks—her old friend had a condo there. I walked her to her gate at the airport and sternly warned her about falling in love with gigolos. I could've packed up and left, too, but I just wallowed in my misery at home. I now understood why Uncle Jari had enjoyed living alone in Hevonpersiinsaari without electricity or television. No stimuli from the outside, nobody telling you what to do. You could just be yourself and sleep away the dark days.

I was on the night shift on the day after Mrs. Voutilainen left for her trip. Half-asleep on my way home, I almost got run over by a car when it ignored a red light and made a turn in the intersection. Pissed off, I gave the car a good kick when it lurched onward. It was yet another freezing day, no surprise, and the biting wind ripped through my jacket hood, numbing my ears. Of course I'd lost my hat at some point. The apartment building stairwell seemed abandoned without the delicious smells of freshly baked ham quiche or apple pie. I should have forced myself to go to the gym, but I didn't have the energy. I'd be lucky if I managed to walk down to Käpygrilli for a beer. Maybe I'd just spend the rest of the day nodding off in front of the television.

On my way in, I checked the mail: an ad for a car and a single envelope. There was no return address. It was hard to tell where it had been postmarked. Was that Spain? The envelope was plain white, the kind that was sold by the millions all over the globe. There was a card inside. I took my time going to the kitchen, getting a pair of scissors and cutting the envelope open carefully, making sure I wasn't damaging whatever was inside.

The card had two sections and opened in the middle, like a book. The front of the card featured a lynx, *el lince ibérico*. The handwritten note inside the card was in Swedish.

Dearest Hilja,

Greetings from the southernmost habitat of the Iberian lynx. It took me almost three months to recover from the frostbite and get my life sorted out. Now I can communicate again with the outside world. I'm staying in the mountains in a small hut, kind of like your cabin in Degerby. The lynx habitat is about six miles away. The nearest town is Huelva, and the easiest way to reach it is to fly to Seville. I'll wait for you here. You can write to me at my e-mail address, lo.lynx@hotmail.com. Come as soon as you can. I miss you terribly.

I couldn't believe my eyes. Was this some diabolical joke? No way could my story end this well. I read the card again and then a third time. It was finally becoming clear that David had survived his crazy stunt and he was waiting for me in Spain. I screamed as if Finland's soccer team had made it to the World Cup. But it had been David who'd won against Gezolian and Vasiliev, six–nil. And I was his prize. I switched my computer on to find the quickest way to get to Seville. A flight to Madrid was departing at five, so I'd be in Seville this evening.

Once I'd bought the ticket, I sent an e-mail to lo.lynx. *Dear Lo, I'll be in Seville tonight at 11:05. My number is still the same. Let me know by text message if you can come pick me up from the airport or if I should continue on my own to somewhere else. I have a layover in Madrid. Your Hilja.*

I quit my job with an e-mail message. That would get messy, but whatever. I packed only the essentials, kissed my lynx painting good-bye, and danced my way to the bus stop in the sleet. I grinned at the bus driver enough to convince him I was insane; all the other passengers were staring at me, too. I had to strain to keep from telling everyone I saw what had just happened. Only a few more hours and I'd see David again.

At the security check, I hugged all of my coworkers. I didn't want to meet David empty-handed, so I bought him a T-shirt with a lynx on the front, size XXL. Right before I got on the plane, I received a text message from him. *Dear Hilja, I'll be at the Seville airport waiting for you. I'll see you soon. Lo.*

I tried to catch some sleep on the plane, but it was useless. I drank a small bottle of sparkling wine, although my mind was bubbling enough already. Once I switched planes in Madrid I began to count the minutes; they went by excruciatingly slowly. I couldn't sleep or listen to music. Below me Spain was an enormous country, freeways and roads forming strips of light that never ended.

David was waiting behind the arrival gate, and as soon as I saw him I began to sprint. He smelled the same, his lips tasted the same, his skin was warm like it used to be. The lynx had called for a mate, and the call had been answered.

ABOUT THE AUTHOR

Photo © Charlotta Boucht

Finland's bestselling female crime author, Leena Lehtolainen first rose to fame with her series starring feisty female detective Mario Kallio. She won the Finnish Whodunit Society's annual prize for the best Finnish crime novel twice and was nominated for the prestigious Glass Key award for the best Nordic crime novel. Her novels have been translated into twenty-nine languages and sold over two million copies. Lehtolainen currently lives in Finland with her husband and two sons.

Learn more about Leena Lehtolainen at:
www.leenalehtolainen.fi
www.ahlbackagency.com/aba_authors/lehtolainen-leena

ABOUT THE TRANSLATOR

Photo © Kochun Hu

Jenni Salmi is a translator and localizer living in Seattle. She was born and raised in Eastern Finland, near the Russian border, where she learned English, Swedish, German, and Russian. After mostly forgetting the other languages, she earned her master's degree in English literature at the University of Joensuu. Leena Lehtolainen's *The Bodyguard* is her first full-length fiction translation.